Beware, The Wheel of Fortune . . .

THE DEAD ZONE

Johnny, the small boy who skated at breakneck speed into an accident that for one horrifying moment plunged him into . . . *the dead zone.*

Johnny Smith, the small-town schoolteacher who spun the wheel of fortune and won a four-and-a-half-year trip into . . . *the dead zone.*

John Smith, who awakened from an interminable coma with an accursed power—the power to see the future and the terrible fate awaiting mankind in . . . *the dead zone.*

"Powerful tension holds the reader to the story like a pin to a magnet!"
—*Houston Post*

STEPHEN KING

THE DEAD ZONE

A SIGNET BOOK

SIGNET
Published by New American Library, a division of
Penguin Putnam Inc., 375 Hudson Street,
New York, New York 10014, U.S.A.
Penguin Books Ltd, 27 Wrights Lane,
London W8 5TZ, England
Penguin Books Australia Ltd, Ringwood,
Victoria, Australia
Penguin Books Canada Ltd, 10 Alcorn Avenue,
Toronto, Ontario, Canada M4V 3B2
Penguin Books (N.Z.) Ltd, 182–190 Wairau Road,
Auckland 10, New Zealand

Penguin Books Ltd, Registered Offices:
Harmondsworth, Middlesex, England

Published by Signet, an imprint of New American Library,
a division of Penguin Putnam Inc.

A hardcover edition of this book was published by The Viking Press. The hardcover edition was published simultaneously in Canada by Penguin Books Canada Limited.

First Signet Printing, August 1980
58   57   56   55   54   53   52

The lyrics on page 64 are from "Back in the U.S.S.R.," words and music by John
Lennon and Paul McCartney. Copyright © 1968 Northern Songs Ltd. All rights
in the United States of America, Mexico, and the Philippines are controlled by
Maclen Music, Inc., c/o ATV Music Corp. Used by permission. All rights reserved.
The lyrics on pages 28 and 47 are from "Whole Lot-ta Shakin' Goin' On" by
Dave Williams and Sonny David.

REGISTERED TRADEMARK—MARCA REGISTRADA

Printed in the United States of America

AUTHOR'S NOTE

What follows is a work of fiction. All of the major characters are made up. Because it plays against the historical backdrop of the last decade, the reader may recognize certain actual figures who played their parts in the 1970s. It is my hope that none of these figures has been misrepresented. There is no third congressional district in New Hampshire and no town of Castle Rock in Maine. Chuck Chatsworth's reading lesson is drawn from *Fire Brain*, by Max Brand, originally published by Dodd, Mead and Company, Inc.

THIS IS FOR OWEN
I LOVE YOU, OLD BEAR

Contents

Prologue

By the time he graduated from college, John Smith had forgotten all about the bad fall he took on the ice that January day in 1953. In fact, he would have been hard put to remember it by the time he graduated from grammar school. And his mother and father never knew about it at all.

They were skating on a cleared patch of Runaround Pond in Durham. The bigger boys were playing hockey with old taped sticks and using a couple of potato baskets for goals. The little kids were just farting around the way little kids have done since time immemorial—their ankles bowing comically in and out, their breath puffing in the frosty twenty-degree air. At one corner of the cleared ice two rubber tires burned sootily, and a few parents sat nearby, watching their children. The age of the snowmobile was still distant and winter fun still consisted of exercising your body rather than a gasoline engine.

Johnny had walked down from his house, just over the Pownal line, with his skates hung over his shoulder. At six, he was a pretty fair skater. Not good enough to join in the big kids' hockey games yet, but able to skate rings around most of the other first graders, who were always pinwheeling their arms for balance or sprawling on their butts.

Now he skated slowly around the outer edge of the clear patch, wishing he could go backward like Timmy Benedix, listening to the ice thud and crackle mysteriously under the snow cover farther out, also listening to the shouts of the hockey players, the rumble of a pulp truck crossing the bridge on its way to U.S. Gypsum in Lisbon Falls, the murmur of conversation from the adults. He was very glad to be alive on that cold, fair winter day. Nothing was wrong with him, nothing troubled his mind, he wanted nothing . . . except to be able to skate backward, like Timmy Benedix.

1

He skated past the fire and saw that two or three of the grown-ups were passing around a bottle of booze.

"Gimme some of that!" he shouted to Chuck Spier, who was bundled up in a big lumberjack shirt and green flannel snowpants.

Chuck grinned at him. "Get outta here, kid, I hear your mother callin you."

Grinning, six-year-old Johnny Smith skated on. And on the road side of the skating area, he saw Timmy Benedix himself coming down the slope, with his father behind him.

"Timmy!" he shouted. "Watch this!"

He turned around and began to skate clumsily backward. Without realizing it, he was skating into the area of the hockey game.

"Hey kid!" someone shouted. "Get out the way!"

Johnny didn't hear. He was *doing* it! He was skating backward! He had caught the rhythm—all at once. It was in a kind of sway of the legs . . .

He looked down, fascinated, to see what his legs were doing.

The big kids' hockey puck, old and scarred and gouged around the edges, buzzed past him, unseen. One of the big kids, not a very good skater, was chasing it with what was almost a blind, headlong plunge.

Chuck Spier saw it coming. He rose to his feet and shouted, *"Johnny! Watch out!"*

John raised his head—and the next moment the clumsy skater, all one hundred and sixty pounds of him, crashed into little John Smith at full speed.

Johnny went flying, arms out. A bare moment later his head connected with the ice and he blacked out.

Blacked out . . . black ice . . . blacked out . . . black ice . . . black. Black.

They told him he had blacked out. All he was really sure of was that strange repeating thought and suddenly looking up at a circle of faces—scared hockey players, worried adults, curious little kids. Timmy Benedix smirking. Chuck Spier was holding him.

Black ice. Black.

"What?" Chuck asked. "Johnny . . . you okay? You took a hell of a knock."

"Black," Johnny said gutturally. "Black ice. Don't jump it no more, Chuck."

Chuck looked around, a little scared, then back at Johnny. He touched the large knot that was rising on the boy's forehead.

"I'm sorry," the clumsy hockey player said. "I never even saw him. Little kids are supposed to stay away from the hockey. It's the rules." He looked around uncertainly for support.

"Johnny?" Chuck said. He didn't like the look of Johnny's eyes. They were dark and faraway, distant and cold. "Are you okay?"

"Don't jump it no more," Johnny said, unaware of what he was saying, thinking only of ice—black ice. "The explosion. The acid."

"Think we ought to take him to the doctor?" Chuck asked Bill Gendron. "He don't know what he's sayin."

"Give him a minute," Bill advised.

They gave him a minute, and Johnny's head did clear. "I'm okay," he muttered. "Lemme up." Timmy Benedix was still smirking, damn him. Johnny decided he would show Timmy a thing or two. He would be skating rings around Timmy by the end of the week . . . backward *and* forward.

"You come on over and sit down by the fire for a while," Chuck said. "You took a hell of a knock."

Johnny let them help him over to the fire. The smell of melting rubber was strong and pungent, making him feel a little sick to his stomach. He had a headache. He felt the lump over his left eye curiously. It felt as though it stuck out a mile.

"Can you remember who you are and everything?" Bill asked.

"Sure. Sure I can. I'm okay."

"Who's your dad and mom?"

"Herb and Vera. Herb and Vera Smith."

Bill and Chuck looked at each other and shrugged.

"I think he's okay," Chuck said, and then, for the third time, "but he sure took a hell of a knock, didn't he? Wow."

"Kids," Bill said, looking fondly out at his eight-year-old twin girls, skating hand in hand, and then back at Johnny. "It probably would have killed a grown-up."

"Not a Polack," Chuck replied, and they both burst out laughing. The bottle of Bushmill's began making its rounds again.

Ten minutes later Johnny was back out on the ice, his headache already fading, the knotted bruise standing out on his forehead like a weird brand. By the time he went home for lunch, he had forgotten all about the fall, and blacking out, in the joy of having discovered how to skate backward.

"God's mercy!" Vera Smith said when she saw him. "How did you get that?"

"Fell down," he said, and began to slurp up Campbell's tomato soup.

"Are you all right, John?" she asked, touching it gently.

"Sure, Mom." He was, too—except for the occasional bad dreams that came over the course of the next month or so . . . the bad dreams and a tendency to sometimes get very dozy at times of the day when he had never been dozy before. And that stopped happening at about the same time the bad dreams stopped happening.

He was all right.

In mid-February, Chuck Spier got up one morning and found that the battery of his old '48 De Soto was dead. He tried to jump it from his farm truck. As he attached the second clamp to the De Soto's battery, it exploded in his face, showering him with fragments and corrosive battery acid. He lost an eye. Vera said it was God's own mercy he hadn't lost them both. Johnny thought it was a terrible tragedy and went with his father to visit Chuck in the Lewiston General Hospital a week after the accident. The sight of Big Chuck lying in that hospital bed, looking oddly wasted and small, had shaken Johnny badly—and that night he had dreamed it was *him* lying there.

From time to time in the years afterward, Johnny had hunches—he would know what the next record on the radio was going to be before the DJ played it, that sort of thing— but he never connected these with his accident on the ice. By then he had forgotten it.

And the hunches were never that startling, or even very frequent. It was not until the night of the county fair and the mask that anything very startling happened. Before the second accident.

Later, he thought of that often.

The thing with the Wheel of Fortune had happened *before* the second accident.

Like a warning from his own childhood.

◆ 2 ◆

The traveling salesman crisscrossed Nebraska and Iowa tirelessly under the burning sun in that summer of 1955. He sat behind the wheel of a '53 Mercury sedan that already had better than seventy thousand miles on it. The Merc was developing a marked wheeze in the valves. He was a big man who still had the look of a cornfed midwestern boy on him; in that summer of 1955, only four months after his Omaha housepainting business had gone broke, Greg Stillson was only twenty-two years old.

The trunk and the back seat of the Mercury were filled with cartons, and the cartons were filled with books. Most of them were Bibles. They came in all shapes and sizes. There was your basic item, The American TruthWay Bible, illustrated with sixteen color plates, bound with airplane glue, for $1.69 and sure to hold together for at least ten months; then for the poorer pocketbook there was The American TruthWay New Testament for sixty-five cents, with no color plates but with the words of Our Lord Jesus printed in red; and for the big spender there was The American TruthWay Deluxe Word of God for $19.95, bound in imitation white leather, the owner's name to be stenciled in gold leaf on the front cover, twenty-four color plates, and a section in the middle to note down births, marriages, and burials. And the Deluxe Word of God might remain in one piece for as long as two years. There was also a carton of paperbacks entitled *America the TruthWay: The Communist-Jewish Conspiracy Against Our United States.*

Greg did better with this paperback, printed on cheap pulp stock, than with all the Bibles put together. It told all about how the Rothschilds and the Roosevelts and the Greenblatts were taking over the U.S. economy and the U.S. government. There were graphs showing how the Jews related directly to the Communist-Marxist-Leninist-Trotskyite axis, and from there to the Antichrist Itself.

The days of McCarthyism were not long over in Washington; in the Midwest Joe McCarthy's star had not yet set, and Margaret Chase Smith of Maine was known as "that bitch" for her famous Declaration of Conscience. In addition to the stuff about Communism, Greg Stillson's rural farm constituency seemed to have a morbid interest in the idea that the Jews were running the world.

Now Greg turned into the dusty driveway of a farmhouse some twenty miles west of Ames, Iowa. It had a deserted, shut-up look to it—the shades down and the barn doors closed—but you could never tell until you tried. That motto had served Greg Stillson well in the two years or so since he and his mother had moved up to Omaha from Oklahoma. The house-painting business had been no great shakes, but he had needed to get the taste of Jesus out of his mouth for a little while, you should pardon the small blasphemy. But now he had come back home—not on the pulpit or revival side this time, though, and it was something of a relief to be out of the miracle business at last.

He opened the car door and as he stepped out into the dust of the driveway a big mean farm dog advanced out of the barn, its ears laid back. It volleyed barks. "Hello, pooch," Greg said in his low, pleasant, but carrying voice—at twenty-two it was already the voice of a trained spellbinder.

The pooch didn't respond to the friendliness in his voice. It kept coming, big and mean, intent on an early lunch of traveling salesman. Greg sat back down in the car, closed the door, and honked the horn twice. Sweat rolled down his face and turned his white linen suit darker gray in circular patches under his arms and in a branching treeshape up his back. He honked again, but there was no response. The clodhoppers had loaded themselves into their International Harvester or their Studebaker and gone into town.

Greg smiled.

Instead of shifting into reverse and backing out of the driveway, he reached behind him and produced a Flit gun—only this one was loaded with ammonia instead of Flit.

Pulling back the plunger, Greg stepped out of the car again, smiling easily. The dog, which had settled down on its haunches, immediately got up again and began to advance on him, growling.

Greg kept smiling. "That's right, poochie," he said in that pleasant, carrying voice. "You just come on. Come on and get it." He hated these ugly farm dogs that ran their half-acre of dooryard like arrogant little Caesars; they told you something about their masters as well.

"Fucking bunch of clodhoppers," he said under his breath. He was still smiling. "Come on, doggie."

The dog came. It tensed its haunches down to spring at him. In the barn a cow mooed, and the wind rustled tenderly through the corn. As it leaped, Greg's smile turned to a hard and bitter grimace. He depressed the Flit plunger and sprayed a stinging cloud of ammonia droplets directly into the dog's eyes and nose.

Its angry barking turned immediately to short, agonized yips, and then, as the bite of ammonia really settled in, to howls of pain. It turned tail at once, a watchdog no longer but only a vanquished cur.

Greg Stillson's face had darkened. His eyes had drawn down to ugly slits. He stepped forward rapidly and administered a whistling kick to the dog's haunches with one of his Stride-King airtip shoes. The dog gave a high, wailing sound, and, driven by its pain and fear, it sealed its own doom by turning around to give battle to the author of its misery rather than running for the barn.

With a snarl, it struck out blindly, snagged the right cuff of Greg's white linen pants, and tore it.

"You sonofabitch!" he cried out in startled anger, and kicked the dog again, this time hard enough to send it rolling in the dust. He advanced on the dog once more, kicked it again, still yelling. Now the dog, eyes watering, nose in fiery agony, one rib broken and another badly sprung, realized its danger from this madman, but it was too late.

Greg Stillson chased it across the dusty farmyard, panting and shouting, sweat rolling down his cheeks, and kicked the dog until it was screaming and barely able to drag itself along through the dust. It was bleeding in half a dozen places. It was dying.

"Shouldn't have bit me," Greg whispered. "You hear? You hear me? You shouldn't have bit me, you dipshit dog. No one gets in my way. You hear? No one." He delivered another kick with one blood-spattered airtip, but the dog could do no more than make a low choking sound. Not much satisfaction in that. Greg's head ached. It was the sun. Chasing the dog around in the hot sun. Be lucky not to pass out.

He closed his eyes for a moment, breathing rapidly, the sweat rolling down his face like tears and nestling in his crew-cut like gems, the broken dog dying at his feet. Colored specks of light, pulsing in rhythm with his heartbeat, floated across the darkness behind his lids.

His head ached.

Sometimes he wondered if he was going crazy. Like now. He had meant to give the dog a burst from the ammonia Flit gun, drive it back into the barn so he could leave his business card in the crack of the screen door. Come back some other time and make a sale. Now look. Look at this mess. Couldn't very well leave his card now, could he?

He opened his eyes. The dog lay at his feet, panting rapidly, drizzling blood from its snout. As Greg Stillson looked down, it licked his shoe humbly, as if to acknowledge that it had been bested, and then it went back to the business of dying.

"Shouldn't have torn my pants," he said to it. "Pants cost me five bucks, you shitpoke dog."

He had to get out of here. Wouldn't do him any good if Clem Kadiddlehopper and his wife and their six kids came back from town now in their Studebaker and saw Fido dying out here with the bad old salesman standing over him. He'd lose his job. The American TruthWay Company didn't hire salesmen who killed dogs that belonged to Christians.

Giggling nervously, Greg went back to the Mercury, got in, and backed rapidly out of the driveway. He turned east on the dirt road that ran straight as a string through the corn, and was soon cruising along at sixty-five, leaving a dust plume two miles long behind him.

He most assuredly didn't want to lose the job. Not yet. He was making good money—in addition to the wrinkles the American TruthWay Company knew about, Greg had added a few of his own that they didn't know about. He was making it now. Besides, traveling around, he got to meet a lot of people . . . a lot of girls. It was a good life, except—

Except he wasn't content.

He drove on, his head throbbing. No, he just wasn't content. He felt that he was meant for bigger things than driving around the Midwest and selling Bibles and doctoring the commission forms in order to make an extra two bucks a day. He felt that he was meant for . . . for . . .

For greatness.

Yes, that was it, that was surely it. A few weeks ago he had taken some girl up in the hayloft, her folks had been in Davenport selling a truckload of chickens, she had started off by asking if he would like a glass of lemonade and one thing had just led to another and after he'd had her she said it was almost like getting diddled by a preacher and he had slapped her, he didn't know why. He had slapped her and then left.

Well, no.

Actually, he had slapped her three or four times. Until she had cried and screamed for someone to come and help her and then he had stopped and somehow—he had had to use every ounce of the charm God had given him—he had made it up with her. His head had been aching then, too, the pulsing specks of brightness shooting and caroming across his field of vision, and he tried to tell himself it was the heat, the explosive heat in the hayloft, but it wasn't just the heat that made his head ache. It was the same thing he had felt in the dooryard when the dog tore his pants, something dark and crazy.

"I'm not crazy," he said aloud in the car. He unrolled the window swiftly, letting in summer heat and the smell of dust and corn and manure. He turned on the radio loud and caught a Patti Page song. His headache went back a little bit.

It was all a matter of keeping yourself under control and—and keeping your record clean. If you did those things, they couldn't touch you. And he was getting better at both of those things. He no longer had the dreams about his father so often, the dreams where his father was standing above him with his hard hat cocked back on his head, bellowing: *"You're no good, runt! You're no fucking good!"*

He didn't have the dreams so much because they just weren't true. He wasn't a runt anymore. Okay, he had been sick a lot as a kid, not much size, but he had gotten his growth, he was taking care of his mother—

And his father was dead. His father couldn't see. He couldn't make his father eat his words because he had died in an oil-derrick blowout and he was dead and once, just once, Greg would like to dig him up and scream into his moldering face *You were wrong, dad, you were wrong about me!* and then give him a good kick the way—

The way he had kicked the dog.

The headache was back, lowering.

"I'm not crazy," he said again below the sound of the music. His mother had told him often that he was meant for something big, something great, and Greg believed it. It was just a matter of getting things—like slapping the girl or kicking the dog—under control and keeping his record clean.

Whatever his greatness was, he would know it when it came to him. Of that he felt quite sure.

He thought of the dog again, and this time the thought

brought a bare crescent of a smile, without humor or compassion.

His greatness was on the way. It might still be years ahead—he was young, sure, nothing wrong with being young as long as you understood you couldn't have everything all at once. As long as you believed it would come eventually. He did believe that.

And God and Sonny Jesus help anyone that got in his way.

Greg Stillson cocked a sunburned elbow out the window and began to whistle along with the radio. He stepped on the go-pedal, walked that old Mercury up to seventy, and rolled down the straight Iowa farm road toward whatever future there might be.

· I ·

The Wheel
of Fortune

Chapter 1

♦ 1 ♦

The two things Sarah remembered about that night later were his run of luck at the Wheel of Fortune and the mask. But as time passed, years of it, it was the mask she thought about—when she could bring herself to think about that horrible night at all.

He lived in an apartment house in Cleaves Mills. Sarah got there at quarter to eight, parking around the corner, and buzzing up to be let in. They were taking her car tonight because Johnny's was laid up at Tibbets' Garage in Hampden with a frozen wheel-bearing or something like that. Something expensive, Johnny had told her over the phone, and then he had laughed a typical Johnny Smith laugh. Sarah would have been in tears if it had been her car—her *pocketbook*.

Sarah went through the foyer to the stairs, past the bulletin board that hung there. It was dotted with file cards advertising motorbikes, stereo components, typing services, and appeals from people who needed rides to Kansas or California, people who were driving to Florida and needed riders to share the driving and help pay for the gas. But tonight the board was dominated by a large placard showing a clenched fist against an angry red background suggesting fire. The one word on the poster was STRIKE! It was late October of 1970.

Johnny had the front apartment on the second floor—the penthouse, he called it—where you could stand in your tux like Ramon Navarro, a big slug of Ripple wine in a balloon glass, and look down upon the vast, beating heart of Cleaves Mills: its hurrying after-show crowds, its bustling taxis, its neon signs. There are almost seven thousand stories in the naked city. This has been one of them.

Actually Cleaves Mills was mostly a main street with a stop-and-go light at the intersection (it turned into a blinker after 6 P.M.), about two dozen stores, and a small moccasin factory. Like most of the towns surrounding Orono, where the Univer-

13

sity of Maine was, its real industry was supplying the things students consumed—beer, wine, gas, rock 'n' roll music, fast food, dope, groceries, housing, movies. The movie house was The Shade. It showed art films and '40's nostalgia flicks when school was in. In the summertime it reverted to Clint Eastwood spaghetti Westerns.

Johnny and Sarah were both out of school a year, and both were teaching at Cleaves Mills High, one of the few high schools in the area that had not consolidated into a three- or four-town district. University faculty and administration as well as university students used Cleaves as their bedroom, and the town had an enviable tax base. It also had a fine high school with a brand-new media wing. The townies might bitch about the university crowd with their smart talk and their Commie marches to end the war and their meddling in town politics, but they had never said no to the tax dollars that were paid annually on the gracious faculty homes and the apartment buildings in the area some students called Fudgey Acres and others called Sleaze Alley.

Sarah rapped on his door and Johnny's voice, oddly muffled, called, "It's open, Sarah!"

Frowning a little, she pushed the door open. Johnny's apartment was in total darkness except for the fitful yellow glow of the blinker half a block up the street. The furniture was so many humped black shadows.

"Johnny . . . ?"

Wondering if a fuse had blown or something, she took a tentative step forward—and then the face appeared before her, floating in the darkness, a horrible face out of a nightmare. It glowed a spectral, rotting green. One eye was wide open, seeming to stare at her in wounded fear. The other was squeezed shut in a sinister leer. The left half of the face, the half with the open eye, appeared to be normal. But the right half was the face of a monster, drawn and inhuman, the thick lips drawn back to reveal snaggle teeth that were also glowing.

Sarah uttered a strangled little shriek and took a stumble-step backward. Then the lights came on and it was just Johnny's apartment again instead of some black limbo, Nixon on the wall trying to sell used cars, the braided rug Johnny's mother had made on the floor, the wine bottles made into candle bases. The face stopped glowing and she saw it was a dime-store Halloween mask, nothing more. Johnny's blue eye was twinkling out of the open eyehole at her.

He stripped it off and stood smiling amiably at her, dressed in faded jeans and a brown sweater.

"Happy Halloween, Sarah," he said.

Her heart was still racing. He had really frightened her. "Very funny," she said, and turned to go. She didn't like being scared like that.

He caught her in the doorway. "Hey . . . I'm sorry."

"Well you ought to be." She looked at him coldly—or tried to. Her anger was already melting away. You just couldn't stay mad at Johnny, that was the thing. Whether she loved him or not—a thing she was still trying to puzzle out—it was impossible to be unhappy with him for very long, or to harbor a feeling of resentment. She wondered if anyone had ever succeeded in harboring a grudge against Johnny Smith, and the thought was so ridiculous she just had to smile.

"There, that's better. Man, I thought you were going to walk out on me."

"I'm not a man."

He cast his eyes upon her. "So I've noticed."

She was wearing a bulky fur coat—imitation raccoon or something vulgar like that—and his innocent lechery made her smile again. "In this thing you couldn't tell."

"Oh, yeah, I can tell," he said. He put an arm around her and kissed her. At first she wasn't going to kiss back, but of course she did.

"I'm sorry I scared you," he said, and rubbed her nose companionably with his own before letting her go. He held up the mask. "I thought you'd get a kick out of it. I'm gonna wear it in homeroom Friday."

"Oh, Johnny, that won't be very good for discipline."

"I'll muddle through somehow," he said with a grin. And the hell of it was, he would.

She came to school every day wearing big, schoolmarmish glasses, her hair drawn back into a bun so severe it seemed on the verge of a scream. She wore her skirts just above the knee in a season when most of the girls wore them just below the edges of their underpants (and my legs are better than any of theirs, Sarah thought resentfully). She maintained alphabetical seating charts which, by the law of averages, at least, should have kept the troublemakers away from each other, and she resolutely sent unruly pupils to the assistant principal, her reasoning being that he was getting an extra five hundred a year to act as ramrod and she wasn't. And still her days were a constant struggle with that freshman teacher demon. Discipline. More disturbing, she had begun to sense that there was a collective, unspoken jury—a kind of school consciousness, maybe—that went into deliberations over every new teacher, and that the verdict being returned on her was not so good.

Johnny, on the face of it, appeared to be the antithesis of everything a good teacher should be. He ambled from class to class in an agreeable sort of daze, often showing up tardy because he had stopped to chat with someone between bells. He let the kids sit where they wanted to so that the same face was never in the same seat from day to day (and the class thugs invariably gravitated to the back of the room). Sarah would not have been able to learn their names that way until March, but Johnny seemed to have them down pat already.

He was a tall man who had a tendency to slouch, and the kids called him Frankenstein. Johnny seemed amused rather than outraged by this. And yet his classes were mostly quiet and well-behaved, there were few skippers (Sarah had a constant problem with kids cutting class), and that same jury seemed to be coming back in his favor. He was the sort of teacher who, in another ten years, would have the school yearbook dedicated to him. She just wasn't. And sometimes wondering why drove her crazy.

"You want a beer before we go? Glass of wine? Anything?"

"No, but I hope you're going well-heeled," she said, taking his arm and deciding not to be mad anymore. "I always eat at least three hot dogs. Especially when it's the last county fair of the year." They were going to Esty, twenty miles north of Cleaves Mills, a town whose only dubious claim to fame was that it held ABSOLUTELY THE LAST AGRICULTURAL FAIR OF THE YEAR IN NEW ENGLAND. The fair would close Friday night, on Halloween.

"Considering Friday's payday, I'm doing good. I got eight bucks."

"Oh . . . my . . . God," Sarah said, rolling her eyes. "I always knew if I kept myself pure I'd meet a sugar daddy someday."

He smiled and nodded. "Us pimps make biiig money, baby. Just let me get my coat and we're off."

She looked after him with exasperated affection, and the

voice that had been surfacing in her mind more and more often—in the shower, while she was reading a book or prepping a class or making her supper for one—came up again, like one of those thirty-second public-service spots on TV. *He's a very nice man and all that, easy to get along with, fun, he never makes you cry. But is that love? I mean, is that all there is to it? Even when you learned to ride your two-wheeler, you had to fall off a few times and scrape both knees. Call it a rite of passage. And that was just a* little *thing.*

"Gonna use the bathroom," he called to her.

"Uh-huh." She smiled a little. Johnny was one of those people who invariably mentioned their nature calls—God knew why.

She went over to the window and looked out on Main Street. Kids were pulling into the parking lot next to O'Mike's, the local pizza-and-beer hangout. She suddenly wished she were back with them, one of them, with this confusing stuff behind her—or still ahead of her. The university was safe. It was a kind of never-never land where everybody, even the teachers, could be a part of Peter Pan's band and never grow up. And there would always be a Nixon or an Agnew to play Captain Hook.

She had met Johnny when they started teaching in September, but she had known his face from the Ed courses they had shared. She had been pinned to a Delta Tau Delta, and none of the judgments that applied to Johnny had applied to Dan. He had been almost flawlessly handsome, witty in a sharp and restless way that always made her a trifle uncomfortable, a heavy drinker, a passionate lover. Sometimes when he drank he turned mean. She remembered a night in Bangor's Brass Rail when that had happened. The man in the next booth had taken joking issue with something Dan had been saying about the UMO football team, and Dan had asked him if he would like to go home with his head on backward. The man had apologized, but Dan hadn't wanted an apology; he had wanted a fight. He began to make personal remarks about the woman with the other man. Sarah had put her hand on Dan's arm and asked him to stop. Dan had shaken her hand off and had looked at her with a queer flat light in his grayish eyes that made any other words she might have spoken dry up in her throat. Eventually, Dan and the other guy went outside and Dan beat him up. Dan had beaten him until the other man, who was in his late thirties and getting a belly, had screamed. Sarah had never heard a man scream before—she never wanted to hear it again. They had to leave quickly because the bartender saw how it was going and called the police. She would have gone home alone that night (*Oh? are you sure?* her mind asked nastily), but it was twelve miles back to the campus and the buses had stopped running at six and she was afraid to hitch.

Dan didn't talk on the way back. He had a scratch on one cheek. Just one scratch. When they got back to Hart Hall, her dorm, she told him she didn't want to see him anymore. "Any way you want it, babe," he said with an indifference that had chilled her—and the second time he called after the Brass Rail incident she had gone out with him. Part of her had hated herself for that.

It had continued all that fall semester of her senior year. He had frightened and attracted her at the same time. He was her first real lover, and even now, two days shy of Halloween 1970, he had been her only real lover. She and Johnny had not been to bed.

Dan had been very good. He had used her, but he had been very good. He would not take any precautions and so she had been forced to go to the university infirmary, where she talked fumblingly about painful menstruation and got the pill. Sexually, Dan had dominated her all along. She did not have many orgasms with him, but his very roughness brought her some, and in the weeks before it had ended she had begun to feel a mature woman's greediness for good sex, a desire that was bewilderingly intermixed with other feelings: dislike for both Dan and herself, a feeling that no sex that depended so much on humiliation and domination could really be called "good sex," and self-contempt for her own inability to call a halt to a relationship that seemed based on destructive feelings.

It had ended swiftly, early this year. He flunked out. "Where will you be going?" she asked him timidly, sitting on his roomie's bed as he threw things into two suitcases. She had wanted to ask other, more personal questions. Will you be near here? Will you take a job? Take night classes? Is there a place for me in your plans? That question, above all others, she had not been able to ask. Because she wasn't prepared for any answer. The answer he gave to her one neutral question was shocking enough.

"Vietnam, I guess."

"What?"

He reached onto a shelf, thumbed briefly through the papers there, and tossed her a letter. It was from the induction center in Bangor: an order to report for his physical exam.

"Can't you get out of it?"

"No. Maybe. I don't know." He lit a cigarette. "I don't think I even want to try."

She had stared at him, shocked.

"I'm tired of this scene. College and get a job and find a little wifey. You've been applying for the little wifey spot, I guess. And don't think I haven't thought it over. It wouldn't work. You know it wouldn't and so do I. We don't fit, Sarah."

She had fled then, all her questions answered, and she never saw him again. She saw his roommate a few times. He got three letters from Dan between January and June. He was inducted and sent down south somewhere for basic training. And that was the last the roommate had heard. It was the last Sarah Bracknell heard, too.

At first she thought she was going to be okay. All those sad, torchy songs, the ones you always seem to hear on the car radio after midnight, they didn't apply to her. Or the clichés about the end of the affair or the crying jags. She didn't pick up a guy on the rebound or start doing the bars. Most evenings that spring she spent studying quietly in her dorm room. It was a relief. It wasn't messy.

It was only after she met Johnny—at a freshman mixer dance last month; they were both chaperoning, purely by luck of the draw—that she realized what a horror her last semester at school had been. It was the kind of thing you couldn't see when you were in it, it was too much a part of you. Two donkeys meet at a hitching rail in a western town. One of them is a town donkey with nothing on his back but a saddle. The other is a prospector's donkey, loaded down with packs, camping and cooking gear, and four fifty-pound sacks of ore. His back is bent into a concertina shape from the weight. The town donkey says, *That's quite a load you got there.* And the prospector's donkey says, *What load?*

In retrospect it was the emptiness that horrified her, it had been five months of Cheyne-Stokes respiration. Eight months if you counted this summer, when she took a small apartment on Flagg Street in Veazie and did nothing but apply for teaching jobs and read paperback novels. She got up, ate breakfast, went out to class or to whatever job interviews she had scheduled, came home, ate, took a nap (the naps were sometimes four hours long), ate again, read until eleven-thirty or so, watched Cavett until she got sleepy, went to bed. She could not remember *thinking* during that period. Life was routine. Sometimes there was a vague sort of ache in her loins, an *unfulfilled ache,* she believed the lady novelists sometimes called it, and for this she would either take a cold shower or a douche. After a while the douches grew painful, and this gave her a bitter, absent sort of satisfaction.

During this period she would congratulate herself from time to time on how adult she was being about the whole thing. She hardly ever thought about Dan—Dan Who, ha-ha. Later she realized that for eight months she had thought of nothing or no one else. The whole country had gone through a spasm of shudders during those eight months, but she had hardly noticed. The marches, the cops in their crash helmets and gas masks, the mounting attacks on the press by Agnew, the Kent State shootings, the summer of violence as blacks and radical groups took to the streets—those things might have happened on some TV late show. Sarah was totally wrapped up in how wonderfully she had gotten over Dan, how well she was adjusting, and how relieved she was to find that everything was just fine. What load?

Then she had started at Cleaves Mills High, and that had been a personal upheaval, being on the other side of the desk after sixteen years as a professional student. Meeting Johnny Smith at that mixer (and with an absurd name like John Smith, could he be completely for real?). Coming out of herself enough to see the way he was looking at her, not lecherously, but with a good healthy appreciation for the way she looked in the light-gray knitted dress she had worn.

He had asked her out to a movie—*Citizen Kane* was playing at The Shade—and she said okay. They had a good time and she was thinking to herself, *No fireworks.* She had enjoyed his kiss goodnight and had thought, *He's sure no Errol Flynn.* He had kept her smiling with his line of patter, which was outrageous, and she had thought, *He wants to be Henny Youngman when he grows up.*

Later that evening, sitting in the bedroom of her apartment and watching Bette Davis play a bitchy career woman on the late movie, some of these thoughts had come back to her and she paused with her teeth sunk into an apple, rather shocked at her own unfairness.

And a voice that had been silent for the best part of a year—not so much the voice of conscience as that of perspective—spoke up abruptly. *What you mean is, he sure isn't Dan. Isn't that it?*

No! she assured herself, not just *rather* shocked now. *I don't think about Dan at all anymore. That . . . was a long time ago.*

Diapers, the voice replied, *that was a long time ago. Dan left yesterday.*

She suddenly realized she was sitting in an apartment by herself late at night, eating an apple and watching a movie on TV that she cared nothing about, and doing it all because it was easier than thinking, thinking was so boring really, when all you had to think about was yourself and your lost love.

Very shocked now.

She had burst into tears.

She had gone out with Johnny the second and third time he asked, too, and that was also a revelation of exactly what she had become. She couldn't very well say that she had another date because it wasn't so. She was a smart, pretty girl, and she had been asked out a lot after the affair with Dan ended, but the only dates she had accepted were hamburger dates at the Den with Dan's roomie, and she realized now (her disgust tempered with rueful humor) that she had only gone on those completely innocuous dates in order to pump the poor guy about Dan. What load?

Most of her college girl friends had dropped over the horizon after graduation. Bettye Hackman was with the Peace Corps in Africa, to the utter dismay of her wealthy old-line-Bangor parents, and sometimes Sarah wondered what the Ugandans must make of Bettye with her white, impossible-to-tan skin and ash-blonde hair and cool, sorority good looks. Deenie Stubbs was at grad school in Houston. Rachel Jurgens had married her fella and was currently gestating somewhere in the wilds of western Massachusetts.

Slightly dazed, Sarah had been forced to the conclusion that Johnny Smith was the first new friend she had made in a long, long time—and she had been her senior high school class's Miss Popularity. She had accepted dates from a couple of the other Cleaves teachers, just to keep things in perspective. One of them was Gene Sedecki, the new math man—but obviously a veteran bore. The other, George Rounds, had immediately tried to make her. She had slapped his face—and the next day he'd had the gall to wink at her as they passed in the hall.

But Johnny was fun, easy to be with. And he did attract her sexually—just how strongly she couldn't honestly say, at least not yet. A week ago, after the Friday they'd had off for the October teachers' convention in Waterville, he had invited her back to his apartment for a home-cooked spaghetti dinner. While the sauce simmered, he had dashed around the corner to get some wine and had come back with two bottles of Apple Zapple. Like announcing his bathroom calls, it was somehow Johnny's style.

After the meal they had watched TV and that had turned to necking and God knew what *that* might have turned into if a couple of his friends, instructors from the university, hadn't turned up with a faculty position paper on academic freedom. They wanted Johnny to look it over and see what he thought. He had done so, but with noticeably less good will than was usual with him. She had noticed that with a warm, secret delight, and the ache in her own loins—the *unfulfilled ache*—had also delighted her, and that night she hadn't killed it with a douche.

She turned away from the window and walked over to the sofa where Johnny had left the mask.

"Happy Halloween," she snorted, and laughed a little.

"What?" Johnny called out.

"I said if you don't come pretty quick I'm going without you."

"Be right out."

"Swell!"

She ran a finger over the Jekyll-and-Hyde mask, kindly Dr. Jekyll the left half, ferocious, subhuman Hyde the right half. Where will we be by Thanksgiving? she wondered. Or by Christmas?

The thought sent a funny, excited little thrill shooting through her.

She liked him. He was a perfectly ordinary, sweet man.

She looked down at the mask again, horrible Hyde growing out of Jekyll's face like a lumpy carcinoma. It had been treated with fluorescent paint so it would glow in the dark.

What's ordinary? Nothing, nobody. Not really. If he was so ordinary, how could he be planning to wear something like that into his homeroom and still be confident of keeping order? And how can the kids call him Frankenstein and still respect and like him? What's ordinary?

Johnny came out, brushing through the beaded curtain that divided the bedroom and bathroom off from the living room.

If he wants me to go to bed with him tonight, I think I'm going to say okay.

And it was a warm thought, like coming home.

"What are you grinning about?"

"Nothing," she said, tossing the mask back to the sofa.

"No, really. Was it something good?"

"Johnny," she said, putting a hand on his chest and standing on tiptoe to kiss him lightly, "some things will never be told. Come on, let's go."

◆ 2 ◆

They paused downstairs in the foyer while he buttoned his denim jacket, and she found her eyes drawn again to the STRIKE! poster with its clenched fist and flaming background.

"There'll be another student strike this year," he said, following her eyes.

"The war?"

"That's only going to be part of it this time. Vietnam and the fight over ROTC and Kent State have activated more students than ever before. I doubt if there's ever been a time when there were so few grunts taking up space at the university."

"What do you mean, grunts?"

"Kids just studying to make grades, with no interest in the system except that it provides them with a ten-thousand-dollar-a-year job when they get out. A grunt is a student who gives a shit about nothing except his sheepskin. That's over. Most of them are awake. There are going to be some big changes."

"Is that important to you? Even though you're out?"

He drew himself up. "Madam, I am an alumnus. Smith, class of '70. Fill the steins to dear old Maine."

She smiled. "Come on, let's go. I want a ride on the whip before they shut it down for the night."

"Very good," he said, taking her arm. "I just happen to have your car parked around the corner."

"And eight dollars. The evening fairly glitters before us."

The night was overcast but not rainy, mild for late October. Overhead, a quarter moon was struggling to make it through the cloud cover. Johnny slipped an arm around her and she moved closer to him.

"You know, I think an awful lot of you, Sarah." His tone was almost offhand, but only almost. Her heart slowed a little and then made speed for a dozen beats or so.

"Really?"

"I guess this Dan guy, he hurt you, didn't he?"

"I don't know what he did to me," she said truthfully. The yellow blinker, a block behind them now, made their shadows appear and disappear on the concrete in front of them.

Johnny appeared to think this over. "I wouldn't want to do that," he said finally.

"No, I know that. But Johnny . . . give it time."

"Yeah," he said. "Time. We've got that, I guess."

And that would come back to her, awake and even more strongly in her dreams, in tones of inexpressible bitterness and loss.

They went around the corner and Johnny opened the passenger door for her. He went around and got in behind the wheel. "You cold?"

"No," she said. "It's a great night for it."

"It is," he agreed, and pulled away from the curb. Her thoughts went back to that ridiculous mask. Half Jekyll with Johnny's blue eye visible behind the widened-O eyesocket of the surprised doctor—*Say, that's some cocktail I invented last night, but I don't think they'll be able to move it in the bars*—and that side was all right because you could see a bit of Johnny inside. It was the Hyde part that had scared her silly, because that eye was closed down to a slit. It could have been anybody. Anybody at all. Dan, for instance.

But by the time they reached the Esty fairgrounds, where the naked bulbs of the midway twinkled in the darkness and the long spokes of the Ferris wheel neon revolved up and down, she had forgotten the mask. She was with her guy, and they were going to have a good time.

◆ 3 ◆

They walked up the midway hand in hand, not talking much, and Sarah found herself reliving the county fairs of her youth. She had grown up in South Paris, a paper town in western Maine, and the big fair had been the one in Fryeburg. For

Johnny, a Pownal boy, it probably would have been Topsham. But they were all the same, really, and they hadn't changed much over the years. You parked your car in a dirt parking lot and paid your two bucks at the gate, and when you were barely inside the fairgrounds you could smell hot dogs, frying peppers and onions, bacon, cotton candy, sawdust, and sweet, aromatic horseshit. You heard the heavy, chain-driven rumble of the baby roller coaster, the one they called The Wild Mouse. You heard the popping of .22s in the shooting galleries, the tinny blare of the Bingo caller from the PA system strung around the big tent filled with long tables and folding chairs from the local mortuary. Rock 'n' roll music vied with the calliope for supremacy. You heard the steady cry of the barkers—two shots for two bits, win one of these stuffed doggies for your baby, hey-hey-over-here, pitch till you win. It didn't change. It turned you into a kid again, willing and eager to be suckered.

"Here!" she said, stopping him. "The whip! The whip!"

"Of course," Johnny said comfortingly. He passed the woman in the ticket cage a dollar bill, and she pushed back two red tickets and two dimes with barely a glance up from her *Photoplay*.

"What do you mean, 'of course'? Why are you 'of coursing' me in that tone of voice?"

He shrugged. His face was much too innocent.

"It wasn't what you said, John Smith. It was how you said it."

The ride had stopped. Passengers were getting off and streaming past them, mostly teenagers in blue melton CPO shirts or open parkas. Johnny led her up the wooden ramp and surrendered their tickets to the whip's starter, who looked like the most bored sentient creature in the universe.

"Nothing," he said as the starter settled them into one of the little round shells and snapped the safety bar into place. "It's just that these cars are on little circular tracks, right?"

"Right."

"And the little circular tracks are embedded on a large circular dish that spins around and around, right?"

"Right."

"Well, when this ride is going full steam, the little car we're sitting in whips around on its little circular track and sometimes develops up to seven g, which is only five less than the astronauts get when they lift off from Cape Kennedy. And I knew this kid . . ." Johnny was leaning solemnly over her now.

"Oh, here comes one of your big lies," Sarah said uneasily.

"When this kid was five he fell down the front steps and put a tiny hairline fracture in his spine at the top of his neck. Then—*ten years later*—he went on the whip at Topsham Fair . . . and . . ." He shrugged and then patted her hand sympathetically. "But you'll probably be okay, Sarah."

"Ohhh . . . I want to get *offfff* . . ."

And the whip whirled them away, slamming the fair and the midway into a tilted blur of lights and faces, and she shrieked and laughed and began to pummel him.

"Hairline fracture!" She shouted at him. "I'll give *you* a hairline fracture when we get off this, you liar!"

"Do you feel anything giving in your neck yet?" he inquired sweetly.

"Oh, you liar!"

They whirled around, faster and faster, and as they snapped past the ride starter for the—tenth? fifteenth?—time, he leaned over and kissed her, and the car whistled around on its track, pressing their lips together in something that was hot and exciting and skintight. Then the ride was slowing down, their car clacked around on its track more reluctantly, and finally came to a swaying, swinging stop.

They got out, and Sarah squeezed his neck. "Hairline fracture, you ass!" she whispered.

A fat lady in blue slacks and penny loafers was passing them. Johnny spoke to her, jerking a thumb back toward Sarah. "That girl is bothering me, ma'am. If you see a policeman would you tell him?"

"You young people think you're smart," the fat lady said disdainfully. She waddled away toward the bingo tent, holding her purse more tightly under her arm. Sarah was giggling helplessly.

"You're impossible."

"I'll come to a bad end," Johnny agreed. "My mother always said so."

They walked up the midway side by side again, waiting for the world to stop making unstable motions before their eyes and under their feet.

"She's pretty religious, your mom, isn't she?" Sarah asked.

"She's as Baptist as you can get," Johnny agreed. "But she's okay. She keeps it under control. She can't resist passing me a few tracts when I'm at home, but that's her thing. Daddy and I put up with it. I used to try to get on her case about it—I'd ask her who the heck was in Nod for Cain to go live with if his dad and mom were the first people on earth, stuff like that—but I decided it was sort of mean and quit it. Two years ago I thought Eugene McCarthy could save the world, and at least the Baptists don't have Jesus running for president."

"Your father's not religious?"

Johnny laughed. "I don't know about that, but he's sure no Baptist." After a moment's thought he added, "Dad's a carpenter," as if that explained it. She smiled.

"What would our mother think if she knew you were seeing a lapsed Catholic?"

"Ask me to bring you home," Johnny said promptly, "so she could slip you a few tracts."

She stopped, still holding his hand. "Would you like to bring me to your house?" she asked, looking at him closely.

Johnny's long, pleasant face became serious. "Yeah," he said. "I'd like you to meet them . . . and vice-versa."

"Why?"

"Don't you know why?" he asked her gently, and suddenly her throat closed and her head throbbed as if she might cry and she squeezed his hand tightly.

"Oh Johnny, I do like you."

"I like you even more than that," he said seriously.

"Take me on the Ferris wheel," she demanded suddenly, smiling. No more talk like this until she had a chance to consider it, to think where it might be leading. "I want to go up high where we can see everything."

"Can I kiss you at the top?"

"Twice, if you're quick."

He allowed her to lead him to the ticket booth, where he surrendered another dollar bill. As he paid he told her, "When I was in high school, I knew this kid who worked at the fair, and he said most of the guys who put these rides together are dead drunk and they leave off all sorts of . . ."

"Go to hell," she said merrily, "nobody lives forever."

"But everybody tries, you ever notice that?" he said, following her into one of the swaying gondolas.

As a matter of fact he got to kiss her several times at the top, with the October wind ruffling their hair and the midway spread out below them like a glowing clockface in the dark.

◆ 4 ◆

After the Ferris wheel they did the carousel, even though he told her quite honestly that he felt like a horse's ass. His legs were so long that he could have stood astride one of the plaster horses. She told him maliciously that she had known a girl in high school who had had a weak heart, except nobody *knew* she had a weak heart, and she had gotten on the carousel with her boyfriend and . . .

"Someday you'll be sorry," he told her with quiet sincerity. "A relationship based on lies is no good, Sarah."

She gave him a very moist raspberry.

After the carousel came the mirror maze, a very good mirror maze as a matter of fact, it made her think of the one in Bradbury's *Something Wicked This Way Comes,* where the little-old-lady schoolteacher almost got lost forever. She could see Johnny in another part of it, fumbling around, waving to her. Dozens of Johnnies, dozens of Sarahs. They bypassed each other, flickered around non-Euclidian angles, and seemed to disappear. She made left turns, right turns, bumped her nose on panes of clear glass, and got giggling helplessly, partly in a nervous claustrophobic reaction. One of the mirrors turned her into a squat Tolkien dwarf. Another created the apotheosis of teenage gangliness with shins a quarter of a mile long.

At last they escaped and he got them a couple of fried hot dogs and a Dixie cup filled with greasy french fries that tasted the way french fries hardly ever do once you've gotten past your fifteenth year.

They passed a kooch joint. Three girls stood out front in sequined skirts and bras. They were shimmying to an old Jerry Lee Lewis tune while the barker hawked them through a microphone. "Come on over baby," Jerry Lee blared, his piano boogying frankly across the sawdust-sprinkled arcades. "Come on over baby, baby got the bull by the horns . . . we ain't fakin . . . whole lotta shakin goin on . . ."

"Club Playboy," Johnny marveled, and laughed. "There used to be a place like this down at Harrison Beach. The barker used to swear the girls could take the glasses right off your nose with their hands tied behind their backs."

"It sounds like an interesting way to get a social disease," Sarah said, and Johnny roared with laughter.

Behind them the barker's amplified voice grew hollow with distance, counterpointed by Jerry Lee's pumping piano, music like some mad, dented hot rod that was too tough to die, rumbling out of the dead and silent fifties like an omen. "Come on, men, come on over, don't be shy because these girls sure aren't, not in the least little bit! It's all on the inside . . . your education isn't complete until you've seen the Club Playboy show . . ."

"Don't you want to go on back and finish your education?" she asked.

He smiled. "I finished my basic course work on that subject some time ago. I guess I can wait a while to get my Ph.D."

She glanced at her watch. "Hey, it's getting late, Johnny. And tomorrow's a school day."

"Yeah. But at least it's Friday."

She sighed, thinking of her fifth-period study hall and her seventh-period New Fiction class, both of them impossibly rowdy.

They had worked their way back to the main part of the midway. The crowd was thinning. The Tilt-A-Whirl had shut down for the evening. Two workmen with unfiltered cigarettes jutting from the corners of their mouths were covering the Wild Mouse with a tarpaulin. The man in the Pitch-Til-U-Win was turning off his lights.

"You doing anything Saturday?" he asked, suddenly diffident. "I know it's short notice, but . . ."

"I have plans," she said.

"Oh."

And she couldn't bear his crestfallen expression, it was really too mean to tease him about that. "I'm doing something with you."

"You are? . . . Oh, you are. Say, that's good." He grinned at her and she grinned back. The voice in her mind, which was sometimes as real to her as the voice of another human being, suddenly spoke up.

You're feeling good again, Sarah. Feeling happy. Isn't it fine?

"Yes, it is," she said. She went up on tiptoe and kissed him quickly. She made herself go on before she could chicken out. "It gets pretty lonely down there in Veazie sometimes, you know. Maybe I could . . . sort of spend the night with you."

He looked at her with warm thoughtfulness, and with a

speculation that made her tingle deep inside. "Would that be what you want, Sarah?"

She nodded. "Very much what I want."

"All right," he said, and put an arm around her.

"Are you sure?" Sarah asked a little shyly.

"I'm just afraid you'll change your mind."

"I won't, Johnny."

He hugged her tighter against him. "Then it's my lucky night."

They were passing the Wheel of Fortune as he said it, and Sarah would later remember that it was the only booth still open on that side of the midway for thirty yards in either direction. The man behind the counter had just finished sweeping the packed dirt inside for any spare dimes that might have fallen from the playing board during the night's action. Probably his last chore before closing up, she thought. Behind him was his large spoked wheel, outlined by tiny electric bulbs. He must have heard Johnny's remark, because he went into his pitch more or less automatically, his eyes still searching the dirt floor of his booth for the gleam of silver.

"Hey-hey-hey, if you feel lucky, mister, spin the Wheel of Fortune, turn dimes into dollars. It's all in the Wheel, try your luck, one thin dime sets this Wheel of Fortune in motion."

Johnny swung back toward the sound of his voice.

"Johnny?"

"I feel lucky, just like the man said." He smiled down at her. "Unless you mind . . . ?"

"No, go ahead. Just don't take too long."

He looked at her again in that frankly speculative way that made her feel a little weak, wondering how it would be with him. Her stomach did a slow roll-over that made her feel a bit nauseated with sudden sexual longing.

"No, not long." He looked at the pitchman. The midway behind them was almost completely empty now, and as the overcast had melted off above them it had turned chilly. The three of them were puffing white vapor as they breathed.

"Try your luck, young man?"

"Yes."

He had switched all his cash to his front pocket when they arrived at the fair, and now he pulled out the remains of his eight dollars. It came to a dollar eighty-five.

The playing board was a strip of yellow plastic with numbers and odds painted on it in squares. It looked a bit like a roulette board, but Johnny saw immediately that the odds here would have turned a Las Vegas roulette player gray. A trip combination paid off at only two to one. There were two house numbers, zero and double zero. He pointed this out to the pitchman who only shrugged.

"You want Vegas, go to Vegas. What can I say?"

But Johnny's good humor tonight was unshakable. Things had gotten off to a poor start with that mask, but it had been all upbeat from there. In fact, it was the best night he could remember in years, maybe the best night ever. He looked at Sarah. Her color was high, her eyes sparkling. "What do you say, Sarah?"

She shook her head. "It's Greek to me. What do you do?"

"Play a number. Or red/black. Or odd/even. Or a ten-number series. They all pay differently." He gazed at the pitchman, who gazed back blandly. "At least, they should."

"Play black," she said. "It is sort of exciting, isn't it?"

"Black," he said and dropped his odd dime on the black square.

The pitchman stared at the single dime on his expanse of playboard and sighed. "Heavy plunger." He turned to the Wheel.

Johnny's hand wandered absently to his forehead and touched it. "Wait," he said abruptly. He pushed one of his quarters onto the square reading 11–20.

"That it?"

"Sure," Johnny said.

The pitchman gave the Wheel a twist and it spun inside its circle of lights, red and black merging. Johnny absently rubbed at his forehead. The Wheel began to slow and now they could hear the metronomelike tick-tock of the small wooden clapper sliding past the pins that divided the numbers. It reached 8, 9, seemed about to stop on 10, and slipped into the 11 slot with a final click and came to rest.

"The lady loses, the gentleman wins," the pitchman said.

"You won, Johnny?"

"Seems like it," Johnny said as the pitchman added two quarters to his original one. Sarah gave a little squeal, barely noticing as the pitchman swept the dime away.

"Told you, my lucky night," Johnny said.

"Twice is luck, once is just a fluke," the pitchman remarked. "Hey-hey-hey."

"Go again, Johnny," she said.

"All right. Just as it is for me."

"Let it ride?"

"Yes."

The pitchman spun the Wheel again, and as it slid around, Sarah murmured quietly to him, "Aren't all these carnival wheels supposed to be fixed?"

"They used to be. Now the state inspects them and they just rely on their outrageous odds system."

The Wheel had slowed to its final unwinding tick-tock. The pointer passed 10 and entered Johnny's trip, still slowing.

"Come on, come *on!*" Sarah cried. A couple of teenagers on their way out paused to watch.

The wooden clapper, moving very slowly now, passed 16 and 17, then came to a stop on 18.

"Gentleman wins again." The pitchman added six more quarters to Johnny's pile.

"You're rich!" Sarah gloated, and kissed him on the cheek.

"You're streaking, fella," the pitchman agreed enthusiastically. "Nobody quits a hot stick. Hey-hey-hey."

"Should I go again?" Johnny asked her.

"Why not?"

"Yeah, go ahead, man," one of the teenagers said. A button on his jacket bore the face of Jimi Hendrix. "That guy took me for four bucks tonight. I love to see him take a beatin."

"You too then," Johnny told Sarah. He gave her the odd quarter off his stack of nine. After a moment's hesitation she laid it down on 21. Single numbers paid off ten to one on a hit, the board announced.

"You're riding the middle trip, right, fella?"

Johnny looked down at the eight quarters stacked on the board, and then he began to rub his forehead again, as if he felt the beginnings of a headache. Suddenly he swept the quarters off the board and jingled them in his two cupped hands.

"No. Spin for the lady. I'll watch this one."

She looked at him, puzzled. "Johnny?"

He shrugged. "Just a feeling."

The pitchman rolled his eyes in a heaven-give-me-strength-to-bear-these-fools gesture and set his Wheel going again. It spun, slowed, and stopped. On double zero. "House numbah, house numbah," the pitchman chanted, and Sarah's quarter disappeared into his apron.

"Is that fair, Johnny?" Sarah asked, hurt.

"Zero and double zero only pay the house," he said.

"Then you were smart to take your money off the board."

"I guess I was."

"You want me to spin this Wheel or go for coffee?" the pitchman asked.

"Spin it," Johnny said, and put his quarters down in two stacks of four on the third trip.

As the Wheel buzzed around in its cage of lights, Sarah asked Johnny, never taking her eyes from the spin, "How much can a place like this take in on one night?"

The teenagers had been joined by a quartet of older people, two men and two women. A man with the build of a construction worker said, "Anywheres from five to seven hundred dollars."

The pitchman rolled his eyes again. "Oh, man, I wish you was right," he said.

"Hey, don't give me that poor mouth," the man who looked like a construction worker said. "I used to work this scam twenty years ago. Five to seven hundred a night, two grand on a Saturday, easy. And that's running a straight Wheel."

Johnny kept his eyes on the Wheel, which was now spinning slowly enough to read the individual numbers as they flashed past. It flashed past 0 and 00, through the first trip, slowing, through the second trip, still slowing.

"Too much legs, man," one of the teenagers said.

"Wait," Johnny said, in a peculiar tone of voice. Sarah glanced at him, and his long, pleasant face looked oddly strained, his blue eyes darker than usual, far away, distant.

The pointer stopped on 30 and came to rest.

"Hot stick, hot stick," the pitchman chanted resignedly as the little crowd behind Johnny and Sarah uttered a cheer. The man who looked like a construction worker clapped Johnny on the back hard enough to make him stagger a bit. The pitchman reached into the Roi-Tan box under the counter and dropped four singles beside Johnny's eight quarters.

"Enough?" Sarah asked.

"One more," Johnny said. "If I win, this guy paid for our fair and your gas. If I lose, we're out half a buck or so."

"Hey-hey-hey," the pitchman chanted. He was brightening up now, getting his rhythm back. "Get it down where you want it down. Step right up, you other folks. This ain't no spectator sport. Round and round she's gonna go and where she's gonna stop ain't nobody knows."

The man who looked like a construction worker and the two teenagers stepped up beside Johnny and Sarah. After a moment's consultation, the teenagers produced half a buck in change between them and dropped it on the middle trip. The man who looked like a construction worker, who introduced himself as Steve Bernhardt, put a dollar on the square marked EVEN.

"What about you, buddy?" the pitchman asked Johnny. "You gonna play it as it lays?"

"Yes," Johnny said.

"Oh man," one of the teenagers said, "that's tempting fate."

"I guess," Johnny said, and Sarah smiled at him.

Bernhardt gave Johnny a speculative glance and suddenly switched his dollar to his third trip. "What the hell," sighed the teenager who had told Johnny he was tempting fate. He switched the fifty cents he and his friend had come up with to the same trip.

"All the eggs in one basket," the pitchman chanted. "That how you want it?"

The players stood silent and affirmative. A couple of roust-abouts had drifted over to watch, one of them with a lady friend; there was now quite a respectable little knot of people in front of the Wheel of Fortune concession in the darkening arcade. The pitchman gave the Wheel a mighty spin. Twelve pairs of eyes watched it revolve. Sarah found herself looking at Johnny again, thinking how strange his face was in this bold yet somehow furtive lighting. She thought of the mask again—Jekyll and Hyde, odd and even. Her stomach turned over again, making her feel a little weak. The Wheel slowed, began to tick. The teenagers began to shout at it, urging it onward.

"Little more, baby," Steve Bernhardt cajoled it. "Little more, honey."

The Wheel ticked into the third trip and came to a stop on 24. A cheer went up from the crowd again.

"Johnny, you did it, you did it!" Sarah cried.

The pitchman whistled through his teeth in disgust and paid off. A dollar for the teenagers, two for Bernhardt, a ten and two ones for Johnny. He now had eighteen dollars in front of him on the board.

"Hot stick, hot stick, hey-hey-hey. One more, buddy? This Wheel's your friend tonight."

Johnny looked at Sarah.

"Up to you, Johnny." But she felt suddenly uneasy.

"Go on, man," the teenager with the Jimi Hendrix button urged. "I *love* to see this guy get a beatin'."

"Okay," Johnny said, "last time."

"Get it down where you want it down."

They all looked at Johnny, who stood thoughtful for a moment, rubbing his forehead. His usually good-humored face was still and serious and composed. He was looking at the Wheel in its cage of lights and his fingers worked steadily at the smooth skin over his right eye.

"As is," he said finally.

A little speculative murmur from the crowd.

"Oh man, that is *really* tempting it."

"He's hot," Bernhardt said doubtfully. He glanced back at his wife, who shrugged to show her complete mystification. "I'll tag along with you, long, tall, and ugly."

The teenager with the button glanced at his friend, who shrugged and nodded. "Okay," he said, turning back to the pitchman. "We'll stick, too."

The Wheel spun. Behind them Sarah heard one of the roustabouts bet the other five dollars against the third trip coming up again. Her stomach did another forward roll but this time it didn't stop; it just went on somersaulting over and over and she became aware that she was getting sick. Cold sweat stood out on her face.

The Wheel began to slow in the first trip, and one of the teenagers flapped his hands in disgust. But he didn't move away. It ticked past 11, 12, 13. The pitchman looked happy at last. Tick-tock-tick, 14, 15, 16.

"It's going through," Bernhardt said. There was awe in his voice. The pitchman looked at his Wheel as if he wished he could just reach out and stop it. It clicked past 20, 21, and settled to a stop in the slot marked 22.

There was another shout of triumph from the crowd, which had now grown almost to twenty. All the people left at the fair were gathered ~~here~~, it seemed. Faintly, Sarah heard the roustabout who had lost his bet grumble something about "Shitass luck," as he paid off. Her head thumped. Her legs felt suddenly, horribly unsteady, the muscles trembling and untrustworthy. She blinked her eyes rapidly several times and got only a nauseating instant of vertigo for her pains. The world seemed to tilt up at a skewed angle, as if they were still on the Whip, and then slowly settle back down.

I got a bad hot dog, she thought dismally. That's what you get for trying your luck at the county fair, Sarah.

"Hey-hey-hey," the pitchman said without much enthusiasm, and paid off. Two dollars for the teenagers, four for Steve Bernhardt, and then a bundle for Johnny—three tens, a five, and a one. The pitchman was not overjoyed, but he was sanguine. If the tall, skinny man with the good-looking blonde tried the third trip again, the pitchman would almost surely gather back in everything he had paid out. It wasn't the skinny man's money until it was off the board. And if he walked? Well, he had cleared a thousand dollars on the Wheel just today, he could afford to pay out a little tonight. The word would get around that Sol Drummore's Wheel had been hit and tomorrow play would be heavier than ever. A winner was a good ad.

"Lay em down where you want em down," he chanted. Several of the others had moved up to the board and were putting down dimes and quarters. But the pitchman looked only at his money player. "What do you say, fella? Want to shoot the moon?"

Johnny looked down at Sarah. "What do you . . . hey, are you all right? You're white as a ghost."

"My stomach," she said, managing a smile. "I think it was my hot dog. Can we go home?"

"Sure. You bet." He was gathering the wad of wrinkled bills up from the board when his eyes happened on the Wheel again. The warm concern for her that had been in them faded out. They seemed to darken again, become speculative in a cold way. *He's looking at that wheel the way a little boy would look at his own private ant colony,* Sarah thought.

"Just a minute," he said.

"All right," Sarah answered. But she felt light-headed now as well as sick to her stomach. And there were rumblings in her lower belly that she didn't like. Not the backdoor trots, Lord. Please.

She thought: *He can't be content until he's lost it all back.*

And then, with strange certainty: *But he's not going to lose.*

"What do you say, buddy?" the pitchman asked. "On or off, in or out."

"Shit or git," one of the roustabouts said, and there was nervous laughter. Sarah's head swam.

Johnny suddenly shoved bills and quarters up to the corner of the board.

"What are you doing?" the pitchman asked, genuinely shocked.

"The whole wad on 19," Johnny said.

Sarah wanted to moan and bit it back.

The crowd murmured.

"Don't push it," Steve Bernhardt said in Johnny's ear. Johnny didn't answer. He was staring at the Wheel with something like indifference. His eyes seemed almost violet.

There was a sudden jingling sound that Sarah at first thought must be in her own ears. Then she saw that the others who had put money down were sweeping it back off the board again, leaving Johnny to make his play alone.

No! She found herself wanting to shout. *Not like that, not alone, it isn't fair . . .*

She bit down on her lips. She was afraid that she might throw up if she opened her mouth. Her stomach was very bad now. Johnny's pile of winnings sat alone under the naked lights. Fifty-four dollars, and the single-number payoff was ten for one.

The pitchman wet his lips. "Mister, the state says I'm not supposed to take any single number bets over two dollars."

"Come on," Bernhardt growled. "You aren't supposed to take trip bets over ten and you just let the guy bet eighteen. What is it, your balls starting to sweat?"

"No, it's just . . ."

"Come on," Johnny said abruptly. "One way or the other. My girl's sick."

The pitchman sized up the crowd. The crowd looked back at him with hostile eyes. It was bad. They didn't understand that the guy was just throwing his money away and he was trying to restrain him. Fuck it. The crowd wasn't going to like it either way. Let the guy do his headstand and lose his money so he could shut down for the night.

"Well," he said, "as long as none of youse is state inspectors . . ." He turned to his Wheel. "Round and round she's gonna go, and where she's gonna stop, ain't nobody knows."

He spun, sending the numbers into an immediate blur. For a time that seemed much longer than it actually could have been, there was no sound but the whirring of the Wheel of Fortune, the night wind rippling a swatch of canvas somewhere, and the sick thump in Sarah's own head. In her mind she begged Johnny to put his arm around her but he only stood quietly with his hands on the playing board and his eyes on the Wheel, which seemed determined to spin forever.

At last it slowed enough for her to be able to read the numbers and she saw 19, the 1 and 9 painted bright red on a black background. Up and down, up and down. The Wheel's smooth whirr broke into a steady ticka-ticka-ticka that was very loud in the stillness.

Now the numbers marched past the pointer with slowing deliberation.

One of the roustabouts called out in wonder: "By the Jesus, it's gonna be close, anyway!"

Johnny stood calmly, watching the Wheel, and now it seemed to her (although it might have been the sickness, which was now rolling through her belly in gripping, peristaltic waves) that his eyes were almost black. Jekyll and Hyde, she thought, and was suddenly, senselessly, afraid of him.

Ticka-ticka-ticka.

The Wheel clicked into the second trip, passed 15 and 16, clicked over 17 and, after an instant's hesitation, 18 as well. With a final *tick!* the pointer dropped into the 19 slot. The crowd held its breath. The Wheel revolved slowly, bringing the pointer up against the small pin between 19 and 20. For a quarter of a second it seemed that the pin could not hold the pointer in the 19 slot; that the last of its dying velocity would carry it over to 20. Then the Wheel rebounded, its force spent, and came to rest.

For a moment there was no sound from the crowd. No sound at all.

Then one of the teenagers, soft and awed: "Hey, man, you just won five hundred and forty dollars."

Steve Bernhardt: "I never seen a run like that. *Never.*"

Then the crowd cheered. Johnny was slapped on the back, pummeled. People brushed by Sarah to get at him, to touch him, and for the moment they were separated she felt miserable, raw panic. Strengthless, she was butted this way and that, her stomach rolling crazily. A dozen afterimages of the Wheel whirled blackly before her eyes.

A moment later Johnny was with her and she saw with weak gladness that it really *was* Johnny and not the composed, mannequinlike figure that had watched the Wheel on its last spin. He looked confused and concerned about her.

"Baby, I'm sorry," he said, and she loved him for that.

"I'm okay," she answered, not knowing if she was or not.

The pitchman cleared his throat. "The Wheel's shut down," he said. "The Wheel's shut down."

An accepting, ill-tempered rumble from the crowd.

The pitchman looked at Johnny. "I'll have to give you a check, young gentleman. I don't keep that much cash in the booth."

"Sure, anything," Johnny said. "Just make it quick. The lady here really is sick."

"Sure, a check," Steve Bernhardt said with infinite contempt. "He'll give you a check that'll bounce as high as the WGAN Tall Tower and *he'll* be down in Florida for the winter."

"My dear sir," the pitchman began, "I assure you . . ."

"Oh, go assure your mother, maybe she'll believe you," Bernhardt said. He suddenly reached over the playing board and groped beneath the counter.

"Hey!" The pitchman yelped. "This is robbery!"

The crowd did not appear impressed with his claim.

"Please," Sarah muttered. Her head was whirling.

"I don't care about the money," Johnny said suddenly. "Let us by, please. The lady's sick."

"Oh, *man*," the teenager with the Jimi Hendrix button said, but he and his buddy drew reluctantly aside.

"No, Johnny," Sarah said, although she was only holding back from vomiting by an act of will now. "Get your money." Five hundred dollars was Johnny's salary for three weeks.

"Pay off, you cheap tinhorn!" Bernhardt roared. He brought up the Roi-Tan cigar box from under the counter, pushed it aside without even looking inside it, groped again, and this time came up with a steel lockbox painted industrial green. He slammed it down on the play-board. "If there ain't five hundred and forty bucks in there, I'll eat my own shirt in front of all these people." He dropped a hard, heavy hand on Johnny's shoulder. "You just wait a minute, sonny. You're gonna have your payday or my name's not Steve Bernhardt."

"Really, sir, I don't have that much . . ."

"You pay," Steve Bernhardt said, leaning over him, "or I'll see you shut down. I mean that. I'm sincere about it."

The pitchman sighed and fished inside his shirt. He produced a key on a fine-link chain. The crowd sighed. Sarah could stay no longer. Her stomach felt bloated and suddenly as still as death. Everything was going to come up, everything, and at express-train speed. She stumbled away from Johnny's side and battered through the crowd.

"Honey, you all right?" a woman's voice asked her, and Sarah shook her head blindly.

"Sarah? *Sarah!*"

You just can't hide . . . from Jekyll and Hyde, she thought incoherently. The fluorescent mask seemed to hang sickly before her eyes in the midway dark as she hurried past the merry-go-round. She struck a light pole with her shoulder, staggered, grabbed it, and threw up. It seemed to come all the way from her heels, convulsing her stomach like a sick, slick fist. She let herself go with it as much as she could.

Smells like cotton candy, she thought, and with a groan she did it again, then again. Spots danced in front of her eyes. The last heave had brought up little more than mucus and air.

"Oh, my," she said weakly, and clung to the light pole to keep from falling over. Somewhere behind her Johnny was calling her name, but she couldn't answer just yet, didn't want to. Her stomach was settling back down a little and for just a moment she wanted to stand here in the dark and congratulate herself on being alive, on having survived her night at the fair.

"Sarah? *Sarah!*"

She spat twice to clear her mouth a little.

"Over here, Johnny."

He came around the carousel with its plaster horses frozen in midleap. She saw he was absently clutching a thick wad of greenbacks in one hand.

"Are you all right?"

"No, but better. I threw up."

"Oh. Oh, Jesus. Let's go home." He took her arm gently.

"You got your money."

He glanced down at the wad of bills and then tucked it absently into his pants pocket. "Yeah. Some of it or all of it, I don't know. That burly guy counted it out."

Sarah took a handkerchief from her purse and began rubbing her mouth with it. Drink of water, she thought. I'd sell my soul for a drink of water.

"You ought to care," she said. "It's a lot of money."

"Found money brings bad luck," he said darkly. "One of my mother's sayings. She had a million of em. And she's death on gambling."

"Dyed-in-the-wool Baptist," Sarah said, and then shuddered convulsively.

"You okay?" he asked, concerned.

"The chills," she said. "When we get in the car I want the heater on full blast, and . . . oh, Lord, I'm going to do it again."

She turned away from him and retched up spittle with a groaning sound. She staggered. He held her gently but firmly. "Can you get back to the car?"

"Yes. I'm all right now." But her head ached and her mouth tasted foul and the muscles of her back and belly all felt sprung out of joint, strained and achey.

They walked slowly down the midway together, scuffing through the sawdust, passing tents that had been closed up and snugged down for the night. A shadow glided up behind them and Johnny glanced around sharply, perhaps aware of how much money he had in his pocket.

It was one of the teenagers—about fifteen years old. He smiled shyly at them. "I hope you feel better," he said to Sarah. "It's those hot dogs, I bet. You can get a bad one pretty easy."

"Ag, don't talk about it," Sarah said.

"You need a hand getting her to the car?" he asked Johnny.

"No, thanks. We're fine."

"Okay. I gotta cut out anyway." But he paused a moment longer, his shy smile widening into a grin "I *love* to see that guy take a beatin."

He trotted off into the dark.

Sarah's small, white station wagon was the only car left in the dark parking lot; it crouched under a sodium light like a forlorn, forgotten pup. Johnny opened the passenger door for Sarah and she folded herself carefully in. He slipped in behind the wheel and started it up.

"It'll take a few minutes for the heater," he said.

"Never mind. I'm hot now."

He looked at her and saw the sweat breaking on her face. "Maybe we ought to trundle you up to the emergency room at Eastern Maine Medical," he said. "If it's salmonella, it could be serious."

"No, I'm okay. I just want to go home and go to sleep, I'm going to get up just long enough tomorrow morning to call in sick at school and then go back to sleep again."

"Don't even bother to get up that long. I'll call you in, Sarah."

She looked at him gratefully. "Would you?"

"Sure."

They were headed back to the main highway now.

"I'm sorry I can't come back to your place with you," Sarah said. "Really and truly."

"Not your fault."

"Sure it is. I ate the bad hot dog. Unlucky Sarah."

"I love you, Sarah," Johnny said. So it was out, it couldn't be called back, it hung between them in the moving car waiting for someone to do something about it.

She did what she could. "Thank you, Johnny."

They drove on in a comfortable silence.

Chapter 2

◆ 1 ◆

It was nearly midnight when Johnny turned the wagon into her driveway. Sarah was dozing.

"Hey," he said, cutting the motor and shaking her gently. "We're here."

"Oh . . . okay." She sat up and drew her coat more tightly about her.

"How do you feel?"

"Better. My stomach's sore and my back hurts, but better. Johnny, you take the car back to Cleaves with you."

"No, I better not," he said. "Someone would see it parked in front of the apartment house all night. That kind of talk we don't need."

"But I was going to come back with you . . ."

Johnny smiled. "And that would have made it worth the risk, even if we had to walk three blocks. Besides, I want you to have the car in case you change your mind about the emergency room."

"I won't."

"You might. Can I come in and call a cab?"

"You sure can."

They went in and Sarah turned on the lights before being attacked by a fresh bout of the shivers.

"The phone's in the living room. I'm going to lie down and cover up with a quilt."

The living room was small and functional, saved from a barracks flavor only by the splashy curtains—flowers in a psychedelic pattern and color—and a series of posters along one wall: Dylan at Forest Hills, Baez at Carnegie Hall, Jefferson Airplane at Berkeley, the Byrds in Cleveland.

Sarah lay down on the couch and pulled a quilt up to her chin. Johnny looked at her with real concern. Her face was paper-white except for the dark circles under her eyes. She looked about as sick as a person can get.

"Maybe I ought to spend the night here," he said. "Just in case something happens, like . . ."

"Like a hairline fracture at the top of my spine?" She looked at him with rueful humor.

"Well, you know. Whatever."

The ominous rumbling in her nether regions decided her. She had fully intended to finish this night by sleeping with John Smith. It wasn't going to work out that way. But that didn't mean she had to end the evening with him in attendance while she threw up, dashed for the w.c., and chugged most of a bottle of Pepto-Bismol.

"I'll be okay," she said. "It was just a bad carnival hot dog, Johnny. You could have just as easily gotten it yourself. Give me a call during your free period tomorrow."

"You sure?"

"Yes, I am."

"Okay, kid." He picked up the phone with no further argument and called his cab. She closed her eyes, lulled and comforted by the sound of his voice. One of the things she liked most about him was that he would always really try to do the right thing, the best thing, with no self-serving bullshit. That was good. She was too tired and feeling too low to play little social games.

"The deed's done," he said, hanging up. "They'll have a guy over in five minutes."

"At least you've got cab fare," she said, smiling.

"And I plan to tip handsomely," he replied, doing a passable W. C. Fields.

He came over to the couch, sat beside her, held her hand.

"Johnny, how did you do it?"

"Hmmm?"

"The Wheel. How could you do that?"

"It was a streak, that's all," he said, looking a little uncomfortable. "Everybody has a streak once in a while. Like at the racetrack or playing blackjack or just matching dimes."

"No," she said.

"Huh?"

"I don't think everybody *does* have a streak once in a while. It was almost uncanny. It . . . scared me a little."

"Did it?"

"Yes."

Johnny sighed. "Once in a while I get feelings, that's all. For as long as I can remember, since I was just a little kid. And I've always been good at finding things people have lost. Like that little Lisa Schumann at school. You know the girl I mean?"

"Little, sad, mousy Lisa?" She smiled. "I know her. She's wandering in clouds of perplexity through my business grammar course."

"She lost her class ring," Johnny said, "and came to me in tears about it. I asked her if she'd checked the back corners of the top shelf in her locker. Just a guess. But it was there."

"And you've always been able to do that?"

He laughed and shook his head. "Hardly ever." The smile slipped a little. "But it was strong tonight, Sarah. I had that Wheel . . ." He closed his fists softly and looked at them, now frowning. "I had it right here. And it had the strangest goddam associations for me."

"Like what?"

"Rubber," he said slowly. "Burning rubber. And cold. And ice. Black ice. Those things were in the back of my mind. God knows why. And a bad feeling. Like to beware."

She looked at him closely, saying nothing, and his face slowly cleared.

"But it's gone now, whatever it was. Nothing probably."

"It was five hundred dollars worth of good luck, anyway," she said. Johnny laughed and nodded. He didn't talk anymore and she drowsed, glad to have him there. She came back to wakefulness when headlights from outside splashed across the wall. His cab.

"I'll call," he said, and kissed her face gently. "You sure you don't want me to hang around?"

Suddenly she did, but she shook her head.

"Call me," she said.

"Period three," he promised. He went to the door.

"Johnny?"

He turned back.

"I love you, Johnny," she said, and his face lit up like a lamp.

He blew a kiss. "Feel better," he said, "and we'll talk."

She nodded, but it was four-and-a-half years before she talked to Johnny Smith again.

♦ 2 ♦

"Do you mind if I sit up front?" Johnny asked the cab driver.

"Nope. Just don't bump your knee on the meter. It's delicate."

Johnny slid his long legs under the meter with some effort and slammed the door. The cabbie, a middle-aged man with a bald head and a paunch, dropped his flag and the cab cruised up Flagg Street.

"Where to?"

"Cleaves Mills," Johnny said. "Main Street. I'll show you where."

"I got to ask you for fare-and-a-half," the cabbie said. "I don't like to, but I got to come back empty from there."

Johnny's hand closed absently over the lump of bills in his pants pocket. He tried to remember if he had ever had so much money on him at one time before. Once. He had bought a two-year-old Chevy for twelve hundred dollars. On a whim, he had asked for cash at the savings bank, just to see what all that cash looked like. It hadn't been all that wonderful, but the surprise on the car dealer's face when Johnny pumped twelve one-hundred-dollar bills into his hand had been wonderful to behold. But this lump of money didn't make him feel good at all, just vaguely uncomfortable, and his mother's axiom recurred to him: *Found money brings bad luck.*

"Fare-and-a-half's okay," he told the cabbie.

"Just as long's we understand each other," the cabbie said more expansively. "I got over so quick on account of I had a call at the Riverside and nobody there would own up when I got over there."

"That so?" Johnny asked without much interest. Dark

houses flashed by outside. He had won five hundred dollars, and nothing remotely like it had ever happened to him before. That phantom smell of rubber burning . . . the sense of partially reliving something that had happened to him when he was very small . . . and that feeling of bad luck coming to balance off the good was still with him.

"Yeah, these drunks call and then they change their minds," the cabbie said. "Damn drunks, I hate em. They call and decide what the hell, they'll have a few more beers. Or they drink up the fare while they're waitin and when I come in and yell 'Who wants the cab?' they don't want to own up."

"Yeah," Johnny said. On their left the Penobscot River flowed by, dark and oily. Then Sarah getting sick and saying she loved him on top of everything else. Probably just caught her in a weak moment, but God! if she had meant it! He had been gone on her almost since the first date. That was the luck of the evening, not beating that Wheel. But it was the Wheel his mind kept coming back to, worrying at it. In the dark he could still see it revolving, and in his ears he could hear the slowing ticka-ticka-ticka of the marker bumping over the pins like something heard in an uneasy dream. Found money brings bad luck.

The cabbie turned off onto Route 6, now well-launched into his own monologue.

"So I says, 'Blow it outcha you-know-where.' I mean, the kid is a smart-aleck, right? I don't have to take a load of horseshit like that from anyone, including my own boy. I been drivin this cab twenty-six years. I been held up six times. I been in fender-benders without number, although I never had a major crash, for which I thank Mary Mother of Jesus and Saint Christopher and God the Father Almighty, know what I mean? And every week, no matter how thin that week was, I put five bucks away for his college. Ever since he was nothin but a pipsqueak suckin a bottle. And what for? So he can come home one fine day and tell me the president of the United States is a pig. Hot damn! The kid probably thinks *I'm* a pig, although he knows if he ever said it I'd rearrange his teeth for him. So that's today's young generation for you. So I says, 'Blow it outcha you-know-where.' "

"Yeah," Johnny said. Now woods were floating by. Carson's Bog was on the left. They were seven miles from Cleaves Mills, give or take. The meter kicked over another dime.

One thin dime, one tenth of a dollar. Hey-hey-hey.

"What's your game, might I ask?" the cabbie said.

"I teach high school in Cleaves."

"Oh, yeah? So you know what I mean. What the hell's wrong with these kids, anyway?"

Well, they ate a bad hot dog called Vietnam and it gave them ptomaine. A guy named Lyndon Johnson sold it to them. So they went to this other guy, see, and they said, "Jesus, mister, I'm sick as hell." And this other guy, his name was Nixon, he said, "I know how to fix that. Have a few more hot dogs." And that's what's wrong with the youth of America.

"I don't know," Johnny said.

"You plan all your life and you do what you can," the cabbie said, and now there was honest bewilderment in his voice, a bewilderment which would not last much longer because the cabbie was embarked upon the last minute of his life. And Johnny, who didn't know that, felt a real pity for the man, a sympathy for his inability to understand.

Come on over baby, whole lotta shakin goin on.

"You never want nothing but the best, and the kid comes home with hair down to his asshole and says the president of the United States is a pig. A pig! Sheeyit, I don't . . ."

"*Look out!*" Johnny yelled.

The cabbie had half-turned to face him, his pudgy American Legionnaire's face earnest and angry and miserable in the dashlights and in the sudden glow of oncoming headlights. Now he snapped forward again, but too late.

"*Jeeesus . . .*"

There were two cars, one on each side of the white line. They had been dragging, side by side, coming up over the hill, a Mustang and a Dodge Charger. Johnny could hear the revved-up whine of their engines. The Charger was boring straight down at them. It never tried to get out of the way and the cabbie froze at the wheel.

"*Jeeeeee . . .*"

Johnny was barely aware of the Mustang flashing by on their left. Then the cab and the Charger met head-on and Johnny felt himself being lifted up and out. There was no pain, although he was marginally aware that his thighs had connected with the taximeter hard enough to rip it out of its frame.

There was the sound of smashing glass. A huge gout of

flame stroked its way up into the night. Johnny's head collided with the cab's windshield and knocked it out. Reality began to go down a hole. Pain, faint and far away, in his shoulders and arms as the rest of him followed his head through the jagged windshield. He was flying. Flying into the October night.

Dim flashing thought: *Am I dying? Is this going to kill me?* Interior voice answering: *Yes, this is probably it.*

Flying. October stars flung across the night. Racketing boom of exploding gasoline. An orange glow. Then darkness.

His trip through the void ended with a hard thump and a splash. Cold wetness as he went into Carson's Bog, twenty-five feet from where the Charger and the cab, welded together, pushed a pyre of flame into the night sky.

Darkness.

Fading.

Until all that was left seemed to be a giant red-and-black wheel revolving in such emptiness as there may be between the stars, try your luck, first time fluky, second time lucky, hey-hey-hey. The wheel revolved up and down, red and black, the marker ticking past the pins, and he strained to see if it was going to come up double zero, house number, house spin, everybody loses but the house. He strained to see but the wheel was gone. There was only blackness and that universal emptiness, negatory, good buddy, el zilcho. Cold limbo.

Johnny Smith stayed there a long, long time.

Chapter 3

◆ 1 ◆

At some time a little past two A.M. on the morning of October 30, 1970, the telephone began to ring in the downstairs hall of a small house about a hundred and fifty miles south of Cleaves Mills.

Herb Smith sat up in bed, disoriented, dragged halfway across the threshold of sleep and left in its doorway, groggy and disoriented.

Vera's voice beside him, muffled by the pillow. "Phone."

"Yeah," he said, and swung out of bed. He was a big, broad-shouldered man in his late forties, losing his hair, now dressed in blue pajama bottoms. He went out into the upstairs hall and turned on the light. Down below, the phone shrilled away.

He went down to what Vera liked to call "the phone nook." It consisted of the phone and a strange little desk-table that she had gotten with Green Stamps about three years ago. Herb had refused from the first to slide his two-hundred-and-forty-pound bulk into it. When he talked on the phone, he stood up. The drawer of the desk-table was full of *Upper Rooms*, *Reader's Digests*, and *Fate* magazine.

Herb reached for the phone, then let it ring again.

A phone call in the middle of the night usually meant one of three things: an old friend had gotten totally shitfaced and had decided you'd be glad to hear from him even at two in the morning; a wrong number; bad news.

Hoping for the middle choice, Herb picked up the phone. "Hello?"

A crisp male voice said: "Is this the Herbert Smith residence?"

"Yes?"

"To whom am I speaking, please?"

"I'm Herb Smith. What . . ."

"Will you hold for a moment?"

"Yes, but who . . ."

Too late. There was a faint clunk in his ear, as if the party on the other end had dropped one of his shoes. He had been put *on hold*. Of the many things he disliked about the telephone—bad connections, kid pranksters who wanted to know if you had Prince Albert in a can, operators who sounded like computers, and smoothies who wanted you to buy magazine subscriptions—the thing he disliked the most was being *on hold*. It was one of those insidious things that had crept into modern life almost unnoticed over the last ten years or so. Once upon a time the fellow on the other end would simply have said, "Hold the phone, willya?" and set it down. At least in those days you were able to hear faraway conversations, a barking dog, a radio, a crying baby. Being *on hold* was a totally different proposition. The line was darkly, smoothly blank. You were nowhere. Why didn't they just say, "Will you hold on while I bury you alive for a little while?"

He realized he was just a tiny bit scared.

"Herbert?"

He turned around, the phone to his ear. Vera was at the top of the stairs in her faded brown bathrobe, hair up in curlers, some sort of cream hardened to a castlike consistency on her cheeks and forehead.

"Who is it?"

"I don't know yet. They've got me on hold."

"On hold? At quarter past two in the morning?"

"Yes."

"It's not Johnny, is it? Nothing's happened to Johnny?"

"I don't know," he said, struggling to keep his voice from rising. Somebody calls you at two in the morning, puts you on hold, you count your relatives and inventory their condition. You make lists of old aunts. You tot up the ailments of grandparents, if you still have them. You wonder if the ticker of one of your friends just stopped ticking. And you try not to think that you have one son you love very much, or about how these calls always seem to come at two in the morning, or how all of a sudden your calves are getting stiff and heavy with tension . . .

Vera had closed her eyes and had folded her hands in the middle of her thin bosom. Herb tried to control his irritation. Restrained himself from saying, "Vera, the Bible makes the strong suggestion that you go and do that in your closet." That would earn him Vera Smith's Sweet Smile for Unbelieving and Hellbound Husbands. At two o'clock in the morning, and *on hold* to boot, he didn't think he could take that particular smile.

The phone clunked again and a different male voice, an older one, said, "Hello, Mr. Smith?"

"Yes, who is this?"

"I'm sorry to have kept you waiting, sir. Sergeant Meggs of the state police, Orono branch."

"Is it my boy? Something about my boy?"

Unaware, he sagged onto the seat of the phone nook. He felt weak all over.

Sergeant Meggs said, "Do you have a son named John Smith, no middle initial?"

"Is he all right? Is he okay?"

Footsteps on the stairs. Vera stood beside him. For a moment she looked calm, and then she clawed for the phone like a tigress. "What is it? What's happened to my Johnny?"

Herb yanked the handset away from her, splintering one of her fingernails. Staring at her hard he said, "I am handling this."

She stood looking at him, her mild, faded blue eyes wide above the hand clapped to her mouth.

"Mr. Smith, are you there?"

Words that seemed coated with novocaine fell from Herb's mouth. "I have a son named John Smith, no middle initial, yes. He lives in Cleaves Mills. He's a teacher at the high school there."

"He's been in a car accident, Mr. Smith. His condition is extremely grave. I'm very sorry to have to give you this news." The voice of Meggs was cadenced, formal.

"Oh, my God," Herb said. His thoughts were whirling. Once, in the army, a great, mean, blond-haired Southern boy named Childress had beaten the crap out of him behind an Atlanta bar. Herb had felt like this then, unmanned, all his thoughts knocked into a useless, smeary sprawl. "Oh, my God," he said again.

"He's dead?" Vera asked. "He's dead? Johnnys *dead?*"

He covered the mouthpiece. "No," he said. "Not dead."

"Not dead! Not dead!" she cried, and fell on her knees in the phone nook with an audible thud. "O God we most heartily thank Thee and ask that You show Thy tender care and loving mercy to our son and shelter him with Your loving hand we ask it in the name of Thy only begotten Son Jesus and . . ."

"Vera shut up!"

For a moment all three of them were silent, as if considering the world and its not-so-amusing ways: Herb, his bulk squashed into the phone nook bench with his knees crushed up against the underside of the desk and a bouquet of plastic flowers in his face; Vera with her knees planted on the hall-way furnace grille; the unseen Sergeant Meggs who was in a strange auditory way witnessing this black comedy.

"Mr. Smith?"

"Yes. I . . . I apologize for the ruckus."

"Quite understandable," Meggs said.

"My boy . . . Johnny . . . was he driving his Volkswagen?"

"Deathtraps, deathtraps, those little beetles are death-traps," Vera babbled. Tears streamed down her face, sliding over the smooth hard surface of the nightpack like rain on chrome.

"He was in a Bangor & Orono Yellow Cab," Meggs said. "I'll give you the situation as I understand it now. There were three vehicles involved, two of them driven by kids from Cleaves Mills. They were dragging. They came up over what's known as Carson's Hill on Route 6, headed east. Your son was in the cab, headed west, toward Cleaves. The cab and the car on the wrong side of the road collided head-on. The cab driver was killed, and so was the boy driving the other car. Your son and a passenger in that other car are at Eastern Maine Med. I understand both of them are listed as critical."

"Critical," Herb said.

"Critical! Critical!" Vera moaned.

Oh, Christ, we sound like one of those weird off-off-Broadway shows, Herb thought. He felt embarrassed for Vera, and for Sergeant Meggs, who must surely be hearing Vera, like some nutty Greek chorus in the background. He wondered how many conversations like this Sergeant Meggs had held in the course of his job. He decided he must have had a good many. Possibly he had already called the cab driver's wife and the dead boy's mother to pass the news. How had they reacted? And what did it matter? Wasn't it Vera's right to weep for her son? And why did a person have to think such crazy things at a time like this?

"Eastern Maine," Herb said. He jotted it on a pad. The drawing on top of the pad showed a smiling telephone handset. The phone cord spelled out the words PHONE PAL. "How is he hurt?"

"I beg your pardon, Mr. Smith?"

"Where did he get it? Head? Belly? What? Is he burned?" Vera shrieked.

"*Vera can you please shut UP!*"

"You'd have to call the hospital for that information," Meggs said carefully. "I'm a couple of hours from having a complete report."

"All right. All right."

"Mr. Smith, I'm sorry to have to call you in the middle of the night with such bad news . . ."

"It's bad, all right," he said, "I've got to call the hospital, Sergeant Meggs. Good-bye."

"Good night, Mr. Smith."

Herb hung up and stared stupidly at the phone. Just like that it happens, he thought. How 'bout that. Johnny.

Vera uttered another shriek, and he saw with some alarm that she had grabbed her hair, rollers and all, and was pulling it. "It's a judgment! A judgment on the way we live, on sin, on something! Herb, get down on your knees with me . . ."

"Vera, I have to call the hospital. I don't want to do it on my knees."

"We'll pray for him . . . promise to do better . . . if you'd only come to church more often with me I know . . . maybe it's your cigars, drinking beer with those men after work . . . cursing . . . taking the name of the Lord God in vain . . . a judgment . . . it's a judgment . . ."

He put his hands on her face to stop its wild, uneasy whipping back and forth. The feel of the night cream was unpleasant, but he didn't take his hands away. He felt pity for her. For the last ten years his wife had been walking somewhere in a gray area between devotion to her Baptist faith and what he considered to be a mild religious mania. Five years after Johnny was born, the doctor had found a number of benign tumors in her uterus and vaginal canal. Their removal had made it impossible for her to have another baby. Five years later, more tumors had necessitated a radical hysterectomy. That was when it had really begun for her, a deep religious feeling strangely coupled with other beliefs. She avidly read pamphlets on Atlantis, spaceships from heaven, races of "pure Christians" who might live in the bowels of the earth. She read *Fate* magazine almost as frequently as the Bible, often using one to illuminate the other.

"Vera," he said.

"We'll do better," she whispered, her eyes pleading with him. "We'll do better and he'll live. You'll see. You'll . . ."

"Vera."

She fell silent, looking at him.

"Let's call the hospital and see just how bad it really is," he said gently.

"A-All right. Yes."

"Can you sit on the stairs there and keep perfectly quiet?"

"I want to pray," she said childishly. "You can't stop me."

"I don't want to. As long as you pray to yourself."

"Yes. To myself. All right, Herb."

She went to the stairs and sat down and pulled her robe primly around her. She folded her hands and her lips began to move. Herb called the hospital. Two hours later they were headed north on the nearly deserted Maine Turnpike. Herb was behind the wheel of their '66 Ford station wagon. Vera sat bolt upright in the passenger seat. Her Bible was on her lap.

◆ 2 ◆

The telephone woke Sarah at quarter of nine. She went to answer it with half her mind still asleep in bed. Her back hurt from the vomiting she had done the night before and the muscles in her stomach felt strained, but otherwise she felt much better.

She picked up the phone, sure it would be Johnny. "Hello?"

"Hi, Sarah." It wasn't Johnny. It was Anne Strafford from school. Anne was a year older than Sarah and in her second year at Cleaves. She taught Spanish. She was a bubbly, effervescent girl and Sarah liked her very much. But this morning she sounded subdued.

"How are you, Annie? It's only temporary. Probably Johnny told you. Carnival hot dogs, I guess . . ."

"Oh, my God, you don't know. You don't . . ." The words were swallowed in odd, choked sounds. Sarah listened to them, frowning. Her initial puzzlement turned to deadly disquiet as she realized Anne was crying.

"Anne? What's wrong? It's not Johnny, is it? Not . . ."

"There was an accident," Anne said. She was now sobbing openly. "He was in a cab. There was a head-on collision. The driver of the other car was Brad Freneau, I had him in Spanish II, he died, his girl friend died this morning, Mary Thibault, she was in one of Johnny's classes, I heard, it's horrible, just horri . . ."

"Johnny!" Sarah screamed into the phone. She was sick to her stomach again. Her hands and feet were suddenly as cold as four gravestones. *"What about Johnny?"*

"He's in critical condition, Sarah. Dave Pelsen called the hospital this morning. He's not expected . . . well, it's very bad."

The world was going gray. Anne was still talking but her voice was far and wee, as e.e cummings had said about the balloon man. Flocked images tumbling over and over one an-

THE WHEEL OF FORTUNE 55

other, none making sense. The carny wheel. The mirror maze. Johnny's eyes, strangely violet, almost black. His dear, homely face in the harsh, county fair lighting, naked bulbs strung on electric wire.

"Not Johnny," she said, far and wee, far and wee. "You're mistaken. He was fine when he left here."

And Anne's voice coming back like a fast serve, her voice so shocked and unbelieving, so affronted that such a thing should have happened to someone her own age, someone young and vital. "They told Dave he'd never wake up even if he survived the operation. They have to operate because his head . . . his head was . . ."

Was she going to say *crushed?* That Johnny's head had been *crushed?*

Sarah fainted then, possibly to avoid that final irrevocable word, that final horror. The phone spilled out of her fingers and she sat down hard in a gray world and then she slipped over and the phone swung back and forth in a decreasing arc, Anne Strafford's voice coming out of it: "Sarah? . . . Sarah? . . . Sarah?"

◆ 3 ◆

When Sarah got to Eastern Maine Medical, it was quarter past twelve. The nurse at the reception desk looked at her white, strained face, estimated her capacity for further truth, and told her that John Smith was still in OR. She added that Johnny's mother and father were in the waiting room.

"Thank you," Sarah said. She turned right instead of left, wound up in a medical closet, and had to backtrack.

The waiting room was done in bright, solid colors that gashed her eyes. A few people sat around looking at tattered magazines or empty space. A gray-haired woman came in from the elevators, gave her visitor's pass to a friend, and sat down. The friend clicked away on high heels. The rest of them went on sitting, waiting their own chance to visit a father who had had gallstones removed, a mother who had discovered a small lump under one of her breasts a bare three days ago, a friend who had been struck in the chest with an invisible sledgehammer while jogging. The faces of the waiters were carefully made-up with composure. Worry was swept under the faces like dirt under a rug. Sarah felt the unreality hov-

ering again. Somewhere a soft bell was ringing. Crepe-soled
shoes squeaked. He had been fine when he left her place.
Impossible to think he was in one of these brick towers, engaged in dying.

She knew Mr. and Mrs. Smith at once. She groped for their
first names and could not immediately find them. They were
sitting together near the back of the room, and unlike the
others here, they hadn't yet had time to come to terms with
what had happened in their lives.

Johnny's mom sat with her coat on the chair behind her
and her Bible clutched in her hands. Her lips moved as she
read, and Sarah remembered Johnny saying she was very religious—maybe too religious, somewhere in that great middle
ground between holy rolling and snake-handling, she remembered him saying. Mr. Smith—*Herb, it came to her, his name
is Herb*—had one of the magazines on his knees, but he wasn't
looking at it. He was looking out the window, where New
England fall burned its way toward November and winter
beyond.

She went over to them. "Mr. and Mrs. Smith?"

They looked up at her, their faces tensed for the dreaded
blow. Mrs. Smith's hands tightened on her Bible, which was
open to the Book of Job, until her knuckles were white. The
young woman before them was not in nurse's or doctor's
whites, but that made no difference to them at this point.
They were waiting for the final blow.

"Yes, we're the Smiths," Herb said quietly.

"I'm Sarah Bracknell. Johnny and I are good friends. Going
together, I suppose you'd say. May I sit down?"

"Johnny's girl friend?" Mrs. Smith asked in a sharp, almost
accusing tone. A few of the others looked around briefly and
then back at their own tattered magazines.

"Yes," she said. "Johnny's girl."

"He never wrote that he had a lady friend," Mrs. Smith
said in that same sharp tone. "No, he never did at all."

"Hush, Mother," Herb said. "Sit down, Miss . . . Bracknell,
wasn't it?"

"Sarah," she said gratefully, and took a chair. "I . . ."

"No, he never did," Mrs. Smith said sharply. "My boy loved
God, but just lately he maybe fell away just a bit. The judgment of the Lord God is sudden, you know. That's what
makes backsliding so dangerous. You know not the day nor
the hour . . ."

"Hush," Herb said. People were looking around again. He fixed his wife with a stern glance. She looked back defiantly for a moment, but his gaze didn't waver. Vera dropped her eyes. She had closed the Bible but her fingers fiddled restlessly along the pages, as if longing to get back to the colossal demolition derby of Job's life, enough bad luck to put her own and her son's in some sort of bitter perspective.

"I was with him last night," Sarah said, and that made the woman look up again, accusingly. At that moment Sarah remembered the biblical connotation of being "with" somebody and felt herself beginning to blush. It was as if the woman could read her thoughts.

"We went to the county fair . . ."

"Places of sin and evil," Vera Smith said clearly.

"I'll tell you one last time to *hush,* Vera," Herb said grimly, and clamped one of his hands over one of his wife's. "I mean it, now. This seems like a nice girl here, and I won't have you digging at her. Understand?"

"Sinful places," Vera repeated stubbornly.

"Will you hush?"

"Let me go. I want to read my Bible."

He let her go. Sarah felt confused embarrassment. Vera opened her Bible and began to read again, lips moving.

"Vera is very upset," Herb said. "We're both upset. You are too, from the look of you."

"Yes."

"Did you and Johnny have a good time last night?" he asked. "At your fair?"

"Yes," she said, the lie and truth of that simple word all mixed up in her mind. "Yes we did, until . . . well, I ate a bad hot dog or something. We had my car and Johnny drove me home to my place in Veazie. I was pretty sick to my stomach. He called a cab. He said he'd call me in sick at school today. And that's the last time I saw him." The tears started to come then and she didn't want to cry in front of them, particularly not in front of Vera Smith, but there was no way to stop it. She fumbled a Kleenex out of her purse and held it to her face.

"There, now," Herb said, and put an arm around her. "There, now." She cried, and it seemed to her in some unclear way that he felt better for having someone to comfort; his wife had found her own dark brand of comfort in Job's story and it didn't include him.

A few people turned around to gawk; through the prisms of her tears they seemed like a crowd. She had a bitter knowledge of what they were thinking: *Better her than me, better all three of them than me or mine, guy must be dying, guy must have gotten his head crushed for her to cry like that. Only a matter of time before some doctor comes down and takes them into a private room to tell them that—*

Somehow she choked off the tears and got hold of herself. Mrs. Smith sat bolt upright, as if startled out of a nightmare, noticing neither Sarah's tears nor her husband's effort to comfort her. She read her Bible.

"Please," Sarah said. "How bad is it? Can we hope?"

Before Herb could answer, Vera spoke up. Her voice was a dry bolt of certified doom: "There's hope in God, Missy."

Sarah saw the apprehensive flicker in Herb's eyes and thought: *He thinks it's driven her crazy. And maybe it has.*

◆ 4 ◆

A long afternoon stretching into evening.

Sometime after two P.M., when the schools began to let out, a number of Johnny's students began to come in, wearing fatigue coats and strange hats and washed-out jeans. Sarah didn't see many of the kids she thought of as the button-down crowd—upward-bound, college-oriented kids, clear of eye and brow. Most of the kids who bothered to come in were the freaks and long-hairs.

A few came over and asked Sarah in quiet tones what she knew about Mr. Smith's condition. She could only shake her head and say she had heard nothing. But one of the girls, Dawn Edwards, who had a crush on Johnny, read the depth of Sarah's fear in her face. She burst into tears. A nurse came and asked her to leave.

"I'm sure she'll be all right," Sarah said. She had a protective arm around Dawn's shoulders. "Just give her a minute or two."

"No, I don't want to stay," Dawn said, and left in a hurry, knocking one of the hard plastic contour chairs over with a clatter. A few moments later Sarah saw the girl sitting out on the steps in the cold, late, October sunshine with her head on her knees.

Vera Smith read her Bible.

By five o'clock most of the students had left. Dawn had also left; Sarah had not seen her go. At seven P.M., a young man with DR. STRAWNS pinned askew to the lapel of his white coat came into the waiting room, glanced around, and walked toward them.

"Mr. and Mrs. Smith?" he asked.

Herb took a deep breath. "Yes. We are."

Vera shut her Bible with a snap.

"Would you come with me, please?"

That's it, Sarah thought. The walk down to the small private room, and then the news. Whatever the news is. She would wait, and when they came back, Herb Smith would tell her what she needed to know. He was a kind man.

"Have you news of my son?" Vera asked in that same clear, strong, and nearly hysterical voice.

"Yes." Dr. Strawns glanced at Sarah. "Are you family, ma'am?"

"No," Sarah said. "A friend."

"A close friend," Herb said. A warm, strong hand closed above her elbow, just as another had closed around Vera's upper arm. He helped them both to their feet. "We'll all go together, if you don't mind."

"Not at all."

He led them past the elevator bank and down a hallway to an office with CONFERENCE ROOM on the door. He let them in and turned on the overhead fluorescent lights. The room was furnished with a long table and a dozen office chairs.

Dr. Strawns closed the door, lit a cigarette, and dropped the burned match into one of the ashtrays that marched up and down the table. "This is difficult," he said, as if to himself.

"Then you had best just say it out," Vera said.

"Yes, perhaps I'd better."

It was not her place to ask, but Sarah could not help it. "Is he dead? Please don't say he's dead . . ."

"He's in a coma." Strawns sat down and dragged deeply on his cigarette. "Mr. Smith has sustained serious head injuries and an undetermined amount of brain damage. You may have heard the phrase 'subdural hematoma' on one or the other of the doctor shows. Mr. Smith has suffered a very grave subdural hematoma, which is localized cranial bleeding. A long operation was necessary to relieve the pressure, and also to remove bone-splinters from his brain."

Herb sat down heavily, his face doughy and stunned. Sarah

noticed his blunt, scarred hands and remembered Johnny telling her his father was a carpenter.

"But God has spared him," Vera said. "I knew he would.
I prayed for a sign. Praise God, Most High! All ye here below
praise His name!"

"Vera," Herb said with no force.

"In a coma,' " Sarah repeated. She tried to fit the information into some sort of emotional frame and found it wouldn't
go. That Johnny wasn't dead, that he had come through a
serious and dangerous operation on his brain—those things
should have renewed her hope. But they didn't. She didn't
like that word *coma*. It had a sinister, stealthy sound. Wasn't
it Latin for "sleep of death"?

"What's ahead for him?" Herb asked.

"No one can really answer that now," Strawns said. He
began to play with his cigarette, tapping it nervously over the
ashtray. Sarah had the feeling he was answering Herb's question literally while completely avoiding the question Herb had
really asked. "He's on life support equipment, of course."

"But you must know something about his chances," Sarah
said. "You must know . . ." She gestured helplessly with her
hands and let them drop to her sides.

"He may come out of it in forty-eight hours. Or a week.
A month. He may never come out of it. And . . . there is a
strong possibility that he may die. I must tell you frankly
that's the most likely. His injuries . . . grave."

"God wants him to live," Vera said. "I know it."

Herb had put his face into his hands and was scrubbing
it slowly.

Dr. Strawns looked at Vera uncomfortably. "I only want
you to be prepared for . . . any eventuality."

"Would you rate his chances for coming out of it?" Herb
asked.

Dr. Strawns hesitated, puffed nervously on his cigarette.
"No, I can't do that," he said finally.

◆ 5 ◆

The three of them waited another hour and then left. It was
dark. A cold and gusty wind had come up and it whistled
across the big parking lot. Sarah's long hair streamed out behind her. Later, when she got home, she would find a crisp

yellow oak leaf caught in it. Overhead, the moon rode the sky, a cold sailor of the night.

Sarah pressed a scrap of paper into Herb's hand. Written on it was her address and phone number. "Would you call me if you hear something? Anything at all?"

"Yes, of course." He bent suddenly and kissed her cheek, and Sarah held his shoulder for a moment in the blowing dark.

"I'm very sorry if I was stiff with you earlier, dear," Vera said, and her voice was surprisingly gentle. "I was upset."

"Of course you were," Sarah said.

"I thought my boy might die. But I've prayed. I've spoken to God about it. As the song says, 'Are we weak and heavy-laden? Cumbered with a load of care? We must never be discouraged. Take it to the Lord in prayer.'"

"Vera, we ought to go along," Herb said. "We ought to get some sleep and see how things look in the . . ."

"But now I've heard from my God," Vera said, looking dreamily up at the moon. "Johnny isn't going to die. It isn't in God's plan for Johnny to die. I listened and I heard that still, small voice speaking in my heart, and I am comforted."

Herb opened the car door. "Come on, Vera."

She looked back at Sarah and smiled. In that smile Sarah suddenly saw Johnny's own easy, devil-may-care grin—but at the same time she thought it was the most ghastly smile she had ever seen in her life.

"God has put his mark on my Johnny," Vera said, "and I rejoice."

"Good night, Mrs. Smith," Sarah said through numb lips.

"Good night, Sarah," Herb said. He got in and started the car. It pulled out of its space and moved across the parking lot to State Street, and Sarah realized she hadn't asked where they were staying. She guessed they might not know themselves yet.

She turned to go to her own car and paused, struck by the river that ran behind the hospital, the Penobscot. It flowed like dark silk, and the reflected moon was caught in its center. She looked up into the sky, standing alone in the parking lot now. She looked at the moon.

God has put his mark on my Johnny and I rejoice.

The moon hung above her like a tawdry carnival toy, a Wheel of Fortune in the sky with the odds all slugged in favor of the house, not to mention the house numbers—zero and double zero. House numbah, house numbah, y'all pay the house, hey-hey-hey.

The wind blew rattling leaves around her legs. She went to her car and sat behind the wheel. She felt suddenly sure she was going to lose him. Terror and loneliness woke in her. She began to shiver. At last she started her car and drove home.

◆ **6** ◆

There was a great outpouring of comfort and good wishes from the Cleaves Mills student body in the following week; Herb Smith told her later that Johnny received better than three hundred cards. Almost all of them contained a hesitant personal note saying they hoped Johnny would be well soon. Vera answered each of them with a thank-you note and a Bible verse.

Sarah's discipline problem in her classes disappeared. Her previous feeling that some returning jury of class consciousness was bringing in an unfavorable verdict changed to just the opposite. Gradually she realized that the kids were viewing her as a tragic heroine, Mr. Smith's lost love. This idea struck her in the teacher's room during her free period on the Wednesday following the accident, and she went off into sudden gales of laughter that turned into a crying jag. Before she was able to get herself under control she had frightened herself badly. Her nights were made restless with incessant dreams of Johnny—Johnny in the Halloween Jekyll-and-Hyde mask, Johnny standing at the Wheel of Fortune concession while some disembodied voice chanted, "Man, I *love* to watch this guy get a beatin," over and over. Johnny saying, "It's all right now, Sarah, everything's *fine*," and then coming into the room with his head gone above the eyebrows.

Herb and Vera Smith spent the week in the Bangor House, and Sarah saw them every afternoon at the hospital, waiting patiently for something to happen. Nothing did. Johnny lay in a room on the intensive care ward on the sixth floor, surrounded by life-support equipment, breathing with the help of a machine. Dr. Strawns had grown less hopeful. On the Friday following the accident, Herb called Sarah on the phone and told her he and Vera were going home.

"She doesn't want to," he said, "but I've gotten her to see reason. I think."

"Is she all right?" Sarah asked.

There was a long pause, long enough to make Sarah think she had overstepped the bounds. Then Herb said, "I don't know. Or maybe I do and I just don't want to say right out that she isn't. She's always had strong ideas about religion and they got a lot stronger after her operation. Her hysterectomy. Now they've gotten worse again. She's been talking a lot about the end of the world. She's connected Johnny's accident with the Rapture, somehow. Just before Armageddon, God is supposed to take all the faithful up to heaven in their actual bodies."

Sarah thought of a bumper sticker she had seen somewhere: IF THE RAPTURE'S TODAY, SOMEBODY GRAB MY STEERING WHEEL! "Yes, I know the idea," she said.

"Well," Herb said uncomfortably, "some of the groups she . . . she corresponds with . . . they believe that God is going to come for the faithful in flying saucers. Take them all up to heaven in flying saucers, that is. These . . . sects . . . have proved, at least to themselves, that heaven is somewhere out in the constellation of Orion. No, don't ask me how they proved it. Vera could tell you. It's . . . well, Sarah, it's all a little hard on me."

"Of course it must be."

Herb's voice strengthened. "But she can still distinguish between what's real and what's not. She needs time to adjust. So I told her she could face whatever's coming at home as easily as here. I've . . ." He paused, sounding embarrassed, then cleared his throat and went on. "I've got to get back to work. I've got jobs. I've signed contracts . . ."

"Sure, of course." She paused. "What about insurance? I mean, this must be costing a Denver mint . . ." It was her turn to feel embarrassed.

"I've talked with Mr. Pelsen, your assistant principal there at Cleaves Mills," Herb said. "Johnny had the standard Blue Cross, but not that new Major Medical. The Blue Cross will cover some of it, though. And Vera and I have our savings."

Sarah's heart sank. *Vera and I have our savings.* How long would one passbook stand up to expenses of two hundred dollars a day or more? And for what purpose in the end? So Johnny could hang on like an insensible animal, pissing brainlessly down a tube while he bankrupted his dad and mom? So his condition could drive his mother mad with unrealized hope? She felt the tears start to slip down her cheeks and for the first time—but not the last—she found herself wishing Johnny would die and be at peace. Part of her revolted in horror at the thought, but it remained.

"I wish you all the best," Sarah said.

"I know that, Sarah. We wish you the best. Will you write?"

"I sure will."

"And come see us when you can. Pownal's not so far away." He hesitated. "Looks to me like Johnny had picked himself out the right girl. It was pretty serious, wasn't it?"

"Yes," Sarah said. The tears were still coming and the past tense was not lost on her. "It was."

"Good-bye, honey."

"Good-bye, Herb."

She hung up the phone, held the buttons down for a second or two, and then called the hospital and asked about Johnny. There had been no change. She thanked the intensive care nurse and walked aimlessly back and forth through the apartment. She thought about God sending out a fleet of flying saucers to pick up the faithful and buzz them off to Orion. It made as much sense as anything else about a God crazy enough to scramble John Smith's brains and put him in a coma that was probably never going to end—except in an unexpected death.

There was a folder of freshman compositions to correct. She made herself a cup of tea and sat down to them. If there was any one moment when Sarah Bracknell picked up the reins of her post-Johnny life again, that was it.

Chapter 4

◆ 1 ◆

The killer was slick.

He sat on a bench in the town park near the bandstand, smoking a Marlboro and humming a song from the Beatles' white album—"you don't know how lucky you are, boy, back in the, back in the, back in the USSR . . ."

He wasn't a killer yet, not really. But it had been on his

mind a long time, killing had. It had been itching at him and itching at him. Not in a bad way, no. He felt quite optimistic about it. The time was right. He didn't have to worry about getting caught. He didn't have to worry about the clothespin. Because he was slick.

A litle snow began to drift down from the sky. It was November 12, 1970, and a hundred and sixty miles northeast of this middle-sized western Maine town, John Smith's dark sleep went on and on.

The killer scanned the park—the town common, the tourists who came to Castle Rock and the Lakes Region liked to call it. But there were no tourists now. The common that was so green in the summer was now yellow, balding, and dead. It waited for winter to cover it decently. The wire-mesh back-stop behind the Little League home plate stood in rusty overlapping diamonds, framed against the white sky. The bandstand needed a fresh coat of paint.

It was a depressing scene, but the killer was not depressed. He was almost manic with joy. His toes wanted to tap, his fingers wanted to snap. There would be no shying away this time.

He crushed his smoke under one boot heel and lit another immediately. He glanced at his watch. 3:02 P.M. He sat and smoked. Two boys passed through the park, tossing a football back and forth, but they didn't see the killer because the benches were down in a dip. He supposed it was a place where the nasty-fuckers came at night when the weather was warmer. He knew all about the nasty-fuckers and the things they did. His mother had told him, and he had *seen* them.

Thinking about his mother made his smile fade a little. He remembered a time when he had been seven, she had come into his room without knocking—she never knocked—and had caught him playing with his thing. She had just about gone crazy. He had tried to tell her it was nothing. Nothing bad. It had just stood up. He hadn't done anything to make it stand up, it did it all on its own. And he just sat there, boinging it back and forth. It wasn't even that much fun. It was sort of boring. But his mother had just about gone crazy.

Do you want to be one of those nasty-fuckers? she had screamed at him. He didn't even know what that word meant—not nasty, he knew that one, but the other one— although he had heard some of the bigger kids use it in the play-yard at the Castle Rock Elementary School. *Do you want to be one of those nasty-fuckers and get one of those diseases? Do you want to have pus running out of it? Do you want it to turn black? Do you want it to rot off? Huh? Huh? Huh?*

She began to shake him back and forth then, and he began to blubber with fear, even then she was a big woman, a dominant and overbearing ocean liner of a woman, and he was not the killer then, he was not slick then, he was a little boy blubbering with fear, and his thing had collapsed and was trying to shrivel back into his body.

She had made him wear a clothespin on it for two hours, so he would know how those diseases felt.

The pain was excruciating.

The little snow flurry had passed. He brushed the image of his mother out of his mind, something he could do effortlessly when he was feeling good, something he couldn't do at all when he was feeling depressed and low.

His thing was standing up now.

He glanced at his watch. 3:07. He dropped his cigarette half-smoked. Someone was coming.

He recognized her. It was Alma, Alma Frechette from the Coffee Pot across the street. Just coming off-shift. He knew Alma; he had dated her up once or twice, shown her a good time. Took her to Serenity Hill over in Naples. She was a good dancer. Nasty-fuckers often were. He was glad it was Alma coming.

She was by herself.

Back in the US, back in the US, back in the USSR—

"Alma!" he called and waved. She started a little, looked around, and saw him. She smiled and walked over to the bench where he sat, saying hello and calling him by name. He stood up, smiling. He wasn't worried about anyone coming. He was untouchable. He was Superman.

"Why you wearing that?" she asked, looking at him.

"Slick, isn't it?" he said, smiling.

"Well, I wouldn't exactly . . ."

"You want to see something?" he asked. "On the bandstand. It's the goddamdest thing."

"What is it?"

"Come and look."

"All right."

As simple as that. She went with him to the bandstand. If anyone had been coming, he still could have called it off. But no one came. No one passed. They had the common to themselves. The white sky brooded over them. Alma was a small girl with light blonde hair. Dyed blonde hair, he was quite sure. Sluts dyed their hair.

He led her up onto the enclosed bandstand. Their feet made hollow, dead echoes on the boards. An overturned music stand lay in one corner. There was an empty Four Roses bottle. This was a place where the nasty-fuckers came, all right.

"What?" she asked, sounding a little puzzled now. A little nervous.

The killer smiled joyously and pointed to the left of the music stand. "There. See?"

She followed his finger. A used condom lay on the boards like a shriveled snakeskin.

Alma's face went tight and she turned to go so quickly that she almost got by the killer. "That's not very funny . . ."

He grabbed her and threw her back. "Where do you think you're going?"

Her eyes were suddenly watchful and frightened. "Let me out of here. Or you'll be sorry. I don't have any time for sick jokes . . ."

"It's no joke," he said. "It's no joke, you nasty-fucker." He was light-headed with the joy of naming her, naming her for what she was. The world whirled.

Alma broke left, heading for the low railing that surrounded the bandstand, meaning to leap over it. The killer caught the back of her cheap cloth coat at the collar and yanked her back again. The cloth ripped with a low purring sound and she opened her mouth to scream.

He slammed his hand over her mouth, mashing her lips back against her teeth. He felt warm blood trickle over his palm. Her other hand was beating at him now, clawing for purchase, but there was no purchase. There was none because he . . . he was . . .

Slick!

He threw her to the board floor. His hand came off her mouth, which was now smeared with blood, and she opened her mouth to scream again, but he landed on top of her, panting, grinning, and the air was driven out of her lungs in a soundless whoosh. She could feel him now, rock hard, gigantic and throbbing, and she quit trying to scream and went on struggling. Her fingers caught and slipped, caught and slipped. He forced her legs rudely apart and lay between them. One of her hands glanced off the bridge of his nose, making his eyes water.

"You nasty-fucker," he whispered, and his hands closed on her throat. He began to throttle her, yanking her head up from the bandstand's board flooring and then slamming it back down. Her eyes bulged. Her face went pink, then red, then a congested purple. Her struggles began to weaken.

"Nasty-fucker, nasty-fucker, nasty-fucker," the killer panted hoarsely. He really was the killer now, Alma Frechette's days of rubbing her body all over people at Serenity Hill were done now. Her eyes bugged out like the eyes of some of those crazy dolls they sold along carnival midways. The killer panted hoarsely. Her hands lay limp on the boards now. His fingers had almost disappeared from sight.

He let go of her throat, ready to grab her again if she stirred. But she didn't. After a moment he ripped her coat open with shaking hands and shoved the skirt of her pink waitress uniform up.

The white sky looked down. The Castle Rock town common was deserted. In fact, no one found the strangled, violated corpse of Alma Frechette until the next day. The sheriff's theory was that a drifter had done it. There were statewide newspaper headlines, and in Castle Rock there was general agreement with the sheriff's idea.

Surely no hometown boy could have done such a dreadful thing.

Chapter 5

◆ 1 ◆

Herb and Vera Smith went back to Pownal and took up the embroidery of their days. Herb finished a house in Durham that December. Their savings did indeed melt away, as Sarah had foreseen, and they applied to the state for Extraordinary Disaster Assistance. That aged Herb almost as much as the accident itself had done. EDA was only a fancy way of saying "welfare" or "charity" in his mind. He had spent a lifetime working hard and honestly with his hands and had thought he would never see the day when he would have to take a state dollar. But here that day was.

Vera subscribed to three new magazines which came through the mail at irregular intervals. All three were badly printed and might have been illustrated by talented children. *God's Saucers*, *The Coming Transfiguration*, and *God's Psychic Miracles*. *The Upper Room*, which still came monthly, now sometimes lay unopened for as long as three weeks at a stretch, but she read these others to tatters. She found a great many things in them that seemed to bear upon Johnny's accident, and she read these nuggets to her tired husband at supper in a high, piercing voice that trembled with exaltation. Herb found himself telling her more and more frequently to be quiet, and on occasion shouting at her to shut up that drivel and let him alone. When he did that, she would give him long-suffering, compassionate, and hurt glances—then slink upstairs to continue her studies. She began to correspond with these magazines, and to exchange letters with the contributors and with other pen-friends who had had similar experiences in their lives.

Most of her correspondents were good-hearted people like Vera herself, people who wanted to help and to ease the nearly insupportable burden of her pain. They sent prayers and prayer stones, they sent charms, they sent promises to include Johnny in their nightly devotions. Yet there were others who were nothing but con-men and -women, and Herb was alarmed by his wife's increasing inability to recognize these. There was an offer to send her a sliver of the One True Cross of Our Lord for just $99.98. An offer to send a vial of water drawn from the spring at Lourdes, which would almost certainly work a miracle when rubbed into Johnny's forehead. That one was $110 plus postage. Cheaper (and more attractive to Vera) was a continuously playing cassette tape of the Twenty-third Psalm and the Lord's Prayer as spoken by southern evangelist Billy Humbarr. Played at Johnny's bedside over a period of weeks it would almost certainly effect a marvelous recovery, according to the pamphlet. As an added blessing (For A Short Time Only) an autographed picture of Billy Humbarr himself would be included.

Herb was forced to step in more and more frequently as her passion for these pseudoreligious geegaws grew. Sometimes he surreptitiously tore up her checks and simply readjusted the checkbook balance upward. But when the offer specified cash and nothing but, he simply had to put his foot down—and Vera began to draw away from him, to view him with distrust as a sinner and an unbeliever.

◆ 2 ◆

Sarah Bracknell kept school during her days. Her afternoons and evenings were not much different than they had been following the breakup with Dan; she was in a kind of limbo, waiting for something to happen. In Paris, the peace talks were stalled. Nixon had ordered the bombing of Hanoi continued in spite of rising domestic and foreign protests. At a press conference he produced pictures proving conclusively that American planes were surely not bombing North Vietnamese hospitals, but he went everywhere by Army helicopter. The investigation into the brutal rape-murder of a Castle Rock waitress was stalled following the release of a wandering sign painter who had once spent three years in the Augusta State Mental Hospital—against everyone's expectations, the sign painter's alibi had turned out to hold water. Janis Joplin was screaming the blues. Paris decreed (for the second year in a row) that hemlines would go down, but they didn't. Sarah was aware of all these things in a vague way, like voices from another room where some incomprehensible party went on and on.

The first snow fell—just a dusting—then a second dusting, and ten days before Christmas there was a storm that closed area schools for the day and she sat home, looking out at the snow as it filled Flagg Street. Her brief thing with Johnny—she could not even properly call it an affair—was part of another season now, and she could feel him beginning to slip away from her. It was a panicky feeling, as if a part of her was drowning. Drowning in days.

She read a good deal about head injuries, comas, and brain damage. None of it was very encouraging. She found out there was a girl in a small Maryland town who had been in a coma for six years; there had been a young man from Liverpool, England, who had been struck by a grappling hook while working on the docks and had remained in a coma for fourteen years before expiring. Little by little this brawny young dock-walloper had severed his connections with the world, wasting away, losing his hair, optic nerves degenerating into oatmeal behind his closed eyes, body gradually drawing up into a fetal position as his ligaments shortened. He had reversed time, had become a fetus again, swimming in the placental waters of coma as his brain degenerated. An autopsy following his death had shown that the folds and convolutions of his cerebrum had smoothed out, leaving the frontal and prefrontal lobes almost utterly smooth and blank.

Oh, Johnny, it just isn't fair, she thought, watching the snow fall outside, filling the world up with blank whiteness, burying fallen summer and red-gold autumn. *It isn't fair, they should let you go to whatever there is to go to.*

There was a letter from Herb Smith every ten days to two weeks—Vera had her pen-friends, and he had his. He wrote in a large, sprawling hand, using an old-fashioned fountain pen. "We are both fine and well. Waiting to see what will happen next as you must be. Yes, I have been doing some reading and I know what you are too kind and thoughtful to say in your letter, Sarah. It looks bad. But of course we hope. I don't believe in God the way Vera does, but I do believe in him after my fashion, and wonder why he didn't take John outright if he was going to. Is there a reason? No one knows, I guess. We only hope."

In another letter:

"I'm having to do most of the Xmas shopping this year as Vera has decided Xmas presents are a sinful custom. This is what I mean about her getting worse all the time. She's always thought it was a holy day instead of a holiday—if you see what I mean—and if she saw me calling it Xmas instead of Christmas I guess she'd 'shoot me for a hossthief.' She was always saying how we should remember it is the birthday of Jesus Christ and not Santa Claus, but she never minded the shopping before. In fact, she used to like it. Now ragging against it is all she talks about, seems like. She gets a lot of these funny ideas from the people she writes back and forth to. Golly I do wish she'd stop and get back to normal. But otherwise we are both fine and well. *Herb.*"

And a Christmas card that she had wept over a little: "Best to you from both of us this holiday season, and if you'd like to come down and spend Xmas with a couple of 'old fogies,' the spare bedroom is made up. Vera and I are both fine and well. Hope the New Year is better for all of us, and am sure it will be. *Herb* and *Vera.*"

She didn't go down to Pownal over the Christmas vacation, partly because of Vera's continued withdrawal into her own world—her progress into that world could be read pretty accurately between the lines of Herb's letters—and partly because their mutual tie now seemed so strange and distant to her. The still figure in the Bangor hospital bed had once been seen in close-up, but now she always seemed to be looking at him through the wrong end of memory's telescope; like the balloon man, he was far and wee. So it seemed best to keep her distance.

Perhaps Herb sensed it as well. His letters became less frequent as 1970 became 1971. In one of them he came as close as he could to saying it was time for her to go on with her life, and closed by saying that he doubted a girl as pretty as she was lacked for dates.

But she hadn't had any dates, hadn't wanted them. Gene Sedecki, the math teacher who had once treated her to an evening that had seemed at least a thousand years long, had begun asking her out indecently soon after Johnny's accident, and he was a hard man to discourage, but she believed that he was finally beginning to get the point. It should have happened sooner.

Occasionally other men would ask her, and one of them, a law student named Walter Hazlett, attracted her quite a bit. She met him at Anne Strafford's New Year's Eve party. She had meant only to make an appearance, but she had stayed quite a while, talking primarily to Hazlett. Saying no had been surprisingly hard, but she had, because she understood the source of attraction too well—Walt Hazlett was a tall man with an unruly shock of brown hair and a slanted, half-cynical smile, and he reminded her strongly of Johnny. That was no basis on which to get interested in a man.

Early in February she was asked out by the mechanic who worked on her car at the Cleaves Mills Chevron. Again she had almost said yes, and then backed away. The man's name was Arnie Tremont. He was tall, olive-skinned, and handsome in a smiling, predatory way. He reminded her a bit of James Brolin, the second banana on that Dr. Welby program, and even more of a certain Delta Tau Delta named Dan.

Better to wait. Wait and see if something was going to happen.

But nothing did.

◆ 3 ◆

In that summer of 1971, Greg Stillson, sixteen years older and wiser than the Bible salesman who had kicked a dog to death in a deserted Iowa dooryard, sat in the back room of his newly incorporated insurance and real estate business in Ridgeway, New Hampshire. He hadn't aged much in the years between. There was a net of wrinkles around his eyes now, and his hair was longer (but still quite conservative). He was still a big man, and his swivel chair creaked when he moved.

He sat smoking a Pall Mall cigarette and looking at the man sprawled comfortably in the chair opposite. Greg was looking at this man the way a zoologist might look at an interesting new specimen.

"See anything green?" Sonny Elliman asked.

Elliman topped six feet, five inches. He wore an ancient, grease-stiffened jeans jacket with the arms and buttons cut off. There was no shirt beneath. A Nazi iron cross, black dressed in white chrome, hung on his bare chest. The buckle of the belt running just below his considerable beer-belly was a great ivory skull. From beneath the pegged cuffs of his jeans poked the scuffed, square toes of a pair of Desert Driver boots. His hair was shoulder-length, tangled, and shining with an accumulation of greasy sweat and engine oil. From one earlobe there dangled a swastika earring, also black dressed in white chrome. He spun a coal-scuttle helmet on the tip of one blunt finger. Stitched on the back of his jacket was a leering red devil with a forked tongue. Above the devil was *The Devil's Dozen.* Below it: *Sonny Elliman, Prez.*

"No," Greg Stillson said. "I don't see anything green, but I do see someone who looks suspiciously like a walking asshole."

Elliman stiffened a little, then relaxed and laughed. In spite of the dirt, the almost palpable body odor, and Nazi regalia, his eyes, a dark green, were not without intelligence and even a sense of humor.

"Rank me to the dogs and back, man," he said. "It's been done before. You got the power now."

"You recognize that, do you?"

"Sure. I left my guys back in the Hamptons, came here alone. Be it on my own head, man." He smiled. "But if we should ever catch you in a similar position, you want to hope your kidneys are wearing combat boots."

"I'll chance it," Greg said. He measured Elliman. They were both big men. He reckoned Elliman had forty pounds on him, but a lot of it was beer muscle. "I could take you, Sonny."

Elliman's face crinkled in amiable good humor again. "Maybe. Maybe not. But that's not the way we play it, man. All that good American John Wayne stuff." He leaned forward, as if to impart a great secret. "Me personally, now, whenever I get me a piece of mom's apple pie, I make it my business to shit on it."

"Foul mouth, Sonny," Greg said mildly.

"What do you want with me?" Sonny asked. "Why don't you get down to it? You'll miss your Jaycee's meeting."

"No," Greg said, still serene. "The Jaycees meet Tuesday nights. We've got all the time in the world."

Elliman made a disgusted blowing sound.

"Now what I thought," Greg went on, "is that *you'd* want something from *me*." He opened his desk drawer and from it took three plastic Baggies of marijuana. Mixed in with the weed were a number of gel capsules. "Found this in your sleeping bag," Greg said. "Nasty, nasty, nasty, Sonny. Bad boy. Do not pass go, do not collect two hundred dollars. Go directly to New Hampshire State Prison."

"You didn't have any search warrant," Elliman said. "Even a kiddy lawyer could get me off, and you know it."

"I don't know any such thing," Greg Stillson said. He leaned back in his swivel chair and cocked his loafers, bought across the state line at L.L. Bean's in Maine, up on his desk. "I'm a big man in this town, Sonny. I came into New Hampshire more or less on my uppers a few years back, and now I've got a nice operation here. I've helped the town council solve a couple of problems, including just what to do about all these kids the chief of police catches doing dope . . . oh, I don't mean bad-hats like you, Sonny, drifters like you we know what to do with when we catch them with a little treasure trove like that one right there on my desk . . . I mean the nice local kids. Nobody really wants to do anything to them at all, you know? I figured that out for them. Put them to work on community projects instead of sending them to jail, I said. It worked out real good. Now we've got the biggest head in the tri-town area coaching Little League and doing a real good job at it."

Elliman was looking bored. Greg suddenly brought his feet down with a crash, grabbed a vase with a UNH logo on the side, and threw it past Sonny Elliman's nose. It missed him by less than an inch, flew end over end across the room, and shattered against the file cabinets in the corner. For the first time Elliman looked startled. And for just a moment the face of this older, wiser Greg Stillson was the face of the younger man, the dog-bludgeoner.

"You want to listen when I talk," he said softly. "Because what we're discussing here is your career over the next ten years or so. Now if you don't have any interest in making a career out of stamping LIVE FREE OR DIE on license plates, you want to listen up, Sonny. You want to pretend this is the first day of school again, Sonny. You want to get it all right the first time. *Sonny.*"

Elliman looked at the smashed fragments of vase, then back at Stillson. His former uneasy calm was being replaced by a feeling of real interest. He hadn't been really interested in anything for quite a while now. He had made the run for beer because he was bored. He had come by himself because he was bored. And when this big guy had pulled him over, using a flashing blue light on the dashboard of his station wagon, Sonny Elliman had assumed that what he had to deal with was just another small-town Deputy Dawg, protecting his territory and rousting the big bad biker on the modified Harley-Davidson. But this guy was something else. He was . . . was . . .

He's crazy! Sonny realized, with dawning delight at the discovery. *He's got two public service awards on his wall, and pictures of him talking to the Rotarians and the Lions, and he's vice president of this dipshit town's Jaycees, and next year he'll be president, and he's just as crazy as a fucking bedbug!*

"Okay," he said. "You got my attention."

"I have had what you might call a checkered career," Greg told him. "I've been up, but I've also been down. I've had a few scrapes with the law. What I'm trying to say, Sonny, is that I don't have any set feelings about you. Not like the other locals. They read in the *Union-Leader* about what you and your bikie friends are doing over in the Hamptons this summer and they'd like to castrate you with a rusty Gillette razor blade."

"That's not the Devil's Dozen," Sonny said. "We came down on a run from upstate New York to get some beachtime, man. We're on vacation. We're not into trashing a bunch of honky-tonk bars. There's a bunch of Hell's Angels tearing ass, and a chapter of the Black Riders from New Jersey, but you know who it is mostly? A bunch of college kids." Sonny's lip curled. "But the papers don't like to report that, do they? They'd rather lay the rap on us than on Susie and Jim."

"You're so much more colorful," Greg said mildly. "And William Loeb over at the *Union-Leader* doesn't like bike clubs."

"That bald-headed creep," Sonny muttered.

Greg opened his desk drawer and pulled out a flat pint of Leader's bourbon. "I'll drink to that," he said. He cracked the seal and drank half the pint at a draught. He blew out a great breath, his eyes watering, and held the pint across the desk. "You?"

Sonny polished the pint off. Warm fire bellowed up from his stomach to his throat.

"Light me up, man," he gasped.

Greg threw back his head and laughed. "We'll get along, Sonny. I have a feeling we'll get along."

"What do you want?" Sonny asked again, holding the empty pint.

"Nothing . . . not now. But I have a feeling . . ." Greg's eyes became far away, almost puzzled. "I told you I'm a big man in Ridgeway. I'm going to run for mayor next time the office comes up, and I'll win. But that's . . ."

"Just the beginning?" Sonny prompted.

"It's a start, anyway." That puzzled expression was still there. "I get things done. People know it. I'm good at what I do. I feel like . . . there's a lot ahead of me. Sky's the limit. But I'm not . . . quite sure . . . what I mean. You know?"

Sonny only shrugged.

The puzzled expression faded. "But there's a story, Sonny. A story about a mouse who took a thorn out of a lion's paw. He did it to repay the lion for not eating him a few years before. You know that story?"

"I might have heard it when I was a kid."

Greg nodded. "Well, it's a few years before . . . whatever it is, Sonny." He shoved the plastic Baggies across the desk. "I'm not going to eat you. I could if I wanted to, you know.

A kiddie lawyer couldn't get you off. In this town, with the riots going on in Hampton less than twenty miles away, Clarence Fucking Darrow couldn't get you off in Ridgeway. These good people would love to see you go up."

Elliman didn't reply, but he suspected Greg was right. There was nothing heavy in his dope stash—two Brown Bombers was the heaviest—but the collective parents of good old Susie and Jim would be glad to see him breaking rocks in Portsmouth, with his hair cut off his head.

"I'm not going to eat you," Greg repeated. "I hope you'll remember that in a few years if I get a thorn in my paw . . . or maybe if I have a job opportunity for you. Keep it in mind?"

Gratitude was not in Sonny Elliman's limited catalogue of human feelings, but interest and curiosity were. He felt both ways about this man Stillson. That craziness in his eyes hinted at many things, but boredom was not one of them.

"Who knows where we'll all be in a few years?" he murmured. "We could all be dead, man."

"Just keep me in mind. That's all I'm asking."

Sonny looked at the broken shards of vase. "I'll keep you in mind," he said.

◆ **4** ◆

1971 passed. The New Hampshire beach riots blew over, and the grumblings of the beachfront entrepreneurs were muted by the increased balances in their bankbooks. An obscure fellow named George McGovern declared for the presidency comically early. Anyone who followed politics knew that the nominee from the Democratic party in 1972 was going to be Edmund Muskie, and there were those who felt he might just wrestle the Troll of San Clemente off his feet and pin him to the mat.

In early June, just before school let out for the summer, Sarah met the young law student again. She was in Day's appliance store, shopping for a toaster, and he had been looking for a gift for his parents' wedding anniversary. He asked her if she'd like to go to the movies with him—the new Clint Eastwood, *Dirty Harry*, was in town. Sarah went. And the two of them had a good time. Walter Hazlett had grown a beard, and he no longer reminded her so much of Johnny. In fact, it had become increasingly difficult for her to remember just what Johnny did look like. His face only came clear in her dreams, dreams where he stood in front of the Wheel of Fortune, watching it spin, his face cold and his blue eyes darkened to that perplexing, and a little fearsome, dark violet shade, watching the Wheel as if it were his own private game preserve.

She and Walt began to see a lot of each other. He was easy to get along with. He made no demands—or, if he did, they were of such a gradually increasing nature as to be unnoticeable. In October he asked her if he could buy her a small diamond. Sarah asked him if she could have the weekend to think it over. That Saturday night she had gone to the Eastern Maine Medical Center, had gotten a special red-bordered pass at the desk, and had gone up to intensive care. She sat beside Johnny's bed for an hour. Outside, the fall wind howled in the dark, promising cold, promising snow, promising a season of death. It lacked sixteen days of a year since the fair, the Wheel, and the head-on collision near the Bog.

She sat and listened to the wind and looked at Johnny. The bandages were gone. The scar began on his forehead an inch above his right eyebrow and twisted up under the hairline. His hair had gone white, making her think of that fictional detective in the 87th Precinct stories—Cotton Hawes, his name was. To Sarah's eyes there seemed to have been no degeneration in him, except for the inevitable weight loss. He was simply a young man she barely knew, fast asleep.

She bent over him and kissed his mouth softly, as if the old fairy tale could be reversed and her kiss could wake him. But Johnny only slept.

She left, went back to her apartment in Veazie, lay down on her bed and cried as the wind walked the dark world outside, throwing its catch of yellow and red leaves before it. On Monday she told Walt that if he really did want to buy her a diamond—a small one, mind—she would be happy and proud to wear it.

That was Sarah Bracknell's 1971.

In early 1972, Edmund Muskie burst into tears during an impassioned speech outside the offices of the man Sonny Elliman had referred to as "that bald-headed creep." George McGovern upset the primary, and Loeb announced gleefully in his paper that the people of New Hampshire didn't like crybabies. In July, McGovern was nominated. In that same month Sarah Bracknell became Sarah Hazlett. She and Walt were married in the First Methodist Church of Bangor.

Less than two miles away, Johnny Smith slept on. And the thought of him came to Sarah, suddenly and horribly, as Walt kissed her in front of the dearly beloved there assembled for the nuptials—*Johnny,* she thought, and saw him as she had when the lights went on, half Jekyll and half snarling Hyde. She stiffened in Walt's arms for a moment, and then it was gone. Memory, vision, whatever it had been, it was gone.

After long thought and discussion with Walt, she had invited Johnny's folks to the wedding. Herb had come alone. At the reception, she asked him if Vera was all right.

He glanced around, saw they were alone for the moment, and rapidly downed the remainder of his Scotch and soda. He had aged five years in the last eighteen months, she thought. His hair was thinning. The lines on his face were deeper. He was wearing glasses in the careful and self-conscious way of people who have just started wearing them, and behind the mild corrective lenses his eyes were wary and hurt.

"No . . . she really isn't, Sarah. The truth is, she's up in Vermont. On a farm. Waiting for the end of the world."

"What?"

Herb told her that six months ago Vera had begun to correspond with a group of about ten people who called themselves The American Society of the Last Times. They were led by Mr. and Mrs. Harry L. Stonkers from Racine, Wisconsin. Mr. and Mrs. Stonkers claimed to have been picked up by a flying saucer while they were on a camping trip. They had been taken away to heaven, which was not out in the constellation Orion but on an earth-type planet that circled Arcturus. There they had communed with the society of angels and had seen Paradise. The Stonkerses had been informed that the Last Times were at hand. They were given the power of telepathy and had been sent back to Earth to gather a few faithful together—for the first shuttle to heaven, as it were. And so the ten of them had gotten together, bought a farm north of St. Johnsbury, and had been settled in there for about seven weeks, waiting for the saucer to come and pick them up.

"It sounds . . ." Sarah began, and then closed her mouth.

"I know how it sounds," Herb said. "It sounds crazy. The place cost them nine thousand dollars. It's nothing but a crashed-in farmhouse with two acres of scrubland. Vera's share was seven hundred dollars—all she could put up. There was no way I could stop her . . . short of committal." He paused, then smiled. "But this is nothing to talk about at your wedding party, Sarah. You and your fellow are going to have all the best. I know you will."

Sarah smiled back as best she could. "Thank you, Herb. Will you . . . I mean, do you think she'll . . ."

"Come back? Oh yes. If the world doesn't end by winter, I think she'll be back."

"Oh, I only wish you the best," she said, and embraced him.

◆ 5 ◆

The farm in Vermont had no furnace, and when the saucer had still not arrived by late October, Vera came home. The saucer had not come, she said, because they were not yet perfect—they had not burned away the nonessential and sinful dross of their lives. But she was uplifted and spiritually exalted. She had had a sign in a dream. She was perhaps not meant to go to heaven in a saucer. She felt more and more strongly that she would be needed to guide her boy, show him the proper way, when he came out of his trance.

Herb took her in, loved her as best he could—and life went on. Johnny had been in his coma for two years.

◆ 6 ◆

Nixon was reinaugurated. The American boys started coming home from Vietnam. Walter Hazlett took his bar exam and was invited to take it again at a later date. Sarah Hazlett kept school while he crammed for his tests. The students who had been silly, gawky freshmen the year she started teaching were now juniors. Flat-chested girls had become bosomy. Shrimps who hadn't been able to find their way around the building were now playing varsity basketball.

The second Arab-Israeli war came and went. The oil boycott came and went. Bruisingly high gasoline prices came and did not go. Vera Smith became convinced that Christ would return from below the earth at the South Pole. This intelligence was based on a new pamphlet (seventeen pages, price $4.50) entitled *God's Tropical Underground*. The startling hypothesis of the pamphleteer was that heaven was actually below our very feet, and that the easiest point of ingress was the South Pole. One of the sections of the pamphlet was "Psychic Experiences of the South Pole Explorers."

Herb pointed out to her that less than a year before she had been convinced that heaven was somewhere Out There, most probably circling Arcturus. "I'd surely be more apt to believe that than this crazy South Pole stuff," he told her. "After all, the Bible says heaven's in the sky. That tropical place below the ground is supposed to be . . ."

"Stop it!" she said sharply, lips pressed into thin white lines. "No need to mock what you don't understand."

"I wasn't mocking, Vera," he said quietly.

"God knows why the unbeliever mocks and the heathen rages," she said. That blank light was in her eyes. They were sitting at the kitchen table, Herb with an old plumbing J-bolt in front of him, Vera with a stack of old *National Geographic*s which she had been gleaning for South Pole pictures and stories. Outside, restless clouds fled west to east and the leaves showered off the trees. It was early October again, and October always seemed to be her worst month. It was the month when that blank light came more frequently to her eyes and stayed longer. And it was always in October that his thoughts turned treacherously to leaving them both. His possibly certifiable wife and his sleeping son, who was probably already dead by any practical definition. Just now he had been turning the J-bolt over in his hands and looking out the window at that restless sky and thinking, *I could pack up. Just throw my things into the back of the pickup and go. Florida, maybe. Nebraska. California. A good carpenter can make good money any damn place. Just get up and go.*

But he knew he wouldn't. It was just that October was his month to think about running away, as it seemed to be Vera's month to discover some new pipeline to Jesus and the eventual salvation of the only child she had been able to nurture in her substandard womb.

Now he reached across the table and took her hand, which was thin and terribly bony—an old woman's hand. She looked up, surprised. "I love you very much, Vera," he said.

She smiled back, and for a glimmering moment she was a great deal like the girl he had courted and won, the girl who had goosed him with a hairbrush on their wedding night. It was a gentle smile, her eyes briefly clear and warm and loving in return. Outside, the sun came out from behind a fat cloud,

dived behind another one, and came out again, sending great
shutter-shadows fleeing across their back field.

"I know you do, Herbert. And I love you."

He put his other hand over hers and clasped it.

"Vera," he said.

"Yes?" Her eyes were so clear . . . suddenly she was with
him, totally *with* him, and it made him realize how dreadfully
far apart they had grown over the last three years.

"Vera, if he never does wake up . . . God forbid, but if he
doesn't . . . we'll still have each other, won't we? I mean . . ."

She jerked her hand away. His two hands, which had been
holding it lightly, clapped on nothing.

"Don't you *ever* say that. Don't you *ever* say that Johnny
isn't going to wake up."

"All I meant was that we . . ."

"Of course he's going to wake up," she said, looking out
the window to the field, where the shadows still crossed and
crossed. "It's God's plan for him. Oh yes. Don't you think I
know? I *know,* believe me. God has great things in store for
my Johnny. I have heard him in my heart."

"Yes, Vera," he said. "Okay."

Her fingers groped for the *National Geographics,* found
them, and began to turn the pages again.

"I *know,*" she said in a childish, petulant voice.

"Okay," he said quietly.

She looked at her magazines. Herb propped his chin in his
palms and looked out at the sunshine and shadow and thought
how soon winter came after golden, treacherous October. He
wished Johnny would die. He had loved the boy from the
very first. He had seen the wonder on his tiny face when Herb
had brought a tiny tree frog to the boy's carriage and had put
the small living thing in the boy's hands. He had taught
Johnny how to fish and skate and shoot. He had sat up with
him all night during his terrible bout with the flu in 1951,
when the boy's temperature had crested at a giddy one hundred and five degrees. He had hidden tears in his hand when
Johnny graduated salutatorian of his high school class and had
made his speech from memory without a slip. So many memories of him—teaching him to drive, standing on the bow of
the *Bolero* with him when they went to Nova Scotia on vacation one year, Johnny eight years old, laughing and excited
by the screwlike motion of the boat, helping him with his
homework, helping him with his treehouse, helping him get

the hang of his Silva compass when he had been in the Scouts. All the memories were jumbled together in no chronological order at all—Johnny was the single unifying thread, Johnny eagerly discovering the world that had maimed him so badly in the end. And now he wished Johnny would die, oh how he wished it, that he would die, that his heart would stop beating, that the final low traces on the EEG would go flat, that he would just flicker out like a guttering candle in a pool of wax: that he would die and release them.

◆ 7 ◆

The seller of lightning rods arrived at Cathy's roadhouse in Somersworth, New Hampshire, in the early afternoon of a blazing summer's day less than a week after the Fourth of July in that year of 1973; and somewhere not so far away there were, perhaps, storms only waiting to be born in the warm elevator shafts of summer's thermal updrafts.

He was a man with a big thirst, and he stopped at Cathy's to slake it with a couple of beers, not to make a sale. But from force of long habit, he glanced up at the roof of the low, ranch-style building, and the unbroken line he saw standing against the blistering gunmetal sky caused him to reach back in for the scuffed suede bag that was his sample case.

Inside, Cathy's was dark and cool and silent except for the muted rumble of the color TV on the wall. A few regulars were there, and behind the bar was the owner, keeping an eye on "As The World Turns" along with his patrons.

The seller of lightning rods lowered himself onto a bar stool and put his sample case on the stool to his left. The owner came over. "Hi, friend. What'll it be?"

"A Bud," the lightning rod salesman said. "And draw another for yourself, if you're a mind."

"I'm always of a mind," the owner said. He returned with two beers, took the salesman's dollar, and left three dimes on the bar. "Bruce Carrick," he said, and offered his hand.

The seller of lightning rods shook it. "Dohay is the name," he said, "Andrew Dohay." He drained off half his beer.

"Pleased to meet you," Carrick said. He wandered off to serve a young woman with a hard face another Tequila Sunrise and eventually wandered back to Dohay. "From out of town?"

"I am," Dohay admitted. "Salesman." He glanced around. "Is it always this quiet?"

"No. It jumps on the weekends and I do a fair trade through the week. Private parties is where we make our dough—if we make it. I ain't starving, but neither am I driving a Cadillac." He pointed a pistol finger at Dohay's glass. "Freshen that?"

"And another for yourself, Mr. Carrick."

"Bruce." He laughed. "You must want to sell me something."

When Carrick returned with the beers the seller of lightning rods said: "I came in to lay the dust, not to sell anything. But now that you mention it . . ." He hauled his sample case up onto the bar with a practiced jerk. Things jingled inside it.

"Oh, here it comes," Carrick said, and laughed.

Two of the afternoon regulars, an old fellow with a wart on his right eyelid and a younger man in gray fatigues, wandered over to see what Dohay was selling. The hard-faced woman went on watching "As The World Turns."

Dohay took out three rods, a long one with a brass ball at the tip, a shorter one, and one with porcelain conductors.

"What the hell . . ." Carrick said.

"Lightning rods," the old campaigner said, and cackled. "He wants to save this ginmill from God's wrath, Brucie. You better listen to what he says."

He laughed again, the man in the gray fatigues joined him, Carrick's face darkened, and the lightning rod salesman knew that whatever chance he had had of making a sale had just flown away. He was a good salesman, good enough to recognize that this queer combination of personalities and circumstances sometimes got together and queered any chance of a deal even before he had a chance to swing into his pitch. He took it philosophically and went into his spiel anyway, mostly from force of habit:

"As I was getting out of my car, I just happened to notice that this fine establishment wasn't equipped with lightning conductors—and that it's constructed of wood. Now for a very small price—and easy credit terms if you should want them—I can guarantee that . . ."

"That lightning'll strike this place at four this afternoon," the man in the gray fatigues said with a grin. The old campaigner cackled.

"Mister, no offense," Carrick said, "but you see that?" He

pointed to a golden nail on a small wooden plaque beside the TV near the glistening array of bottles. Spiked on the nail was a drift of papers. "All of those things are bills. They got to be paid by the fifteenth of the month. They get written in red ink. Now you see how many people are in here drinking right now? I got to be careful. I got to . . ."

"Just my point," Dohay broke in smoothly. "You have to be careful. And the purchase of three or four lightning rods is a careful purchase. You've got a going concern here. You wouldn't want it wiped out by one stroke of lightning on a summer's day, would you?"

"He wouldn't mind," the old campaigner said. "He'd just collect the insurance and go down to Florida. Woon'tchoo, Brucie?"

Carrick looked at the old man with distaste.

"Well, then, let's talk about insurance," the lightning rod salesman interposed. The man in the gray fatigues had lost interest and had wandered away. "Your fire insurance premiums will go down . . ."

"The insurance is all lumped together," Carrick said flatly. "Look, I just can't afford the outlay. Sorry. Now if you was to talk to me again next year . . ."

"Well, perhaps I will," the lightning rod salesman said, giving up. "Perhaps I will." No one thought they could be struck by lightning until they were struck; it was a constant fact of this business. You couldn't make a fellow like this Carrick see that it was the cheapest form of fire insurance he could buy. But Dohay was a philosopher. After all, he had told the truth when he said he came in to lay the dust.

To prove it, and to prove there were no hard feelings, he ordered another beer. But this time he did not match it with one for Carrick.

The old campaigner slid onto the stool beside him.

"About ten years ago there was a fella got hit by lightning out on the golf course," he said. "Killed him just as dead as shit. Now, there's a man could have used a lightning rod right up on his head, am I right?" He cackled, sending out a lot of stale beer-breath into Dohay's face. Dohay smiled dutifully. "All the coins in his pockets were fused together. That's what I heard. Lightning's a funny thing. Sure is. Now, I remember one time . . ."

A funny thing, Dohay thought, letting the old man's words flow harmlessly over him, nodding in the right places out of instinct. A funny thing, all right, because it doesn't care who or what it hits. Or when.

He finished his beer and went out, carrying his satchelful of insurance against the wrath of God—maybe the only kind ever invented—with him. The heat struck him like a hammerblow, but still he paused for a moment in the mostly deserted parking lot, looking up at the unbroken line of roof-ridge. $19.95, $29.95 tops, and the man couldn't afford the outlay. He'd save seventy bucks on his combined insurance the first year, but he couldn't afford the outlay—and you couldn't tell him different why those clowns standing around yukking it up.

Maybe some day he would be sorry.

The seller of lightning rods got into his Buick, cranked up the air conditioning, and drove away west toward Concord and Berlin, his sample case on the seat beside him, running ahead of whatever storms might be whistling up the wind behind.

◆ 8 ◆

In early 1974 Walt Hazlett passed his bar exams. He and Sarah threw a party for all of his friends, her friends, and their mutual friends—more than forty people in all. The beer flowed like water, and after it was over Walt said they could count themselves damn lucky not to have been evicted. When the last of the guests were seen out (at three in the morning), Walt had come back from the door to find Sarah in the bedroom, naked except for her shoes and the diamond chip earrings he had gone into hock to give her for her birthday. They had made love not once but twice before falling into sodden slumber from which they awoke at nearly noon, with paralyzing hangovers. About six weeks later Sarah discovered that she was pregnant. Neither of them ever doubted that conception had occurred on the night of the big party.

In Washington, Richard Nixon was being pressed slowly into a corner, wrapped in a snarl of magnetic tapes. In Georgia, a peanut farmer, ex-Navy man and current governor named James Earl Carter had begun talking with a number of close friends about running for the job Mr. Nixon would soon be vacating.

In Room 619 of the Eastern Maine Medical Center, Johnny Smith still slept. He had begun to pull into a fetal shape.

Dr. Strawns, the doctor who had talked to Herb and Vera and Sarah in the conference room on the day following the accident, had died of burns in late 1973. His house had caught fire on the day after Christmas. The Bangor fire department had determined that the fire had been caused by a faulty set of Christmas tree ornaments. Two new doctors, Weizak and Brown, interested themselves in Johnny's case.

Four days before Nixon resigned, Herb Smith fell into the foundation of a house he was building in Gray, landed on a wheelbarrow, and broke his leg. The bone was a long time healing, and it never really felt good again. He limped, and on wet days he began to use a cane. Vera prayed for him, and insisted that he wrap a cloth that had been personally blessed by the Reverend Freddy Coltsmore of Bessemer, Alabama, around the leg each night when he went to bed. The price of the Blessed Coltsmore Cloth (as Herb called it) was $35. It did no good that he was aware of.

In the middle of October, shortly after Gerald Ford had pardoned the ex-president, Vera became sure that the world was going to end again. Herb realized what she was about barely in time; she had made arrangements to give what little cash and savings they had recouped since Johnny's accident to the Last Times Society of America. She had tried to put the house up for sale, and had made an arrangement with the Goodwill, which was going to send a van out in two days' time to pick up all the furniture. Herb found out when the realtor called him to ask if a prospective buyer could come and look at the house that afternoon.

For the first time he had genuinely lost his temper with Vera.

"What in *Christ's* name did you think you were doing?" he roared, after dragging the last of the incredible story out of her. They were in the living room. He had just finished calling Goodwill to tell them to forget the van. Outside, rain fell in monotonous gray sheets.

"Don't blaspheme the name of the Savior, Herbert. Don't . . ."

"Shut up! Shut up! I'm tired of listening to you rave about that *crap*!"

She drew in a startled gasp.

He limped over to her, his cane thumping the floor in counterpoint. She flinched back a little in her chair and then looked up at him with that sweet martyr's expression that made him want, God forgive him, to bust her one across the head with his own damn walking stick.

"You're not so far gone that you don't know what you're doing," he said. "You don't have that excuse. You snuck around behind my back, Vera. You . . ."

"I did not! That's a lie! I did no such . . ."

"*You did!*" he bellowed. "Well, you listen to me, Vera. This is where I'm drawing the line. You pray all you want. Praying's free. Write all the letters you want, a stamp still only costs thirteen cents. If you want to take a bath in all the cheap, shitty lies those Jesus-jumpers tell, if you want to go on with the delusions and the make-believe, you go on. But I'm not a part of it. Remember that. *Do you understand me?*"

"Our-father-who-art-in-heaven-hallow'd-be-thy-name . . ."

"*Do you understand me?*"

"*You think I'm crazy!*" she shouted at him, and her face crumpled and squeezed together in a terrible way. She burst into the braying, ugly tears of utter defeat and disillusion.

"No," he said more quietly. "Not yet. But maybe it's time for a little plain talk, Vera, and the truth is, I think you will be if you don't pull out of this and start facing reality."

"You'll see," she said through her tears. "You'll see. God knows the truth but waits."

"Just as long as you understand that he's not going to have our furniture while he's waiting," Herb said grimly. "As long as we see eye to eye on that."

"It's Last Times!" she told him. "The hour of the Apocalypse is at hand."

"Yeah? That and fifteen cents will buy you a cup of coffee, Vera."

Outside the rain fell in steady sheets. That was the year Herb turned fifty-two, Vera fifty-one, and Sarah Hazlett twenty-seven.

Johnny had been in his coma for four years.

◆ 9 ◆

The baby came on Halloween night. Sarah's labor lasted nine hours. She was given mild whiffs of gas when she needed them, and at some point in her extremity it occurred to her that she was in the same hospital as Johnny, and she called his name over and over again. Afterward she barely remembered this, and certainly never told Walt. She thought she might have dreamed it.

The baby was a boy. They named him Dennis Edward Hazlett. He and his mother went home three days later, and Sarah was teaching again after the Thanksgiving holiday. Walt had landed what looked like a fine job with a Bangor firm of lawyers, and if all went well they planned for Sarah to quit teaching in June of 1975. She wasn't all that sure she wanted to. She had grown to like it.

◆ 10 ◆

On the first day of 1975, two small boys, Charlie Norton and Norm Lawson, both Otisfield, Maine, were in the Nortons' back yard, having a snowball fight. Charlie was eight, Norm was nine. The day was overcast and drippy.

Sensing that the end of the snowball fight was nearing—it was almost time for lunch—Norm charged Charlie, throwing a barrage of snowballs. Ducking and laughing, Charlie was at first forced back, and then turned tail and ran, jumping the low stone wall that divided the Norton back yard from the woods. He ran down the path that led toward Strimmer's Brook. As he went, Norm caught him a damn good one on the back of the hood.

Then Charlie disappeared from sight.

Norm jumped the wall and stood there for a moment, looking into the snowy woods and listening to the drip of meltwater from the birches, pines, and spruces.

"Come on back, chicken!" Norm called, and made a series of high gobbling sounds.

Charlie didn't rise to the bait. There was no sign of him now, but the path descended steeply as it went down toward the brook. Norm gobbled again and shifted irresolutely from one foot to the other. These were Charlie's woods, not his. Charlie's territory. Norm loved a good snowball fight when he was winning, but he didn't really want to go down there if Charlie was lying in ambush for him with half a dozen good hard slushballs all ready to go.

Nonetheless he had taken half a dozen steps down the path when a high, breathless scream rose from below.

Norm Lawson went as cold as the snow his green gum-rubber boots were planted in. The two snowballs he had been holding dropped from his hands and plopped to the ground. The scream rose again, so thin it was barely audible.

Jeepers-creepers, he went and fell in the brook, Norm thought, and that broke the paralysis of his fear. He ran down the path, slipping and sliding, falling right on his can once. His heartbeat roared in his ears. Part of his mind saw him fishing Charlie from the brook just before he went down for the third time and getting written up in *Boy's Life* as a hero.

Three-quarters of the way down the slope the path dog-legged, and when he got around the corner he saw that Charlie Norton hadn't fallen in Strimmer's Brook after all. He was standing at the place where the path leveled out, and he was staring at something in the melting snow. His hood had fallen back and his face was nearly as white as the snow itself. As Norm approached, he uttered that horrible gasping out-of-breath scream again.

"What is it?" Norm asked, approaching. "Charlie, what's wrong?"

Charlie turned to him, his eyes huge, his mouth gaping. He tried to speak but nothing came out of his mouth but two inarticulate grunts and a silver cord of saliva. He pointed instead.

Norm came closer and looked. Suddenly all the strength went out of his legs and he sat down hard. The world swam around him.

Protruding from the melting snow were two legs clad in blue jeans. There was a loafer on one foot, but the other was bare, white, and defenseless. One arm stuck out of the snow, and the hand at the end of it seemed to plead for a rescue that had never come. The rest of the body was still merci-fully hidden.

Charlie and Norm had discovered the body of seventeen-year-old Carol Dunbarger, the fourth victim of the Castle Rock Strangler.

It had been almost two years since he had last killed, and the people of Castle Rock (Strimmer's Brook formed the southern borderline between the towns of Castle Rock and Otisfield) had begun to relax, thinking the nightmare was fi-nally over.

It wasn't.

Chapter 6

◆ 1 ◆

Eleven days after the discovery of the Dunbarger girl's body, a sleet-and-ice storm struck northern New England. On the sixth floor of the Eastern Maine Medical Center, everything was running just a little bit late in consequence. A lot of the staff had run into problems getting to work, and those that made it found themselves running hard just to stay even.

It was after nine A.M. when one of the aides, a young woman named Allison Conover, brought Mr. Starret his light breakfast. Mr. Starret was recovering from a heart attack and was "doing his sixteen" in intensive care—a sixteen-day stay following a coronary was standard operation procedure. Mr. Starret was doing nicely. He was in Room 619, and he had told his wife privately that the biggest incentive to his recovery was the prospect of getting away from the living corpse in the room's second bed. The steady whisper of the poor guy's respirator made it hard to sleep, he told her. After a while it got so you didn't know if you wanted it to go on whispering—or stop. Stop dead, so to speak.

The TV was on when Allison came in. Mr. Starret was sitting up in bed with his control button in one hand. "Today" had ended, and Mr. Starret had not yet decided to blank out "My Back Yard," the cartoon show that followed it. That would have left him alone with the sound of Johnny's respirator.

"I'd about given up on you this morning," Mr. Starret said, looking at his breakfast tray of orange juice, plain yogurt, and wheat flakes with no great joy. What he really craved was two cholesterol-filled eggs, fried over easy and sweating butter, with five slices of bacon on the side, not too crisp. The sort of fare that had, in fact, landed him here in the first place. At least according to his doctor—the birdbrain.

"The going's bad outside," Allison said shortly. Six patients had already told her they had about given up on her this morning, and the line was getting old. Allison was a pleasant girl, but this morning she was feeling harried.

"Oh, sorry," Mr. Starret said humbly. "Pretty slippery on the roads, is it?"

"It sure is," Allison said, thawing slightly. "If I didn't have my husband's four-wheel drive today, I never would have made it."

Mr. Starret pushed the button that raised his bed so he could eat his breakfast comfortably. The electric motor that raised and lowered it was small but loud. The TV was also quite loud—Mr. Starret was a little deaf, and as he had told his wife, the guy in the other bed had never complained about a little extra volume. Never asked to see what was on the other channels, either. He supposed a joke like that was in pretty poor taste, but when you'd had a heart attack and wound up in intensive care sharing a room with a human vegetable, you either learned a little black humor or you went crazy.

Allison raised her voice a little to be heard over the whining motor and the TV as she finished setting up Mr. Starret's tray. "There were cars off the road all up and down State Street hill."

In the other bed Johnny Smith said softly, "The whole wad on nineteen. One way or the other. My girl's sick."

"You know, this yogurt isn't half bad," Mr. Starret said. He hated yogurt, but he didn't want to be left alone until absolutely necessary. When he was alone he kept taking his own pulse. "It tastes a little bit like wild hickory n . . ."

"Did you hear something?" Allison asked. She looked around doubtfully.

Mr. Starret let go of the control button on the side of the bed and the whine of the electric motor died. On the TV, Elmer Fudd took a potshot at Bugs Bunny and missed.

"Nothing but the TV," Mr. Starret said. "What'd I miss?"

"Nothing, I guess. It must have been the wind around that window." She could feel a stress headache coming on—too much to do and not enough people this morning to help her do it—and she rubbed at her temples, as if to drive the pain away before it could get properly seated.

On her way out she paused and looked down at the man in the other bed for a moment. Did he look different somehow? As if he had shifted position? Surely not.

Allison left the room and went on down the hall, pushing

her breakfast cabinet ahead of her. It was as terrible a morning as she had feared it would be, everything out of kilter, and by noon her head was pounding. She had quite understandably forgotten all about anything she might have heard that morning in Room 619.

But in the days that followed she found herself looking more and more often at Smith, and by March Allison had become almost sure that he had straightened a bit—come out of what the doctors called his prefetal position a little. Not much—just a little. She thought of mentioning it to someone, but in the end did not. After all, she was only an aide, little more than kitchen help.

It really wasn't her place.

◆ 2 ◆

It was a dream, he guessed.

He was in a dark, gloomy place—a hallway of some kind. The ceiling was too high to see. It was lost in the shadows. The walls were dark chromed steel. They opened out as they went upward. He was alone, but a voice floated up to where he stood, as if from a great distance. A voice he knew, words that had been spoken to him in another place, at another time. The voice frightened him. It was groaning and lost, echoing back and forth between that dark chromed steel like a trapped bird he remembered from his childhood. The bird had flown into his father's toolshed and hadn't the wit to get back out. He had panicked and had gone swooping back and forth, cheeping in desperate alarm, battering itself against the walls until it had battered itself to death. This voice had the same doomed quality as that long-ago bird's cheeping. It was never going to escape this place.

"You plan all your life and you do what you can," this spectral voice groaned. "You never want nothing but the best, and the kid comes home with hair down to his asshole and says the president of the United States is a pig. A pig! Sheeyit, I don't . . ."

Look out, he wanted to say. He wanted to warn the voice, but he was mute. Look out for what? He didn't know. He didn't even know for sure who he was, although he had a suspicion that he had once been a teacher or preacher.

"*Jeeeesus!*" The faraway voice screamed. Lost voice, doomed, drowned. "*Jeeeee . . .*"

Silence then. Echoes dying away. Then, in a little while, it would start again.

So after a while—he did not know how long, time seemed to have no meaning or relevance in this place—he began to grope his way down the hall, calling in return (or perhaps only calling in his mind), perhaps hoping that he and the owner of the voice could find their way out together, perhaps only hoping to give some comfort and receive some in return.

But the voice kept getting further and further away, dimmer and fainter

(far and wee)

until it was just an echo of an echo. And then it was gone. He was alone now, walking down this gloomy and deserted hall of shadows. And it began to seem to him that it wasn't an illusion or a mirage or a dream—at least not of the ordinary kind. It was as if he had entered limbo, a weird conduit between the land of the living and that of the dead. But toward which end was he moving?

Things began to come back. Disturbing things. They were like ghosts that joined him on his walk, fell in on either side of him, in front of him, behind him, until they circled him in an eldritch ring—weave a circle round him thrice and touch his eyes with holy dread, was that how it went? He could almost see them. All the whispering voices of purgatory. There was a Wheel turning and turning in the night, a Wheel of the Future, red and black, life and death, slowing. Where had he laid his bet? He couldn't remember and he should be able to, because the stakes were his existence. In or out? It had to be one or the other. His girl was sick. He had to get her home.

After a while, the hallway began to seem brighter. At first he thought it was imagination, a sort of dream within a dream if that were possible, but after an unknown length of time the brightness became too marked to be an illusion. The whole experience of the corridor seemed to become less dreamlike. The walls drew back until he could barely see them, and the dull dark color changed to a sad and misty gray, the color of twilight on a warm and overcast March afternoon. It began to seem that he was not in a hallway at all anymore, but in a room—*almost* in a room, separated from it by the thinnest of membranes, a sort of placental sac, like a baby waiting to be born. Now he heard other voices, not echoey but dull and thudding, like the voices of nameless gods speaking in forgotten tongues. Little by little these voices came clearer, until he could nearly make out what they were saying.

He began to open his eyes from time to time (or thought he did) and he could actually see the owners of those voices: bright, glowing, spectral shapes with no faces at first, sometimes moving about the room, sometimes bending over him. It didn't occur to him to try speaking to them, at least not at first. It came to him that this might be some sort of afterlife, and these bright shapes the shapes of angels.

The faces, like the voices, began to come clearer with time. He saw his mother once, leaning into his field of vision and slowly thundering something totally without meaning into his upturned face. His father was there another time. Dave Pelsen from school. A nurse he came to know; he believed her name was Mary or possibly Marie. Faces, voices, coming closer, jelling together.

Something else crept in: a feeling that he had *changed*. He didn't like the feeling. He distrusted it. It seemed to him that whatever the change was, it was nothing good. It seemed to him that it meant sorrow and bad times. He had gone into the darkness with everything, and now it felt to him that he was coming out of it with nothing at all—except for some secret strangeness.

The dream was ending. Whatever it had been, the dream was ending. The room was very real now, very *close*. The voices, the faces—

He was going to come into the room. And it suddenly seemed to him that what he wanted to do was turn and run— to go back down that dark hallway forever. The dark hallway was not good, but it was better than this new feeling of sadness and impending loss.

He turned and looked behind him and yes, it was there, the place where the room's walls changed to dark chrome, a corner beside one of the chairs where, unnoticed by the bright people who came and went, the room became a passageway into what he now suspected was eternity. The place where that other voice had gone, the voice of—

The cab driver.

Yes. That memory was all there now. The cab ride, the driver bemoaning his son's long hair, bemoaning the fact that his son thought Nixon was a pig. Then the headlights breasting the hall, a pair on each side of the white line. The crash. No pain, but the knowledge that his thighs had connected with the taximeter hard enough to rip it out of its frame. There had been a sensation of cold wetness and then the dark hallway and now this.

Choose, something inside whispered. *Choose or they'll choose for you, they'll rip you out of this place, whatever and wherever it is, like doctors ripping a baby out of its mother's womb by cesarian section.*

And then Sarah's face came to him—she had to be out there someplace, although hers had not been one of the bright faces bending over his. She had to be out there, worried and scared. She was almost his, now. He felt that. He was going to ask her to marry him.

That feeling of unease came back, stronger than ever, and this time it was all mixed up with Sarah. But wanting her was stronger, and he made his decision. He turned his back on the dark place, and when he looked back over his shoulder later on, it had disappeared; there was nothing beside the chair but the smooth white wall of the room where he lay. Not long after he began to know where the room must be— it was a hospital room, of course. The dark hallway faded to a dreamy memory, never completely forgotten. But more important, more immediate, was the fact that he was John Smith, he had a girl named Sarah Bracknell, and he had been in a terrible car accident. He suspected that he must be very lucky to be alive, and he could only hope that all his original equipment was still there and still functioning. He might be in Cleaves Mills Community Hospital, but he guessed the EMMC was more likely. From the way he felt he guessed he had been here for some time—he might have been blacked out for as long as a week or ten days. It was time to get going again.

Time to get going again. That was the thought in Johnny's mind when things finally jelled all the way back together and he opened his eyes.

It was May 17, 1975. Mr. Starret had long since gone home with standing orders to walk two miles a day and mend his high-cholesterol ways. Across the room was an old man engaged in a weary fifteenth round with that all-time heavy-weight champ, carcinoma. He slept the sleep of morphia, and the room was otherwise empty. It was 3:15 P.M. The TV screen was a drawn green shade.

"Here I am," Johnny Smith croaked to no one at all. He was shocked by the weakness of his voice. There was no calendar in the room, and he had no way of knowing that he had been out of it four-and-a-half years.

♦ 3 ♦

The nurse came in some forty minutes later. She went over to the old man in the other bed, changed his IV feed, went into the bathroom, and came out with a blue plastic pitcher. She watered the old man's flowers. There were over half a dozen bouquets, and a score of get-well cards standing open on his table and windowsill. Johnny watched her perform this homey chore, feeling as yet no urge to try his voice again.

She put the pitcher back and came over to Johnny's bed. *Going to turn my pillows,* he thought. Their eyes met briefly, but nothing in hers changed. *She doesn't know I'm awake. My eyes have been open before. It doesn't mean anything to her.*

She put her hand on the back of his neck. It was cool and comforting and Johnny knew she had three children and that the youngest had lost most of the sight in one eye last Fourth of July. A firecracker accident. The boy's name was Mark.

She lifted his head, flipped his pillow over, and settled him back. She started to turn away, adjusting her nylon uniform at the hips, and then turned back, puzzled. Belatedly thinking that there had been someting new in his eyes, maybe. Something that hadn't been there before.

She glanced at him thoughtfully, started to turn away again, and he said, "Hello, Marie."

She froze, and he could hear an ivory click as her teeth came suddenly and violently together. Her hand pressed against her chest just above the swell of her breasts. A small gold crucifix hung there. "O-my-God," she said. "You're awake. I *thought* you looked different. How did you know my name?"

"I suppose I must have heard it." It was hard to talk, terribly hard. His tongue was a sluggish worm, seemingly unlubricated by saliva.

She nodded. "You've been coming up for some time now. I'd better go down to the nurses' station and have Dr. Brown or Dr. Weizak paged. They'll want to know you're back with us." But she stayed a moment longer, looking at him with a frank fascination that made him uneasy.

"Did I grow a third eye?" he asked.

She laughed nervously. "No . . . of course not. Excuse me."

His eye caught on his own window ledge and his table pushed up against it. On the ledge was a faded African violet and a picture of Jesus Christ—it was the sort of picture of Jesus his mother favored, with Christ looking as if he was ready to bat clean-up for the New York Yankees or something of a similar clean and athletic nature. But the picture was—yellow. *Yellow and beginning to curl at the corners.* Sudden fear dropped over him like a suffocating blanket. "Nurse!" he called. "Nurse!"

In the doorway she turned back.

"Where are my get-well cards?" Suddenly it was hard for him to breathe. "That other guy's got . . . didn't anyone send me a card?"

She smiled, but it was forced. It was the smile of someone who is hiding something. Suddenly Johnny wanted her by his bed. He would reach out and touch her. If he could touch her, he would know what she was hiding.

"I'll have the doctor paged," she said, and left before he could say anything else. He looked at the African violet, at the aging picture of Jesus, baffled and afraid. After a little while, he drifted off to sleep again.

◆ 4 ◆

"He *was* awake," Marie Michaud said. "He was completely coherent."

"Okay," Dr. Brown answered. "I'm not doubting you. If he woke up once, he'll wake up again. Probably. It's just a matter of . . ."

Johnny moaned. His eyes opened. They were blank, half rolled up. Then he seemed to see Marie, and his eyes came into focus. He smiled a little. But his face was still slack, as if only his eyes were awake and the rest of him still slept. She had a sudden feeling that he was not looking at her but *into* her.

"I think he'll be okay," Johnny said. "Once they clean that impacted cornea, the eye'll be as good as new. Should be."

Marie gasped harshly, and Brown glanced at her. "What is it?"

"He's talking about my boy," she whispered. "My Mark."

"No," Brown said. "He's talking in his sleep, that's all. Don't make a picture out of an inkblot, Nurse."

"Yes. Okay. But he's not asleep now, is he?"

"Marie?" Johnny asked. He smiled tentatively. "I dozed off, didn't I?"

"Yes," Brown said. "You were talking in your sleep. Gave Marie here a turn. Were you dreaming?"

"No-oo . . . not that I remember. What did I say? And who are you?"

"I'm Dr. James Brown. Just like the soul singer. Only I'm a neurologist. You said, 'I think he'll be okay once they clean that impacted cornea.' I think that was it, wasn't it, Nurse?"

"My boy's going to have that operation," Marie said. "My boy Mark."

"I don't remember anything," Johnny said. "I guess I was sleeping." He looked at Brown. His eyes were clear now, and scared. "I can't lift my arms. Am I paralyzed?"

"Nope. Try your fingers."

Johnny did. They all wiggled. He smiled.

"Superfine," Brown said. "Tell me your name."

"John Smith."

"Good, and your middle name?"

"I don't have one."

"That's fine, who needs one? Nurse, go down to your station and find out who's in neurology tomorrow. I'd like to start a whole series of tests on Mr. Smith."

"Yes, Doctor."

"And you might call Sam Weizak. You'll get him at home or at the golf course."

"Yes, Doctor."

"And no reporters, please . . . for your life!" Brown was smiling but serious.

"No, of course not." She left, white shoes squeaking faintly. Her little boy's going to be just fine, Johnny thought. I'll be sure to tell her.

"Dr. Brown," he said, "where are my get-well cards? Didn't anybody send me a card?"

"Just a few more questions," Dr. Brown said smoothly. "Do you recall your mother's name?"

"Of course I do. Vera."

"Her maiden name?"

"Nason."

"Your father's name?"

"Herbert. Herb. And why did you tell her no reporters?"

"Your mailing address?"

"RFD #1, Pownal," Johnny said promptly, and then stopped. An expression of comic surprise passed across his face. "I mean . . . well, I live in Cleaves Mills now, at 110 North Main Street. Why the hell did I give you my parents' address? I haven't lived there since I was eighteen."

"And how old are you now?"

"Look it up on my driver's license," Johnny said. "I want to know why I don't have any get-well cards. How long have I been in the hospital, anyway? And which hospital is this?"

"It's the Eastern Maine Medical Center. And we'll get to all the rest of your questions if you'll just let me . . ."

Brown was sitting by the bed in a chair he had drawn over from the corner—the same corner where Johnny had once seen the passage leading away. He was making notes on a clipboard with a type of pen Johnny couldn't remember ever having seen before. It had a thick blue plastic barrel and a fibrous tip. It looked like the strange hybrid offspring of a fountain pen and a ballpoint.

Just looking at it made that formless dread come back, and without thinking about it, Johnny suddenly seized Dr. Brown's left hand in one of his own. His arm moved creakily, as if there were invisible sixty-pound weights tied to it—a couple below the elbow and a couple above. He captured the doctor's hand in a weak grip and pulled. The funny pen left a thick blue line across the paper.

Brown looked at him, at first only curious. Then his face drained of color. The sharp expression of interest left his eyes and was replaced with a muddy look of fear. He snatched his hand away—Johnny had no power to hold it—and for an instant a look of revulsion crossed the doctor's face, as if he had been touched by a leper.

Then it was gone, and he only looked surprised and disconcerted. "What did you do that for? Mr. Smith . . ."

His voice faltered. Johnny's face had frozen in an expression of dawning comprehension. His eyes were the eyes of a man who has seen something terrible moving and shifting in the shadows, something too terrible to be described or even named.

But it was a fact. It had to be named.

"Fifty-five *months*?" Johnny asked hoarsely. "Going on five *years*? *No.* Oh my God, *no.*"

"Mr. Smith," Brown said, now totally flustered. "Please, it's not good for you to excite . . ."

Johnny raised his upper body perhaps three inches from the bed and then slumped back, his face shiny with sweat. His eyes rolled helplessly in their sockets. "I'm twenty-seven?" he muttered. "Twenty-*seven*? Oh my *Jesus.*"

Brown swallowed and heard an audible click. When Smith had grabbed his hand, he had felt a sudden onrush of bad feelings, childlike in their intensity; crude images of revulsion had assaulted him. He had found himself remembering a picnic in the country when he had been seven or eight, sitting down and putting his hand in something warm and slippery. He had looked around and had seen that he had put his hand into the maggoty remains of a woodchuck that had lain under a laurel bush all that hot August. He had screamed then, and he felt a little bit like screaming now—except that the feeling was fading, dwindling, to be replaced with a question: *How did he know? He touched me and he knew.*

Then twenty years of education rose up strongly in him, and he pushed the notion aside. There were cases without number of comatose patients who had awakened with a dreamlike knowledge of many things that had gone on around them while they were in coma. Like anything else, coma was a matter of degree. Johnny Smith had never been a vegetable; his EEG had never gone flatline, and if it had, Brown would not be talking with him now. Sometimes being in a coma was a little like being behind a one-way glass. To the beholding eye the patient was completely conked out, but the patient's senses might still continue to function in some low, power-down fashion. And that was the case here, of course.

Marie Michaud came back in. "Neurology is confirmed, and Dr. Weizak is on his way."

"I think Sam will have to wait until tomorrow to meet Mr. Smith," Brown said. "I want him to have five milligrams of Valium."

"I don't want a sedative," Johnny said. "I want to get *out* of here. I want to know what happened!"

"You'll know everything in time," Brown said. "Right now it's important that you rest."

"I've been resting for four-and-a-half years!"

"Then another twelve hours won't make much difference," Brown said inexorably.

A few moments later the nurse swabbed his upper arm with alcohol, and there was the sting of a needle. Johnny began to feel sleepy almost at once. Brown and the nurse began to look twelve feet tall.

"Tell me one thing, at least," he said. His voice seemed to come from far, far away. Suddenly it seemed terribly important. "That pen. What do you call that pen?"

"This?" Brown held it out from his amazing height. Blue plastic body, fibrous tip. "It's called a Flair. Now go to sleep, Mr. Smith."

And Johnny did, but the word followed him down into his sleep like a mystic incantation, full of idiot meaning: *Flair* . . . *Flair* . . . *Flair* . . .

◆ 5 ◆

Herb put the telephone down and looked at it. He looked at it for a long time. From the other room came the sound of the TV, turned up almost all the way. Oral Roberts was talking about football and the healing love of Jesus—there was a connection there someplace, but Herb had missed it. Because of the telephone call. Oral's voice boomed and roared. Pretty soon the show would end and Oral would close it out by confidently telling his audience that something *good* was going to happen to *them*. Apparently Oral was right.

My boy, Herb thought. While Vera had prayed for a miracle, Herb had prayed for his boy to die. It was Vera's prayer that had been answered. What did that mean, and where did it leave him? And what was it going to do to her?

He went into the living room. Vera was sitting on the couch. Her feet, encased in elastic pink mules, were up on a hassock. She was wearing her old gray robe. She was eating popcorn straight from the popper. Since Johnny's accident she had put on nearly forty pounds and her blood pressure had skyrocketed. The doctor wanted to put her on medication, but Vera wouldn't have it—if it was the will of the Lord for her to have the high blood, she said, then she would have it. Herb had once pointed out that the will of the Lord had never stopped her from taking Bufferin when she had a headache.

She had answered with her sweetest long-suffering smile and her most potent weapon: silence.

"Who was on the phone?" she asked him, not looking away from the TV. Oral had his arm around the well-known quarterback of an NFC team. He was talking to a hushed multitude. The quarterback was smiling modestly.

". . . and you have all heard this fine athlete tell you tonight how he abused his body, his Temple of God. And you have heard . . ."

Herb snapped it off.

"Herbert *Smith*!" She nearly spilled her popcorn sitting up. "I was watching! That was . . ."

"Johnny woke up."

". . . Oral Roberts and . . ."

The words snapped off in her mouth. She seemed to crouch back in her chair, as if he had taken a swing at her. He looked back, unable to say more, wanting to feel joy but afraid. So afraid.

"Johnny's . . ." She stopped, swallowed, then tried again. "Johnny . . . *our* Johnny?"

"Yes. He spoke with Dr. Brown for nearly fifteen minutes. Apparently it wasn't that thing they thought . . . false-waking . . . after all. He's coherent. He can move."

"*Johnny's awake?*"

Her hands came up to her mouth. The popcorn popper, half-full, did a slow dipsy-doodle off her lap and thumped to the rug, spilling popcorn everywhere. Her hands covered the lower half of her face. Above them her eyes got wider and wider still until, for a dreadful second, Herb was afraid that they might fall out and dangle by their stalks. Then they closed. A tiny mewing sound came from behind her hands.

"Vera? Are you all right?"

"O my God I thank You for Your will be done my Johnny You brought me my I knew You would, my Johnny, o dear God I will bring You my thanksgiving every day of my life for my Johnny *Johnny JOHNNY*—" Her voice was rising to a hysterical, triumphant scream. He stepped forward, grabbed the lapels of her robe, and shook her. Suddenly time seemed to have reversed, doubled back on itself like strange cloth— they might have been back on the night when the news of the accident came to them, delivered through that same telephone in that same nook.

By nook or by crook, Herb Smith thought crazily.

"O my precious God my Jesus oh my Johnny the miracle like I said the *miracle* . . ."

"*Stop it, Vera!*"

Her eyes were dark and hazy and hysterical. "Are you sorry he's awake again? After all these years of making fun of me? Of telling people I was crazy?"

"Vera, I never told anyone you were crazy."

"*You told them with your eyes!*" she shouted at him. "But my God wasn't mocked. Was he, Herbert? *Was he?*"

"No," he said. "I guess not."

"I told you. I told you God had a plan for my Johnny. Now you see his hand beginning to work." She got up. "I've got to go to him. I've got to tell him." She walked toward the closet where her coat hung, seemingly unaware that she was in her robe and nightgown. Her face was stunned with rapture. In some bizarre and almost blasphemous way she reminded him of the way she had looked on the day they were married. Her pink mules crunched popcorn into the rug.

"Vera."

"I've got to tell him that God's plan . . ."

"Vera."

She turned to him, but her eyes were far away, with her Johnny.

He went to her and put his hands on her shoulders.

"You tell him that you love him . . . that you prayed . . . waited . . . watched. Who has a better right? You're his mother. You bled for him. Haven't I watched you bleed for him over the last five years? I'm not sorry he's back with us, you were wrong to say that. I don't think I can make of it what you do, but I'm not sorry. I bled for him, too."

"Did you?" Her eyes were flinty, proud, and unbelieving.

"Yes. And I'm going to tell you something else, Vera. You're going to keep your trap shut about God and miracles and Great Plans until Johnny's up on his feet and able to . . ."

"I'll say what I have to say!"

". . . and able to think what he's doing. What I'm saying is that you're going to give him a chance to make something of it for himself before you start in on him."

"You have no right to talk to me that way! No right at all!"

"I'm exercising my right as Johnny's dad," he said grimly. "Maybe for the last time in my life. And you better not get in my way, Vera. You understand? Not you, not God, not the bleeding holy Jesus. You follow?"

She glared at him sullenly and said nothing.

"He's going to have enough to do just coping with the idea that he's been out like a light for four-and-a-half years. We don't know if he'll be able to walk again, in spite of the therapist that came in. We do know there'll have to be an operation on his ligaments, if he even wants to try; Weizak told us that. Probably more than one. And more therapy, and a lot of it's going to hurt him like hell. So tomorrow you're just going to be his mother."

"Don't you dare talk to me that way! *Don't you dare!*"

"If you start in sermonizing, Vera, I'll drag you out of his room by the hair of your head."

She stared at him, white-faced and trembling. Joy and fury were at war in her eyes.

"You better get dressed," Herb said. "We ought to get going."

It was a long, silent ride up to Bangor. The happiness they should have felt between them was not there; only Vera's hot and militant joy. She sat bolt upright in the passenger seat, her Bible in her lap, open to the twenty-third Psalm.

◆ 6 ◆

At quarter of nine the next morning, Marie came into Johnny's room and said, "Your mom and dad are here, if you're up to seeing them."

"Yes, I'd like that." He felt much better this morning, stronger and less disoriented. But the thought of seeing them scared him a little. In terms of his conscious recollection, he had seen them about five months ago. His father had been working on the foundation of a house that had now probably been standing for three years or more. His mom had fixed him home-baked beans and apple pie for dessert and had clucked over how thin he was getting.

He caught Marie's hand weakly as she turned to go.

"Do they look all right? I mean . . ."

"They look fine."

"Oh. Good."

"You can only have half an hour with them now. Some more time this evening if the neurology series doesn't prove too tiring."

"Dr. Brown's orders?"

"And Dr. Weizak's."

"All right. For a while. I'm not sure how long I want to be poked and prodded."

Marie hesitated.

"Something?" Johnny asked.

"No . . . not now. You must be anxious to see your folks. I'll send them in."

He waited, nervous. The other bed was empty; the cancer patient had been moved out while Johnny slept off his Valium pop.

The door opened. His mother and father came in. Johnny felt simultaneous shock and relief: shock because they *had* aged, it *was* all true; relief because the changes in them did not yet seem mortal. And if that could be said of them, perhaps it could be said of him as well.

But something in him had changed, changed drastically—and it *might* be mortal.

That was all he had time to think before his mother's arms were around him, her violet sachet strong in his nostrils, and she was whispering: "Thank God, Johnny, thank God, thank God you're awake."

He hugged her back as best he could—his arms still had no power to grip and fell away quickly—and suddenly, in six seconds, he knew how it was with her, what she thought, and what was going to happen to her. Then it was gone, fading like that dream of the dark corridor. But when she broke the embrace to look at him, the look of zealous joy in her eyes had been replaced with one of thoughtful consideration.

The words seemed to come out of him of their own: "Let them give you the medicine, Mom. That's best."

Her eyes widened, she wet her lips—and then Herb was beside her, his eyes filled with tears. He had lost some weight—not as much as Vera had put on, but he was noticeably thinner. His hair was going fast but the face was the same, homely and plain and well-loved. He took a large brakeman's bandanna from his back pocket and wiped his eyes with it. Then he stuck out his hand.

"Hi, son," he said. "Good to have you back."

Johnny shook his father's hand as well as he could; his pale and strengthless fingers were swallowed up in his father's red hand. Johnny looked from one to the other—his mother in a bulky powder-blue pantsuit, his father in a really hideous houndstooth jacket that looked as if it should belong to a vacuum-cleaner salesman in Kansas—and he burst into tears.

"I'm sorry," he said. "I'm sorry, it's just that . . ."

"You go on," Vera said, sitting on the bed beside him. Her face was calm and clear now. There was more mother than madness in it. "You go on and cry, sometimes that's best."

And Johnny did.

◆ 7 ◆

Herb told him his Aunt Germaine had died. Vera told him that the money for the Pownal Community Hall had finally been raised and the building had commenced a month ago, as soon as the frost was out of the ground. Herb added that he had put in a bid, but he guessed honest work cost too dear for them to want to pay. "Oh, shush, you sore loser," Vera said.

There was a little silence and then Vera spoke again. "I hope you realize that your recovery is a miracle of God, Johnny. The doctors despaired. In Matthew, chapter nine, we read . . ."

"Vera," Herb said warningly.

"Of course it was a miracle, Mom. I know that."

"You . . . you do?"

"Yes. And I want to talk about it with you . . . hear your ideas about what it means . . . just as soon as I get on my feet again."

She was staring at him, open-mouthed. Johnny glanced past her at his father and their eyes met for a moment. Johnny saw great relief in his father's eyes. Herb nodded imperceptibly.

"A Conversion!" Vera ejaculated loudly. "My boy has had a Conversion! Oh, praise God!"

"Vera, hush," Herb said. "Best to praise God in a lower voice when you're in the hospital."

"I don't see how anybody could not call it a miracle, Mom. And we're going to talk about it a lot. Just as soon as I'm out of here."

"You're going to come home," she said. "Back to the house where you were raised. I'll nurse you back to health and we'll pray for understanding."

He was smiling at her, but holding the smile was an effort. "You bet. Mom, would you go down to the nurses' station and ask Marie if I can have some juice? Or maybe some ginger ale? I guess I'm not used to talking, and my throat . . ."

"Of course I will." She kissed his cheek and stood up. "Oh, you're so thin. But I'll fix that when I get you home." She left the room, casting a single victorious glance at Herb as she went. They heard her shoes tapping off down the hall.

"How long has she been that way?" Johnny asked quietly.

Herb shook his head. "It's come a little at a time since your accident. But it had its start long before that. You know. You remember."

"Is she . . ."

"I don't know. There are people down South that handle snakes. I'd call them crazy. She doesn't do that. How are you, Johnny? Really?"

"I don't know," Johnny said. "Daddy, where's Sarah?"

Herb leaned forward and clasped his hands between his knees. "I don't like to tell you this, John, but . . ."

"She's married? She got *married*?"

Herb didn't answer. Without looking directly at Johnny, he nodded his head.

"Oh, God," Johnny said hollowly. "I was afraid of that."

"She's been Mrs. Walter Hazlett for going on three years. He's a lawyer. They have a baby boy. John . . . no one really believed you were going to wake up. Except for your mother, of course. None of us had any *reason* to believe you would wake up." His voice was trembling now, hoarse with guilt. "The doctors said . . . ah, never mind what they said. Even I gave you up. I hate like hell to admit it, but it's true. All I can ask you is to try to understand about me . . . and Sarah."

He tried to say that he did understand, but all that would come out was a sickly sort of croak. His body felt sick and old, and suddenly he was drowning in his sense of loss. The lost time was suddenly sitting on him like a load of bricks— a real thing, not just a vague concept.

"Johnny, don't take on. There are other things. Good things."

"It's . . . going to take some getting used to," he managed.

"Yeah. I know."

"Do you ever see her?"

"We write back and forth once in a while. We got acquainted after your accident. She's a nice girl, real nice. She's still teaching at Cleaves, but I understand she is getting done this June. She's happy, John."

"Good," he said thickly. "I'm glad someone is."

"Son . . ."

"I hope you're not telling secrets," Vera Smith said brightly, coming back into the room. She had an ice-clogged pitcher in one hand. "They said you weren't ready for fruit juice, Johnny, so I brought you the ginger ale."

"That's fine, Mom."

She looked from Herb to Johnny and back to Herb again. "*Have* you been telling secrets? Why the long faces?"

"I was just telling Johnny he's going to have to work hard if he wants to get out of here," said Herb. "Lots of therapy."

"Now why would you want to talk about that now?" She poured ginger ale into Johnny's glass. "Everything's going to be fine now. You'll see."

She popped a flexible straw into the glass and handed it to him.

"Now you drink all of it," she said, smiling. "It's good for you."

Johnny did drink all of it. It tasted bitter.

Chapter 7

◆ 1 ◆

"Close your eyes," Dr. Weizak said.

He was a small, roly-poly man with an incredible styled head of hair and spade sideburns. Johnny couldn't get over all that hair. A man with a haircut like that in 1970 would have had to fight his way out of every bar in eastern Maine, and a man Weizak's age would have been considered ripe for committal.

All that hair. Man.

He closed his eyes. His head was covered with electrical contact points. The contacts went to wires that fed into a wall-console EEG. Dr. Brown and a nurse stood by the console, which was calmly extruding a wide sheet of graph paper. Johnny wished the nurse could have been Marie Michaud. He was a little scared.

Dr. Weizak touched his eyelids and Johnny jerked.

"Nuh . . . hold still, Johnny. These are the last two. Just . . . there."

"All right, Doctor," the nurse said.

A low hum.

"All right, Johnny. Are you comfortable?"

"Feels like there are pennies on my eyelids."

"Yes? You'll get used to that in no time. Now let me explain to you this procedure. I am going to ask you to visualize a number of things. You will have about ten seconds on each, and there are twenty things to visualize in all. You understand?"

"Yes."

"Very fine. We begin. Dr. Brown?"

"All ready."

"Excellent. Johnny, I ask you to see a table. On this table there is an orange."

Johnny thought about it. He saw a small card-table with folding steel legs. Resting on it, a little off-center, was a large orange with the word SUNKIST stamped on its pocky skin.

"Good," Weizak said.

"Can that gadget see my orange?"

"Nuh . . . well, yes; in a symbolic way it can. The machine is tracing your brainwaves. We are searching for blocks, Johnny. Areas of impairment. Possible indications of continuing intercranial pressure. Now I ask you to shush with the questions."

"All right."

"Now I ask you to see a television. It is on, but not receiving a station."

Johnny saw the TV that was in the apartment—*had* been in his apartment. The screen was bright gray with snow. The tips of the rabbit ears were wrapped with tinfoil for better reception.

"Good."

The series went on. For the eleventh item Weizak said, "Now I ask you to see a picnic table on the left side of a green lawn."

Johnny thought about it, and in his mind he saw a lawn chair. He frowned.

"Something wrong?" Weizak asked.

"No, not at all," Johnny said. He thought harder. Picnics. Weiners, a charcoal brazier . . . associate, dammit, associate. How hard can it be to see a picnic table in your mind, you've only seen a thousand of them in your life; associate your way to it. Plastic spoons and forks, paper plates, his father in a chef's hat, holding a long fork in one hand and wearing an apron with a motto printed across it in tipsy letters. THE COOK NEEDS A DRINK. His father making burgers and then they would all go sit at the—

Ah, here it came!

Johnny smiled, and then the smile faded. This time the image in his mind was of a hammock. "Shit!"

"No picnic table?"

"It's the weirdest thing. I can't quite . . . seem to think of it. I mean, I know what it is, but I can't see it in my mind. Is that weird, or is that weird?"

"Never mind. Try this one: a globe of the world, sitting on the hood of a pickup truck."

That one was easy.

On the nineteenth item, a rowboat lying at the foot of a street sign (who thinks these things up? Johnny wondered), it happened again. It was frustrating. He saw a beachball lying beside a gravestone. He concentrated harder and saw a turnpike overpass. Weizak soothed him, and a few moments later the wires were removed from his head and eyelids.

"Why couldn't I see those things?" he asked, his eyes moving from Weizak to Brown. "What's the problem?"

"Hard to say with any real certainty," Brown said. "It may be a kind of spot amnesia. Or it may be that the accident destroyed a small portion of your brain—and I mean a really microscopic bit. We don't really know what the problem is, but it's pretty obvious that you've lost a number of trace memories. We happened to strike two. You'll probably come across more."

Weizak said abruptly, "You sustained a head injury when you were a child, yes?"

Johnny looked at him doubtfully.

"There is an old scar," Weizak said. "There is a theory, Johnny, backed by a good deal of statistical research . . ."

"Research that is nowhere near complete," Brown said, almost primly.

"That is true. But this theory supposes that the people who tend to recover from long-term coma are people who have sustained some sort of brain injury at a previous time . . . it is as though the brain has made some adaptation as the result of the first injury that allows it to survive the second."

"It's not proven," Brown said. He seemed to disapprove of Weizak even bringing it up.

"The scar is there," Weizak said. "Can you not remember what happened to you, Johnny? I would guess you must have blacked out. Did you fall down the stairs? A bicycle accident, perhaps? The scar says this happened to a young boy."

Johnny thought hard, then shook his head. "Have you asked my mom and dad?"

"Neither of them can remember any sort of head injury . . . nothing occurs to you?"

For a moment, something did—a memory of smoke, black and greasy and smelling like rubber. Cold. Then it was gone. Johnny shook his head.

Weizak sighed, then shrugged. "You must be tired."

"Yes. A little bit."

Brown sat on the edge of the examination table. "It's quarter of eleven. You've worked hard this morning. Dr. Weizak and I will answer a few questions, if you like, then you go up to your room for a nap. Okay?"

"Okay," Johnny said. "The pictures you took of my brain . . ."

"The CAT-scan," Weizak nodded. "Computerized Axial Tomography." He took a box of Chiclets and shook three of them into his mouth. "The CAT-scan is really a series of brain X-rays, Johnny. The computer highlights the pictures and . . ."

"What did it tell you? How long have I got?"

"What is this how long have I got stuff?" Brown asked. "It sounds like a line from an old movie."

"I've heard that people who come out of long-term comas don't always last so long," Johnny said. "They lapse back. It's like a light bulb going really bright before it burns out for good."

Weizak laughed hard. It was a hearty, bellowing laugh, and it was something of a wonder that he didn't choke on his gum. "Oh, such melodrama." He put a hand on Johnny's chest. "You think Jim and I are babies in this field? Nuh. We are neurologists. What you Americans call high-priced talent. Which means we are only stupid about the functions of the human brain instead of out-and-out ignoramuses. So I tell you, yes, there have been lapse-backs. But you will not lapse. I think we can say that, Jim, yes, okay?"

"Yes," Brown said. "We haven't been able to find very much in the way of significant impairment. Johnny, there's a guy in Texas who was in a coma for nine years. Now he's a bank loan officer, and he's been doing that job for six years. Before that he was a teller for two years. There's a woman in Arizona who was down for twelve years. Something went wrong with the anesthesia while she was in labor. Now she's in a wheelchair, but she's alive and aware. She came out of it in 1969 and met the baby she had delivered twelve years before. The baby was in the seventh grade and an honors student."

"Am I going to be in a wheelchair?" Johnny asked. "I can't straighten my legs out. My arms are a little better, but my legs . . ." He trailed off, shaking his head.

"The ligaments shorten," Weizak said. "Yes? That's why comatose patients begin to pull into what we call the prefetal position. But we know more about the physical degeneration that occurs in coma than we used to, we are better at holding it off. You have been exercised regularly by the hospital physical therapist, even in your sleep. And different patients react to coma in different ways. Your deterioration has been quite slow, Johnny. As you say, your arms are remarkably responsive and able. But there *has* been deterioration. Your therapy will be long and . . . should I lie to you? Nuh, I don't think so. It will be long and painful. You will shed your tears. You may come to hate your therapist. You may come to fall in love with your bed. And there will be operations—only one if you are very, very lucky, but perhaps as many as four—to lengthen those ligaments. These operations are still new. They may succeed completely, partially, or not at all. And yet as God wills it, I believe you will walk again. I don't believe you will ever ski or leap hurdles, but you may run and you will certainly swim."

"Thank you," Johnny said. He felt a sudden wave of affection for this man with the accent and the strange haircut. He wanted to do something for Weizak in return—and with that feeling came the urge, almost the *need,* to touch him.

He reached out suddenly and took Weizak's hand in both of his own. The doctor's hand was big, deeply lined, warm.

"Yes?" Weizak said kindly. "And what is this?"

And suddenly things changed. It was impossible to say how. Except that suddenly Weizak seemed very clear to him. Weizak seemed to . . . to *stand forth,* outlined in a lovely, clear light. Every mark and mole and line on Weizak's face stood in relief. And every line told its own story. *He began to understand.*

"I want your wallet," Johnny said.

"My . . . ?" Weizak and Brown exchanged a startled glance.

"There's a picture of your mother in your wallet and I need to have it," Johnny said. *"Please."*

"How did you know that?"

"Please!"

Weizak looked into Johnny's face for a moment, and then slowly dug under his smock and produced an old Lord Buxton, bulgy and out of shape.

"How did you know I carry a picture of my mother? She is dead, she died when the Nazis occupied Warsaw . . ."

Johnny snatched the wallet from Weizak's hand. Both he and Brown looked stunned. Johnny opened it, dismissed the plastic picture-pockets, and dug in the back instead, his fingers hurrying past old business cards, receipted bills, a canceled check, an old ticket to some political function. He came up with a small snapshot that had been laminated in plastic. The picture showed a young woman, her features plain, her hair drawn back under a kerchief. Her smile was radiant and youthful. She held the hand of a young boy. Beside her was a man in the uniform of the Polish army.

Johnny pressed the picture between his hands and closed his eyes and for a moment there was darkness and then rushing out of the darkness came a wagon . . . no, not a wagon, a hearse. A horse-drawn hearse. The lamps had been muffled in black sacking. Of course it was a hearse because they were

(dying by the hundreds, yes, by the thousands, no match for the panzers, the wehrmacht, nineteenth-century cavalry against the tanks and machine guns. explosions. screaming, dying men, a horse with its guts blown out and its eyes rolling wildly, showing the white, an overturned cannon behind it and still they come. weizak comes, standing in his stirrups, his sword held high in the slanting rain of late summer 1939, his men following him, stumbling through the mud, the turret gun of the nazi tiger tank tracks him, braces him, brackets him, fires, and suddenly he is gone below the waist, the sword flying out of his hand; and down the road is warsaw. the nazi wolf is loose in europe)

"Really, we have to put a stop to this," Brown said, his

voice faraway and worried. "You're overexciting yourself, Johnny."

The voices came from far away, from a hallway in time.

"He's put himself in some kind of trance," Weizak said.

Hot in here. He was sweating. He was sweating because

(the city's on fire, thousands are fleeing, a truck is roaring from side to side down a cobbled street, and the back of the truck is full of waving german soldiers in coal-scuttle helmets and the young woman is not smiling now, she is fleeing, no reason not to flee. the child has been sent to safety and now the truck jumps the curb, the mudguard strikes her, shattering her hip and sending her flying through a plateglass window and into a clock shop and everything begins to chime. chime because of the time. the chime time is)

"Six o'clock," Johnny said thickly. His eyes had rolled up to straining, bulging whites. "September 2, 1939, and all the cuckoo birds are singing."

"Oh my God, what is it we have?" Weizak whispered. The nurse had backed up against the EEG console, her face pale and scared. Everyone is scared now because death is in the air. It's always in the air in this place, this

(hospital. smell of ether. they're screaming in the place of death. poland is dead, poland has fallen before the lightning warfare wehrmacht blitzkrieg. shattered hip. the man in the next bed calling for water, calling, calling, calling. she remembers "THE BOY IS SAFE." what boy? she doesn't know. what boy? what is her name? she doesn't remember. only that)

"The boy is safe," Johnny said thickly. "Uh-huh. Uh-huh."

"We have to put a stop to this," Brown repeated.

"How do you suggest we do that?" Weizak asked, his voice brittle. "It has gone too far to . . ."

Voices fading. The voices are under the clouds. Everything is under the clouds. Europe is under the clouds of war. Everything is under the clouds but the peaks, the mountain peaks of

(switzerland. switzerland and now her name is BORENTZ. her name is JOHANNA BORENTZ and her husband is an engineer or an architect, whichever it is that builds the bridges. he builds in switzerland and there is goat's milk, goat's cheese. a baby. ooooh the labor! the labor is terrible and she needs drugs, morphine, this JOHANNA BORENTZ, because of the hip. the broken hip. it has mended, it has gone to sleep, but now it awakes and begins

to scream as her pelvis spreads to let the baby out. one baby.
two. and three. and four. they don't come all at once, no—
they are a harvest of years. they are)

"The babies," Johnny lilted, and now he spoke in a woman's voice, not his own voice at all. It was the voice of a woman. Then gibberish in song came from his mouth.

"What in the name of God . . ." Brown began.

"Polish, it is Polish!" Weizak cried. His eyes were bulging, his face pale. "It is a cradle song and it is in Polish, my God, my Christ, what is it we have here?"

Weizak leaned forward as if to cross the years with Johnny, as if to leap them, as if to

(bridge, a bridge, it's in turkey. then a bridge somewhere hot
in the far east, is it Laos? can't tell, lost a man there, we lost
HANS there, then a bridge in virginia, a bridge over the RAP-
PAHANNOCK RIVER and another bridge in california. we
are applying for citizenship now and we go to classes in a hot
little room in the back of a post-office where it always smells
of glue. it is 1963, november, and when we hear kennedy has
been killed in dallas we weep and when the little boy salutes
his father's coffin she thinks "THE BOY IS SAFE" and it
brings back memories of some burning, some great burning
and sorrow, what boy? she dreams about the boy. it makes her
head hurt. and the man dies, HELMUT BORENTZ dies and
she and the children live in carmel california. in a house on.
on. on. can't see the street sign, it's in the dead zone, like the
rowboat, like the picnic table on the lawn. it's in the dead zone.
like warsaw. the children go away, she goes to their graduation
ceremonies one by one, and her hip hurts. one dies in vietnam.
the rest of them are fine. one of them is building bridges. her
name is JOHANNA BORENTZ and late at night alone now
she sometimes thinks in the ticking darkness: "THE BOY IS
SAFE.")

Johnny looked up at them. His head felt strange. That peculiar light around Weizak had gone. He felt like himself again, but weak and a little pukey. He looked at the picture in his hands for a moment and then handed it back.

"Johnny?" Brown said. "Are you all right?"

"Tired," he muttered.

"Can you tell us what happened to you?"

He looked at Weizak. "Your mother is alive," he said.

"No, Johnny. She died many years ago. In the war."

"A German trooptruck knocked her through a plate-glass

show window and into a clock shop," Johnny said. "She woke up in a hospital with amnesia. She had no identification, no papers. She took the name Johanna . . . somebody. I didn't get that, but when the war was over she went to Switzerland and married a Swiss . . . engineer, I think. His specialty was building bridges, and his name was Helmut Borentz. So her married name was—is—Johanna Borentz."

The nurse's eyes were getting bigger and bigger. Dr. Brown's face was tight, either because he had decided Johnny was having them all on or perhaps just because he didn't like to see his neat schedule of tests disrupted. But Weizak's face was still and thoughtful.

"She and Helmut Borentz had four children," Johnny said in that same, calm, washed-out voice. "His job took him all over the world. He was in Turkey for a while. Somewhere in the Far East, Laos. I think, maybe Cambodia. Then he came here. Virginia first, then some other places I didn't get, finally California. He and Johanna became U.S. citizens. Helmut Borentz is dead. One of the children they had is also dead. The others are alive and fine. But she dreams about you sometimes. And in the dreams she thinks, 'the boy is safe.' But she doesn't remember your name. Maybe she thinks it's too late."

"California?" Weizak said thoughtfully.

"Sam," Dr. Brown said. "Really, you mustn't encourage this."

"Where in California, John?"

"Carmel. By the sea. But I couldn't tell which street. It was there, but I couldn't tell. It was in a dead zone. Like the picnic table and the rowboat. But she's in Carmel, California. Johanna Borentz. She's not old."

"No, of course she would not be old," Sam Weizak said in that same thoughtful, distant tone. "She was only twenty-four when the Germans invaded Poland."

"Dr. Weizak, I have to insist," Brown said harshly.

Weizak seemed to come out of a deep study. He looked around as if noticing his younger colleague for the first time. "Of course," he said. "Of course you must. And John has had his question-and-answer period . . . although I believe he has told us more than we have told him."

"That's nonsense," Brown said curtly, and Johnny thought: *He's scared. Scared spitless.*

Weizak smiled at Brown, and then at the nurse. She

was eyeing Johnny as if he were a tiger in a poorly built cage. "Don't talk about this, Nurse. Not to your supervisor, your mother, your brother, your lover, or your priest. Understood?"

"Yes, Doctor," the nurse said. *But she'll talk,* Johnny thought, and then glanced at Weizak. *And he knows it.*

◆ 2 ◆

He slept most of the afternoon. Around four P.M. he was rolled down the corridor to the elevator, taken down to neurology, and there were more tests. Johnny cried. He seemed to have very little control over the functions adults are supposed to be able to control. On his way back up, he urinated on himself and had to be changed like a baby. The first (but far from the last) wave of deep depression washed over him, carried him limply away, and he wished himself dead. Self-pity accompanied the depression and he thought how unfair this was. He had done a Rip van Winkle. He couldn't walk. His girl had married another man and his mother was in the grip of a religious mania. He couldn't see anything ahead that looked worth living for.

Back in his room, the nurse asked him if he would like anything. If Marie had been on duty, Johnny would have asked for ice water. But she had gone off at three.

"No," he said, and rolled over to face the wall. After a little while, he slept.

Chapter 8

◆ 1 ◆

His father and mother came in for an hour that evening, and Vera left a bundle of tracts.

"We're going to stay until the end of the week," Herb said, "and then, if you're still doing fine, we'll be going back to Pownal for a while. But we'll be back up every weekend."

"I want to stay with my boy," Vera said loudly.

"It's best that you don't, Mom," Johnny said. The depression had lifted a little bit, but he remembered how black it had been. If his mother started to talk about God's wonderful plan for him while he was in that state, he doubted if he would be able to hold back his cackles of hysterical laughter.

"You need me, John. You need me to explain . . ."

"First I need to get well," Johnny said. "You can explain after I can walk. Okay?"

She didn't answer. There was an almost comically stubborn expression on her face—except there was nothing very funny about it. Nothing at all. *Nothing but a quirk of fate, that's all. Five minutes earlier or later on that road could have changed everything. Now look at us, all of us fucked over royally. And she believes it's God's plan. It's either that or go completely crazy, I suppose.*

To break the awkward silence, Johnny said: "Well, did Nixon get reelected, dad? Who ran against him?"

"He got reelected," Herb said. "He ran against McGovern."

"Who?"

"McGovern. George McGovern. Senator from South Dakota."

"Not Muskie?"

"No. But Nixon's not president anymore. He resigned."

"*What?*"

"He was a liar," Vera said dourly. "He became swollen with pride and the Lord brought him low."

"Nixon resigned?" Johnny was flabbergasted. "*Him?*"

"It was either quit or be fired," Herb said. "They were getting ready to impeach him."

Johnny suddenly realized that there had been some great and fundamental upheaval in American politics—almost surely as a result of the war in Vietnam—and he had missed it. For the first time he really *felt* like Rip van Winkle. How much had things changed? He was almost afraid to ask. Then a really chilling thought occurred.

"Agnew . . . Agnew's president?"

"Ford," Vera said. "A good, honest man."

"*Henry Ford is president of the United States?*"

"Not Henry," she said. "Jerry."

He stared from one to the other, more than half convinced that all this was a dream or a bizarre joke.

"Agnew resigned, too," Vera said. Her lips were pressed

thin and white. "He was a thief. He accepted a bribe right in his office. That's what they say."

"He didn't resign over the bribe," Herb said. "He resigned over some mess back in Maryland. He was up to his neck in it, I guess. Nixon nominated Jerry Ford to become vice president. Then Nixon resigned last August and Ford took over. *He* nominated Nelson Rockefeller to be vice president. And that's where we are now."

"A divorced man," Vera said grimly. "God forbid he ever becomes the president."

"What did Nixon do?" Johnny asked. "Jesus Christ. I . . ." He glanced at his mother, whose brow had clouded instantly. "I mean, holy crow, if they were going to impeach him . . ."

"You needn't take the Savior's name in vain over a bunch of crooked politicians," Vera said. "It was Watergate."

"Watergate? Was that an operation in Vietnam? Something like that?"

"The Watergate Hotel in Washington," Herb said. "Some Cubans broke into the offices of the Democratic Committee there and got caught. Nixon knew about it. He tried to cover it up."

"Are you kidding?" Johnny managed at last.

"It was the tapes," Vera said. "And that John Dean. Nothing but a rat deserting a sinking ship, that's what I think. A common tattletale."

"Daddy, can you explain this to me?"

"I'll try," Herb said, "but I don't think the whole story has come out, even yet. And I'll bring you the books. There's been about a million books written on it already, and I guess there'll be a million more before it's finally done. Just before the election, in the summer of 1972 . . ."

◆ 2 ◆

It was ten-thirty and his parents were gone. The lights on the ward had been dimmed. Johnny couldn't sleep. It was all dancing around in his head, a frightening jumble of new input. The world had changed more resoundingly than he would have believed possible in so short a time. He felt out of step and out of tune.

Gas prices had gone up nearly a hundred percent, his father had told him. At the time of his accident, you could buy regular gas for thirty or thirty-two cents a gallon. Now it was fifty-four cents and sometimes there were lines at the pumps. The legal speed limit all over the country was fifty-five miles an hour and the long-haul truckers had almost revolted over that.

But all of that was nothing. Vietnam was over. It had ended. The country had finally gone Communist. Herb said it had happened just as Johnny began to show signs that he might come out of his coma. After all those years and all that bloodshed, the heirs of·Uncle Ho had rolled up the country like a windowshade in a matter of days.

The president of the United States had been to Red China. Not Ford, but Nixon. He had gone before he resigned. *Nixon,* of all people. The old witch-hunter himself. If anyone but his dad had told him that, Johnny would have flatly refused to believe.

It was all too much, it was too scary. Suddenly he didn't want to know any more, for fear it might drive him totally crazy. That pen Dr. Brown had had, that Flair—how many other things were there like that? How many hundreds of little things, all of them making the point over and over again: You lost part of your life, almost six percent, if the actuarial tables are to be believed. You're behind the times. You missed out.

"John?" The voice was soft. "Are you asleep, John?"

He turned over. A dim silhouette stood in his doorway. A small man with rounded shoulders. It was Weizak.

"No. I'm awake."

"I hoped so. May I come in?"

"Yes. Please do."

Weizak looked older tonight. He sat by Johnny's bed.

"I was on the phone earlier," he said. "I called directory assistance for Carmel, California. I asked for a Mrs. Johanna Borentz. Do you think there was such a number?"

"Unless it's unlisted or she doesn't have a phone at all," Johnny said.

"She has a phone. I was given the number."

"Ah," Johnny said. He was interested because he liked Weizak, but that was all. He felt no need to have his knowledge of Johanna Borentz validated, because he knew it was valid knowledge—he knew in the same way he knew he was right-handed.

"I sat for a long time and thought about it," Weizak said.

"I told you my mother was dead, but that was really only an assumption. My father died in the defense of Warsaw. My mother simply never turned up, nuh? It was logical to assume that she had been killed in the shelling . . . during the occupation . . . you understand. She never turned up, so it was logical to assume that. Amnesia . . . as a neurologist I can tell you that permanent, general amnesia is very, very rare. Probably rarer than true schizophrenia. I have never read of a documented case lasting thirty-five years."

"She recovered from her amnesia long ago," Johnny said. "I think she simply blocked everything out. When her memory did come back, she had remarried and was the mother of two children . . . possibly three. Remembering became a guilt trip, maybe. But she dreams of you. 'The boy is safe.' Did you call her?"

"Yes," Weizak said. "I dialed it direct. Did you know you could do that now? Yes. It is a great convenience. You dial one, the area code, the number. Eleven digits and you can be in touch with any place in the country. It is an amazing thing. In some ways a frightening thing. A boy—no, a young man—answered the telephone. I asked if Mrs. Borentz was at home. I heard him call, 'Mom, it's for you.' Clunk went the receiver on the table or desk or whatever. I stood in Bangor, Maine, not forty miles from the Atlantic Ocean and listened to a young man put the phone down on a table in a town on the Pacific Ocean. My heart . . . it was pounding so hard it frightened me. The wait seemed long. Then she picked up the phone and said, 'Yes? Hello?' "

"What did you say? How did you handle it?"

"I did not, as you say, handle it," Weizak replied, and smiled crookedly. "I hung up the telephone. And I wished for a strong drink, but I did not have one."

"Are you satisfied it was her?"

"John, what a naive question! I was nine years old in 1939. I had not heard my mother's voice since then. She spoke only Polish when I knew her. I speak only English now . . . I have forgotten much of my native language, which is a shameful thing. How could I be satisfied one way or the other?"

"Yes, but *were* you?"

Weizak scrubbed a hand slowly across his forehead. "Yes," he said. "It was her. It was my mother."

"But you couldn't talk to her?"

"Why should I?" Weizak asked, sounding almost angry.

"Her life is her life, nuh? It is as you said. The boy is safe. Should I upset a woman that is just coming into her years of peace? Should I take the chance of destroying her equilibrium forever? Those feelings of guilt you mentioned . . . should I set them free? Or even run the risk of so doing?"

"I don't know," Johnny said. They were troublesome questions, and the answers were beyond him—but he felt that Weizak was trying to say something about what he had done by articulating the questions. The questions he could not answer.

"The boy is safe, the woman is safe in Carmel. The country is between them, and we let that be. But what about you, John? What are we going to do about you?"

"I don't understand what you mean."

"I will spell it out for you then, nuh? Dr. Brown is angry. He is angry at me, angry at you, and angry at himself, I suspect, for half-believing something he has been sure is total poppycock for his whole life. The nurse who was a witness will never keep her silence. She will tell her husband tonight in bed, and it may end there, but her husband may tell his boss, and it is very possible that the papers will have wind of this by tomorrow evening. 'Coma Patient Re-Awakens with Second Sight.' "

"Second sight," Johnny said. "Is that what it is?"

"I don't know what it is, not really. Is it psychic? Seer? Handy words that describe nothing, nothing at all. You told one of the nurses that her son's optic surgery was going to be successful . . ."

"Marie," Johnny murmured. He smiled a little. He liked Marie.

". . . and that is already all over the hospital. Did you see the future? Is that what second sight is? I don't know. You put a picture of my mother between your hands and were able to tell me where she lives today. Do you know where lost things and lost people may be found? Is *that* what second sight is? I don't know. Can you read thoughts? Influence objects of the physical world? Heal by the laying on of hands? These are all things that some call 'psychic.' They are all related to the idea of 'second sight.' They are things that Dr. Brown laughs at. Laughs? No. He doesn't laugh. He scoffs."

"And you don't?"

"I think of Edgar Cayce. And Peter Hurkos. I tried to tell

Dr. Brown about Hurkos and he scoffed. He doesn't want to talk about it; he doesn't want to know about it."

Johnny said nothing.

"So . . . what are we going to do about you?"

"Does something need to be done?"

"I think so," Weizak said. He stood up. "I'll leave you to think it out for yourself. But when you think, think about this: some things are better not seen, and some things are better lost than found."

He bade Johnny good night and left quietly. Johnny was very tired now, but still sleep did not come for a long time.

Chapter 9

◆ 1 ◆

Johnny's first surgery was scheduled for May 28. Both Weizak and Brown had explained the procedure carefully to him. He would be given a local anesthetic—neither of them felt a general could be risked. This first operation would be on his knees and ankles. His own ligaments, which had shortened during his long sleep, would be lengthened with a combination of plastic wonder-fibers. The plastic to be used was also employed in heart valve bypass surgery. The question was not so much one of his body's acceptance or rejection of the artificial ligaments, Brown told him, as it was a question of his legs' ability to adjust to the change. If they had good results with the knees and the ankles, three more operations were on the boards: one on the long ligaments of his thighs, one on the elbow-strap ligaments, and possibly a third on his neck, which he could barely turn at all. The surgery was to be performed by Raymond Ruopp, who had pioneered the technique. He was flying in from San Francisco.

"What does this guy Ruopp want with me, if he's such a superstar?" Johnny asked. *Superstar* was a word he had learned from Marie. She had used it in connection with a balding, bespectacled singer with the unlikely name of Elton John.

"You're underestimating your own superstar qualities," Brown answered. "There are only a handful of people in the United States who have recovered from comas as long as yours was. And of that handful, your recovery from the accompanying brain damage has been the most radical and pleasing."

Sam Weizak was more blunt. "You're a guinea pig, nuh?"

"What?"

"Yes. Look into the light, please." Weizak shone a light into the pupil of Johnny's left eye. "Did you know I can look right at your optic nerve with this thing? Yes. The eyes are more than the windows of the soul. They are one of the brain's most crucial maintenance points."

"Guinea pig," Johnny said morosely, staring into the savage point of light.

"Yes." The light snapped off. "Don't feel so sorry for yourself. Many of the techniques to be employed in your behalf—and some of those already employed—were perfected during the Vietnam war. No shortage of guinea pigs in the V.A. hospitals, nuh? A man like Ruopp is interested in you because you are unique. Here is a man who has slept four-and-a-half years. Can we make him walk again? An interesting problem. He sees the monograph he will write on it for *The New England Journal of Medicine*. He looks forward to it the way a child looks forward to new toys under the Christmas tree. He does not see you, he does not see Johnny Smith in his pain, Johnny Smith who must take the bedpan and ring for the nurse to scratch if his back itches. That's good. His hands will not shake. Smile, Johnny. This Ruopp looks like a bank clerk, but he is maybe the best surgeon in North America."

But it was hard for Johnny to smile.

He had read his way dutifully through the tracts his mother had left him. They depressed him and left him frightened all over again for her sanity. One of them, by a man named Salem Kirban, struck him as nearly pagan in its loving contemplation of a bloody apocalypse and the yawning barbecue pits of hell. Another described the coming Anti-christ in pulp-horror terms. The others were a dark carnival of craziness: Christ was living under the South Pole, God drove flying saucers, New York was Sodom, L.A. was Gomorrah. They dealt with exorcism, with witches, with all manner of things seen and unseen. It was impossible for him to reconcile the pamphlets with the religious yet earthy woman he had known before his coma.

Three days after the incident involving Weizak's snapshot of his mother, a slim and dark-haired reporter from the Bangor *Daily News* named David Bright showed up at the door of Johnny's room and asked if he could have a short interview.

"Have you asked the doctors?" Johnny asked.

Bright grinned. "Actually, no."

"All right," Johnny said. "In that case, I'd be happy to talk to you."

"You're a man after my own heart," Bright said. He came in and sat down.

His first questions were about the accident and about Johnny's thoughts and feelings upon slipping out of a coma and discovering he had misplaced nearly half a decade. Johnny answered these questions honestly and straightforwardly. Then Bright told him that he had heard from "a source" that Johnny had gained some sort of sixth sense as a result of the accident.

"Are you asking me if I'm psychic?"

Bright smiled and shrugged. "That'll do for a start."

Johnny had thought carefully about the things Weizak had said. The more he thought, the more it seemed to him that Weizak had done exactly the right thing when he hung up the phone without saying anything. Johnny had begun to associate it in his mind with that W. W. Jacobs story, "The Monkey's Paw." The paw was for wishing, but the price you paid for each of your three wishes was a black one. The old couple had wished for one hundred pounds and had lost their son in a mill accident—the mill's compensation had come to exactly one hundred pounds. Then the old woman had wished for her son back and he had come—but before she could open the door and see what a horror she had summoned out of its grave, the old man had used the last wish to send it back. As Weizak had said, maybe some things were better lost than found.

"No," he said. "I'm no more psychic than you are."

"According to my source, you . . ."

"No, it isn't true."

Bright smiled a trifle cynically, seemed to debate pressing the matter further, then turned to a fresh page in his notebook. He began to ask about Johnny's prospects for the future, his feelings about the road back, and Johnny also answered these questions as honestly as he could.

"So what are you going to do when you get out of here?" Bright asked, closing his notebook.

"I haven't really thought about that. I'm still trying to adjust to the idea that Gerald Ford is the president."

Bright laughed. "You're not alone in that, my friend."

"I suppose I'll go back to teaching. It's all I know. But right now that's too far ahead to think about."

Bright thanked him for the interview and left. The article appeared in the paper two days later, the day before his leg surgery. It was on the bottom of the front page, and the headline read: JOHN SMITH, MODERN RIP VAN WINKLE, FACES LONG ROAD BACK. There were three pictures, one of them Johnny's picture for the Cleaves Mills High School yearbook (it had been taken barely a week before the accident), a picture of Johnny in his hospital bed, looking thin and twisted with his arms and legs in their bent positions. Between these two was a picture of the almost totally demolished taxi, lying on its side like a dead dog. There was no mention in Bright's article of sixth senses, precognitive powers, or wild talents.

"How did you turn him off the ESP angle?" Weizak asked him that evening.

Johnny shrugged. "He seemed like a nice guy. Maybe he didn't want to stick me with it."

"Maybe not," Weizak said. "But he won't forget it. Not if he's a good reporter, and I understand that he is."

"You understand?"

"I asked around."

"Looking out for my best interests?"

"We all do what we can, nuh? Are you nervous about tomorrow, Johnny?"

"Not nervous, no. Scared is a more accurate word."

"Yes, of course you are. I would be."

"Will you be there?"

"Yes, in the observation section of the operating theater. Above. You won't be able to tell me from the others in my greens, but I will be there."

"Wear something," Johnny said. "Wear something so I'll know it's you."

Weizak looked at him, and smiled. "All right. I'll pin my watch to my tunic."

"Good," Johnny said. "What about Dr. Brown? Will he be there?"

"Dr. Brown is in Washington. Tomorrow he will present you to the American Society of Neurologists. I have read his paper. It is quite good. Perhaps overstated."

"You weren't invited?"

Weizak shrugged. "I don't like to fly. That is something that scares me."

"And maybe you wanted to stay here?"

Weizak smiled crookedly, spread his hands, and said nothing.

"He doesn't like me much, does he?" Johnny asked. "Dr. Brown?"

"No, not much," Weizak said. "He thinks you are having us on. Making things up for some reason of your own. Seeking attention, perhaps. Don't judge him solely on that, John. His cast of mind makes it impossible for him to think otherwise. If you feel anything for Jim, feel a little pity. He is a brilliant man, and he will go far. Already he has offers, and someday soon he will fly from these cold north woods and Bangor will see him no more. He will go to Houston or Hawaii or possibly even to Paris. But he is curiously limited. He is a mechanic of the brain. He has cut it to pieces with his scalpel and found no soul. Therefore there is none. Like the Russian astronauts who circled the earth and did not see God. It is the empiricism of the mechanic, and a mechanic is only a child with superior motor control. You must never tell him I said that."

"No."

"And now you must rest. Tomorrow you have a long day."

◆ 2 ◆

All Johnny saw of the world-famous Dr. Ruopp during the operation was a pair of thick horn-rimmed glasses and a large wen at the extreme left side of the man's forehead. The rest of him was capped, gowned, and gloved.

Johnny had been given two preop injections, one of demerol and one of atropine, and when he was wheeled in he was as high as a kite. The anesthetist approached with the biggest novocaine needle Johnny had ever seen in his life. He expected that the injection would hurt, and he was not wrong. He was injected between L4 and L5, the fourth and fifth lumbar vertebrae, high enough up to avoid the *cauda equina,* that bundle of nerves at the base of the spine that vaguely resembles a horse's tail.

Johnny lay on his stomach and bit his arm to keep from screaming.

After an endless time, the pain began to fade to a dull sensation of pressure. Otherwise, the lower half of his body was totally gone.

Ruopp's face loomed over him. The green bandit, Johnny thought. Jesse James in horn-rims. Your money or your life.

"Are you comfortable, Mr. Smith?" Ruopp asked.

"Yes. But I'd just as soon not go through that again."

"You may read magazines, if you like. Or you may watch in the mirror, if you feel it will not upset you."

"All right."

"Nurse, give me a blood pressure, please."

"One-twenty over seventy-six, Doctor."

"That's lovely. Well, group, shall we begin?"

"Save me a drumstick," Johnny said weakly, and was surprised by the hearty laughter. Ruopp patted his sheet-covered shoulder with one thinly gloved hand.

He watched Ruopp select a scalpel and disappear behind the green drapes hung over the metal hoop that curved above Johnny. The mirror was convex, and Johnny had a fairly good if slightly distorted view of everything.

"Oh yes," Ruopp said. "Oh yes, dee-de-dee . . . here's what we want . . . hum-de-dum . . . okay . . . clamp, please, Nurse, come on, wake up for Christ's sake . . . yes sir . . . now I believe I'd like one of those . . . no, hold it . . . don't give me what I ask for, give me what I need . . . yes, okay. Strap, please."

With forceps, the nurse handed Ruopp something that looked like a bundle of thin wires twisted together. Ruopp picked them delicately out of the air with tweezers.

Like an Italian dinner, Johnny thought, *and look at all that spaghetti sauce.* That was what made him feel ill, and he looked away. Above him, in the gallery, the rest of the bandit gang looked down at him. Their eyes looked pale and merciless and frightening. Then he spotted Weizak, third from the right, his watch pinned neatly to the front of his gown.

Johnny nodded.

Weizak nodded back.

That made it a little better.

◆ 3 ◆

Ruopp finished the connections between his knees and calves, and Johnny was turned over. Things continued. The anesthesiologist asked him if he felt all right. Johnny told her he thought he felt as well as possible under the circumstances. She asked him if he would like to listen to a tape and he said that would be very nice. A few moments later the clear, sweet voice of Joan Baez filled the operating room. Ruopp did his thing. Johnny grew sleepy and dozed off. When he woke up the operation was still going on. Weizak was still there. Johnny raised one hand, acknowledging his presence, and Weizak nodded again.

◆ 4 ◆

An hour later it was done. He was wheeled into a recovery room where a nurse kept asking him if he could tell her how many of his toes she was touching. After a while, Johnny could.

Ruopp came in, his bandit's mask hanging off to one side. "All right?" he asked.

"Yes."

"It went very well," Ruopp said. "I'm optimistic."

"Good."

"You'll have some pain," Ruopp said. "Quite a lot of it, perhaps. The therapy itself will give you a lot of pain at first. Stick with it."

"Stick with it," Johnny muttered.

"Good afternoon," Ruopp said, and left. Probably, Johnny thought, to play a quick nine on the local golf course before it got too dark.

◆ 5 ◆

Quite a lot of pain.

By nine P.M. the last of the local had worn off, and Johnny was in agony. He was forbidden to move his legs without the help of two nurses. It felt as if nail-studded belts had been looped around his knees and then cinched cruelly tight. Time slowed to an inchworm's crawl. He would glance at his watch, sure that an hour had passed since the last time he had looked at it, and would see instead that it had only been four minutes. He became sure he couldn't stand the pain for another minute, then the minute would pass, and he would become sure he couldn't stand it for another minute.

He thought of all the minutes stacked up ahead, like coins in a slot five miles high, and the blackest depression he had ever known swept over him in a smooth solid wave and carried him down. They were going to torture him to death. Operations on his elbows, thighs, his neck. Therapy. Walkers, wheelchairs, canes.

You're going to have pain . . . stick with it.

No, you *stick with it,* Johnny thought. *Just leave me alone. Don't come near me again with your butchers' knives. If this is your idea of helping, I want no part of it.*

Steady throbbing pain, digging into the meat of him.

Warmth on his belly, trickling.

He had wet himself.

Johnny Smith turned his face toward the wall and cried.

◆ 6 ◆

Ten days after that first operation and two weeks before the next one was scheduled, Johnny looked up from the book he was reading—Woodward and Bernstein's *All the President's Men*—and saw Sarah standing in the doorway, looking at him hesitantly.

"Sarah," he said. "It is you, isn't it?"

She let out her breath shakily. "Yes. It's me, Johnny."

He put the book down and looked at her. She was smartly dressed in a light-green linen dress, and she held a small, brown clutch bag in front of her like a shield. She had put a streak in her hair and it looked good. It also made him feel a sharp and twisting stab of jealousy—had it been her idea, or that of the man she lived and slept with? She was beautiful.

"Come in," he said. "Come in and sit down."

She crossed the room and suddenly he saw himself as she must see him—too thin, his body slumped a little to one side in the chair by the window, his legs stuck out straight on the hassock, dressed in a Johnny and a cheap hospital bathrobe.

"As you can see, I put on my tux," he said.

"You look fine." She kissed his cheek and a hundred memories shuffled brightly through his mind like a doubled pack of cards. She sat in the other chair, crossed her legs, and tugged at the hem of her dress.

They looked at each other without saying anything. He saw that she was very nervous. If someone were to touch her on the shoulder, she would probably spring right out of her seat.

"I didn't know if I should come," she said, "but I really wanted to."

"I'm glad you did."

Like strangers on a bus, he thought dismally. *It's got to be more than this, doesn't it?*

"So how're you doing?" she asked.

He smiled. "I've been in the war. Want to see my battle scars?" He raised his gown over his knees, showing the S-shaped incisions that were now beginning to heal. They were still red and hashmarked with stitches.

"Oh, my Lord, what are they *doing* to you?"

"They're trying to put Humpty Dumpty back together again," Johnny said. "All the king's horses, all the king's men, and all the king's doctors. So I guess . . ." And then he stopped, because she was crying.

"Don't say it like that, Johnny," she said. "Please don't say it like that."

"I'm sorry. It was just . . . I was trying to joke about it." Was that it? Had he been trying to laugh it off or had it been a way of saying, *Thanks for coming to see me, they're cutting me to pieces?*

"Can you? Can you joke about it?" She had gotten a Kleenex from the clutch bag and was wiping her eyes with it.

"Not very often. I guess seeing you again . . . the defenses go up, Sarah."

"Are they going to let you out of here?"

"Eventually. It's like running the gauntlet in the old days, did you ever read about that? If I'm still alive after every Indian in the tribe has had a swing at me with his tomahawk, I get to go free."

"This summer?"

"No, I . . . I don't think so."

"I'm so sorry it happened," she said, so low he could barely hear her. "I try to figure out why . . . or how things could have been changed . . . and it just robs me of sleep. If I hadn't eaten that bad hot dog . . . if you had stayed instead of going back . . ." She shook her head and looked at him, her eyes red. "It seems sometimes there's no percentage."

Johnny smiled. "Double zero. House spin. Hey, you remember that? I clobbered that Wheel, Sarah."

"Yes. You won over five hundred dollars."

He looked at her, still smiling, but now the smile was puzzled, wounded almost. "You want to know something funny? My doctors think maybe the reason I lived was because I had some sort of head injury when I was young. But I couldn't remember any, and neither could my mom and dad. But it seems like every time I think of it, I flash on that Wheel of Fortune . . . and a smell like burning rubber."

"Maybe you were in a car accident . . ." she began doubtfully.

"No, I don't think that's it. But it's like the Wheel was my warning . . . and I ignored it."

She shifted a little and said uneasily, "Don't, Johnny."

He shrugged. "Or maybe it was just that I used up four years of luck in one evening. But look at this, Sarah." Carefully, painfully, he took one leg off the hassock, bent it to a ninety-degree angle, then stretched it out on the hassock again. "Maybe they can put Humpty back together again. When I woke up, I couldn't do that, and I couldn't get my legs to straighten out as much as they are now, either."

"And you can *think*, Johnny," she said. "You can *talk*. We all thought that . . . you know."

"Yeah, Johnny the turnip." A silence fell between them again, awkward and heavy. Johnny broke it by saying with forced brightness, "So how's by you?"

"Well . . . I'm married. I guess you knew that."

"Dad told me."

"He's such a fine man," Sarah said. And then, in a burst, "I couldn't wait, Johnny. I'm sorry about that, too. The doctors said you'd never come out of it, and you'd get lower and lower until you just . . . just slipped away. And even if I had known . . ." She looked up at him with an uneasy expression of defense on her face. "Even if I'd known, Johnny, I don't think I could have waited. Four-and-a-half years is a long time."

"Yeah, it is," he said. "That's a hell of a long time. You want to hear something morbid? I got them to bring me four years worth of news magazines just so I could see who died. Truman. Janis Joplin. Jimi Hendrix—Jesus, I thought of him doing "Purple Haze" and I could hardly believe it. Dan Blocker. And you and me. We just slipped away."

"I feel so bad about it," she said, nearly whispering. "So damn guilty. But I love the guy, Johnny. I love him a lot."

"Okay, that's what matters."

"His name is Walt Hazlett, and he's a . . ."

"I think I'd rather hear about your kid," Johnny said. "No offense, huh?"

"He's a peach," she said, smiling. "He's seven months old now. His name is Dennis but we call him Denny. He's named after his paternal grandfather."

"Bring him in sometime. I'd like to see him."

"I will," Sarah said, and they smiled at each other falsely, knowing that nothing of the kind was ever going to happen. "Johnny, is there anything that you need?"

Only you, babe. And the last four-and-a-half years back again.

"Nah," he said. "You still teachin?"

"Still teachin, for a while yet," she agreed.

"Still snortin that wicked cocaine?"

"Oh Johnny, you haven't changed. Same old tease."

"Same old tease," he agreed, and the silence fell between them again with an almost audible thump.

"Can I come see you again?"

"Sure," he said. "That would be fine, Sarah." He hesitated, not wanting it to end so inconclusively, not wanting to hurt her or himself if it could be avoided. Wanting to say something honest.

"Sarah," he said, "you did the right thing."

"Did I?" she asked. She smiled, and it trembled at the corners of her mouth. "I wonder. It all seems so cruel and . . . I can't help it, so *wrong.* I love my husband and my baby, and when Walt says that someday we're going to be living in the finest house in Bangor, I believe him. He says someday he's going to run for Bill Cohen's seat in the House, and I believe that, too. He says someday someone from Maine is going to be elected president, and I can almost believe that. And I come in here and look at your poor legs . . ." She was beginning to cry again now. "They look like they went through a Mixmaster or something and you're so *thin* . . ."

"No, Sarah, don't."

"You're so thin and it seems wrong and cruel and I *hate* it, I *hate* it, because it isn't right at all, none of it!"

"Sometimes nothing is right, I guess," he said. "Tough old world. Sometimes you just have to do what you can and try to live with it. You go and be happy, Sarah. And if you want to come and see me, come on and come. Bring a cribbage board."

"I will," she said. "I'm sorry to cry. Not very cheery for you, huh?"

"It's all right," he said, and smiled. "You want to get off that cocaine, baby. Your nose'll fall off."

She laughed a little. "Same old Johnny," she said. Suddenly she bent and kissed his mouth. "Oh, Johnny, be well soon."

He looked at her thoughtfully as she drew away.

"Johnny?"

"You didn't leave it," he said. "No, you didn't leave it at all."

"Leave what?" She was frowning in puzzlement.

"Your wedding ring. You didn't leave it in Montreal."

He had put his hand up to his forehead and was rubbing the patch of skin over his right eye with his fingers. His arm cast a shadow and she saw with something very like superstitious fear that his face was half-light, half-dark. It made her think of the Halloween mask he had scared her with. She and Walt had honeymooned in Montreal, but how could Johnny know that? Unless maybe Herb had told him. Yes, that was almost certainly it. But only she and Walt knew that she had lost her wedding ring somewhere in the hotel room. No one else knew because he had bought her another ring before they flew home. She had been too embarrassed to tell anyone, even her mother.

"How . . ."

Johnny frowned deeply, then smiled at her. His hand fell away from his forehead and clasped its mate in his lap.

"It wasn't sized right," he said. "You were packing, don't you remember, Sarah? He was out buying something and you were packing. He was out buying . . . buying . . . don't know. It's in the dead zone."

Dead zone?

"He went out to a novelty shop and bought a whole bunch of silly stuff as souvenirs. Whoopee cushions and things like that. But Johnny, how could you know I lost my r . . ."

"You were packing. The ring wasn't sized right, it was a lot too big. You were going to have it taken care of when you got back. But in the meantime, you . . . you . . ." That puzzled frown began to return, then cleared immediately. He smiled at her. "You stuffed it with toilet paper!"

There was no question about the fear now. It was coiling lazily in her stomach like cold water. Her hand crept up to her throat and she stared at him, nearly hypnotized. *He's got the same look in his eyes, that same cold amused look that he had when he was beating the Wheel that night. What's happened to you, Johnny? What are you?* The blue of his eyes had darkened to a near violet, and he seemed far away. She wanted to run. The room itself seemed to be darkening, as if he were somehow tearing the fabric of reality, pulling apart the links between past and present.

"It slipped off your finger," he said. "You were putting his shaving stuff into one of those side pockets and it just slipped off. You didn't notice you'd lost it until later, and so you thought it was somewhere in the room." He laughed, and it was a high, tinkling, tripping sound—not like Johnny's usual laugh at all—but cold . . . cold. "Boy, you two turned that room upside down. But you packed it. It's still in that suitcase pocket. All this time. You go up in the attic and look, Sarah. You'll see."

In the corridor outside, someone dropped a water glass or something and cursed in surprise when it broke. Johnny glanced toward the sound, and his eyes cleared. He looked back, saw her frozen, wide-eyed face, and frowned with concern.

"What? Sarah, did I say something wrong?"

"How did you know?" she whispered. "How could you know those things?"

"I don't know," he said. "Sarah, I'm sorry if I . . ."

"Johnny, I ought to go, Denny's with the sitter."

"All right. Sarah, I'm sorry I upset you."

"How could you know about my ring, Johnny?"

He could only shake his head.

◆ **7** ◆

Halfway down the first-floor corridor, her stomach began to feel strange. She found the ladies' just in time. She hurried in, closed the door of one of the stalls, and threw up violently. She flushed and then stood with her eyes closed, shivering, but also close to laughter. The last time she had seen Johnny she had thrown up, too. Rough justice? Brackets in time, like bookends? She put her hands over her mouth to stifle whatever might be trying to get out—laughter or maybe a scream. And in the darkness the world seemed to tilt irrationally, like a dish. Like a spinning Wheel of Fortune.

◆ 8 ◆

She had left Denny with Mrs. Labelle, so when she got home the house was silent and empty. She went up the narrow stairway to the attic and turned the switch that controlled the two bare, dangling light bulbs. Their luggage was stacked up in one corner, the Montreal travel stickers still pasted to the sides of the orange Grants' suitcases. There were three of them. She opened the first, felt through the elasticized side pouches, and found nothing. Likewise the second. Likewise the third.

She drew in a deep breath and then let it out, feeling foolish and a little disappointed—but mostly relieved. Overwhelmingly relieved. No ring. Sorry, Johnny. But on the other hand, I'm not sorry at all. It would have been just a little bit too spooky.

She started to slide the suitcases back into place between a tall pile of Walt's old college texts and the floor lamp that crazy woman's dog had knocked over and which Sarah had never had the heart to throw out. And as she dusted off her hands preparatory to putting the whole thing behind her, a small voice far inside her whispered, almost too low to hear, *Sort of a flying search, wasn't it? Didn't really want to find anything, did you, Sarah?*

No. No, she really hadn't wanted to find anything. And if that little voice thought she was going to open all those suitcases again, it was crazy. She was fifteen minutes late in picking up Denny, Walt was bringing home one of the senior partners in his firm for dinner (a *very* big deal), and she owed Betty Hackman a letter—from the Peace Corps in Uganda, Betty had gone directly into marriage with the son of a staggeringly rich Kentucky horse breeder. Also, she ought to clean both bathrooms, set her hair, and give Denny a bath. There was really too much to do to be frigging around up in this hot, dirty attic.

So the pulled all three suitcases open again and this time

she searched the side pockets *very* carefully, and tucked all the way down in the corner of the third suitcase she found her wedding ring. She held it up to the glare of one of the naked bulbs and read the engraving inside, still as fresh as it had been on the day Walt slipped the ring on her finger: WALTER AND SARAH HAZLETT—JULY 9, 1972.

Sarah looked at it for a long time.

Then she put the suitcases back, turned off the lights, and went back downstairs. She changed out of the linen dress, which was now streaked with dust, and into slacks and a light top. She went down the block to Mrs. Labelle's and picked up her son. They went home and Sarah put Denny in the living room, where he crawled around vigorously while she prepared the roast and peeled some potatoes. With the roast in the oven, she went into the living room and saw that Denny had gone to sleep on the rug. She picked him up and put him in his crib. Then she began to clean the toilets. And in spite of everything, in spite of the way the clock was racing toward dinnertime, her mind never left the ring. Johnny had known. She could even pinpoint the moment he had come by his knowledge: When she had kissed him before leaving.

Just thinking about him made her feel weak and strange, and she wasn't sure why. It was all mixed up. His crooked smile, so much the same, his body, so terribly changed, so slight and undernourished, the lifeless way his hair lay against his scalp contrasting so blindingly with the rich memories she still held of him. She had *wanted* to kiss him.

"Stop it," she muttered to herself. Her face in the bathroom mirror looked like a stranger's face. Flushed and hot and— let's face it, gang, sexy.

Her hand closed on the ring in the pocket of her slacks, and almost—but not quite—before she was aware of what she was going to do, she had thrown it into the clean, slightly blue water of the toilet bowl. All sparkly clean so that if Mr. Treaches of Baribault, Treaches, Moorehouse, and Gendron had to take a leak sometime during the dinner party, he wouldn't be offended by any unsightly ring around the bowl, who knows what roadblocks may stand in the way of a young man on his march toward the counsels of the mighty, right? Who knows anything in this world?

It made a tiny splash and sank slowly to the bottom of the clear water, turning lazily over and over. She thought she heard a small clink when it struck the porcelain at the bottom, but that was probably just imagination. Her head throbbed. The attic had been hot and stale and musty. But Johnny's kiss—that had been sweet. So sweet.

Before she could think about what she was doing (and thus allow reason to reassert itself), she reached out and flushed the toilet. It went with a bang and a roar. It seemed louder, maybe, because her eyes were squeezed shut. When she opened them, the ring was gone. It had been lost, and now it was lost again.

Suddenly her legs felt weak and she sat down on the edge of the tub and put her hands over her face. Her hot, hot face. She wouldn't go back and see Johnny again. It wasn't a good idea. It had upset her. Walt was bringing home a senior partner and she had a bottle of Mondavi and a budget-fracturing roast, those were the things she would think about. She should be thinking about how much she loved Walt, and about Denny asleep in his crib. She should think about how, once you made your choices in this crazy world, you had to live with them. And she would not think about Johnny Smith and his crooked, charming smile anymore.

◆ 9 ◆

The dinner that night was a great success.

Chapter 10

◆ 1 ◆

The doctor put Vera Smith on a blood-pressure drug called Hydrodiural. It didn't lower her blood pressure much ("not a dime's worth," she was fond of writing in her letters), but it did make her feel sick and weak. She had to sit down and rest after vacuuming the floor. Climbing a flight of stairs made her stop at the top and pant like a doggy on a hot August afternoon. If Johnny hadn't told her it was for the best, she would have thrown the pills out the window right then.

The doctor tried her on another drug, and that made her heart race so alarmingly that she did stop taking it.

"This is a trial-and-error procedure," the doctor said. "We'll get you fixed up eventually, Vera. Don't worry."

"I don't worry," Vera said. "My faith is in the Lord God."

"Yes, of course it is. Just as it should be, too."

By the end of June, the doctor had settled on a combination of Hydrodiural and another drug called Aldomet—fat, yellow, expensive pills, nasty things. When she started taking the two drugs together, it seemed like she had to make water every fifteen minutes. She had headaches. She had heart palpitations. The doctor said her blood pressure was down into the normal range again, but she didn't believe him. What good were doctors, anyway? Look what they were doing to her Johnny, cutting him up like butcher's meat, three operations already, he looked like a monster with stitches all over his arms and legs and neck, and he still couldn't get around without one of those walkers, like old Mrs. Sylvester had to use. If her blood pressure was down, why did she feel so crummy all the time?

"You've got to give your body time enough to get used to the medication," Johnny said. It was the first Saturday in July, and his parents were up for the weekend. Johnny had just come back from hydrotherapy, and he looked pale and haggard. In each hand he held a small lead ball, and he was raising them and then lowering them into his lap as they talked, flexing his elbows, building up his biceps and triceps. The healing scars which ran like slashmarks across his elbows and forearms expanded and contracted.

"Put your faith in God, Johnny," Vera said. "There's no need of all this foolishness. Put your faith in God and he'll heal you."

"Vera . . ." Herb began.

"Don't you Vera me. This is *foolishness*! Doesn't the Bible say, ask and it shall be given, knock and it shall be opened unto you? There's no need for me to take that evil medicine and no need for my boy to let those doctors go on torturing him. It's wrong, it's not helping, and *it's sinful*!"

Johnny put the balls of lead shot on the bed. The muscles in his arms were trembling. He felt sick to his stomach and exhausted and suddenly furious at his mother.

"The Lord helps those who help themselves," he said. "You don't want the Christian God at all, Mom. You want a magic genie that's going to come out of a bottle and give you three wishes."

"Johnny!"

"Well, it's true."

"Those doctors put that idea in your head! All of these crazy ideas!" Her lips were trembling; her eyes wide but tearless. "God brought you out of that coma to do his will, John. These others, they're just . . ."

"Just trying to get me back on my feet so I won't have to do God's will from a wheelchair the rest of my life."

"Let's not have an argument," Herb said. "Families shouldn't argue." And hurricanes shouldn't blow, but they do every year, and nothing he could say was going to stop this. It had been coming.

"If you put your trust in God, Johnny . . ." Vera began, taking no notice of Herb at all.

"I don't trust anything anymore."

"I'm sorry to hear you say that," she said. Her voice was stiff and distant. "Satan's agents are everywhere. They'll try to turn you from your destiny. Looks like they are getting along with it real well."

"You have to make some kind of . . . of eternal thing out of it, don't you? I'll tell you what it was, it was a stupid accident, a couple of kids were dragging and I just happened to get turned into dog meat. You know what I want, Mom? I want to get out of here. That's all I want. And I want you to go on taking your medicine and . . . and try to get your feet back on the ground. That's all I want."

"I'm leaving." She stood up. Her face was pale and drawn. "I'll pray for you, Johnny."

He looked at her, helpless, frustrated, and unhappy. His anger was gone. He had taken it out on her. "Keep taking your medicine!" he said.

"I pray that you'll see the light."

She left the room, her face set and as grim as stone.

Johnny looked helplessly at his father.

"John, I wish you hadn't done that," Herb said.

"I'm tired. It doesn't do a thing for my judgment. Or my temper."

"Yeah," Herb said. He seemed about to say more and didn't.

"Is she still planning to go out to California for that flying saucer symposium or whatever it is?"

"Yes. But she may change her mind. You never know from one day to the next, and it's still a month away."

"You ought to do something."

"Yeah? What? Put her away? Commit her?"

Johnny shook his head. "I don't know. But maybe it's time you thought about that seriously instead of just acting like it's out of the question. She's sick. You have to see that."

Herb said loudly: "She was all right before you . . ."

Johnny winced, as if slapped.

"Look, I'm sorry. John, I didn't mean that."

"Okay, Dad."

"No, I really didn't." Herb's face was a picture of misery. "Look, I ought to go after her. She's probably leafleting the hallways by now."

"Okay."

"Johnny, just try to forget this and concentrate on getting well. She does love you, and so do I. Don't be hard on us."

"No. It's all right, dad."

Herb kissed Johnny's cheek. "I have to go after her."

"All right."

Herb left. When they were gone, Johnny got up and tottered the three steps between his chair and the bed. Not much. But something. A start. He wished more than his father knew that he hadn't blown up at his mother like that. He wished it because an odd sort of certainty was growing in him that his mother was not going to live much longer.

◆ 2 ◆

Vera stopped taking her medication. Herb talked to her, then cajoled, finally demanded. It did no good. She showed him the letters of her "correspondents in Jesus," most of them scrawled and full of misspellings, all of them supporting her stand and promising to pray for her. One of them was from a lady in Rhode Island who had also been at the farm in Vermont, waiting for the end of the world (along with her pet Pomeranian, Otis). "*GOD* is the best medicine," this lady wrote, "ask *GOD* and YOU WILL BE HEALED, not DRS who OSURP the POWER of *GOD,* it is DRS who have caused all the CANCER in this evil world with there DEVIL'S MEDDLING, anyone who has had SURGERY for instance, even MINOR like TONSILS OUT, sooner or later they will end up with CANCER, this is a proven fact, so ask *GOD,* pray *GOD,* merge YOUR WILL with HIS WILL and YOU WILL BE *HEALED!!*"

Herb talked to Johnny on the phone, and the next day Johnny called his mother and apologized for being so short with her. He asked her to please start taking the medicine again—for him. Vera accepted his apology, but refused to go back to the medication. If God needed her treading the earth, then he would see she continued to tread it. If God wanted to call her home, he would do that even if she took a barrel of pills a day. It was a seamless argument, and Johnny's only possible rebuttal was the one that Catholics and Protestants alike have rejected for eighteen hundred years: that God works His will through the mind of man as well as through the spirit of man.

"Momma," he said, "haven't you thought that God's will was for some doctor to invent that drug so you could live longer? Can't you even consider that idea?"

Long distance was no medium for theological argument. She hung up.

The next day Marie Michaud came into Johnny's room, put her head on his bed, and wept.

"Here, here," Johnny said, startled and alarmed. "What's this? What's wrong?"

"My boy," she said, still crying. "My Mark. They operated on him and it was just like you said. He's fine. He's going to see out of his bad eye again. Thank God."

She hugged Johnny and he hugged her back as best he could. With her warm tears on his own cheek, he thought that whatever had happened to him wasn't all bad. Maybe some things should be told, or seen, or found again. It wasn't even so farfetched to think that God *was* working through him, although his own concept of God was fuzzy and ill-defined. He held Marie and told her how glad he was. He told her to remember that he wasn't the one who had operated on Mark, and that he barely remembered what it was that he had told her. She left shortly after that, drying her eyes as she went, leaving Johnny alone to think.

◆ **3** ◆

Early in August, Dave Pelsen came to see Johnny. The Cleaves Mills High assistant principal was a small, neat man who wore thick glasses and Hush Puppies and a series of loud sports jackets. Of all the people who came to see Johnny during that almost endless summer of 1975, Dave had changed the least. The gray was speckled a little more fully through his hair, but that was all.

"So how are you doing? Really?" Dave asked, when they had finished the amenities.

"Not so bad," Johnny said. "I can walk alone now if I don't overdo it. I can swim six laps in the pool. I get headaches sometimes, real killers, but the doctors say I can expect that to go on for some time. Maybe the rest of my life."

"Mind a personal question?"

"If you're going to ask me if I can still get it up," Johnny said with a grin, "that's affirmative."

"That's good to know, but what I wanted to know about is the money. Can you pay for this?"

Johnny shook his head. "I've been in the hospital for going on five years. No one but a Rockefeller could pay for that. My father and mother got me into some sort of state-funded program. Total Disaster, or something like that."

Dave nodded. "The Extraordinary Disaster program. I figured that. But how did they keep you out of the state hospital, Johnny? That place is the pits."

"Dr. Weizak and Dr. Brown saw to that. And they're largely responsible for my having been able to come back as far as I have. I was a . . . a guinea pig, Dr. Weizak says. How long can we keep this comatose man from turning into a total vegetable? The physical therapy unit was working on me the last two years I was in coma. I had megavitamin shots . . . my ass still looks like a case of smallpox. Not that they expected any return on the project from me personally. I was assumed to be a terminal case almost from the time I came in. Weizak says that what he and Brown did with me is 'aggressive life support.' He thinks it's the beginning of a response to all the criticism about sustaining life after hope of recovery is gone. Anyway, they couldn't continue to use me if I'd gone over to the state hospital, so they kept me here. Eventually, they would have finished with me and then I *would* have gone to the state hospital."

"Where the most sophisticated care you would have gotten would have been a turn every six hours to prevent bedsores," Dave said. "And if you'd waked up in 1980, you would have been a basket case."

"I think I would have been a basket case no matter what," Johnny said. He shook his head slowly. "I think if someone proposes one more operation on me, I'll go nuts. And I'm still going to have a limp and I'll never be able to turn my head all the way to the left."

"When are they letting you out?"

"In three weeks, God willing."

"Then what?"

Johnny shrugged. "I'm going down home, I guess. To Pownal. My mother's going to be in California for a while on a . . . a religious thing. Dad and I can use the time to get reacquainted. I got a letter from one of the big literary agents in New York . . . well, not *him*, exactly, but one of his assistants. They think there might be a book in what happened to me. I thought I'd try to do two or three chapters and an outline, maybe this guy or his assistant can sell it. The money would come in pretty damn handy, no kidding there."

"Has there been any other media interest?"

"Well, the guy from the Bangor *Daily News* who did the original story . . ."

"Bright? He's good."

"He'd like to come down to Pownal after I blow this joint and do a feature story. I like the guy, but right now I'm holding him off. There's no money in it for me, and right now, frankly, that's what I'm looking for. I'd go on 'To Tell the Truth' if I thought I could make two hundred bucks out of it. My folks' savings are gone. They sold their car and bought a clunker. Dad took a second mortgage on the house when he should have been thinking about retiring and selling it and living on the proceeds."

"Have you thought about coming back into teaching?"

Johnny glanced up. "Is that an offer?"

"It ain't chopped liver."

"I'm grateful," Johnny said. "But I'm just not going to be ready in September, Dave."

"I wasn't thinking about September. You must remember Sarah's friend, Anne Strafford?" Johnny nodded. "Well, she's Anne Beatty now, and she's going to have a baby in December. So we need an English teacher second semester. Light schedule. Four classes, one senior study hall, two free periods."

"Are you making a firm offer, Dave?"

"Firm."

"That's pretty damn good of you," Johnny said hoarsely.

"Hell with that," Dave said easily. "You were a pretty damn good teacher."

"Can I have a couple of weeks to think it over?"

"Until the first of October, if you want," Dave said. "You'd still be able to work on your book, I think. If it looks like there might be a possibility there."

Johnny nodded.

"And you might not want to stay down there in Pownal too long," Dave said. "You might find it . . . uncomfortable."

Words rose to Johnny's lips and he had to choke them off. *Not for long, Dave. You see, my mother's in the process of blowing her brains out right now. She's just not using a gun. She's going to have a stroke. She'll be dead before Christmas unless my father and I can persuade her to start taking her medicine again, and I don't think we can. And I'm a part of it—how much of a part I don't know. I don't think I want to know.*

Instead he replied, "News travels, huh?"

Dave shrugged. "I understand through Sarah that your mother has had problems adjusting. She'll come around, Johnny. In the meantime, think about it."

"I will. In fact, I'll give you a tentative yes right now. It would be good to teach again. To get back to normal."

"You're my man," Dave said.

After he left, Johnny lay down on his bed and looked out the window. He was very tired. *Get back to normal.* Somehow he didn't think that was ever really going to happen.

He felt one of his headaches coming on.

◆ 4 ◆

The fact that Johnny Smith had come out of his coma with something extra finally did get into the paper, and it made page one under David Bright's by-line. It happened less than a week before Johnny left the hospital.

He was in physical therapy, lying on his back on a floor-pad. Resting on his belly was a twelve-pound medicine ball. His physical therapist, Eileen Magown, was standing above him and counting off situps. He was supposed to do ten of them, and he was currently struggling over number eight. Sweat was streaming down his face, and the healing scars on his neck stood out bright red.

Eileen was a small, homely woman with a whipcord body, a nimbus of gorgeous, frizzy red hair, and deep green eyes flecked with hazel. Johnny sometimes called her—with a mixture of irritation and amusement—the world's smallest Marine D.I. She had ordered and cajoled and demanded him back from a bed-fast patient who could barely hold a glass of water to a man who could walk without a cane, do three chinups at a time, and do a complete turn around the hospital pool in fifty-three seconds—not Olympic time, but not bad. She was unmarried and lived in a big house on Center Street in Oldtown with her four cats. She was slate-hard and she wouldn't take no for an answer.

Johnny collapsed backward. "Nope," he panted. "Oh, I don't think so, Eileen."

"Up, boy!" she cried in high and sadistic good humor. "Up! Up! Just three more and you can have a Coke!"

"Give me my ten-pound ball and I'll give you two more."

"That ten-pound ball is going into the *Guinness Book of Records* as the world's biggest suppository if you don't give me three more. *Up!*"

"*Urrrrrrgrah!*" Johnny cried, jerking through number eight. He flopped back down, then jerked up again.

"Great!" Eileen cried. "One more, one more!"

"*OOOOARRRRRRRRUNCH!*" Johnny screamed, and sat up for the tenth time. He collapsed to the mat, letting the medicine ball roll away. "I ruptured myself, are you happy, all my guts just came loose, they're floating around inside me, I'll sue you, you goddam harpy."

"Jeez, what a baby," Eileen said, offering him her hand. "This is nothing compared to what I've got on for next time."

"Forget it," Johnny said. "All I'm gonna do next time is swim in the . . ."

He looked at her, an expression of surprise spreading over his face. His grip tightened on her hand until it was almost painful.

"Johnny? What's wrong? Is it a charley horse?"

"Oh gosh," Johnny said mildly.

"*Johnny?*"

He was still gripping her hand, looking into her face with a faraway, dreamy contemplation that made her feel nervous. She had heard things about Johnny Smith, rumors that she had disregarded with her own brand of hard-headed Scots pragmatism. There was a story that he had predicted Marie Michaud's boy was going to be all right, even before the doctors were one hundred percent sure they wanted to try the risky operation. Another rumor had something to do with Dr.

Weizak; it was said Johnny had told him his mother was not dead but living someplace on the West Coast under another name. As far as Eileen Magown was concerned, the stories were so much eyewash, on a par with the confession magazines and sweet-savage love stories so many nurses read on station. But the way he was looking at her now made her feel afraid. It was as if he was looking inside her.

"Johnny, are you okay?" They were alone in the physical therapy room. The big double doors with the frosted glass panels which gave on the pool area were closed.

"Gosh sakes," Johnny said. "You better . . . yes, there's still time. Just about."

"What are you talking about?"

He snapped out of it then. He let go of her hand . . . but he had gripped it tightly enough to leave white indentations along the back.

"Call the fire department," he said. "You forgot to turn off the burner. The curtains are catching on fire."

"What . . . ?"

"The burner caught the dish towel and the dish towel caught the curtains," Johnny said impatiently. "Hurry up and call them. Do you want your house to burn down?"

"Johnny, you can't know . . ."

"Never mind what I can't know," Johnny said, grabbing her elbow. He got her moving and they walked across to the doors. Johnny was limping badly on his left leg, as he always did when he was tired. They crossed the room that housed the swimming pool, their heels clacking hollowly on the tiles, then went out into the first floor hallway and down to the nurses' station. Inside, two nurses were drinking coffee and a third was on the phone, telling someone on the other end how she had redone her apartment.

"Are you going to call or should I?" Johnny asked.

Eileen's mind was in a whirl. Her morning routine was as set as a single person's is apt to be. She had gotten up and boiled herself a single egg while she ate a whole grapefruit, unsweetened, and a bowl of All-Bran. After breakfast she had dressed and driven to the hospital. *Had* she turned off the burner? Of course she had. She couldn't specifically remember doing it, but it was habit. She must have.

"Johnny, really, I don't know where you got the idea . . ."

"Okay, I will."

They were in the nurses' station now, a glassed-in booth

furnished with three straight-backed chairs and a hot plate. The little room was dominated by the callboard—rows of small lights that flashed red when a patient pushed his call button. Three of them were flashing now. The two nurses went on drinking their coffee and talking about some doctor who had turned up drunk at Benjamin's. The third was apparently talking with her beautician.

"Pardon me, I have to make a call," Johnny said.

The nurse covered the phone with her hand. "There's a pay phone in the lob . . ."

"Thanks," Johnny said, and took the phone out of her hand. He pushed for one of the open lines and dialed 0. He got a busy signal. "What's wrong with this thing?"

"Hey!" The nurse who had been talking to her beautician cried. "What the hell do you think you're doing? Give me that!"

Johnny remembered that he was in a hospital with its own switchboard and dialed 9 for an outside line. Then he redialed the 0.

The deposed nurse, her cheeks flaming with anger, grabbed for the phone. Johnny pushed her away. She whirled, saw Eileen, and took a step toward her. "Eileen, what's with this crazy guy?" she asked stridently. The other two nurses had put down their coffee cups and were staring gape-mouthed at Johnny.

Eileen shrugged uncomfortably. "I don't know, he just . . ."

"Operator."

"Operator, I want to report a fire in Oldtown," Johnny said. "Can you give me the correct number to call, please?"

"Hey," one of the nurses said. "Whose house is on fire?"

Eileen shifted her feet nervously. "He says mine is."

The nurse who had been talking about her apartment to her beautician did a double take. "Oh my God, it's *that* guy," she said.

Johnny pointed at the callboard, where five or six lights were flashing now. "Why don't you go see what those people want?"

The operator had connected him with the Oldtown Fire Department.

"My name is John Smith and I need to report a fire. It's at . . ." He looked at Eileen. "What's your address?"

For a moment Johnny didn't think she was going to tell him. Her mouth worked, but nothing came out. The two coffee-drinkers had now forsaken their cups and withdrawn to the station's far corner. They were whispering together like little girls in a grammar school john. Their eyes were wide.

"Sir?" the voice on the other end asked.

"Come *on*," Johnny said, "do you want your cats to fry?"

"624 Center Street," Eileen said reluctantly. "Johnny, you've wigged out."

Johnny repeated the address into the phone. "It's in the kitchen."

"Your name, Sir?"

"John Smith. I'm calling from the Eastern Maine Medical Center in Bangor."

"May I ask how you came by your information?"

"We'd be on the phone the rest of the day. My information is correct. Now go put it out." He banged the phone down.

". . . and he said Sam Weizak's mother was still . . ."

She broke off and looked at Johnny. For a moment he felt all of them looking at him, their eyes lying on his skin like tiny, hot weights, and he knew what would come of this and it made his stomach turn.

"Eileen," he said.

"What?"

"Do you have a friend next door?"

"Yes . . . Burt and Janice are next door . . ."

"Either of them home?"

"I guess Janice probably would be, sure."

"Why don't you give her a call?"

Eileen nodded, suddenly understanding what he was getting at. She took the phone from his hand and dialed an 827 exchange number. The nurses stood by watching avidly, as if they had stepped into a really exciting TV program by accident.

"Hello? Jan? It's Eileen. Are you in your kitchen? . . . Would you take a look out your window and tell me if everything looks, well, all right over at my place? . . . Well, a friend of mine says . . . I'll tell you after you go look, okay?" Eileen was blushing. "Yes, I'll wait." She looked at Johnny and repeated, "You've wigged out, Johnny."

There was a pause that seemed to go on and on. Then Eileen began listening again. She listened for a long time and then said in a strange, subdued voice totally unlike her usual one: "No, that's all right, Jan. They've been called. No . . . I can't explain right now but I'll tell you later." She looked at Johnny. "Yes, it is funny how I could have known . . . but I can explain. At least I think I can. Good-bye."

She hung up the telephone. They all looked at her, the nurses with avid curiosity, Johnny with only dull certainty.

"Jan says there's smoke pouring out of my kitchen window," Eileen said, and all three nurses sighed in unison. Their eyes, wide and somehow accusing, turned to Johnny again. *Jury's eyes,* he thought dismally.

"I ought to go home," Eileen said. The aggressive, cajoling, positive physical therapist was gone, replaced by a small woman who was worried about her cats and her house and her things. "I . . . I don't know how to thank you, Johnny . . . I'm sorry I didn't believe you, but . . ." She began to weep.

One of the nurses moved toward her, but Johnny was there first. He put an arm around her and led her out into the hall.

"You really can," Eileen whispered. "What they said . . ."

"You go on," Johnny said. "I'm sure it's going to be fine. There's going to be some minor smoke and water damage, and that's all. That movie poster from *Butch Cassidy and the Sundance Kid,* I think you're going to lose that, but that's all."

"Yes, okay. Thank you, Johnny. God bless you." She kissed him on the cheek and then began to trot down the hall. She looked back once, and the expression on her face was very much like superstitious dread.

The nurses were lined up against the glass of the nurses' station, staring at him. Suddenly they reminded him of crows on a telephone line, crows staring down at something bright and shiny, something to be pecked at and pulled apart.

"Go on and answer your calls," he said crossly, and they flinched back at the sound of his voice. He began to limp up the hall toward the elevator, leaving them to start the gossip on its way. He was tired. His legs hurt. His hip joints felt as if they had broken glass in them. He wanted to go to bed.

Chapter 11

◆ 1 ◆

"What are you going to do?" Sam Weizak asked.

"Christ, I don't know," Johnny said. "How many did you say are down there?"

"About eight. One of them is the northern New England

AP stringer. And there are people from two of the TV sta-
tions with cameras and lights. The hospital director is quite
angry with you, Johnny. He feels you have been naughty."

"Because a lady's house was going to burn down?" Johnny
asked. "All I can say is it must have been one frigging slow
news day."

"As a matter of fact, it wasn't. Ford vetoed two bills. The
P.L.O. blew up a restaurant in Tel Aviv. And a police dog
sniffed out four hundred pounds of marijuana at the airport."

"Then what are they doing here?" Johnny asked. When
Sam had come in with the news that reporters were gathering
in the lobby, his first sinking thought was what his mother
might make of this. She was with his father in Pownal, making
ready for her California pilgrimage, which began the following
week. Neither Johnny nor his father believed the trip was a
good idea, and the news that her son had somehow turned
psychic might make her cancel it, but in this case Johnny was
very much afraid that the cure might be the greater of two
evils. Something like this could set her off for good.

On the other hand—this thought suddenly blossomed in his
mind with all the force of inspiration—it might persuade her
to start taking her medicine again.

"They're here because what happened is news," Sam said.
"It has all the classic ingredients."

"I didn't do anything, I just . . ."

"You just told Eileen Magown her house was on fire and
it was," Sam said softly. "Come on, Johnny, you must have
known this was going to happen sooner or later."

"I'm no publicity hound," Johnny said grimly.

"No. I didn't mean to suggest you were. An earthquake is
no publicity hound. But the reporters cover it. People want
to know."

"What if I just refuse to talk to them?"

"That is not much of an option," Sam replied. "They will
go away and publish crazy rumors. Then, when you leave the
hospital, they will fall on you. They will shove microphone in
your face as if you were a senator or a crime boss, nuh?"

Johnny thought about it. "Is Bright down there?"

"Yes"

"Suppose I ask him to come up? He can get the story and
give it to the rest of them."

"You can do that, but it would make the rest of them extremely unhappy. And an unhappy reporter will be your

enemy. Nixon made them unhappy and they tore him to pieces."

"I'm not Nixon," Johnny said.

Weizak grinned radiantly. "Thank God," he said.

"What do you suggest?" Johnny asked.

◆ 2 ◆

The reporters stood up and crowded forward when Johnny stepped through the swing doors and into the west lobby. He was wearing a white shirt, open at the collar, and a pair of blue jeans that were too big for him. His face was pale but composed. The scars from the tendon operations stood out clearly on his neck. Flash-paks popped warm fire at him and made him wince. Questions were babbled.

"Here! Here!" Sam Weizak shouted. "This is a convalescent patient! He wants to make a brief statement and he will answer some of your questions, but only if you behave in an orderly fashion! Now fall back and let him breathe!"

Two sets of TV light bars flashed on, bathing the lobby in an unearthly glare. Doctors and nurses gathered by the lounge doorway to watch. Johnny winced away from the lights, wondering if this was what they meant by the lime-light. He felt as if all of it might be a dream.

"Who're you?" one of the reporters yelled at Weizak.

"I am Samuel Weizak, this young man's doctor, and that name is spelled with two X's."

There was general laughter and the mood eased a little.

"Johnny, you feel all right?" Weizak asked. It was early evening, and his sudden insight that Eileen Magown's kitchen was catching fire seemed distant and unimportant, the memory of a memory.

"Sure," he said.

"What's your statement?" one of the reporters called.

"Well," Johnny said, "it's this. My physical therapist is a woman named Eileen Magown. She's a very nice lady, and she's been helping me get my strength back. I was in an accident, you see, and . . ." One of the TV cameras moved in, goggling at him blankly, throwing him offstride for a moment. ". . . and I got pretty weak. My muscles sort of collapsed. We were in the physical therapy room this morning, just finishing up, and I got the feeling that her house was on fire. That is, to be more specific . . ." *Jesus, you sound like an asshole!* "I felt that she had forgotten to turn off her stove and that the curtains in the kitchen were about to catch fire. So we just went and called the fire department and that's all there was to it."

There was a moment's gaping pause as they digested that— *I sort of got the feeling, and that's all there was to it*—and then the barrage of questions came again, everything mixed together into a meaningless stew of human voices. Johnny looked around helplessly, feeling disoriented and vulnerable.

"One at a time!" Weizak yelled. "Raise your hands! Were you never schoolchildren?"

Hands waved, and Johnny pointed at David Bright.

"Would you call this a psychic experience, Johnny?"

"I would call it a feeling," Johnny answered. "I was doing situps and I finished. Miss Magown took my hand to help me up and I just knew."

He pointed at someone else.

"Mel Allen, Portland *Sunday Telegram*, Mr. Smith. Was it like a picture? A picture in your head?"

"No, not at all," Johnny said, but he was not really able to remember what it *had* been like.

"Has this happened to you before, Johnny?" A young woman in a slacksuit asked.

"Yes, a few times."

"Can you tell us about the other incidents?"

"No, I'd rather not."

One of the TV reporters raised his hand and Johnny nodded at him. "Did you have any of these flashes *before* your accident and the resulting coma, Mr. Smith?"

Johnny hesitated.

The room seemed very still. The TV lights were warm on his face, like a tropical sun. "No," he said.

Another barrage of questions. Johnny looked helplessly at Weizak again.

"Stop! Stop!" He bellowed. He looked at Johnny as the roar subsided. "You are done, Johnny?"

"I'll answer two more questions," Johnny said. "Then . . . really . . . it's been a long day for me . . . yes, Ma'am?"

He was pointing to a stout woman who had wedged herself in between two young reporters. "Mr. Smith," she said in a loud, carrying, tubalike voice, "who will be the Democrats' nominee for president next year?"

"I can't tell you that," Johnny said, honestly surprised at the question. "How could I tell you that?"

More hands were raised. Johnny pointed to a tall, sober-faced man in a dark suit. He took one step forward. There was something prim and coiled about him.

"Mr. Smith, I'm Roger Dussault, from the Lewiston *Sun,* and I would like to know if you have any idea why you should have such an extraordinary ability as this . . . if indeed you do. Why you, Mr. Smith?"

Johnny cleared his throat. "As I understand your question . . . you're asking me to justify something I don't understand. I can't do that."

"Not justify, Mr. Smith. Just explain."

He thinks I'm hoaxing them. Or trying.

Weizak stepped up beside Johnny. "I wonder if I might answer that," he said. "Or at least attempt to explain why it cannot be answered."

"Are you psychic, too?" Dussault asked coldly.

"Yes, all neurologists must be, it's a requirement," Weizak said. There was a burst of laughter and Dussault flushed.

"Ladies and gentlemen of the press. This man spent four-and-a-half years in a coma. We who study the human brain have no idea why he did, or why he came out of it, and this is for the simple reason that we do not understand what a coma really is, any more than we understand sleep or the simple act of waking. Ladies and gentlemen, we do not understand the brain of a frog or the brain of an ant. You may quote me on these things . . . you see I am fearless, nuh?"

More laughter. They liked Weizak. But Dussault did not laugh.

"You may also quote me as saying I believe that this man is now in possession of a very new human ability, or a very old one. Why? If I and my colleagues do not understand the brain of an ant, can I tell you why? I cannot. I can suggest some interesting things to you, however, things which may or may not have bearing. A part of John Smith's brain has been damaged beyond repair—a very small part, but all parts of the brain may be vital. He calls this his 'dead zone,' and there, apparently, a number of trace memories were stored. All of these wiped-out memories seem to be part of a 'set'—that of street, road, and highway designations. A subset of a larger overall set, that of where is it. This is a small but total aphasia which seems to include both language and visualization skills.

"Balancing this off, another tiny part of John Smith's brain appears to have *awakened*. A section of the cerebrum within the parietal lobe. This is one of the deeply grooved sections of the 'forward' or 'thinking' brain. The electrical responses from this section of Smith's brain are way out of line from what they should be, nuh? Here is one more thing. The parietal lobe has something to do with the sense of touch—how much or how little we are not completely sure—and it is very near to that area of the brain that sorts and identifies various shapes and textures. And it has been my own observation that John's 'flashes' are always preceded by some sort of touching."

Silence. Reporters were scribbling madly. The TV cameras, which had moved in to focus on Weizak, now pulled back to include Johnny in the picture.

"Is that it, Johnny?" Weizak asked again.

"I guess . . ."

Dussault suddenly shouldered his way through the knot of reporters. For a bemused moment Johnny thought he was going to join them in front of the doors, possibly for the purpose of rebuttal. Then he saw that Dussault was slipping something from around his neck.

"Let's have a demonstration," he said. He was holding a medallion on a fine-link gold chain. "Let's see what you can do with this."

"We'll see no such thing," Weizak said. His bushy salt-and-pepper eyebrows had drawn thunderously together and he stared down at Dussault like Moses. "This man is not a carnival performer, sir!"

"You sure could have fooled me," Dussault said. "Either he can or he can't, right? While you were busy suggesting things, I was busy suggesting something to myself. What I was suggesting was that these guys can never perform on demand, because they're all as genuine as a pile of three-dollar bills."

Johnny looked at the other reporters. Except for Bright, who looked rather embarrassed, they were watching avidly. Suddenly he felt like a Christian in a pitful of lions. They win either way, he thought. If I can tell him something, they've got a front-page story. If I can't, or if I refuse to try, they've got another kind of story.

"Well?" Dussault asked. The medallion swung back and forth below his fist.

Johnny looked at Weizak, but Weizak was looking away, disgusted.

"Give it to me," Johnny said.

Dussault handed it over. Johnny put the medallion in his palm. It was a St. Christopher medal. He dropped the fine-link chain on top of it in a crisp little yellow heap and closed his hand over it.

Dead silence fell in the room. The handful of doctors and nurses standing by the lounge doorway had been joined by half a dozen others, some of them dressed in streetclothes and on their way out of the hospital for the night. A crowd of patients had gathered at the end of the hallway leading to the first-floor TV and game lounge. The people who had come for the regular early evening visiting hours had drifted over from the main lobby. A feeling of thick tension lay in the air like a humming power cable.

Johnny stood silently, pale and thin in his white shirt and oversized blue jeans. The St. Christopher medal was clamped so tightly in his right hand that the cords in his wrist stood out clearly in the glare of the TV light bars. In front of him, sober, impeccable, and judgmental in his dark suit, Dussault stood in the adversary position. The moment seemed to stretch out interminably. No one coughed or whispered.

"Oh," Johnny said softly . . . then: "Is that it?"

His fingers loosened slowly. He looked at Dussault.

"Well?" Dussault asked, but the authority was suddenly gone from his voice. The tired, nervous young man who had answered the reporters' questions seemed also to be gone. There was a half-smile on Johnny's lips, but there was nothing warm about it. The blue of his eyes had darkened. They had grown cold and distant. Weizak saw it and felt a chill of goose-flesh. He later told his wife that it had been the face of a man looking through a high-powered microscope and observing an interesting species of paramecium.

"It's your sister's medallion," he said to Dussault. "Her name was Anne but everyone called her Terry. Your older sister. You loved her. You almost worshipped the ground she walked on."

Suddenly, terribly, Johnny Smith's voice began to climb and change. It became the cracked and unsure voice of an adolescent.

"It's for when you cross Lisbon Street against the lights,

Terry, or when you're out parking with one of those guys from E.L. Don't forget, Terry . . . don't forget . . ."

The plump woman who had asked Johnny who the Democrats would nominate next year uttered a frightened little moan. One of the TV camermen muttered "Holy Jesus" in a hoarse voice.

"Stop it," Dussault whispered. His face had gone a sick shade of gray. His eyes bulged and spittle shone like chrome on his lower lip in this harsh light. His hands moved for the medallion, which was now looped on its fine gold chain over Johnny's fingers. But his hands moved with no power or authority. The medallion swung back and forth, throwing off hypnotic gleams of light.

"Remember me, Terry," the adolescent voice begged. "Stay clean, Terry . . . please, for God's sake stay clean . . ."

"*Stop it! Stop it, you bastard!*"

Now Johnny spoke in his own voice again. "It was speed, wasn't it? Then meth. She died of a heart attack at twenty-seven. But she wore it ten years, Rog. She remembered you. She never forgot. Never forgot . . . never . . . never . . . never."

The medallion slipped from his fingers and struck the floor with a small, musical sound. Johnny stared away into emptiness for a moment, his face calm and cool and distant. Dussault grubbed at his feet for the medallion, sobbing hoarsely in the stunned silence.

A flash-pak popped, and Johnny's face cleared and became his own again. Horror touched it, and then pity. He knelt clumsily beside Dussault.

"I'm sorry," he said. "I'm sorry, I didn't mean . . ."

"You cheapjack, bastard hoaxer!" Dussault screamed at him. "It's a lie! All a lie! All a *lie*!" He struck Johnny a clumsy, open-handed blow on the neck and Johnny fell over, striking his head on the foor, hard. He saw stars.

Uproar.

He was dimly aware that Dussault was pushing his way blindly through the crowd and toward the doors. People milled around Dussault, around Johnny. He saw Dussault through a forest of legs and shoes. Then Weizak was beside him, helping him to sit up.

"John, are you all right? Did he hurt you?"

"Not as bad as I hurt him. I'm okay." He struggled to his feet. Hands—maybe Weizak's, maybe someone else's—helped him. He felt dizzy and sick; almost revolted. This had been a mistake, a terrible mistake.

Someone screamed piercingly—the stout woman who had asked about the Democrats. Johnny saw Dussault pitch forward to his knees, grope at the sleeve of the stout woman's print blouse and then slide tiredly forward onto the tile near the doorway he had been trying to reach. The St. Christopher medal was still in one hand.

"Fainted," someone said. "Fainted dead away. I'll be damned."

"My fault," Johnny said to Sam Weizak. His throat felt close and tight with shame, with tears. "All my fault."

"No," Sam said. "No, John."

But it was. He shook loose of Weizak's hands and went to where Dussault lay, coming around now, eyes blinking dazedly at the ceiling. Two of the doctors had come over to where he lay.

"Is he all right?" Johnny asked. He turned toward the woman reporter in the slacksuit and she shrank away from him. A cramp of fear passed over her face.

Johnny turned the other way, toward the TV reporter who had asked him if he'd had any flashes before his accident. It suddenly seemed very important that he explain to someone. "I didn't mean to hurt him," he said. "Honest to God, I never meant to hurt him. I didn't know . . ."

The TV reporter backed up a step. "No," he said. "Of course you didn't. He was asking for it, anybody could see that. Just . . . don't touch me, huh?"

Johnny looked at him dumbly, lips quivering. He was still in shock but beginning to understand. Oh yes. He was beginning to understand. The TV reporter tried to smile and could only produce a death's-head rictus.

"Just don't touch me, Johnny. Please."

"It's not like that," Johnny said—or tried to. Later, he was never sure if any sound had come out.

"Don't touch me, Johnny, okay?"

The reporter backed up to where his cameraman was packing his gear. Johnny stood and watched him. He began to shake all over.

◆ 3 ◆

"It's for your own good, John," Weizak said. The nurse stood behind him, a white ghost, a sorcerer's apprentice with her hands hovering above the small, wheeled medication table, a junkie's paradise of sweet dreams.

"No," Johnny said. He was still shaking, and now there was cold sweat as well. "No more shots. I've had it up to here with shots."

"A pill, then."

"No more pills, either."

"To help you sleep."

"Will *he* be able to sleep? That man Dussault?"

"He asked for it," the nurse murmured, and then flinched as Weizak turned toward her. But Weizak smiled crookedly.

"She is right, nuh?" he said. "The man asked for it. He thought you were selling empty bottles, John. A good night's sleep and you'll be able to put this in perspective."

"I'll sleep on my own."

"Johnny, please."

It was quarter past eleven. The TV across the room had just gone off. Johnny and Sam had watched the filmed story together; it had been second-lined right after the bills Ford had vetoed. My own story made better theater, Johnny thought with morbid amusement. Film footage of a bald-headed Republican mouthing platitudes about the national budget just didn't compare with the film clip that WABI cameraman had gotten here earlier this evening. The clip had ended with Dussault plunging across the floor with his sister's medal clutched in his hand and then crashing down in a faint, clutching at the woman reporter the way a drowning man might clutch at a straw.

When the TV anchorman went on to the police dog and the four hundred pounds of pot, Weizak had left briefly and had come back with the news that the hospital switchboard had jammed up with calls for him even before the report was over. The nurse with the medication had shown up a few minutes later, leading Johnny to believe that Sam had gone down to the nurse's station to do more than check on incoming calls.

At that instant, the telephone rang.

Weizak swore softly under his breath. "I told them to hold them all. Don't answer it, John, I'll . . ."

But Johnny already had it. He listened for a moment, then nodded. "Yes, that was right." He put a hand over the receiver. "It's my dad," he said. He uncovered the receiver. "Hi, Dad. I guess you . . ." He listened. The small smile on his lips faded and was replaced by an expression of dawning horror. His lips moved silently.

"John, what is it?" Weizak asked sharply.

"All right, Daddy," Johnny said, almost in a whisper. "Yes. Cumberland General. I know where it is. Just above Jerusalem's Lot. Okay. All right. Daddy . . ."

His voice broke. His eyes were tearless but glistening.

"I know that, Daddy. I love you too. I'm sorry."

Listened.

"Yes. Yes it was," Johnny said. "I'll see you, Daddy. Yes. Good-bye."

He hung up the phone, put the heels of his hands to his eyes, and pressed.

"Johnny?" Sam leaned forward, took one of his hands away and held it gently. "Is it your mother?"

"Yeah. It's my mother."

"Heart attack?"

"Stroke," Johnny said, and Sam Weizak made a small, pained hissing between his teeth. "They were watching the TV news . . . neither of them had any idea . . . and I came on . . . and she had a stroke. Christ. She's in the hospital. Now if something happens to my dad, we got a triple play." He uttered a high scream of laughter. His eyes rolled wildly from Sam to the nurse and back to Sam again. "It's a good talent," he said. "Everybody should have it." The laugh came again, so like a scream.

"How bad is she?" Sam asked.

"He doesn't know." Johnny swung his legs out of bed. He had changed back to a hospital gown and his feet were bare.

"What do you think you are doing?" Sam asked sharply.

"What does it look like?"

Johnny got up, and for a moment it seemed that Sam would push him back onto the bed. But he only watched Johnny limp over to the closet. "Don't be ridiculous. You're not ready for this, John."

Unmindful of the nurse—they had seen his bare tail enough times, God knew—Johnny let the gown drop around his feet.

The thick, twisting scars stood out on the backs of his knees and dimpled into the scant swell of his calves. He began to rummage in the closet for clothes, and came up with the white shirt and jeans he had worn to the news conference.

"John, I absolutely forbid this. As your doctor and your friend. I tell you, it is madness."

"Forbid all you want, I'm going," Johnny said. He began to dress. His face wore that expression of distant preoccupation that Sam associated with his trances. The nurse gawped.

"Nurse, you might as well go back to your station," Sam said.

She backed to the door, stood there for a moment, and then left. Reluctantly.

"Johnny," Sam said. He got up, went to him, and put a hand on his shoulder. "You didn't do it."

Johnny shook the hand off. "I did it, all right," he said. "She was watching me when it happened." He began to button the shirt.

"You urged her to take her medicine and she stopped."

Johnny looked at Weizak for a moment and then went back to buttoning his shirt.

"If it hadn't happened tonight, it would have happened tomorrow, next week, next month . . ."

"Or next year. Or in ten years."

"No. It would not have been ten years, or even one. And you know it. Why are you so anxious to pin this tail on yourself? Because of that smug reporter? Is it maybe an inverted kind of self-pity? An urge to believe that you have been cursed?"

Johnny's face twisted. "She was watching *me* when it happened. Don't you get that? Are you so fucking soft you don't get that?"

"She was planning a strenuous trip, all the way to California and back, you told me that yourself. A symposium of some kind. A highly emotional sort of thing, from what you have said. Yes? Yes. It would almost certainly have happened then. A stroke is not lightning from a blue sky, Johnny."

Johnny buttoned the jeans and then sat down as if the act of dressing had tired him out too much to do more. His feet were still bare. "Yeah," he said. "Yeah, you may be right."

"Sense! He sees sense! Thank the Lord!"

"But I still have to go, Sam."

Weizak threw up his hands. "And do what? She is in the

hands of her doctors and her God. That is the situation. Better than anyone else, you must understand."

"My dad will need me," Johnny said softly. "I understand that, too."

"How will you go? It's nearly midnight."

"By bus. I'll grab a cab over to Peter's Candlelighter. The Greyhounds still stop there, don't they?"

"You don't have to do that," Sam said.

Johnny was groping under the chair for his shoes and not finding them. Sam got them from under the bed and handed them to him.

"I'll drive you down."

Johnny looked up at him. "You'd do that?"

"If you'll take a mild tranquilizer, yes."

"But your wife . . ." He realized in a confused sort of way that the only concrete thing he knew about Weizak's personal life was that his mother was living in California.

"I am divorced," Weizak said. "A doctor has to be out all hours of the night . . . unless he is a podiatrist or a dermatologist, nuh? My wife saw the bed as half-empty rather than half-full. So she filled it with a variety of men."

"I'm sorry," Johnny said, embarrassed.

"You spend far too much time being sorry, John." Sam's face was gentle, but his eyes were stern. "Put on your shoes."

Chapter 12

◆ 1 ◆

Hospital to hospital, Johnny thought dreamily, flying gently along on the small blue pill he had taken just before he and Sam left the EMMC and climbed into Sam's '75 El Dorado. *Hospital to hospital, person to person, station to station.*

In a queer, secret way, he enjoyed the trip—it was his first time out of the hospital in almost five years. The night was clear, the Milky Way sprawled across the sky in an unwinding clockspring of light, a half-moon followed them over the dark tree line as they fled south through Palmyra, Newport, Pitts-

field, Benton, Clinton. The car whispered along in near total
silence. Low music, Haydn, issued from the four speakers of
the stereo tape player.

*Came to one hospital in the Cleaves Mills Rescue Squad
ambulance, went to another in a Cadillac,* he thought. He
didn't let it bother him. It was just enough to ride, to float
along on the track, to let the problem of his mother, his new
ability, and the people who wanted to pry into his soul (*He
asked for it . . . just don't touch me, huh?*) rest in a temporary
limbo. Weizak didn't talk. Occasionally he hummed snatches
of the music.

Johnny watched the stars. He watched the turnpike, nearly
deserted this late. It unrolled ceaselessly in front of them.
They went through the tollgate at Augusta and Weizak took
a time-and-toll ticket. Then they went on again—Gardener,
Sabbatus, Lewiston.

*Nearly five years, longer than some convicted murderers
spend in the slam.*

He slept.

Dreamed.

"Johnny," his mother said in his dream. "Johnny, make me
better, make me well." She was in a beggar's rags. She was
crawling toward him over cobblestones. Her face was white.
Thin blood ran from her knees. White lice squirmed in her
thin hair. She held shaking hands out to him. "It's the power
of God working in you," she said. "It's a great responsibility,
Johnny. A great trust. You must be worthy."

He took her hands, closed his own over them, and said,
"Spirits, depart from this woman."

She stood up. "Healed!" she cried in a voice that was filled
with a strange and terrible triumph. "*Healed! My son has
healed me! His work is great upon the earth!*"

He tried to protest, to tell her that he didn't want to do
great works, or heal, or speak in tongues, or divine the future,
or find those things that had been lost. He tried to tell her,
but his tongue wouldn't obey the command of his brain. Then
she was past him, striding off down the cobbled street, her
posture cringing and servile but somehow arrogant at the
same time; her voice belled like a clarion: "*Saved! Savior!
Saved! Savior!*"

And to his horror he saw that there had been thousands of
others behind her, maybe millions, all of them maimed or
deformed or in terror. The stout lady reporter was there,

needing to know who the Democrats would nominate for the presidency in 1976; there was a death-eyed farmer in biballs with a picture of his son, a smiling young man in Air Force blues, who had been reported MIA over Hanoi in 1972, he needed to know if his son was dead or alive; a young woman who looked like Sarah with tears on her smooth cheeks, holding up a baby with a hydrocephalic head on which blue veins were traced like runes of doom; an old man with his fingers turned into clubs by arthritis; others. They stretched for miles, they would wait patiently, they would kill him with their mute, bludgeoning need.

"*Saved!*" His mother's voice carried back imperatively. "*Savior! Saved! Saved!*"

He tried to tell them that he could neither heal nor save, but before he could open his mouth to make the denial, the first had laid hands on him and was shaking him.

The shaking was real enough. It was Weizak's hand on his arm. Bright orange light filled the car, turning the interior as bright as day—it was nightmare light, turning Sam's kind face into the face of a hobgoblin. For a moment he thought the nightmare was still going on and then he saw the light was coming from parking-lot lamps. They had changed those, too, apparently, while he was in his coma. From hard white to a weird orange that lay on the skin like paint.

"Where are we?" he asked thickly.

"The hospital," Sam said. "Cumberland General."

"Oh. All right."

He sat up. The dream seemed to slide off him in fragments, still littering the floor of his mind like something broken and not yet swept up.

"Are you ready to go in?"

"Yes," Johnny said.

They crossed the parking lot amid the soft creak of summer crickets in the woods. Fireflies stitched through the darkness. The image of his mother was very much on him—but not so much that he was unable to enjoy the soft and fragrant smell of the night and the feel of the faint breeze against his skin. There was time to enjoy the health of the night, and the feeling of health coming inside him. In the context of why he was here, the thought seemed almost obscene—but only almost. And it wouldn't go away.

◆ 2 ◆

Herb came down the hallway to meet them, and Johnny saw that his father was wearing old pants, shoes with no socks, and his pajama shirt. It told Johnny a lot about the suddenness with which it had come. It told him more than he wanted to know.

"Son," he said. He looked smaller, somehow. He tried to say more and couldn't. Johnny hugged him and Herb burst into tears. He sobbed against Johnny's shirt.

"Daddy," he said. "That's all right, Daddy, that's all right."

His father put his arms on Johnny's shoulders and wept. Weizak turned away and began to inspect the pictures on the walls, indifferent water colors by local artists.

Herb began to recover himself. He swiped his arm across his eyes and said, "Look at me, still in my pj top. I had time to change before the ambulance came. I guess I never thought of it. Must be getting senile."

"No, you're not."

"Well." He shrugged. "Your doctor friend brought you down? That was nice of you, Dr. Weizak."

Sam shrugged. "It was nothing."

Johnny and his father walked toward the small waiting room and sat down. "Daddy, is she . . ."

"She's sinking," Herb said. He seemed calmer now. "Conscious, but sinking. She's been asking for you, Johnny. I think she's been holding on for you."

"My fault," Johnny said. "All this is my f . . ."

The pain in his ear startled him, and he stared at his father, astonished. Herb had seized his ear and twisted it firmly. So much for the role reversal of having his father cry in his arms. The old twist-the-ear trick had been a punishment Herb had reserved for the gravest of errors. Johnny couldn't remember having his ear twisted since he was thirteen, and had gotten fooling around with their old Rambler. He had inadvertently pushed in the clutch and the old car had rumbled silently downhill to crash into their back shed.

"Don't you ever say that," Herb said.

"*Jeez Dad!*"

Herb let go, a little smile lurking just below the corners of his mouth. "Forgot all about the old twist-the-ear, huh? Probably thought I had, too. No such luck, Johnny."

Johnny stared at his father, still dumbfounded.

"Don't you *ever* blame yourself."

"But she was watching that damned . . ."

"News, yes. She was ecstatic, she was thrilled . . . then she was on the floor, her poor old mouth opening and closing like she was a fish out of water." Herb leaned closer to his son. "The doctor won't come right out and tell me, but he asked me about 'heroic measures.' I told him none of that stuff. She committed her own kind of sin, Johnny. She presumed to know the mind of God. So don't you ever blame yourself for her mistake." Fresh tears glinted in his eyes. His voice roughened. "God knows I spent my life loving her and it got hard in the late going. Maybe this is just the best thing."

"Can I see her?"

"Yes, she's at the end of the hall, Room 35. They're expecting you, and so is she. Just one thing, Johnny. Agree with anything and everything she might say. Don't . . . let her die thinking it was all for nothing."

"No." He paused. "Are you coming with me?"

"Not now. Maybe later."

Johnny nodded and walked up the hall. The lights were turned down low for the nighttime. The brief moment in the soft, kind summer night seemed far away now, but his nightmare in the car seemed very close.

Room 35. VERA HELEN SMITH, the little card on the door read. Had he known her middle name was Helen? It seemed he must have, although he couldn't remember. But he could remember other things: her bringing him an ice-cream bar wrapped in her handkerchief one bright summer day at Old Orchard Beach, smiling and gay. He and his mother and father playing rummy for matches—later, after the religion business began to deepen its hold on her, she wouldn't have cards in the house, not even to play cribbage with. He remembered the day the bee had stung him and he ran to her, bawling his head off, and she had kissed the swelling and pulled out the stinger with tweezers and then had wrapped the wound in a strip of cloth that had been dipped in baking soda.

He pushed the door open and went in. She was a vague hump in the bed and Johnny thought, *That's what I looked like.* A nurse was taking her pulse; she turned when the door opened and the dim hall lights flashed on her spectacles.

"Are you Mrs. Smith's son?"

"Yes."

"*Johnny?*" Her voice rose from the hump in the bed, dry and hollow, rattling with death as a few pebbles will rattle in an empty gourd. The voice—God help him—made his skin crawl. He moved closer. Her face was twisted into a snarling mask on the left-hand side. The hand on the counterpane was a claw. *Stroke,* he thought. *What the old people call a shock. Yes. That's better. That's what she looks like. Like she's had a bad shock.*

"Is that you, John?"

"It's me, Ma."

"Johnny? Is that you?"

"Yes, Ma."

He came closer yet, and forced himself to take the bony claw.

"I want my Johnny," she said querulously.

The nurse shot him a pitying look, and he found himself wanting to smash his fist through it.

"Would you leave us alone?" he asked.

"I really shouldn't while . . ."

"Come on, she's my mother and I want some time alone with her," Johnny said. "What about it?"

"Well . . ."

"Bring me my juice, Dad!" his mother cried hoarsely. "Feel like I could drink a quart!"

"Would you get *out* of here?" he cried at the nurse. He was filled with a terrible sorrow of which he could not even find the focus. It seemed like a whirlpool going down into darkness.

The nurse left.

"Ma," he said, sitting beside her. That weird feeling of doubled time, of reversal, would not leave him. How many times had she sat over his bed like this, perhaps holding his dry hand and talking to him? He recalled the timeless period when the room had seemed so close to him—seen through a gauzy placental membrane, his mother's face bending over him, thundering senseless sounds slowly into his upturned face.

"Ma," he said again, and kissed the hook that had replaced her hand.

"Gimme those nails, I can do that," she said. Her left eye seemed frozen in its orbit; the other rolled wildly. It was the eye of a gutshot horse. "I want Johnny."

"Ma, I'm here."

"*John-ny! John-ny! JOHN-NY!*"

"*Ma,*" he said, afraid the nurse would come back.

"You . . ." She broke off and her head turned toward him a little. "Bend over here where I can see," she whispered.

He did as she asked.

"You came," she said. "Thank you. Thank you." Tears began to ooze from the good eye. The bad one, the one on the side of her face that had been frozen by the shock, stared indifferently upward.

"Sure I came."

"I saw you," she whispered. "What a power God has given you, Johnny! Didn't I tell you? Didn't I say it was so?"

"Yes, you did."

"He has a job for you," she said. "Don't run from him, Johnny. Don't hide away in a cave like Elijah or make him send a big fish to swallow you up. Don't do that, John."

"No. I won't." He held her claw-hand. His head throbbed.

"Not the potter but the potter's clay, John. Remember."

"All right."

"*Remember that!*" she said stridently, and he thought, *She's going back into nonsense land.* But she didn't; at least she went no further into nonsense land than she had been since he came out of his coma.

"Heed the still, small voice when it comes," she said.

"Yes, Ma. I will."

Her head turned a tiny bit on the pillow, and—was she *smiling?*

"You think I'm crazy, I guess." She twisted her head a little more, so she could look directly at him. "But that doesn't matter. You'll know the voice when it comes. It'll tell you what to do. It told Jeremiah and Daniel and Amos and Abraham. It'll come to you. It'll tell you. And when it does, Johnny . . . *do your duty.*"

"Okay, Ma."

"What a power," she murmured. Her voice was growing furry and indistinct. "What a power God has given you . . . I knew . . . I always knew . . ." Her voice trailed off. The good eye closed. The other stared blankly forward.

Johnny sat with her another five minutes, then got up to leave. His hand was on the doorknob and he was easing the door open when her dry, rattling voice came again, chilling him with its implacable, positive command.

"*Do your duty, John.*"

"Yes, Ma."

It was the last time he ever spoke to her. She died at five minutes past eight on the morning of August 20. Somewhere north of them, Walt and Sarah Hazlett were having a discussion about Johnny that was almost an argument, and somewhere south of them, Greg Stillson was cutting himself some prime asshole.

Chapter 13

◆ 1 ◆

"You don't understand," Greg Stillson said in a voice of utter, reasonable patience to the kid sitting in the lounge at the back of the Ridgeway police station. The kid, shirtless, was tilted back in a padded folding chair and drinking a bottle of Pepsi. He was smiling indulgently at Greg Stillson, not understanding that twice was all Greg Stillson ever repeated himself, understanding that there was one prime asshole in the room, but not yet understanding who it was.

That realization would have to be brought home to him.

Forcibly, if necessary.

Outside, the late August morning was bright and warm. Birds sang in the trees. And Greg felt his destiny was closer than ever. That was why he would be careful with this prime asshole. This was no long-haired bike-freak with a bad case of bowlegs and B.O.; this kid was a college boy, his hair was moderately long but squeaky clean, and he was George Harvey's nephew. Not that George cared for him much (George had fought his way across Germany in 1945, and he had two words for these long-haired freaks, and those two words were not Happy Birthday), but he was blood. And George was a man to be reckoned with on the town council. *See what you can do with him,* George had told Greg when Greg informed him that Chief Wiggins had arrested his sister's kid. But his eyes said, *Don't hurt him. He's blood.*

The kid was looking at Greg with lazy contempt. "I understand," he said. "Your Deputy Dawg took my shirt and I want it back. And *you* better understand something. If I don't get it back, I'm going to have the American Civil Liberties Union down on your red neck."

Greg got up, went to the steel-gray file cabinet opposite the soda machine, pulled out his keyring, selected a key, and opened the cabinet. From atop a pile of accident and traffic forms, he took a red T-shirt. He spread it open so the legend on it was clear: BABY LET'S FUCK.

"You were wearing this," Greg said in that same mild voice. "On the street."

The kid rocked on the back legs of his chair and swigged some more Pepsi. The little indulgent smile playing around his mouth—almost a sneer—did not change. "That's right," he said. "And I want it back. It's my property."

Greg's head began to ache. This smartass didn't realize how easy it would be. The room was soundproofed, and there had been times when that soundproofing had muffled screams. No—he didn't realize. He didn't *understand*.

But keep your hand on it. Don't go overboard. Don't upset the applecart.

Easy to think. Usually easy to do. But sometimes, his temper—his temper got out of hand.

Greg reached into his pocket and pulled out his Bic lighter.

"So you just go tell your gestapo chief and my fascist uncle that the First Amendment . . ." He paused, eyes widening a little. "What are you . . . ? Hey! *Hey!*"

Taking no notice and at least outwardly calm, Greg struck a light. The Bic's gas flame vroomed upward, and Greg lit the kid's T-shirt on fire. It burned quite well, actually.

The front legs of the kid's chair came down with a bang and he leaped toward Greg with his bottle of Pepsi still in his hand. The self-satisfied little smirk was gone, replaced with a look of wide-eyed shock and surprise—and the anger of a spoiled brat who has had everything his own way for too long.

No one ever called him *runt,* Greg Stillson thought, and his headache worsened. Oh, he was going to have to be careful.

"Gimme that!" the kid shouted. Greg was holding the shirt out, pinched together in two fingers at the neck, ready to drop it when it got too hot. "Gimme that, you asshole! That's mine! That's . . ."

Greg planted his hand in the middle of the kid's bare chest and shoved him as hard as he could—which was hard indeed. The kid went flying across the room, the anger dissolving into total shock, and—at last—what Greg needed to see: fear.

He dropped the shirt on the tile floor, picked up the kid's Pepsi, and poured what was left in the bottle onto the smouldering T-shirt. It hissed balefully.

The kid was getting up slowly, his back pressed against the

wall. Greg caught his eyes with his own. The kid's eyes were brown and very, very wide.

"We're going to reach an understanding," Greg said, and the words seemed distant to him, behind the sick thud in his head. "We're going to have a little seminar right here in this back room about just who's the asshole. You got my meaning? We're gonna reach some conclusions. Isn't that what you college boys like to do? Reach conclusions?"

The kid drew breath in hitches. He wet his lips, seemed about to speak, and then yelled: *"Help!"*

"Yeah, you need help, all right," Greg said. "I'm going to give you some, too."

"You're crazy," George Harvey's nephew said, and then yelled again, louder: "HELP!"

"I may be," Greg said. "Sure. But what we got to find out, Sonny, is who the prime asshole is. See what I mean?"

He looked down at the Pepsi bottle in his hand, and suddenly he swung it savagely against the corner of the steel cabinet. It shattered, and when the kid saw the scatter of glass on the floor and the jagged neck in Greg's hand pointing toward him, he screamed. The crotch of his jeans, faded almost white, suddenly darkened. His face went the color of old parchment. And as Greg walked toward him, gritting glass under the workboots he wore summer and winter, he cringed against the wall.

"When I go out on the street, I wear a white shirt," Greg said. He was grinning, showing white teeth. "Sometimes a tie. When you go out on the street, you wear some rag with a filthy saying on it. So who's the asshole, kiddo?"

George Harvey's nephew whined something. His bulging eyes never left the spears of glass jutting from the bottle neck in Greg's hand.

"I'm standing here high and dry," Greg said, coming a little closer, "and you got piss running down both legs into your shoes. So who's the asshole?"

He began to jab the bottle neck lightly toward the kid's bare and sweaty midriff, and George Harvey's nephew began to cry. This was the sort of kid that was tearing the country in two, Greg thought. The thick wine of fury buzzed and coursed in his head. Stinking yellow lowbelly crybaby assholes like this.

Ah, but don't hurt him—don't kick over the applecart—

"I sound like a human being," Greg said, "and you sound like a pig in a grease-pit, boy. So who's the asshole?"

He jabbed with the bottle again; one of the jagged glass points dimpled the kid's skin just below the right nipple and brought a tiny bead of blood. The kid howled.

"I'm talking to you," Greg said. "You better answer up, same as you'd answer up one of your professors. Who's the asshole?"

The kid sniveled but made no coherent sound.

"You answer up if you want to pass this exam," Greg said. "I'll let your guts loose all over this floor, boy." And in that instant, he meant it. He couldn't look directly at this welling drop of blood; it would send him crazy if he did, George Harvey's nephew or not. "Who's the asshole?"

"Me," the kid said, and began to sob like a small child afraid of the bogeyman, the Allamagoosalum that waits behind the closet door in the dead hours of the night.

Greg smiled. The headache thumped and flared. "Well, that's pretty good, you know. That's a start. But it's not quite good enough. I want you to say, 'I'm an asshole.' "

"I'm an asshole," the kid said, still sobbing. Snot flowed from his nose and hung there in a runner. He wiped it away with the back of his hand.

"Now I want you to say, 'I'm a prime asshole.' "

"I . . . I'm a prime asshole."

"Now you just say one more thing and maybe we can be done here. You say, 'Thank you for burning up that dirty shirt, Mayor Stillson.' "

The kid was eager now. The kid saw his way clear. "Thanks for burning up that dirty shirt."

In a flash, Greg ran one of the jagged points from left to right across the kid's soft belly, bringing a line of blood. He barely broke the skin, but the kid howled as if all the devils of hell were behind him.

"You forgot to say 'Mayor Stillson,' " Greg said, and just like that it broke. The headache gave one more massive beat right between his eyes and was gone. He looked down stupidly at the bottle neck in his hand and could barely remember how it had gotten there. Stupid damn thing. He had almost thrown everything away over one numbnuts kid.

"Mayor Stillson!" The kid was screaming. His terror was perfect and complete. "Mayor Stillson! Mayor Stillson! Mayor Still . . ."

"That's good," Greg said.

". . . son! Mayor Stillson! Mayor Stillson! Mayor . . ."

Greg whacked him hard across the face, and the kid rapped his head on the wall. He fell silent, his eyes wide and blank.

Greg stepped very close to him. He reached out. He closed one hand around each of the kid's ears. He pulled the kid's face forward until their noses were touching. Their eyes were less than half an inch apart.

"Now, your uncle is a power in this town," he said softly, holding the kid's ears like handles. The kid's eyes were huge and brown and swimming. "I'm a power too—coming to be one—but I ain't no George Harvey. He was born here, raised here, everything. And if you was to tell your uncle what went on in here, he might take a notion to finish me in Ridgeway."

The kid's lips were twitching in a nearly soundless blubber. Greg shook the boy's head slowly back and forth by the ears, banging their noses together.

"He might not . . . he was pretty damn mad about that shirt. But he might. Blood ties are strong ties. So you think about this, son. If you was to tell your uncle what went on here and your uncle squeezed me out, I guess I would come along and kill you. Do you believe that?"

"Yeah," the kid whispered. His cheeks were wet, gleaming.

" 'Yes sir, Mayor Stillson.' "

"Yessir, Mayor Stillson."

Greg let go of his ears. "Yeah," he said. "I'd kill you, but first I'd tell anybody that'd listen about how you pissed yourself and stood there crying with snot running out of your nose."

He turned and walked away quickly, as if the kid smelled bad, and went to the cabinet again. He got a box of Band-Aids from one of the shelves and tossed them across to the kid, who flinched back and fumbled them. He hastened to pick them up off the floor, as if Stillson might attack him again for missing.

Greg pointed. "Bathroom over there. You clean yourself up. I'm gonna leave you a Ridgeway PAL sweatshirt. I want it mailed back, clean, no bloodstains. You understand?"

"Yes," the kid whispered.

"SIR!" Stillson screamed at him. "*SIR! SIR! SIR! Can't you remember that?*"

"Sir," the kid moaned. "Yessir, yessir."

"They don't teach you kids respect for *nothing*," Greg said. "Not for *nothing*."

The headache was trying to come back. He took several deep breaths and quelled it—but his stomach felt miserably upset. "Okay, that's the end. I just want to offer you one good piece of advice. Don't you make the mistake of getting back to your damn college this fall or whenever and start thinking this was some way it wasn't. Don't you try to kid yourself about Greg Stillson. Best forgotten, kid. By you, me, and George. Working this around in your mind until you think you could have another swing at it would be the worst mistake of your life. Maybe the last."

With that Greg left, taking one last contemptuous look at the kid standing there, his chest and belly caked with a few minor smears of dried blood, his eyes wide, his lips trembling. He looked like an overgrown ten-year-old who has struck out in the Little League playoffs.

Greg made a mental bet with himself that he would never see or hear from this particular kid again, and it was a bet he won. Later that week, George Harvey stopped by the barbershop where Greg was getting a shave and thanked him for "talking some sense" into his nephew. "You're good with these kids, Greg," he said. "I dunno . . . they seem to respect you."

Greg told him not to mention it.

◆ 2 ◆

While Greg Stillson was burning a shirt with an obscene saying on it in New Hampshire, Walt and Sarah Hazlett were having a late breakfast in Bangor, Maine. Walt had the paper.

He put his coffee cup down with a clink and said, "Your old boyfriend made the paper, Sarah."

Sarah was feeding Denny. She was in her bathrobe, her hair something of a mess, her eyes still only about a quarter open. Eighty percent of her mind was still asleep. There had been a party last night. The guest of honor had been Harrison Fisher, who had been New Hampshire's third district congressman since dinosaurs walked the earth, and a sure candidate for reelection next year. It had been politic for her and Walt to go. *Politic.* That was a word that Walt used a lot lately. He had had lots more to drink than she had, and this morning he was dressed and apparently chipper while she felt buried in a pile of sludge. It wasn't fair.

"Blue!" Denny remarked, and spat back a mouthful of mixed fruit.

"That's not nice," Sarah said to Denny. To Walt: "Are you talking about Johnny Smith?"

"The one and only."

She got up and came around to Walt's side of the table. "He's all right, isn't he?"

"Feeling good and kicking up dickens by the sound of this," Walt said dryly.

She had a hazy idea that it might be related to what had happened to her when she went to see Johnny, but the size of the headline shocked her: REAWAKENED COMA PATIENT DEMONSTRATES PSYCHIC ABILITY AT DRAMATIC NEWS CONFERENCE. The story was under David Bright's by-line. The accompanying photo showed Johnny, still looking thin and, in the unsparing glare of the flash, pitifully confused, standing over the sprawled body of a man the caption identified as Roger Dussault, a reporter for the Lewiston paper. *Reporter Faints after Revelation,* the caption read.

Sarah sank down into the chair next to Walt and began to read the article. This did not please Denny, who began to pound on the tray of his highchair for his morning egg.

"I believe you're being summoned," Walt said.

"Would you feed him, honey? He eats better for you anyway." *Story Continued Page 9, Col. 3.* She folded the paper open to page nine.

"Flattery will get you everywhere," Walt said agreeably. He slipped off his sports coat and put on her apron. "Here it comes, guy," he said, and began feeding Denny his egg.

When she had finished the story, Sarah went back and read it again. Her eyes were drawn again and again to the picture, to Johnny's confused, horror-struck face. The people loosely grouped around the prone Dussault were looking at Johnny with an expression close to fear. She could understand that. She remembered kissing him, and the strange, preoccupied look that had slipped over his face. And when he told her where to find the lost wedding ring, *she* had been afraid.

But Sarah, what you were afraid of wasn't quite the same thing, was it?

"Just a little more, big boy," Walt was saying, as if from a thousand miles away. Sarah looked up at them, sitting together in a bar of mote-dusted sunlight, her apron flapping between Walt's knees, and she was suddenly afraid again. She saw the ring sinking to the bottom of the toilet bowl, turning over and over. She heard the small clink as it struck the porcelain. She thought of Halloween masks, of the kid saying, *I love to see this guy take a beatin*. She thought of promises made and never kept, and her eyes went to this thin newsprint face, looking out at her with such haggard, wretched surprise.

". . . gimmick, anyway," Walt said, hanging up her apron. He had gotten Denny to eat the egg, every bit of it, and now their son and heir was sucking contentedly away at a juice-bottle.

"Huh?" Sarah looked up as he came over to her.

"I said that for a man who must have almost half a million dollars' worth of hospital bills outstanding, it's a helluva good gimmick."

"What are you *talking* about? What do you mean, *gimmick?*"

"Sure," he said, apparently missing her anger. "He could make seven, maybe ten thousand dollars doing a book about the accident and the coma. But if he came out of the coma psychic, the sky's the limit."

"That's one *hell* of an allegation!" Sarah said, and her voice was thin with fury.

He turned to her, his expression first one of surprise and then of understanding. The understanding look made her angrier than ever. If she had a nickel for every time Walt Hazlett had thought he understood her, they could fly first-class to Jamaica.

"Look, I'm sorry I brought it up," he said.

"Johnny would no more lie than the Pope would . . . would . . . you know."

He bellowed laughter, and in that moment she nearly picked up his own coffee cup and threw it at him. Instead, she locked her hands together tightly under the table and squeezed them. Denny goggled at his father and then burst into his own peal of laughter.

"Honey," Walt said. "I have nothing against him, I have nothing against what he's doing. In fact, I respect him for it. If that fat old mossback Fisher can go from a broke lawyer to a millionaire during fifteen years in the House of Representatives, then this guy should have a perfect right to pick up as much as he can playing psychic . . ."

"Johnny doesn't lie," she repeated tonelessly.

"It's a gimmick for the blue-rinse brigade who read the

weekly tabloids and belong to the Universe Book Club," he said cheerily. "Although I will admit that a little second sight would come in handy during jury selection in this damn Timmons trial."

"Johnny Smith doesn't lie," she repeated, and heard him saying: *It slipped off your finger. You were putting his shaving stuff into one of those side pockets and it just slipped off . . . you go up in the attic and look, Sarah. You'll see.* But she couldn't tell Walt that. Walt didn't know she had been to see Johnny.

Nothing wrong in going to see him, her mind offered uneasily.

No, but how would he react to the news that she had thrown her original wedding ring into the toilet and flushed it away? He might not understand the sudden twitch of fear that had made her do it—the same fear she saw mirrored on those other newsprint faces, and, to some degree, on Johnny's own. No, Walt might not understand that at all. After all, throwing your wedding ring into the toilet and then pushing the flush did suggest a certain vulgar symbolism.

"All right," Walt was saying, "he doesn't lie. But I just don't believe . . ."

Sarah said softly, "Look at the people behind him, Walt. Look at their faces. *They* believe."

Walt gave them a cursory glance. "Sure, the way a kid believes in a magician as long as the trick is ongoing."

"You think this fellow Dussault was a, what-do-you-call-it, a shill? According to the article, he and Johnny had never met before."

"That's the only way the illusion will work, Sarah," Walt said patiently. "It doesn't do a magician any good to pull a bunny out of a rabbit hutch, only out of a hat. Either Johnny Smith knew something or he made a terribly good guess based on this guy Dussault's behavior at the time. But I repeat, I respect him for it. He got a lot of mileage out of it. If it turns him a buck, more power to him."

In that moment she hated him, loathed him, this good man she had married. There was really nothing so terrible on the reverse side of his goodness, his steadiness, his mild good humor—just the belief, apparently grounded in the bedrock of his soul, that everybody was looking out for number one, each with his or her own little racket. This morning he could call Harrison Fisher a fat old mossback; last night he had been bellowing with laughter at Fisher's stories about Greg Stillson, the funny mayor of some-town-or-other and who might just be crazy enough to run as an independent in the House race next year.

No, in the world of Walt Hazlett, no one had psychic powers and there were no heroes and the doctrine of *we-have-to-change-the-system-from-within* was all-powerful. He was a good man, a steady man, he loved her and Denny, but suddenly her soul cried out for Johnny and the five years together of which they had been robbed. Or the lifetime together. A child with darker hair.

"You better get going, babe," she said quietly. "They'll have your guy Timmons in stocks and bonds, or whatever they are."

"Sure." He smiled at her, the summation done, session adjourned. "Still friends?"

"Still friends." *But he knew where the ring was. He* knew.

Walt kissed her, his right hand resting lightly on the back of her neck. He always had the same thing for breakfast, he always kissed her the same way, some day they were going to Washington, and no one was psychic.

Five minutes later he was gone, backing their little red Pinto out onto Pond Street, giving his usual brief toot on the horn, and putting away. She was left alone with Denny, who was in the process of strangling himself while he tried to wiggle under his highchair tray.

"You're going at that all wrong, Sluggo," Sarah said, crossing the kitchen and unlatching the tray.

"Blue!" Denny said, disgusted with the whole thing.

Speedy Tomato, their tomcat, sauntered into the kitchen at his usual slow, hipshot juvenile delinquent's stride, and Denny grabbed him, making little chuckling noises. Speedy laid his ears back and looked resigned.

Sarah smiled a little and cleared the table. Inertia. A body at rest tends to remain at rest, and she was at rest. Never mind Walt's darker side; she had her own. She had no intention of doing more than sending Johnny a card at Christmas. It was better, safer, that way—because a body in motion tends to keep moving. Her life here was good. She had survived Dan, she had survived Johnny, who had been so unfairly taken from her (but so much in this world was unfair), she had come through her own personal rapids to this smooth water, and here she would stay. This sunshiny kitchen was not a bad place. Best to forget county fairs, Wheels of Fortune, and Johnny Smith's face.

As she ran water into the sink to do the dishes she turned

on the radio and caught the beginning of the news. The first item made her freeze with a just-washed plate in one hand, her eyes looking out over their small backyard in startled contemplation. Johnny's mother had had a stroke while watching a TV report on her son's press conference. She had died this morning, not an hour ago.

Sarah dried her hands, snapped off the radio, and pried Speedy Tomato out of Denny's hands. She carried her boy into the living room and popped him into his playpen. Denny protested this indignity with loud, lusty howls of which she took no notice. She went to the telephone and called the EMMC. A switchboard operator who sounded tired of repeating the same piece of intelligence over and over again told her that John Smith had discharged himself the night before, slightly before midnight.

She hung up the phone and sat down in a chair. Denny continued to cry from his playpen. Water ran into the kitchen sink. After a while she got up, went into the kitchen, and turned it off.

Chapter 14

◆ 1 ◆

The man from *Inside View* showed up on October 16, not long after Johnny had walked up to get the mail.

His father's house was set well back from the road; their graveled driveway was nearly a quarter of a mile long, running through a heavy stand of second-growth spruce and pine. Johnny did the total round trip every day. At first he had returned to the porch trembling with exhaustion, his legs on fire, his limp so pronounced that he was really lurching along. But now, a month and a half after the first time (when the half a mile had taken him an hour to do), the walk had become one of his day's pleasures, something to look forward to. Not the mail, but the walk.

He had begun splitting wood for the coming winter, a chore Herb had been planning to hire out since he himself had landed a contract to do some inside work on a new housing project in Libertyville. "You know when old age has started lookin over your shoulder, John," he had said with a smile. "It's when you start lookin for inside work as soon as fall rolls around."

Johnny climbed the porch and sat down in the wicker chair beside the glider, uttering a small sound of relief. He propped his right foot on the porch railing, and with a grimace of pain, used his hands to lift his left leg over it. That done, he began to open his mail.

It had tapered off a lot just lately. During the first week he had been back here in Pownal, there had sometimes been as many as two dozen letters and eight or nine packages a day, most of them forwarded through the EMMC, a few of them sent to General Delivery, Pownal (and assorted variant spellings: Pownell, Poenul, and, in one memorable case, Poonuts).

Most of them were from disassociated people who seemed to be drifting through life in search of any rudder. There were children who wanted his autograph, women who wanted to sleep with him, both men and women seeking advice to the lovelorn. Some sent lucky charms. Some sent horoscopes. A great many of the letters were religious in nature, and in these badly spelled missives, usually written in a large and careful handwriting but one step removed from the scrawl of a bright first-grader, he seemed to feel the ghost of his mother.

He was a prophet, these letters assured him, come to lead the weary and disillusioned American people out of the wilderness. He was a sign that the Last Times were at hand. To this date, October 16, he had received eight copies of Hal Lindsey's *The Late Great Planet Earth*—his mother surely would have approved of that one. He was urged to proclaim the divinity of Christ and put a stop to the loose morals of youth.

These letters were balanced off by the negative contingent, which was smaller but just as vocal—if usually anonymous. One correspondent, writing in grubby pencil on a sheet of yellow legal paper proclaimed him the Antichrist and urged him to commit suicide. Four or five of the letter writers had inquired about how it felt to murder your own mother. A great many wrote to accuse him of perpetrating a hoax. One wit wrote, "PRECOGNITION, TELEPATHY, BULLSHIT! EAT MY DONG, YOU EXTRASENSORY TURKEY!"

And then they sent *things*. That was the worst of it.

Every day on his way home from work, Herb would stop at the Pownal post office and pick up the packages that were too big to fit in their mailbox. The notes accompanying the things were all essentially the same; a lowgrade scream. *Tell me, tell me, tell me.*

This scarf belonged to my brother, who disappeared on a fishing trip in the Allagash in 1969. I feel very strongly that he is still alive. Tell me where he is.

This lipstick came from my wife's dressing table. I think she's having an affair, but I'm not sure. Tell me if she is.

This is my son's ID bracelet. He never comes home after school anymore, he stays out until all hours, I'm worried sick. Tell me what he's doing.

A woman in North Carolina—God knew how she had found out about him; the press conference in August had not made the national media—sent a charred piece of wood. Her house had burned down, her letter explained, and her husband and two of her five children had died in the blaze. The Charlotte fire department said it was faulty wiring, but she simply couldn't accept that. It had to be arson. She wanted Johnny to feel the enclosed blackened relic and tell her who had done it, so the monster would spend the rest of his life rotting in prison.

Johnny answered none of the letters and returned all the objects (even the charcoaled hunk of wood) at his cost and with no comment. He *did* touch some of them. Most, like the charred piece of wallboard from the grief-stricken woman in Charlotte, told him nothing at all. But when he touched a few of them, disquieting images came, like waking dreams. In most cases there was barely a trace; a picture would form and fade in seconds, leaving him with nothing concrete at all, only a feeling. But one of them . . .

It had been the woman who sent the scarf in hopes of finding out what had happened to her brother. It was a white knitted scarf, no different from a million others. But as he handled it, the reality of his father's house had suddenly been gone, and the sound of the television in the next room rose and flattened, rose and flattened, until it was the sound of drowsing summer insects and the faraway babble of water.

Woods smells in his nostrils. Green shafts of sunlight falling through great old trees. The ground had been soggy for the last three hours or so, squelchy, almost swamplike. He was scared, plenty scared, but he had kept his head. If you were lost in the big north country and panicked, they might as well carve your headstone. He had kept pushing south. It had been two days since he had gotten separated from Stiv and Rocky and Logan. They had been camping near

(but that wouldn't come, it was in the dead zone)

some stream, trout-fishing, and it had been his own damn fault; he had been pretty damn drunk.

Now he could see his pack leaning against the edge of an old and moss-grown blowdown, white deadwood poking through the green here and there like bones, he could see his pack, yes, but he couldn't reach it because he had walked a few yards away to take a leak and he had walked into a really squelchy place, mud almost to the tops of his L.L. Bean's boots, and he tried to back out, find a dryer place to do his business, but he couldn't get out. He couldn't get out because it wasn't mud at all. It was . . . something else.

He stood there, looking around fruitlessly for something to grab onto, almost laughing at the idiocy of having walked right into a patch of quicksand while looking for a place to take a piss.

He stood there, at first positive that it must be a shallow patch of quicksand, at the very worst over his boot-tops, another tale to tell when he was found.

He stood there, and real panic did not begin to set in until the quicksand oozed implacably over his knees. He began to struggle then, forgetting that if you got your stupid self into quicksand you were supposed to remain very still. In no time at all the quicksand was up to his waist and now it was chest-high, sucking at him like great brown lips, constricting his breathing; he began to scream and no one came, nothing came except for a fat brown squirrel that picked its way down the side of the mossy deadfall and perched on his pack and watched him with his bright, black eyes.

Now it was up to his neck, the rich, brown smell of it in his nose and his screams became thin and gasping as the quicksand implacably pressed the breath out of him. Birds flew swooping and cheeping and scolding, and green shafts of sunlight like tarnished copper fell through the trees, and the quicksand rose over his chin. Alone, he was going to die alone, and he opened his mouth to scream one last time and there was no scream because the quicksand flowed into his mouth, it flowed over his tongue, it flowed between his teeth in thin ribbons, he was *swallowing* quicksand and the scream was never uttered—

Johnny had come out of that in a cold sweat, his flesh marbled into goosebumps, the scarf wrapped tightly between his hands, his breath coming in short, strangled gasps. He had thrown the scarf on the floor where it lay like a twisted white snake. He would not touch it again. His father had put it in a return envelope and sent it back.

But now, mercifully, the mail was beginning to taper off. The crazies had discovered some fresher object for their public and private obsessions. Newsmen no longer called for interviews, partly because the phone number had been changed and unlisted, partly because the story was old hat.

Roger Dussault had written a long and angry piece for his paper, of which he was the feature editor. He proclaimed the whole thing a cruel and tasteless hoax. Johnny had undoubtedly boned up on incidents from the pasts of several reporters who were likely to attend the press conference, just in case. Yes, he admitted, his sister Anne's nickname had been Terry. She had died fairly young, and amphetamines might have been a contributing cause. But all of that was accessible information to anyone who wanted to dig it up. He made it all seem quite logical. The article did not explain how Johnny, who had not been out of the hospital, could have come by this "accessible information," but that was a point most readers seemed to have overlooked. Johnny could not have cared less. The incident was closed, and he had no intention of creating new ones. What good could it possibly do to write the lady who had sent the scarf and tell her that her brother had drowned, screaming, in quicksand because he had gone the wrong way while looking for a place to take a piss? Would it ease her mind or help her live her life any better?

Today's mail was a mere six letters. A power bill. A card from Herb's cousin out in Oklahoma. A lady who had sent Johnny a crucifix with MADE IN TAIWAN stamped on Christ's feet in tiny gold letters. There was a brief note from Sam Weizak. And a small envelope with a return address that made him blink and sit up straighter. *S. Hazlett, 12 Pond Street, Bangor.*

Sarah. He tore it open.

He had received a sympathy card from her two days after the funeral services for his mother. Written on the back of it in her cool, backslanting hand had been: "Johnny—I'm so sorry that this has happened. I heard on the radio that your mom had passed away—in some ways that seemed the most unfair thing of all, that your private grief should have been made a thing of public knowledge. You may not remember, but we talked a little about your mom the night of your accident. I asked you what she'd do if you brought home a lapsed Catholic and you said she would smile and welcome me in and slip me a few tracts. I could see your love for her in the way you smiled. I know from your father that she had changed, but much of the change was because she loved you so much and just couldn't accept what had happened. And in the end I guess her faith was rewarded. Please accept my warm sympathy, and if there's anything I can do, now or later on, please count on your friend—*Sarah*."

That was one note he had answered, thanking her for both the card and the thought. He had written it carefully, afraid that he might betray himself and say the wrong thing. She was a married woman now, that was beyond his control or ability to change. But he *did* remember their conversation about his mother—and so many other things about that night. Her note had summoned up the whole evening, and he answered in a bittersweet mood that was more bitter than sweet. He still loved Sarah Bracknell, and he had to remind himself constantly that she was gone, replaced by another woman who was five years older and the mother of a small boy.

Now he pulled a single sheet of stationery out of the envelope and scanned it quickly. She and her boy were headed down to Kennebunk to spend a week with Sarah's freshman and sophomore roommate, a girl named Stephanie Constantine now, Stephanie Carsleigh then. She said that Johnny might remember her, but Johnny didn't. Anyway, Walt was stuck in Washington for three weeks on combined firm and Republican party business, and Sarah thought she might take one afternoon and come by Pownal to see Johnny and Herb, if it was no trouble.

"You can reach me at Steph's number, 814-6219, any time between Oct. 17th and the 23rd. Of course, if it would make you feel uncomfortable in any way, just call me and say so, either up here or down there in K'bunk. I'll understand. Much love to both of you—*Sarah*."

Holding the letter in one hand, Johnny looked across the yard and into the woods, which had gone russet and gold, seemingly just in the last week. The leaves would be falling soon, and then it would be time for winter.

Much love to both of you—Sarah. He ran his thumb across the words thoughtfully. It would be better not to call, nor to write, not to do anything, he thought. She would get the message. Like the woman who mailed the scarf—what possible good could it do? Why kick a sleeping dog? Sarah might be able to use that phrase, much love, blithely, but he could not. He wasn't over the hurt of the past. For him, time had been crudely folded, stapled, and mutilated. In the progression of his own interior time, she had been his girl only six months ago. He could accept the coma and the loss of time in an intellectual way, but his emotions stubbornly resisted. Answering her condolence note had been difficult, but with a note it was always possible to crumple the thing up and start again if it began to go in directions it shouldn't go, if it began to overstep the bounds of friendship, which was all they were now allowed to share. If he saw her, he might do or say something stupid. Better not to call. Better just to let it sink.

But he would call, he thought. Call and invite her over.

Troubled, he slipped the note back into the envelope.

The sun caught on bright chrome, twinkled there, and tossed an arrow of light back into his eyes. A Ford sedan was crunching its way down the driveway. Johnny squinted and tried to make out if it was a familiar car. Company out here was rare. There had been lots of mail, but people had only stopped by on three or four occasions. Pownal was small on the map, hard to find. If the car did belong to some seeker after knowledge, Johnny would send him or her away quickly, as kindly as possible, but firmly. That had been Weizak's parting advice. Good advice, Johnny thought.

"Don't let anyone rope you into the role of consulting swami, John. Give no encouragement and they will forget. It may seem heartless to you at first—most of them are misguided people with too many problems and only the best of intentions—but it is a question of your life, your privacy. So be firm." And so he had been.

The Ford pulled into the turnaround between the shed and the woodpile, and as it swung around, Johnny saw the small Hertz sticker in the corner of the windshield. A very tall man in a very new blue jeans and a red plaid hunting shirt that looked as if it had just come out of an L.L. Bean box got out of the car and glanced around. He had the air of a man who is not used to the country, a man who knows there are no more wolves or cougars in New England, but who wants to make sure all the same. A city man. He glanced up at the porch, saw Johnny, and raised one hand in greeting.

"Good afternoon," he said. He had a flat city accent as well—Brooklyn, Johnny thought—and he sounded as if he were talking through a Saltine box.

"Hi," Johnny said. "Lost?"

"Boy, I hope not," the stranger said, coming over to the foot of the steps. "You're either John Smith or his twin brother."

Johnny grinned. "I don't have a brother, so I guess you found your way to the right door. Can I do something for you?"

"Well, maybe we can do something for each other." The stranger mounted the porch steps and offered his hand. Johnny shook it. "My name is Richard Dees. *Inside View* magazine."

His hair was cut in a fashionable ear-length style, and it was mostly gray. Dyed gray, Johnny thought with some amusement. What could you say about a man who sounded as if he were talking through a Saltine box and dyed his hair gray?

"Maybe you've seen the magazine."

"Oh, I've seen it. They sell it at the checkout counters in the supermarket. I'm not interested in being interviewed. Sorry you had to make a trip out here for nothing." They sold it in the supermarket, all right. The headlines did everything but leap off the pulp-stock pages and try to mug you. CHILD KILLED BY CREATURES FROM SPACE, DISTRAUGHT MOTHER CRIES. THE FOODS THAT ARE POISONING YOUR CHILDREN. 12 PSYCHICS PREDICT CALIFORNIA EARTHQUAKE BY 1978.

"Well now, an interview wasn't exactly what we were thinking of," Dees said. "May I sit down?"

"Really, I . . ."

"Mr. Smith, I've flown all the way up from New York, and from Boston I came on a little plane that had me wondering what would happen to my wife if I died intestate."

"Portland-Bangor Airways?" Johnny asked, grinning.

"That's what it was," Dees agreed.

"All right," Johnny said. "I'm impressed with your valor and your dedication to your job. I'll listen, but only for fifteen minutes or so. I'm supposed to sleep every afternoon." This was a small lie in a good cause.

"Fifteen minutes should be more than enough." Dees leaned forward. "I'm just making an educated guess, Mr. Smith, but I'd estimate that you must owe somewhere in the neighborhood of two hundred thousand dollars. That roll somewhere within putting distance of the pin, does it?"

Johnny's smile thinned. "What I owe or don't owe," he said, "is my business."

"All right, of course, sure. I didn't mean to offend, Mr. Smith. *Inside View* would like to offer you a job. A rather lucrative job."

"No. Absolutely not."

"If you'll just give me a chance to lay this out for you . . ."

Johnny said, "I'm not a practicing psychic. I'm not a Jeane Dixon or an Edgar Cayce or an Alex Tannous. That's over with. The last thing I want to do is rake it up again."

"Can I have just a few moments?"

"Mr. Dees, you don't seem to understand what I'm . . ."

"Just a few moments?" Dees smiled winningly.

"How did you find out where I was, anyway?"

"We have a stringer on a mid-Maine paper called the Kennebec *Journal.* He said that although you'd dropped out of the public view, you were probably staying with your father."

"Well, I owe him a real debt of thanks, don't I?"

"Sure," Dees said easily. "I'm betting you'll think so when you hear the whole deal. May I?"

"All right," Johnny said. "But just because you flew up here on Panic Airlines, I'm not going to change my mind."

"Well, however you see it. It's a free country, isn't it? Sure it is. *Inside View* specializes in a psychic view of things, Mr. Smith, as you probably know. Our readers, to be perfectly frank, are out of their gourds for this stuff. We have a weekly circulation of three million. Three million readers every week, Mr. Smith, how's that for a long shot straight down the fairway? How do we do it? We stick with the upbeat, the spiritual . . ."

"Twin Babies Eaten By Killer Bear," Johnny murmured.

Dees shrugged. "Sure, well; it's a tough old world, isn't it? People have to be informed about these things. It's their right to know. But for every downbeat article we've got three others telling our readers how to lose weight painlessly, how to find sexual happiness and compatibility, how to get closer to God . . ."

"Do you believe in God, Mr. Dees?"

"Actually, I don't," Dees said, and smiled his winning smile. "But we live in a democracy, greatest country on earth, right? Everyone is the captain of his own soul. No, the point is, our *readers* believe in God. They believe in angels and miracles . . ."

"And exorcisms and devils and Black Masses . . ."

"Right, right, right. You catch. It's a *spiritual* audience. They *believe* all this psychic bushwah. We have a total of ten psychics under contract, including Kathleen Nolan, the most famous seer in America. We'd like to put you under contract, Mr. Smith."

"Would you?"

"Indeed we would. What would it mean for you? Your picture and a short column would appear roughly twelve times a year, when we run one of our All-Psychic issues. *Inside View*'s Ten Famous Psychics Preview the Second Ford Administration, that sort of thing. We always do a New Year's issue, and one each Fourth of July on the course of America over the next year—that's always a very informative issue, lots of chip shots on foreign policy and economic policy in that one—plus assorted other goodies."

"I don't think you understand," Johnny said. He was speaking very slowly, as if to a child. "I've had a couple of precognitive bursts—I suppose you could say I 'saw the future'—but I don't have any control over it. I could no more come up with a prediction for the second Ford administration—if there ever is one—than I could milk a bull."

Dees looked horrified. "Who said you could? Staff writers do all those columns."

"Staff . . . ?" Johnny gaped at Dees, finally shocked.

"Of course," Dees said impatiently. "Look. One of our most popular guys over the last couple of years has been Frank Ross, the guy who specializes in natural disasters. Hell of a nice guy, but Jesus Christ, he quit school in the ninth grade. He did two hitches in the Army and was swamping out Greyhound buses at the Port Authority terminal in New York when we found him. You think we'd let him write his own column? He'd misspell cat."

"But the predictions . . ."

"A free hand, nothing but a free hand. But you'd be surprised how often these guys and gals get stuck for a real whopper."

"Whopper," Johnny repeated, bemused. He was a little surprised to find himself getting angry. His mother had bought *Inside View* for as long as he could remember, all the way back to the days when they had featured pictures of bloody car wrecks, decapitations, and bootlegged execution photos. She had sworn by every word. Presumably the greater part of *Inside View*'s other 2,999,999 readers did as well. And here sat this fellow with his dyed gray hair and his forty-dollar shoes and his shirt with the store-creases still in it, talking about *whoppers*.

"But it all works out," Dees was saying. "If you ever get stuck, all you have to do is call us collect and we all take it into the pro-shop together and come up with something. We have the right to anthologize your columns in our yearly book, *Inside Views of Things to Come*. You're perfectly free to sign any contract you can get with a book publisher, however. All we get is first refusal on the magazine rights, and we hardly ever refuse, I can tell you. And we pay very handsomely. That's over and above whatever figure we contract for. Gravy on your mashed potatoes, you might say." Dees chuckled.

"And what might that figure be?" Johnny asked slowly. He was gripping the arms of his rocker. A vein in his right temple pulsed rhythmically.

"Thirty thousand dollars per year for two years," Dees said. "And if you prove popular, that figure would become negotiable. Now, all our psychics have some area of expertise. I understand that you're good with objects." Dees's eyes became half-lidded, dreamy. "I see a regular feature. Twice monthly, maybe—we don't want to run a good thing into the ground. 'John Smith invites *Inside View*-ers to send in personal belongings for psychic examination . . .' Something like that. We'd make it clear, of course, that they should send in inexpensive stuff because nothing could be returned. But you'd be surprised. Some people are crazy as bedbugs, God love em. You'd be surprised at some of the stuff that would come in. Diamonds, gold coins, wedding rings . . . and we could attach a rider to the contract specifying that all objects mailed in would become your personal property."

Now Johnny began to see tones of dull red before his eyes. "People would send things in and I'd just keep them. That's what you're saying."

"Sure, I don't see any problem with that. It's just a question of keeping the ground rules clear up front. A little extra gravy for those mashed potatoes."

"Suppose," Johnny said, carefully keeping his voice even and modulated, "suppose I got . . . stuck for a whopper, as you put it . . . and I just called in and said President Ford was going to be assassinated on September 31, 1976? Not because I felt he was, but because I was stuck?"

"Well, September only has thirty days, you know," Dees said. "But otherwise, I think it's a hole in one. You're going to be a natural, Johnny. You think big. That's good. You'd be surprised how many of these people think small. Afraid to put their mouths where their money is, I suppose. One of our guys—Tim Clark out in Idaho—wrote in two weeks ago and said he'd had a flash that Earl Butz was going to be forced to resign next year. Well pardon my French, but who gives a fuck? Who's Earl Butz to the American housewife? But you have good waves, Johnny. You were made for this stuff."

"Good waves," Johnny muttered.

Dees was looking at him curiously. "You feel all right, Johnny? You look a little white."

Johnny was thinking of the lady who had sent the scarf. Probably she read *Inside View,* too. "Let me see if I can summarize this," he said. "You'd pay me thirty thousand dollars a year for my name . . ."

"And your picture, don't forget."

"*And* my picture, for a few ghost-written columns. Also a feature where I tell people what they want to know about objects they send in. As an extra added attraction, I get to keep the stuff . . ."

"If the lawyers can work it out . . ."

". . . as my personal property. That the deal?"

"That's the *bare bones* of the deal, Johnny. The way these things feed each other, it's just amazing. You'll be a household word in six months, and after that, the sky is the limit. The Carson show. Personal appearances. Lecture tours. Your book, of course, pick your house, they're practically throwing money at psychics along Publisher's Row. Kathy Nolan started with a contract like the one we're offering you, and she makes over two hundred thou a year now. Also, she founded her own church and the IRS can't touch dime-one of her money. She doesn't miss a trick, does our Kathy."

Dees leaned forward, grinning. "I tell you, Johnny, the sky is the limit."

"I'll bet."

"Well? What do you think?"

Johnny leaned forward toward Dees. He grabbed the sleeve of Dees's new L.L. Bean shirt in one hand and the collar of Dees's new L.L. Bean shirt in the other.

"Hey! What the hell do you think you're d . . ."

Johnny bunched the shirt in both hands and drew Dees forward. Five months of daily exercise had toned up the muscles in his hands and arms to a formidable degree.

"You asked me what I thought," Johnny said. His head was beginning to throb and ache. "I'll tell you. I think you're a ghoul. A grave robber of people's dreams. I think someone ought to put you to work at Roto-Rooter. I think your mother should have died of cancer the day after she conceived you. If there's a hell, I hope you burn there."

"You can't talk to me like that!" Dees cried. His voice rose to a fishwife's shriek. "You're fucking crazy! Forget it! Forget the whole thing, you stupid hick sonofabitch! You had your chance! Don't come crawling around . . ."

"Furthermore, you sound like you're talking through a Saltine box," Johnny said, standing up. He lifted Dees with him. The tails of his shirt popped out of the waistband of his new jeans, revealing a fishnet undershirt beneath. Johnny began to shake Dees methodically back and forth. Dees forgot about being angry. He began to blubber and roar.

Johnny dragged him to the porch steps, raised one foot, and planted it squarely in the seat of the new Levi's. Dees went down in two big steps, still blubbering and roaring. He fell in the dirt and sprawled full-length. When he got up and turned around to face Johnny, his country-cousin duds were caked with dooryard dust. It made them look more real, somehow, Johnny thought, but doubted if Dees would appreciate that.

"I ought to put the cops on you," he said hoarsely. "And maybe I will."

"You do whatever turns you on," Johnny said. "But the law around here doesn't take too kindly to people who stick their noses in where they haven't been invited."

Dees's face worked in an uneasy contortion of fear, anger, and shock. "God help you if you ever need us," he said.

Johnny's head was aching fiercely now, but he kept his

voice even. "That's just right," he said. "I couldn't agree more."

"You're going to be sorry, you know. Three million readers. That cuts both ways. When we get done with you the people in this country wouldn't believe you if you predicted spring in April. They wouldn't believe you if you said the World Series is going to come in October. They wouldn't believe you if . . . if . . ." Dees spluttered, furious.

"Get out of here, you cheap cocksucker," Johnny said.

"*You can kiss off that book!*" Dees screamed, apparently summoning up the worst thing he could think of. With his working, knotted face and his dust-caked shirt, he looked like a kid having a class-A tantrum. His Brooklyn accent had deepened and darkened to the point where it was almost a patois. "They'll laugh you out of every publishing house in New York! Nightstand Readers wouldn't touch you when I get done with you! There are ways of fixing smart guys like you and we got em, fuckhead! We . . ."

"I guess I'll go get my Remmy and shoot myself a trespasser," Johnny remarked.

Dees retreated to his rental car, still shouting threats and obscenities. Johnny stood on the porch and watched him, his head thudding sickly. Dees got in, revved the car's engine mercilessly, and then screamed out, throwing dirt into the air in clouds. He let the car drift just enough on his way out to knock the chopping block by the shed flying. Johnny grinned a little at that in spite of his bad head. He could set up the chopping block a lot more easily than Dees was going to be able to explain the big dent in that Ford's front fender to the Hertz people.

Afternoon sun twinkled on chrome again as Dees sprayed gravel all the way up the driveway to the road. Johnny sat down in the rocker again and put his forehead in his hand and got ready to wait out the headache.

◆ 2 ◆

"You're going to do *what*?" the banker asked. Outside and below, traffic passed back and forth along the bucolic main street of Ridgeway, New Hampshire. On the walls of the banker's pine-panelled, third-floor office were Frederick Remington prints and photographs of the banker at local functions.

On his desk was a lucite cube, and embedded in this cube were pictures of his wife and his son.

"I'm going to run for the House of Representatives next year," Greg Stillson repeated. He was dressed in khaki suntan pants, a blue shirt with the sleeves rolled up, and a black tie with a single blue figure. He looked out of place in the banker's office, somehow, as if at any moment he might rise to his feet and begin an aimless, destructive charge around the room, knocking over furniture, sweeping the expensively framed Remington prints to the floor, pulling the drapes from their rods.

The banker, Charles "Chuck" Gendron, president of the local Lions Club, laughed—a bit uncertainly. Stillson had a way of making people feel uncertain. As a boy he had been scrawny, perhaps; he liked to tell people that "a high wind woulda blowed me away"; but in the end his father's genes had told, and sitting here in Gendron's office, he looked very much like the Oklahoma oilfield roughneck that his father had been.

He frowned at Gendron's chuckle.

"I mean, George Harvey might have something to say about that, mightn't he, Greg?" George Harvey, besides being a mover and a shaker in town politics, was the third district Republican godfather.

"George won't say boo," Greg said calmly. There was a salting of gray in his hair, but his face suddenly looked very much like the face of the man who long ago had kicked a dog to death in an Iowa farmyard. His voice was patient. "George is going to be on the sidelines, but he's gonna be on my side of the sidelines, if you get my meaning. I ain't going to be stepping on his toes, because I'm going to run as an independent. I don't have twenty years to spend learning the ropes and licking boots."

Chuck Gendron said hesitantly, "You're kidding, aren't you, Greg?"

Greg's frown returned. It was forbidding. "Chuck, I never kid. People . . . they *think* I kid. The *Union-Leader* and those yo-yos on the *Daily Democrat*, they think I kid. But you go see George Harvey. You ask *him* if I kid around, or if I get the job done. You ought to know better, too. After all, we buried some bodies together, didn't we, Chuck?"

The frown metamorphosed into a somehow chilling grin—chilling to Gendron, perhaps, because he had allowed himself to be pulled along on a couple of Greg Stillson's development schemes. They had made money, yes, of course they had, that wasn't the problem. But there had been a couple of aspects of the Sunningdale Acres development (and the Laurel Estates deal as well, to be honest) that hadn't been—well, strictly legal. A bribed EPA agent for one thing, but that wasn't the worst thing.

On the Laurel Estates thing there had been an old man out on the Back Ridgeway Road who hadn't wanted to sell, and first the old man's fourteen-or-so chickens had died of some mysterious ailment and second there had been a fire in the old man's potato house and third when the old man came back from visiting his sister, who was in a nursing home in Keene, one weekend not so long ago, someone had smeared dogshit all over the old man's living room and dining room and fourth the old man had sold and fifth Laurel Estates was now a fact of life.

And, maybe sixth: That motorcycle spook, Sonny Elliman, was hanging around again. He and Greg were good buddies, and the only thing that kept that from being town gossip was the counterbalancing fact that Greg was seen in the company of a lot of heads, hippies, freaks, and cyclists—as a direct result of the Drug Counselling Center he had set up, plus Ridgeway's rather unusual program for young drug, alcohol, and road offenders. Instead of fining them or locking them up, the town took out their services in trade. It had been Greg's idea—and a good one, the banker would be the first to admit. It had been one of the things that had helped Greg to get elected mayor.

But this—this was utter craziness.

Greg had said something else. Gendron wasn't sure what.

"Pardon me," he said.

"I asked you how you'd like to be my campaign manager," Greg repeated.

"Greg . . ." Gendron had to clear his throat and start again. "Greg, you don't seem to understand. Harrison Fisher is the Third District representative in Washington. Harrison Fisher is Republican, respected, and probably eternal."

"No one is eternal," Greg said.

"Harrison is damn close," Gendron said. "Ask Harvey. They went to school together. Back around 1800, I think."

Greg took no notice of this thin witticism. "I'll call myself a Bull Moose or something . . . and everyone will think I'm

kidding around . . . and in the end, the good people of the
Third District are going to laugh me all the way to
Washington."

"Greg, you're crazy."

Greg's smile disappeared as if it had never been there.
Something frightening happened to his face. It became very
still, and his eyes widened to show too much of the whites.
They were like the eyes of a horse that smells bad water.

"You don't want to say something like that, Chuck. *Ever.*"

The banker felt more than chilled now.

"Greg, I apologize. It's just that . . ."

"No, you don't ever want to say that to me, unless you
want to find Sonny Elliman waiting for you some afternoon
when you go out to get your big fucking Imperial."

Gendron's mouth moved but no sound came out.

Greg smiled again, and it was like the sun suddenly breaking through threatening clouds. "Never mind. We don't want
to be kicking sand if we're going to be working together."

"Greg . . ."

"I want you because you know every damn businessman in
this part of New Hampshire. We're gonna have plenty good
money once we get this thing rolling, but I figure we'll have
to prime the pump. Now's the time for me to expand a little,
and start looking like the state's man as well as Ridgeway's
man. I figure fifty thousand dollars ought to be enough to
fertilize the grass roots."

The banker, who had worked for Harrison Fisher in his last
four canvasses, was so astounded by Greg's political naiveté
that at first he was at a loss on how to proceed. At last he
said, "Greg. Businessmen contribute to campaigns not out of
the goodness of their hearts but because the winner ends up
owing them something. In a close campaign they'll contribute
to any candidate who has a chance of winning, because they
can write off the loser as a tax loss as well. But the operant
phrase is *chance of winning*. Now Fisher is a . . ."

"Shoo-in," Greg supplied. He produced an envelope from
his back pocket. "Want you to look at these."

Gendron looked doubtfully at the envelope, then up at
Greg. Greg nodded encouragingly. The banker opened the
envelope.

There was a long silence in the pine-panelled office after
Gendron's initial harsh gasp for breath. It was unbroken except for the faint hum of the digital clock on the banker's

desk and the hiss of a match as Greg lit a Phillies cheroot. On the walls of the office were Frederick Remington pictures. In the lucite cube were family pictures. Now, spread on the desk, were pictures of the banker with his head buried between the thighs of a young woman with black hair—or it might have been red, the pictures were high-grain black-and-white glossies and it was hard to tell. The woman's face was very clear. It was not the face of the banker's wife. Some residents of Ridgeway would have recognized it as the face of one of the waitresses at Bobby Strang's truckstop two towns over.

The pictures of the banker with his head between the legs of the waitress were the safe ones—her face was clear but his was not. In others, his own grandmother would have recognized him. There were pictures of Gendron and the waitress involved in a whole medley of sexual delights—hardly all the positions of the Kama Sutra, but there were several positions represented that had never made the "Sexual Relationships" chapter of the Ridgeway High health textbook.

Gendron looked up, his face cheesy, his hands trembling. His heart was galloping in his chest. He feared a heart attack.

Greg was not even looking at him. He was looking out the window at the bright blue slice of October sky visible between the Ridgeway Five and Ten and the Ridgeway Card and Notion Shoppe.

"The winds of change have started to blow," he said, and his face was distant and preoccupied; almost mystical. He looked back at Gendron. "One of those drug-freaks down at the Center, you know what he gave me?"

Chuck Gendron shook his head numbly. With one of his shaking hands he was massaging the left side of his chest—just in case. His eyes kept falling to the photographs. The damning photographs. What if his secretary came in right now? He stopped massaging his chest and began gathering up the pictures, stuffing them back into the envelope.

"He gave me Chairman Mao's little red book," Greg said. A chuckle rumbled up from the barrel chest that had once been so thin, part of a body that had mostly disgusted his idolized father. "And one of the proverbs in there . . . I can't remember exactly how it went, but it was something like, 'The man who senses the wind of change should build not a windbreak but a windmill.' That was the flavor of it, anyway."

He leaned forward.

"Harrison Fisher's not a shoo-in, he's a has-been. Ford is a has-been. Muskie's a has-been. Humphrey's a has-been. A lot of local and state politicians all the way across this country are going to wake up the day after election day and find out that they're as dead as dodo birds. They forced Nixon out, and the next year they forced out the people who stood behind him in the impeachment hearings, and next year they'll force out Jerry Ford for the same reason."

Greg Stillson's eyes blazed at the banker.

"You want to see the wave of the future? Look up in Maine at this guy Longley. The Republicans ran a guy named Erwin and the Demos ran a guy named Mitchell and when they counted the votes for governor, they both got a big surprise, because the people went and elected themselves an insurance man from Lewiston that didn't want any part of either party. Now they're talking about him as a dark horse candidate for president."

Gendron still couldn't talk.

Greg drew in his breath. "They're all gonna think I'm kiddin, see? They thought *Longley* was kiddin. But I'm not kiddin. I'm building windmills. And you're gonna supply the building materials."

He ceased. Silence fell in the office, except for the hum of the clock. At last Gendron whispered, "Where did you get these pictures? Was it that Elliman?"

"Aw, hey. You don't want to talk about that. You forget all about those pictures. Keep them."

"And who keeps the negatives?"

"Chuck," Greg said earnestly, "you don't understand. I'm offering you Washington. Sky's the limit, boy! I'm not even asking you to raise that much money. Like I said, just a bucket of water to help prime the pump. When we get rolling, plenty of money is going to come in. Now, you know the guys that have money. You have lunch with them down at the Caswell House. You play poker with them. You have written them commercial loans tied to the prime rate at no more than their say so. And you know how to put an armlock on them."

"Greg you don't understand, you don't . . ."

Greg stood up. "The way I just put an armlock on you," he said.

The banker looked up at him. His eyes rolled helplessly. Greg Stillson thought he looked like a sheep that had been led neatly to the slaughter.

"Fifty thousand dollars," he said. "You find it."

He walked out, closing the door gently behind him. Gendron heard his booming voice even through the thick walls, bandying with his secretary. His secretary was a sixty-year-old flat-chested biddy, and Stillson probably had her giggling like a schoolgirl. He was a buffoon. It was that as much as his programs for coping with youthful crime that had made him mayor of Ridgeway. But the people didn't elect buffoons to Washington.

Well—hardly ever.

That wasn't his problem. Fifty thousand dollars in campaign contributions, that was his problem. His mind began to scurry around the problem like a trained white rat scurrying around a piece of cheese on a plate. It could probably be done. Yes, it could probably be done—but would it end there?

The white envelope was still on his desk. His smiling wife looked at it from her place in the lucite cube. He scooped the envelope up and jammed it into the inner pocket of his suitcoat. It had been Elliman, somehow Elliman had found out and had taken the pictures, he was sure of it.

But it had been Stillson who told him what to do.

Maybe the man wasn't such a buffoon after all. His assessment of the political climate of 1975–76 wasn't completely stupid. *Building windmills instead of windbreaks . . . the sky's the limit.*

But that wasn't his problem.

Fifty thousand dollars was his problem.

Chuck Gendron, president of the Lions and all-round good fellow (last year he had ridden one of those small, funny motorcycles in the Ridgeway Fourth of July parade), pulled a yellow legal tablet out of the top drawer of his desk and began jotting down a list of names. The trained white rat at work. And down on Main Street Greg Stillson turned his face up into the strong autumn sunlight and congratulated himself on a job well-done—or well-begun.

Chapter 15

◆ 1 ◆

Later, Johnny supposed that the reason he ended up finally making love to Sarah—almost five years to the day after the fair—had a lot to do with the visit of Richard Dees, the man from *Inside View*. The reason he finally weakened and called Sarah and invited her to come and visit was little more than a wistful urge to have someone nice come to call and take the nasty taste out of his mouth. Or so he told himself.

He called her in Kennebunk and got the former roommate, who said Sarah would be right with him. The phone clunked down and there was a moment of silence when he contemplated (but not very seriously) just hanging up and closing the books for good. Then Sarah's voice was in his ear.

"Johnny? Is it you?"

"The very same."

"How are you?"

"Fine. How's by you?"

"I'm fine," she said. "Glad you called. I . . . didn't know if you would."

"Still sniffin that wicked cocaine?"

"No, I'm on heroin now."

"You got your boy with you?"

"I sure do. Don't go anywhere without him."

"Well, why don't the two of you truck on out here some day before you have to go back up north?"

"I'd like that, Johnny," she said warmly.

"Dad's working in Westbrook and I'm chief cook and bottlewasher. He gets home around four-thirty and we eat around five-thirty. You're welcome to stay for dinner, but be warned: all my best dishes use Franco-American spaghetti as their base."

She giggled. "Invitation accepted. Which day is best?"

"What about tomorrow or the day after, Sarah?"

"Tomorrow's fine," she said after the briefest of hesitations. "See you then."

"Take care, Sarah."

"You too."

He hung up thoughtfully, feeling both excited and guilty—for no good reason at all. But your mind went where it wanted to, didn't it? And where his mind wanted to go now was to examine possibilities maybe best left unconsidered.

Well, she knows the thing she needs to know. She knows what time dad comes home—what else does she need to know?

And his mind answered itself: *What you going to do if she shows up at noon?*

Nothing, he answered, and didn't wholly believe it. Just thinking about Sarah, the set of her lips, the small, upward tilt of her green eyes—those were enough to make him feel weak and sappy and a little desperate.

Johnny went out to the kitchen and slowly began to put together this night's supper, not so important, just for two. Father and son batching it. It hadn't been all that bad. He was still healing. He and his father had talked about the four-and-a-half years he had missed, about his mother—working around that carefully but always seeming to come a little closer to the center, in a tightening spiral. Not needing to understand, maybe, but needing to come to terms. No, it hadn't been that bad. It was a way to finish putting things together. For both of them. But it would be over in January when he returned to Cleaves Mills to teach. He had gotten his half-year contract from Dave Pelsen the week before, had signed it and sent it back. What would his father do then? Go on, Johnny supposed. People had a way of doing that, just going on, pushing through with no particular drama, no big drumrolls. He would get down to visit Herb as often as he could, every weekend, if that felt like the right thing to do. So many things had gotten strange so fast that all he could do was feel his way slowly along, groping like a blind man in an unfamiliar room.

He put the roast in the oven, went into the living room, snapped on the TV, then snapped it off again. He sat down and thought about Sarah. *The baby,* he thought. *The baby will be our chaperon if she comes early.* So that was all right, after all. All bases covered.

But his thoughts were still long and uneasily speculative.

◆ 2 ◆

She came at quarter past twelve the next day, wheeling a snappy little red Pinto into the driveway and parking it, getting out, looking tall and beautiful, her dark blonde hair caught in the mild October wind.

"Hi, Johnny!" she called, raising her hand.

"Sarah!" He came down to meet her; she lifted her face and he kissed her cheek lightly.

"Just let me get the emperor," she said, opening the passenger door.

"Can I help?"

"Naw, we get along just fine together, don't we, Denny? Come on, kiddo." Moving deftly, she unbuckled the straps holding a pudgy little baby in the car seat. She lifted him out. Denny stared around the yard with wild, solemn interest, and then his eyes fixed on Johnny and held there. He smiled.

"Vig!" Denny said, and waved both hands.

"I think he wants to go to you," Sarah said. "Very unusual. Denny has his father's Republican sensibilities—he's rather standoffish. Want to hold him?"

"Sure," Johnny said, a little doubtfully.

Sarah grinned. "He won't break and you won't drop him," she said, and handed Denny over. "If you did, he'd probably bounce right up like Silly Putty. *Disgustingly* fat baby."

"Vun bunk!" Denny said, curling one arm nonchalantly around Johnny's neck and looking comfortably at his mother.

"It really is amazing," Sarah said. "He never takes to people like . . . Johnny? *Johnny?*"

When the baby put his arm around Johnny's neck, a confused rush of feelings had washed over him like mild warm water. There was nothing dark, nothing troubling. Everything was very simple. There was no concept of the future in the baby's thoughts. No feeling of trouble. No sense of past unhappiness. And no words, only strong images: warmth, dryness, the mother, the man that was himself.

"Johnny?" She was looking at him apprehensively.

"Hmmmm?"

"Is everything all right?"

She's asking me about Denny, he realized. Is everything all right with Denny? Do you see trouble? Problems?

"Everything's fine," he said. "We can go inside if you want, but I usually roost on the porch. It'll be time to crouch around the stove all day long soon enough."

"I think the porch will be super. And Denny looks as if he'd like to try out the yard. *Great* yard, he says. Right, kiddo?" She ruffled his hair and Denny laughed.

"He'll be okay?"

"As long as he doesn't try to eat any of those woodchips."

"I've been splitting stove-lengths," Johnny said, setting Denny down as carefully as a Ming vase. "Good exercise."

"How are you? Physically?"

"I think," Johnny said, remembering the heave-ho he had given Richard Dees a few days ago, "that I'm doing as well as could be expected."

"That's good. You were kinda low the last time I saw you."

Johnny nodded. "The operations."

"Johnny?"

He glanced at her and again felt that odd mix of speculation, guilt, and something like anticipation in his viscera. Her eyes were on his face, frankly and openly.

"Yeah?"

"Do you remember . . . about the wedding ring?"

He nodded.

"It was there. Where you said it would be. I threw it away."

"Did you?" He was not completely surprised.

"I threw it away and never mentioned it to Walt." She shook her head. "And I don't know why. It's bothered me ever since."

"Don't let it."

They were standing on the steps, facing each other. Color had come up in her cheeks, but she didn't drop her eyes.

"There's something I'd like to finish," she said simply. "Something we never had the chance to finish."

"Sarah . . ." he began, and stopped. He had absolutely no idea what to say next. Below them, Denny tottered six steps and then sat down hard. He crowed, not put out of countenance at all.

"Yes," she said. "I don't know if it's right or wrong. I love Walt. He's a good man, easy to love. Maybe the one thing I know is a good man from a bad one. Dan—that guy I went with in college—was one of the bad guys. You set my mouth for the other kind, Johnny. Without you, I never could have appreciated Walt for what he is."

"Sarah, you don't have to . . ."

"I *do* have to," Sara contradicted. Her voice was low and

intense. "Because things like this you can only say once. And you either get it wrong or right, it's the end either way, because it's too hard to ever try to say again." She looked at him pleadingly. "Do you understand?"

"Yes, I suppose I do."

"I love you, Johnny," she said. "I never stopped. I've tried to tell myself that it was an act of God that split us up. I don't know. Is a bad hot dog an act of God? Or two kids dragging on a back road in the middle of the night? All I want . . ." Her voice had taken on a peculiar flat emphasis that seemed to beat its way into the cool October afternoon like an artisan's small hammer into thin and precious foil ". . . all I want is what was taken from us." Her voice faltered. She looked down. "And I want it with all my heart, Johnny. Do you?"

"Yes," he said. He put his arms out and was confused when she shook her head and stepped away.

"Not in front of Denny," she said. "It's stupid, maybe, but that would be a little bit too much like public infidelity. I want everything, Johnny." Her color rose again, and her pretty blush began to feed his own excitement. "I want you to hold me and kiss me and love me," she said. Her voice faltered again, nearly broke. "I think it's wrong, but I can't help it. It's wrong but it's right. It's *fair*."

He reached out one finger and brushed away a tear that was moving slowly down her cheek.

"And it's only this once, isn't it?"

She nodded. "Once will have to put paid to everything. Everything that would have been, if things hadn't gone wrong." She looked up, her eyes brighter green than ever, swimming with tears. "Can we put paid to everything with only the one time, Johnny?"

"No," he said, smiling. "But we can try, Sarah."

She looked fondly down at Denny, who was trying to climb up onto the chopping block without much success. "He'll sleep," she said.

◆ 3 ◆

They sat on the porch and watched Denny play in the yard under the high blue sky. There was no hurry, no impatience between them, but there was a growing electricity that they both felt. She had opened her coat and sat on the porch glider in a powder-blue wool dress, her ankles crossed, her hair blown carelessly on her shoulders where the wind had spilled it. The blush never really left her face. And high white clouds fled across the sky, west to east.

They talked of inconsequential things—there was no hurry. For the first time since he had come out of it, Johnny felt that time was not his enemy. Time had provided them with this little air pocket in exchange for the main flow of which they had been robbed, and it would be here for as long as they needed it. They talked about people who had been married, about a girl from Cleaves Mills who had won a Merit scholarship, about Maine's independent governor. Sarah said he looked like Lurch on the old Addams Family show and thought like Herbert Hoover, and they both laughed over that.

"Look at him," Sarah said, nodding toward Denny.

He was sitting on the grass by Vera Smith's ivy trellis, his thumb in his mouth, looking at them sleepily.

She got his car-bed out of the Pinto's back seat.

"Will he be okay on the porch?" she asked Johnny. "It's so mild. I'd like to have him nap in the fresh air."

"He'll be fine on the porch," Johnny said.

She set the bed in the shade, popped him into it, and pulled the two blankets up to his chin. "Sleep, baby," Sara said.

He smiled at her and promptly closed his eyes.

"Just like that?" Johnny asked.

"Just like that," she agreed. She stepped close to him and put her arms around his neck. Quite clearly he could hear the faint rustle of her slip beneath her dress. "I'd like you to kiss me," she said calmly. "I've waited five years for you to kiss me again, Johnny."

He put his arms around her waist and kissed her gently. Her lips parted.

"Oh, Johnny," she said against his neck. "I love you."

"I love you too, Sarah."

"Where do we go?" she asked, stepping away from him. Her eyes were as clear and dark as emeralds now. "Where?"

◆ 4 ◆

He spread the faded army blanket, which was old but clean, on the straw of the second loft. The smell was fragrant and sweet. High above them there was the mysterious coo and flutter of the barn swallows, and then they settled down again. There was a small, dusty window which looked down on the house and porch. Sarah wiped a clean place on the glass and looked down at Denny.

"It's okay?" Johnny asked.

"Yes. Better here than in the house. That would have been like . . ." She shrugged.

"Making my dad a part of it?"

"Yes. This is between us."

"Our business."

"Our business," she agreed. She lay on her stomach, her face turned to one side on the faded blanket, her legs bent at the knee. She pushed her shoes off, one by one. "Unzip me, Johnny."

He knelt beside her and pulled the zipper down. The sound was loud in the stillness. Her back was the color of coffee with cream against the whiteness of her slip. He kissed her between the shoulder blades and she shivered.

"Sarah," he murmured.

"What?"

"I have to tell you something."

"What?"

"The doctor made a mistake during one of those operations and gelded me."

She punched him on the shoulder. "Same old Johnny," she said. "And you had a friend once who broke his neck on the crack-the-whip at Topsham Fair."

"Sure," he said.

Her hand touched him like silk, moving gently up and down.

"It doesn't feel like they did anything terminal to you," she said. Her luminous eyes searched his. "Not at all. Shall we look and see?"

There was the sweet smell of the hay. Time spun out. There was the rough feel of the army blanket, the smooth feel of her flesh, the naked reality of her. Sinking into her was like sinking into an old dream that had never been quite forgotten.

"Oh, Johnny, my dear . . ." Her voice in rising excitement.

Her hips moving in a quickening tempo. Her voice was far away. The touch of her hair was like fire on his shoulder and chest. He plunged his face deeply into it, losing himself in that dark-blonde darkness.

Time spinning out in the sweet smell of hay. The rough-textured blanket. The sound of the old barn creaking gently, like a ship, in the October wind. Mild white light coming in through the roof chinks, catching motes of chaff in half a hundred pencil-thin sunbeams. Motes of chaff dancing and revolving.

She cried out. At some point she cried out his name, again and again and again, like a chant. Her fingers dug into him like spurs. Rider and ridden. Old wine decanted at last, a fine vintage.

Later they sat by the window, looking out into the yard. Sarah slipped her dress on over bare flesh and left him for a little bit. He sat alone, not thinking, content to watch her reappear in the window, smaller, and cross the yard to the porch. She bent over the baby bed and readjusted the blankets. She came back, the wind blowing her hair out behind her and tugging playfully at the hem of her dress.

"He'll sleep another half hour," she said.

"Will he?" Johnny smiled. "Maybe I will, too."

She walked her bare toes across his belly. "You better not."

And so again, and this time she was on top, almost in an attitude of prayer, her head bent, her hair swinging forward and obscuring her face. Slowly. And then it was over.

◆ 5 ◆

"Sarah . . ."

"No, Johnny. Better not say it. Time's up."

"I was going to say that you're beautiful."

"Am I?"

"You are," he said softly. "Dear Sarah."

"Did we put paid to everything?" she asked him.

Johnny smiled. "Sarah, we did the best we could."

◆ 6 ◆

Herb didn't seem surprised to see Sarah when he got home from Westbrook. He welcomed her, made much of the baby, and then scolded Sarah for not bringing him down sooner.

"He has your color and complexion," Herb said. "And I

think he's going to have your eyes, when they get done changing."

"If only he has his father's brains," Sarah said. She had put an apron on over the blue wool dress. Outside, the sun was going down. Another twenty minutes and it would be dark.

"You know, the cooking is supposed to be Johnny's job," Herb said.

"Couldn't stop her. She put a gun to my head."

"Well, maybe it's all for the best," Herb said. "Everything you make comes out tasting like Franco-American spaghetti."

Johnny shied a magazine at him and Denny laughed, a high, piercing sound that seemed to fill the house.

Can he see? Johnny wondered. *It feels like it's written all over my face.* And then a startling thought came to him as he watched his father digging in the entryway closet for a box of Johnny's old toys that he had never let Vera give away: *Maybe he understands.*

They ate. Herb asked Sarah what Walt was doing in Washington and she told them about the conference he was attending, which had to do with Indian land claims. The Republican meetings were mostly wind-testing exercises, she said.

"Most of the people he's meeting with think that if Reagan is nominated over Ford next year, it's going to mean the death of the party," Sarah said. "And if the Grand Old Party dies, that means Walt won't be able to run for Bill Cohen's seat in 1978 when Cohen goes after Bill Hathaway's Senate seat."

Herb was watching Denny eat string beans, seriously, one by one, using all six of his teeth on them. "I don't think Cohen will be able to wait until '78 to get in the Senate. He'll run against Muskie next year."

"Walt says Bill Cohen's not that big a dope," Sarah said. "He'll wait. Walt says his own chance is coming, and I'm starting to believe him."

After supper they sat in the living room, and the talk turned away from politics. They watched Denny play with the old wooden cars and trucks that a much younger Herb Smith had made for his own son over a quarter of a century ago. A younger Herb Smith who had been married to a tough, good-humored woman who would sometimes drink a bottle of Black Label beer in the evening. A man with no gray in his hair and nothing but the highest hopes for his son.

He does understand, Johnny thought, sipping his coffee.

Whether he knows what went on between Sarah and me this afternoon, whether or not he suspects what might have gone on, he understands the basic cheat. You can't change it or rectify it, the best you can do is try to come to terms. This afternoon she and I consummated a marriage that never was. And tonight he's playing with his grandson.

He thought of the Wheel of Fortune, slowing, stopping.

House number. Everyone loses.

Gloom was trying to creep up, a dismal sense of finality, and he pushed it away. This wasn't the time; he wouldn't let it be the time.

By eight-thirty Denny had begun to get scratchy and cross and Sarah said, "Time for us to go, folks. He can suck a bottle on our way back to Kennebunk. About three miles from here, he'll have corked off. Thanks for having us." Her eyes, brilliant green, found Johnny's for a moment.

"Our pleasure entirely," Herb said, standing up. "Right, Johnny?"

"Right," he said. "Let me carry that car-bed out for you, Sarah."

At the door, Herb kissed the top of Denny's head (and Denny grabbed Herb's nose in his chubby fist and honked it hard enough to make Herb's eyes water) and Sarah's cheek. Johnny carried the car-bed down to the red Pinto and Sarah gave him the keys so he could put everything in the back.

When he finished, she was standing by the driver's side door, looking at him. "It was the best we could do," she said, and smiled a little. But the brilliance of her eyes told him the tears were close again.

"It wasn't so bad at all," Johnny said.

"We'll stay in touch?"

"I don't know, Sarah. Will we?"

"No, I suppose not. It would be too easy, wouldn't it?"

"Pretty easy, yes."

She stepped close and stretched to kiss his cheek. He could smell her hair, clean and fragrant.

"Take care," she whispered. "I'll think about you."

"Be good, Sarah," he said, and touched her nose.

She turned then, got in behind the wheel, a smart young matron whose husband was on the way up. *I doubt like hell if they'll be driving a Pinto next year,* Johnny thought.

The lights came on, then the little sewing machine motor roared. She raised a hand to him and then she was pulling out of the driveway. Johnny stood by the chopping block, hands in his pockets, and watched her go. Something in his heart seemed to have closed. It was not a major feeling. That was the worst of it—it wasn't a major feeling at all.

He watched until the taillights were out of sight and then he climbed the porch steps and went back into the house. His dad was sitting in the big easy chair in the living room. The TV was off. The few toys he had found in the closet were scattered on the rug and he was looking at them.

"Good to see Sarah," Herb said. "Did you and she have . . ." there was the briefest, most minute hesitation . . . "a nice visit?"

"Yes," Johnny said.

"She'll be down again?"

"No, I don't think so."

He and his father were looking at each other.

"Well now, maybe that's for the best," Herb said finally.

"Yes. Maybe so."

"You played with these toys," Herb said, getting down on his knees and beginning to gather them up. "I gave a bunch of them to Lottie Gedreau when she had her twins, but I knew I had a few of them left. I saved a few back."

He put them back in the box one by one, turning each of them over in his hands, examining them. A race car. A bull-dozer. A police car. A small hook-and-ladder truck from which most of the red paint had been worn away where a small hand would grip. He took them back to the entryway closet and put them away.

Johnny didn't see Sarah Hazlett again for three years.

Chapter 16

◆ 1 ◆

The snow came early that year. There were six inches on the ground by November 7, and Johnny had taken to lacing on a pair of old green gumrubber boots and wearing his old parka for the trek up to the mailbox. Two weeks before, Dave

Pelsen had mailed down a package containing the texts he would be using in January, and Johnny had already begun making tentative lesson plans. He was looking forward to getting back. Dave had also found him an apartment on Howland Street in Cleaves. 24 Howland Street. Johnny kept that on a scrap of paper in his wallet, because the name and number had an irritating way of slipping his mind.

On this day the skies were slatey and lowering, the temperature hovering just below the twenty-degree mark. As Johnny tramped up the driveway, the first spats of snow began to drift down. Because he was alone, he didn't feel too self-conscious about running his tongue out and trying to catch a flake on it. He was hardly limping at all, and he felt good. There hadn't been a headache in two weeks or more.

The mail consisted of an advertising circular, a *Newsweek,* and a small manila envelope addressed to John Smith, no return address. Johnny opened it on the way back, the rest of the mail stuffed into his hip pocket. He pulled out a single page of newsprint, saw the words *Inside View* at the top, and came to a halt halfway back to the house.

It was page three of the previous week's issue. The headline story dealt with a reporter's "exposé" on the handsome second banana of a TV crime show; the second banana had been suspended from high school twice (twelve years ago) and busted for possession of cocaine (six years ago). Hot news for the *hausfraus* of America. There was also an all-grain diet, a cute baby photo, and the story of a nine-year-old girl who had been miraculously cured of cerebral palsy at Lourdes (DOCTORS MYSTIFIED, the headline trumpeted gleefully). A story near the bottom of the page had been circled. MAINE "PSYCHIC" ADMITS HOAX, the headline read. The story was not by-lined.

IT HAS ALWAYS BEEN THE POLICY of *Inside View* not only to bring you the fullest coverage of the psychics which the so-called "National Press" ignores, but to expose the tricksters and charlatans who have held back true acceptance of legitimate psychic phenomena for so long.

One of these tricksters admitted his own hoax to an *Inside View* source recently. This so-called "psychic," John Smith of Pownal, Maine, admitted to our source that "it was all a gimmick to pay back my hospital bills.

If there's a book in it, I might come out with enough to pay off what I owe and retire for a couple of years in the bargain," Smith grinned. "These days, people will believe anything—why shouldn't I get on the gravy train?"

Thanks to *Inside View,* which has always cautioned readers that there are two phony psychics for each real one, John Smith's gravy train has just been derailed. And we reiterate our standing offer of $1000 to anyone who can prove that any nationally known psychic is a fraud.

Hoaxers and charlatans, be warned!

Johnny read the article twice as the snow began to come down more heavily. A reluctant grin broke over his features. The ever-vigilant press apparently didn't enjoy being thrown off some bumpkin's front porch, he thought. He tucked the tear sheet back into its envelope and stuffed it into his back pocket with the rest of the mail.

"Dees," he said aloud, "I hope you're still black and blue."

◆ 2 ◆

His father was not so amused. Herb read the clipping and then slammed it down on the kitchen table in disgust. "You ought to sue that son of a whore. That's nothing but slander, Johnny. A deliberate hatchet job."

"Agreed and agreed," Johnny said. It was dark outside. This afternoon's silently falling snow had developed into tonight's early winter blizzard. The wind shrieked and howled around the eaves. The driveway had disappeared under a dunelike progression of drifts. "But there was no third party when we talked, and Dees damn well knows it. It's his word against mine."

"He didn't even have the guts to put his own name to this lie," Herb said. "Look at this 'an *Inside View* source.' What's this source? Get him to name it, that's what I say."

"Oh, you can't do that," Johnny said, grinning. "That's like walking up to the meanest street-fighter on the block with a KICK ME HARD sign taped to your crotch. Then they turn it into a holy war, page one and all. No thanks. As far as I'm concerned, they did me a favor. I don't want to make a career out of telling people where gramps hid his stock certificates or who's going to win the fourth at Scarborough Downs. Or take this lottery." One of the things that had most surprised Johnny on coming out of his coma was to discover that Maine and about a dozen other states had instituted a legal numbers game. "In the last month I've gotten sixteen letters from people who want me to tell them what the number's going to be. It's insane. Even if I could tell them, which I couldn't, what good would it do them? You can't pick your own number in the Maine lottery, you get what they give you. But still I get the letters."

"I don't see what that has to do with this crappy article."

"If people think I'm a phony, maybe they'll leave me alone."

"Oh," Herb said. "Yeah, I see what you mean." He lit his pipe. "You've never really been comfortable with it, have you?"

"No," Johnny said. "We never talk much about it, either, which is something of a relief. It seems like the only thing other people *do* want to talk about." And it wasn't just that they wanted to talk; that wouldn't have bothered him so much. But when he *was* in Slocum's Store for a sixpack or a loaf of bread, the girl would try to take his money without touching his hand, and the frightened, skittish look in her eyes was unmistakable. His father's friends would give him a little wave instead of a handshake. In October Herb had hired a local high school girl to come in once a week to do some dusting and vacuum the floors. After three weeks she had quit for no stated reason at all—probably someone at her high school had told her who she was cleaning for. It seemed that for everyone who was anxious to be touched, to be informed, to be in contact with Johnny's peculiar talent, there was another who regarded him as a kind of leper. At times like these, Johnny would think of the nurses staring at him the day he had told Eileen Magown that her house was on fire, staring at him like magpies on a telephone wire. He would think of the way the TV reporter had drawn back from him after the press conference's unexpected conclusion, agreeing with everything he said but not wanting to be touched. Unhealthy either way.

"No, we don't talk about it," Herb agreed. "It makes me think of your mother, I suppose. She was so sure you'd been given the . . . the whatever-it-is for some reason. Sometimes I wonder if she wasn't right."

Johnny shrugged. "All I want is a normal life. I want to

bury the whole damn thing. And if this little squib helps me do it, so much the better."

"But you still can do it, can't you?" Herb asked. He was looking closely at his son.

Johnny thought about a night not quite a week ago. They had gone out to dinner, a rare happening on their strapped budget. They had gone to Cole's Farm in Gray, probably the best restaurant in the area, a place that was always packed. The night had been cold, the dining room cheery and warm. Johnny had taken his father's coat and his own into the cloak-room, and as he thumbed through the racked coats, looking for empty hangers, a whole series of clear impressions had cascaded through his mind. It was like that sometimes, and on another occasion he could have handled every coat for twenty minutes and gotten nothing at all. Here was a lady's coat with a fur collar. She was having an affair with one of her husband's poker buddies, was scared sick about it, but didn't know how to close it off. A man's denim jacket, sheep-skin-lined. This guy was also worried—about his brother, who had been badly hurt on a construction project the week be-fore. A small boy's parka—his grandmother in Durham had given him a Snoopy transistor radio just today and he was mad because his father hadn't let him bring it into the dining room with him. And another one, a plain, black topcoat, that had turned him cold with terror and robbed him of his appe-tite. The man who owned this coat was going mad. So far he had kept up appearances—not even his wife suspected—but his vision of the world was being slowly darkened by a series of increasingly paranoid fantasies. Touching that coat had been like touching a writhing coil of snakes.

"Yes, I can still do it," Johnny said briefly. "I wish to hell I couldn't."

"You really mean that?"

Johnny thought of the plain, black topcoat. He had only picked at his meal, looking this way and that, trying to single the man out of the crowd, unable to do so.

"Yes," he said. "I mean it."

"Best forgotten then," Herb said, and clapped his son on the shoulder.

◆ 3 ◆

And for the next month or so it seemed that it would be forgotten. Johnny drove north to attend a meeting at the high school for mid-year teachers and to take a load of his personal things up to his new apartment, which he found small but liveable.

He went in his father's car, and as he was getting ready to leave Herb asked him, "You're not nervous? About driving?"

Johnny shook his head. Thoughts of the accident itself troubled him very little now. If something was going to happen to him, it would. And deep down he felt confident that lightning would not strike in the same place again—when he died, he didn't believe it would be in a car accident.

In fact, the long trip was quiet and soothing, the meeting a little bit like Old Home Week. All of his old colleagues who were still teaching at CMHS dropped by to wish him the best. But he couldn't help noticing how few of them actually shook hands with him, and he seemed to sense a certain reserve, a wariness in their eyes. Driving home, he convinced himself it was probably imagination. And if not, well . . . even that had its amusing side. If they had read their *Inside View,* they would know he was a hoax and nothing to worry about.

The meeting over, there was nothing to do but go back to Pownal and wait for the Christmas holidays to come and go. The packages containing personal objects stopped coming, almost as if a switch had been thrown—the power of the press, Johnny told his father. They were replaced by a brief spate of angry—and mostly anonymous—letters and cards from people who seemed to feel personally cheated.

"You ort to burn in H!E!L!L! for your slimey skeems to bilk this American Republic," a typical one read. It had been written on a crumpled sheet of Ramada Inn stationery and was postmarked York, Pennsylvania. "You are nothing but a *Con Artist* and a *dirty rotten cheet.* I bless God for that paper that saw thru you. You ort to be ashamed of yourself Sir. The Bible says an ordinary sinner will be cast into the Lake OF F!I!R!E! and be consomed but a F!A!U!L!S!E P!R!O!F!I!T shall burn *forever* and *EVER!* Thats you a False Profit who sold your Immortal Soul for a few cheep bucks. So thats the end of my letter and I hope for your sake I never catch you out on the Streets of your Home Town. Signed, A FRIEND (of God not you Sir)!"

Over two dozen letters in this approximate vein came in during the course of about twenty days following the appearance of the *Inside View* story. Several enterprising souls expressed an interest in joining in with Johnny as partners. "I used to be a magician's assistant," one of these latter missives bragged, "and I could trick an old whore out of her g-string. If you're planning a mentalist gig, you need me in!"

Then the letters dried up, as had the earlier influx of boxes and packages. On a day in late November when he had checked the mailbox and found it empty for the third afternoon in a row, Johnny walked back to the house remembering that Andy Warhol had predicted that a day would come when everyone in America would be famous for fifteen minutes. Apparently his fifteen minutes had come and gone, and no one was any more pleased about it than he was.

But as things turned out, it wasn't over yet.

♦ 4 ♦

"Smith?" The telephone voice asked. "John Smith?"

"Yes." It wasn't a voice he knew, or a wrong number. That made it something of a puzzle since his father had had the phone unlisted about three months ago. This was December 17, and their tree stood in the corner of the living room, its base firmly wedged into the old tree stand Herb had made when Johnny was just a kid. Outside it was snowing.

"My name is Bannerman. Sheriff George Bannerman, from Castle Rock." He cleared his throat. "I've got a . . . well, I suppose you'd say I've got a proposal for you."

"How did you get this number?"

Bannerman cleared his throat again. "Well, I could have gotten it from the phone company, I suppose, it being police business. But actually I got it from a friend of yours. Doctor by the name of Weizak."

"Sam Weizak gave you my number?"

"That's right."

Johnny sat down in the phone nook, utterly perplexed. Now the name Bannerman meant something to him. He had come across the name in a Sunday supplement article only recently. He was the sheriff of Castle County, which was considerably west of Pownal, in the Lakes region. Castle Rock was the county seat, about thirty miles from Norway and twenty from Bridgton.

"Police business?" he repeated.

"Well, I guess you'd say so, ayuh. I was wondering if maybe the two of us could get together for a cup of coffee . . ."

"It involves Sam?"

"No. Dr. Weizak has nothing to do with it," Bannerman said. "He gave me a call and mentioned your name. That was . . . oh, a month ago, at least. To be frank, I thought he was nuts. But now we're just about at our wits' end."

"About what? Mr.—*Sheriff*—Bannerman, I don't understand what you're talking about."

"It'd really be a lot better if we could get together for coffee," Bannerman said. "Maybe this evening? There's a place called Jon's on the main drag in Bridgton. Sort of half-way between your town and mine."

"No, I'm sorry," Johnny said. "I'd have to know what it was about. And how come Sam never called me?"

Bannerman sighed. "I guess you're a man who doesn't read the papers," he said.

But that wasn't true. He had read the papers compulsively since he had regained consciousness, trying to pick up on the things he had missed. And he had seen Bannerman's name just recently. Sure. Because Bannerman was on a pretty hot seat. He was the man in charge of—

Johnny held the phone away from his ear and looked at it with sudden understanding. He looked at it the way a man might look at a snake he has just realized is poisonous.

"Mr. Smith?" It squawked tinnily. "Hello? Mr. Smith?"

"I'm here," Johnny said, putting the phone back to his ear. He was conscious of a dull anger at Sam Weizak, Sam who had told him to keep his head down only this summer, and then had turned around and given this local-yokel sheriff an earful—behind Johnny's back.

"It's that strangling business, isn't it?"

Bannerman hesitated a long time. Then he said, "Could we talk, Mr. Smith?"

"No. Absolutely not." The dull anger had ignited into sudden fury. Fury and something else. He was scared.

"Mr. Smith, it's important. Today . . ."

"No. I want to be left alone. Besides, don't you read the goddam *Inside View*? I'm a fake anyway."

"Dr. Weizak said . . ."

"He had no business saying anything!" Johnny shouted. He was shaking all over. "Good-bye!" He slammed the phone into its cradle and got out of the phone nook quickly, as if that would prevent it from ringing again. He could feel a headache beginning in his temples. Dull drill-bits. Maybe I should call his mother out there in California, he thought. Tell her where her little sonny-buns is. Tell her to get in touch. Tit for tat.

Instead he hunted in the address book in the phone-table drawer, found Sam's office number in Bangor, and called it. As soon as it rang once on the other end he hung up, scared again. Why had Sam done that to him? Goddammit, why?

He found himself looking at the Christmas tree.

Same old decorations. They had dragged them down from the attic again and taken them out of their tissue-paper cradles again and hung them up again, just two evenings ago. It was a funny thing about Christmas decorations. There weren't many things that remained intact year after year as a person grew up. Not many lines of continuity, not many physical objects that could easily serve both the states of childhood and adulthood. Your kid clothes were handed down or packed off to the Salvation Army; your Donald Duck watch sprung its mainspring; your Red Ryder cowboy boots wore out. The wallet you made in your first camp handicrafts class got replaced by a Lord Buxton, and you traded your red wagon and your bike for more adult toys—a car, a tennis racket, maybe one of those new TV hockey games. There were only a few things you could hang onto. A few books, maybe, or a lucky coin, or a stamp collection that had been preserved and improved upon.

Add to that the Christmas tree ornaments in your parents' house.

The same chipped angels year after year, and the same tinsel star on top; the tough surviving platoon of what had once been an entire battalion of glass balls (and we never forget the honored dead, he thought—this one died as a result of a baby's clutching hand, this one slipped as dad was putting it on and crashed to the floor, the red one with the Star of Bethlehem painted on it was simply and mysteriously broken one year when we took them down from the attic, and I cried); the tree stand itself. But sometimes, Johnny thought, absently massaging his temples, it seemed it would be better,

more merciful, if you lost touch with even these last vestiges
of childhood. You could never discover the books that had
first turned you on in quite the same way. The lucky coin had
not protected you from any of the ordinary whips and scorns
and scrapes of an ordinary life. And when you looked at the
ornaments you remembered that there had once been a
mother in the place to direct the tree-trimming operation,
always ready and willing to piss you off by saying "a little
higher" or "a little lower" or "I think you've got too much
tinsel on that left side, dear." You looked at the ornaments
and remembered that just the two of you had been around
to put them up this year, just the two of you because your
mother went crazy and then she died, but the fragile Christmas tree ornaments were still here, still hanging around to
decorate another tree taken from the small back woodlot and
didn't they say more people committed suicide around Christmas than at any other time of the year? By God, it was no
wonder.

What a power God has given you, Johnny.

Sure, that's right, God's a real prince. He knocked me
through the windshield of a cab and I broke my legs and
spent five years or so in a coma and three people died. The
girl I loved got married. She had the son who should have
been mine by a lawyer who's breaking his ass to get to Washington so he can help run the big electric train set. If I'm on
my feet for more than a couple of hours at a time it feels like
somebody took a long splinter and rammed it straight up my
leg to my balls. God's a real sport. He's such a sport that he
fixed up a funny comic-opera world where a bunch of glass
Christmas tree globes could outlive you. Neat world, and a
really first-class God in charge of it. He must have been on
our side during Vietnam, because that's the way he's been
running things ever since time began.

He has a job for you, Johnny.

Bailing some half-assed country cop out of a jam so he can
get reelected next year?

Don't run from him, Johnny. Don't hide away in a cave.

He rubbed his temples. Outside, the wind was rising. He
hoped dad would be careful coming home from work.

Johnny got up and pulled on a heavy sweatshirt. He went
out into the shed, watching his breath frost the air ahead of
him. To the left was a large pile of wood he had split in the
autumn just past, all of it cut into neat stove lengths. Next to

it was a box of kindling, and beside that was a stack of old newspapers. He squatted down and began to thumb through them. His hands went numb quickly but he kept going and eventually he came to the one he was looking for. The Sunday paper from three weeks ago.

He took it into the house, slapped it down on the kitchen table, and began to root through it. He found the article he was looking for in the features section and sat down to re-read it.

The article was accompanied by several photos, one of them showing an old woman locking a door, another showing a police car cruising a nearly deserted street, two others showing a couple of businesses that were nearly deserted. The headline read: THE HUNT FOR THE CASTLE ROCK STRANGLER GOES ON . . . AND ON.

Five years ago, according to the story, a young woman named Alma Frechette who worked at a local restaurant had been raped and strangled on her way home from work. A joint investigation of the crime had been conducted by the state attorney general's office and the Castle County sheriff's department. The result had been a total zero. A year later an elderly woman, also raped and strangled, had been discovered in her tiny third-floor apartment on Carbine Street in Castle Rock. A month later the killer had struck again; this time the victim had been a bright young junior high school girl.

There had been a more intensive investigation. The investigative facilities of the FBI had been utilized, all to no result. The following November Sheriff Carl M. Kelso, who had been the county's chief law officer since approximately the days of the Civil War, had been voted out and George Bannerman had been voted in, largely on an aggressive campaign to catch the "Castle Rock Strangler."

Two years passed. The strangler had not been apprehended, but no further murders occurred, either. Then, last January, the body of seventeen-year-old Carol Dunbarger had been found by two small boys. The Dunbarger girl had been reported as a missing person by her parents. She had been in and out of trouble at Castle Rock High School where she had a record of chronic tardiness and truancy, she had been busted twice for shoplifting, and had run away once before, getting as far as Boston. Both Bannerman and the state police assumed she had been thumbing a ride—and the killer had picked her up. A midwinter thaw had uncovered her body near Strimmer's Brook, where two small boys had found it. The state medical examiner said she had been dead about two months.

Then, this November 2, there had been yet another murder. The victim was a well-liked Castle Rock grammar school teacher named Etta Ringgold. She was a lifetime member of the local Methodist church, holder of an M.B.S. in elementary education, and prominent in local charities. She had been fond of the works of Robert Browning, and her body had been found stuffed into a culvert that ran beneath an unpaved secondary road. The uproar over the murder of Miss Ringgold had rumbled over all of northern New England. Comparisons to Albert DeSalvo, the Boston Strangler, were made—comparisons that did nothing to pour oil on the troubled waters. William Loeb's *Union-Leader* in not-so-distant Manchester, New Hampshire, had published a helpful editorial titled THE DO-NOTHING COPS IN OUR SISTER STATE.

This Sunday supplement article, now nearly four weeks old and smelling pungently of shed and woodbox, quoted two local psychiatrists who had been perfectly happy to blue-sky the situation as long as their names weren't printed. One of them mentioned a particular sexual aberration—the urge to commit some violent act at the moment of orgasm. Nice, Johnny thought, grimacing. He strangled them to death as he came. His headache was getting worse all the time.

The other shrink pointed out the fact that all five murders had been committed in late fall or early winter. And while the manic-depressive personality didn't conform to any one set pattern, it was fairly common for such a person to have mood-swings closely paralleling the change of the seasons. He might have a "low" lasting from mid-April until about the end of August and then begin to climb, "peaking" at around the time of the murders.

During the manic or "up" state, the person in question was apt to be highly sexed, active, daring, and optimistic. "He would be likely to believe the police unable to catch him," the unnamed psychiatrist had finished. The article concluded by saying that, so far, the person in question had been right.

Johnny put the paper down, glanced at the clock, and saw his father should be home almost anytime, unless the snow was holding him up. He took the old newspaper over to the wood stove and poked it into the firebox.

Not my business. Goddam Sam Weizak anyway.

Don't hide away in a cave, Johnny.

He wasn't hiding away in a cave, that wasn't it at all. It just so happened that he'd had a fairly tough break. Losing a big chunk of your life, that qualified you for tough-break status, didn't it?

And all the self-pity you can guzzle?

"Fuck you," he muttered to himself. He went to the window and looked out. Nothing to see but snow falling in heavy, wind-driven lines. He hoped dad was being careful, but he also hoped his father would show up soon and put an end to this useless rat-run of introspection. He went over to the telephone again and stood there, undecided.

Self-pity or not, he *had* lost a goodish chunk of his life. His *prime,* if you wanted to put it that way. He had worked hard to get back. Didn't he deserve some ordinary privacy? Didn't he have a right to what he had just been thinking of a few minutes ago—an ordinary life?

There is no such thing, my man.

Maybe not, but there sure was such a thing as an *ab*normal life. That thing at Cole's Farm. Feeling people's clothes and suddenly knowing their little dreads, small secrets, petty triumphs—that was abnormal. It was a talent, it was a curse.

Suppose he did meet this sheriff? There was no guarantee he could tell him a thing. And suppose he could? Just suppose he could hand him his killer on a silver platter? It would be the hospital press conference all over again, a three-ring circus raised to the grisly nth power.

A little song began to run maddeningly through his aching head, little more than a jingle, really. A Sunday-school song from his early childhood: *This little light of mine . . . I'm gonna let it shine . . . this little light of mine . . . I'm gonna let it shine . . . let it shine, shine, shine, let it shine . . .*

He picked up the phone and dialed Weizak's office number. Safe enough now, after five. Weizak would have gone home, and big-deal neurologists don't list their home phones. The phone rang six or seven times and Johnny was going to put it down when it was answered and Sam himself said, "Hi? Hello?"

"Sam?"

"John Smith?" The pleasure in Sam's voice was unmistakable—but was there also an undercurrent of unease in it?

"Yeah, it's me."

"How do you like this snow?" Weizak said, maybe a little too heartily. "Is it snowing where you are?"

"It's snowing."

"Just started here about an hour ago. They say . . . John? Is it the sheriff? Is that why you sound so cold?"

"Well, he called me," Johnny said, "and I've been sort of wondering what happened. Why you gave him my name. Why you didn't call me and say you had . . . and why you didn't call me first and ask if you could."

Weizak sighed. "Johnny, I could maybe give you a lie, but that would be no good. I didn't ask you first because I was afraid you would say no. And I didn't tell you I'd done it afterward because the sheriff laughed at me. When someone laughs at one of my suggestions, I assume, nuh, that the suggestion is not going to be taken."

Johnny rubbed at one aching temple with his free hand and closed his eyes. "But why, Sam? You know how I feel about that. You were the one who told me to keep my head down and let it blow over. You told me that yourself."

"It was the piece in the paper," Sam said. "I said to myself, Johnny lives down that way. And I said to myself, five dead women. Five." His voice was slow, halting, and embarrassed. It made Johnny feel much worse to hear Sam sounding like this. He wished he hadn't called.

"Two of them teen-age girls. A young mother. A teacher of young children who loved Browning. All of it so corny, nuh? So corny I suppose they would never make a movie or a TV show out of it. But nonetheless true. It was the teacher I thought about most. Stuffed into a culvert like a bag of garbage . . ."

"You had no damn right to bring me into your guilt fantasies," Johnny said thickly.

"No, perhaps not."

"No perhaps about it!"

"Johnny, are you all right? You sound . . ."

"I'm fine!" Johnny shouted.

"You don't sound fine."

"I've got a shitter of a headache, is that so surprising? I wish to *Christ* you'd left this alone. When I told you about your mother you didn't call her. Because you said . . ."

"I said some things are better lost than found. But that is not always true, Johnny. This man, whoever he is, has a terribly disturbed personality. He may kill himself. I am sure that

when he stopped for two years the police thought he had.
But a manic-depressive sometimes has long level periods—it
is called a 'plateau of normality'—and then goes back to the
same mood-swings. He may have killed himself after murder-
ing that teacher last month. But if he hasn't, what then? He
may kill another one. Or two. Or four. Or . . ."

"Stop it."

Sam said, "Why did Sheriff Bannerman call you? What
made him change his mind?"

"I don't know. I suppose the voters are after him."

"I'm sorry I called him, Johnny, and that this has upset you
so. But even more I am sorry that I did not call you and tell
you what I had done. I was wrong. God knows you have a
right to live your life quietly."

Hearing his own thoughts echoed did not make him feel
better. Instead he felt more miserable and guilty than ever.

"All right," he said. "That's okay, Sam."

"I'll not say anything to anyone again. I suppose that is like
putting a new lock on the barn door after a horse theft, but
it's all I can say. I was indiscreet. In a doctor, that's bad."

"All right," Johnny said again. He felt helpless, and the
slow embarrassment with which Sam spoke made it worse.

"I'll see you soon?"

"I'll be up in Cleaves next month to start teaching. I'll
drop by."

"Good. Again, my sincere apologies, John."

Stop saying that!

They said their good-byes and Johnny hung up, wishing he
hadn't called at all. Maybe he hadn't wanted Sam to agree so
readily that what he had done was wrong. Maybe what he
had really wanted Sam to say was, *Sure I called him. I wanted
you to get off your ass and do something.*

He wandered across to the window and looked out into the
blowing darkness. *Stuffed into a culvert like a bag of garbage.*

God, how his head ached.

◆ **5** ◆

Herb got home half an hour later, took one look at Johnny's
white face and said, "Headache?"

"Yeah."

"Bad?"

"Not too bad."

"We want to watch the national news," Herb said. "Glad I got home in time. Bunch of people from NBC were over in Castle Rock this afternoon, filming. That lady reporter you think is so pretty was there. Cassie Mackin."

He blinked at the way Johnny turned on him. For a moment it seemed that Johnny's face was all eyes, staring out at him and full of a nearly inhuman pain.

"Castle Rock? Another murder?"

"Yeah. They found a little girl on the town common this morning. Saddest damn thing you ever heard of. I guess she had a pass to go across the common to the library for some project she was working on. She got to the library but she never got back . . . Johnny, you look terrible, boy."

"How old was she?"

"Just nine," Herb said. "A man who'd do a thing like that should be strung up by the balls. That's my view on it."

"Nine," Johnny said, and sat down heavily. "Stone the crows."

"Johnny, you sure you feel okay? You're white as paper."

"Fine. Turn on the news."

Shortly, John Chancellor was in front of them, bearing his nightly satchel of political aspirations (Fred Harris's campaign was not catching much fire), government edicts (the cities of America would just have to learn common budgetary sense, according to President Ford), international incidents (a nationwide strike in France), the Dow Jones (up), and a "heart-warming" piece about a boy with cerebral palsy who was raising a 4-H cow.

"Maybe they cut it," Herb said.

But after a commercial, Chancellor said: "In western Maine, there's a townful of frightened, angry people tonight. The town is Castle Rock, and over the last five years there have been five nasty murders—five women ranging in age from seventy-one to fourteen have been raped and strangled. Today there was a sixth murder in Castle Rock, and the victim was a nine-year-old girl. Catherine Mackin is in Castle Rock with the story."

And there she was, looking like a figment of make-believe carefully superimposed on a real setting. She was standing across from the Town Office Building. The first of that afternoon's snow which had developed into tonight's blizzard was powdering the shoulders of her coat and her blonde hair.

"A sense of quietly mounting hysteria lies over this small New England mill town this afternoon," she began. "The townspeople of Castle Rock have been nervous for a long time over the unknown person the local press calls 'the Castle Rock Strangler' or sometimes 'the November Killer.' That nervousness has changed to terror—no one here thinks that word is too strong—following the discovery of Mary Kate Hendrasen's body on the town common, not far from the bandstand where the body of the November Killer's first victim, a waitress named Alma Frechette, was discovered."

A long panning shot of the town common, looking bleak and dead in the falling snow. This was replaced with a school photograph of Mary Kate Hendrasen, grinning brashly through a heavy set of braces. Her hair was a fine white-blonde. Her dress was an electric blue. Most likely her best dress, Johnny thought sickly. Her mother put her into her best dress for her school photo.

The reporter went on—now they were recapitulating the past murders—but Johnny was on the phone, first to directory assistance and then to the Castle Rock town offices. He dialed slowly, his head thudding.

Herb came out of the living room and looked at him curiously. "Who are you calling, son?"

Johnny shook his head and listened to the phone ring on the other end. It was picked up. "Castle County sheriff's office."

"I'd like to talk to Sheriff Bannerman, please."

"Could I have your name?"

"John Smith, from Pownal."

"Hold on, please."

Johnny turned to look at the TV and saw Bannerman as he had been that afternoon, bundled up in a heavy parka with county sheriff patches on the shoulders. He looked uncomfortable and dogged as he fielded the reporters' questions. He was a broad-shouldered man with a big, sloping head capped with curly dark hair. The rimless glasses he wore looked strangely out of place, as spectacles always seem to look out of place on very big men.

"We're following up a number of leads," Bannerman said.

"Hello? Mr. Smith?" Bannerman said.

Again that queer sense of doubling. Bannerman was in two places at one time. Two *times* at one time, if you wanted to look at it that way. Johnny felt an instant of helpless vertigo.

He felt the way, God help him, you felt on one of those cheap carnival rides, the Tilt-A-Whirl or the Crack-The-Whip.

"Mr. Smith? Are you there, man?"

"Yes, I'm here." He swallowed. "I've changed my mind."

"Good boy! I'm damned glad to hear it."

"I still may not be able to help you, you know."

"I know that. But . . . no venture, no gain." Bannerman cleared his throat. "They'd run me out of this town on a rail if they knew I was down to consulting a psychic."

Johnny's face was touched with a ghost of a grin. "And a *discredited* psychic, at that."

"Do you know where Jon's in Bridgton is?"

"I can find it."

"Can you meet me there at eight o'clock?"

"Yes, I think so."

"Thank you, Mr. Smith."

"All right."

He hung up. Herb was watching him closely. Behind him, the "Nightly News" credits were rolling.

"He called you earlier, huh?"

"Yeah, he did. Sam Weizak told him I might be able to help."

"Do you think you can?"

"I don't know," Johnny said, "but my headache feels a little better."

◆ 6 ◆

He was fifteen minutes late getting to Jon's Restaurant in Bridgton; it seemed to be the only business establishment on Bridgton's main drag that was still open. The plows were falling behind the snow, and there were drifts across the road in several places. At the junction of Routes 302 and 117, the blinker light swayed back and forth in the screaming wind. A police cruiser with CASTLE COUNTY SHERIFF in gold leaf on the door was parked in front of Jon's. He parked behind it and went inside.

Bannerman was sitting at a table in front of a cup of coffee and a bowl of chili. The TV had misled. He wasn't a big man; he was a huge man. Johnny walked over and introduced himself.

Bannerman stood up and shook the offered hand. Looking

at Johnny's white, strained face and the way his thin body seemed to float inside his Navy pea jacket, Bannerman's first thought was: *This guy is sick—he's maybe not going to live too long.* Only Johnny's eyes seemed to have any real life— they were a direct, piercing blue, and they fixed firmly on Bannerman's own with sharp, honest curiosity. And when their hands clasped, Bannerman felt a peculiar kind of sur- prise, a sensation he would later describe as a *draining*. It was a little like getting a shock from a bare electrical wire. Then it was gone.

"Glad you could come," Bannerman said. "Coffee?"

"Yes."

"How about a bowl of chili? They make great damn chili here. I'm not supposed to eat it because of my ulcer, but I do anyway." He saw the look of surprise on Johnny's face and smiled. "I know, it doesn't seem right, a great big guy like me having an ulcer, does it?"

"I guess anyone can get one."

"You're damn tooting," Bannerman said. "What changed your mind?"

"It was the news. The little girl. Are you sure it was the same guy?"

"It was the same guy. Same M.O. And the same sperm type."

He watched Johnny's face as the waitress came over. "Cof- fee?" she asked.

"Tea," Johnny said.

"And bring him a bowl of chili, Miss," Bannerman said. When the waitress had gone he said, "This doctor, he says that if you touch something, sometimes you get ideas about where it came from, who might have owned it, that sort of thing."

Johnny smiled. "Well," he said, "I just shook your hand and I know you've got an Irish setter named Rusty. And I know he's old and going blind and you think it's time he was put to sleep, but you don't know how you'd explain it to your girl."

Bannerman dropped his spoon back into his chili—*plop*. He stared at Johnny with his mouth open. "By God," he said. "You got that from me? Just now?"

Johnny nodded.

Bannerman shook his head and muttered, "It's one thing

to hear something like that and another to . . . doesn't it tire you out?"

Johnny looked at Bannerman, surprised. It was a question he had never been asked before. "Yes. Yes, it does."

"But you knew. I'll be *damned*."

"But look, Sheriff."

"George. Just plain George."

"Okay, I'm Johnny, just Johnny. George, what I don't know about you would fill about five books. I don't know where you grew up or where you went to police school or who your friends are or where you live. I know you've got a little girl, and her name's something like Cathy, but that's not quite it. I don't know what you did last week or what beer you favor or what your favorite TV program is."

"My daughter's name is Katrina," Bannerman said softly. "She's nine, too. She was in Mary Kate's class."

"What I'm trying to say is that the . . . the knowing is sometimes a pretty limited thing. Because of the dead zone."

"Dead zone?"

"It's like some of the signals don't conduct," Johnny said. "I can never get streets or addresses. Numbers are hard but they sometimes come." The waitress returned with Johnny's tea and chili. He tasted the chili and nodded at Bannerman. "You're right. It's good. Especially on a night like this."

"Go to it," Bannerman said. "Man, I love good chili. My ulcer hollers bloody hell about it. Fuck you, ulcer, I say. Down the hatch."

They were quiet for a moment. Johnny worked on his chili and Bannerman watched him curiously. He supposed Smith could have found out he had a dog named Rusty. He even could have found out that Rusty was old and nearly blind. Take it a step farther: if he knew Katrina's name, he might have done that "something like Cathy but that's not quite it" routine just to add the right touch of hesitant realism. But *why?* And none of that explained that queer, zapped feeling he'd gotten in his head when Smith touched his hand. If it was a con, it was a damned good one.

Outside, the wind gusted to a low shriek that seemed to rock the small building on its foundations. A flying veil of snow lashed the Pondicherry Bowling Lanes across the street.

"Listen to that," Bannerman said. "Supposed to keep up all night. Don't tell *me* the winters're getting milder."

"Have you got something?" Johnny asked. "Something that belonged to the guy you're looking for?"

"We think we might," Bannerman said, and then shook his head. "But it's pretty thin."

"Tell me."

Bannerman laid it out for him. The grammar school and the library sat facing each other across the town common. It was standard operating procedure to send students across when they needed a book for a project or a report. The teacher gave them a pass and the librarian initialed it before sending them back. Near the center of the common, the land dipped slightly. On the west side of the dip was the town bandstand. In the dip itself were two dozen benches where people sat during band concerts and football rallies in the fall.

"We think he just sat himself down and waited for a kid to come along. He would have been out of sight from both sides of the common. But the footpath runs along the north side of the dip, close to those benches."

Bannerman shook his head slowly.

"What makes it worse is that the Frechette woman was killed right *on* the bandstand. I am going to face a shitstorm about that at town meeting in March—that is, if I'm still around in March. Well, I can show them a memo I wrote to the town manager, requesting adult crossing guards on the common during school hours. Not that it was this killer that I was worried about, Christ, no. Never in my wildest dreams did I think he'd go back to the same spot a second time."

"The town manager turned down the crossing guards?"

"Not enough money," Bannerman said. "Of course, he can spread the blame around to the town selectmen, and they'll try to spread it back on me, and the grass will grow up on Mary Kate Hendrasen's grave and . . ." He paused a moment, or perhaps choked on what he was saying. Johnny gazed at his lowered head sympathetically.

"It might not have made any difference anyhow," Bannerman went on in a dryer voice. "Most of the crossing guards we use are women, and this fuck we're after doesn't seem to care how old or young they are."

"But you think he waited on one of those benches?"

Bannerman did. They had found an even dozen fresh cigarette butts near the end of one of the benches, and four more behind the bandstand itself, along with an empty box. Marlboros, unfortunately—the second or third most popular brand in the country. The cellophane on the box had been dusted for prints and had yielded none at all.

"None at all?" Johnny said. "That's a little funny, isn't it?"

"Why do you say so?"

"Well, you'd guess the killer was wearing gloves even if he wasn't thinking about prints—it was cold out—but you'd think the guy that sold him the cigarettes . . ."

Bannerman grinned. "You've got a head for this work," he said, "but you're not a smoker."

"No," Johnny said. "I used to smoke a few cigarettes when I was in college, but I lost the habit after my accident."

"A man keeps his cigarettes in his breast pocket. Take them out, get a cigarette, put the pack back. If you're wearing gloves and not leaving fresh prints every time you get a butt, what you're doing is polishing that cellophane wrapper. Get it? And you missed one other thing, Johnny. Need me to tell you?"

Johnny thought it over and then said, "Maybe the pack of cigarettes came out of a carton. And those cartons are packed by machine."

"That's it," Bannerman said. "You *are* good at this."

"What about the tax stamp on the package?"

"Maine," Bannerman said.

"So if the killer and the smoker were the same man . . ." Johnny said thoughtfully.

Bannerman shrugged. "Sure, there's the technical possibility that they weren't. But I've tried to imagine who else would want to sit on a bench in the town common on a cold, cloudy winter morning long enough to smoke twelve or sixteen cigarettes, and I come up a blank."

Johnny sipped his tea. "None of the other kids that crossed saw anything?"

"Nothing," Bannerman said. "I've talked to every kid that had a library pass this morning."

"That's a lot weirder than the fingerprint business. Doesn't it strike you that way?"

"It strikes me as goddam scary. Look, the guy is sitting there, and what he's waiting for is one kid—one *girl*—by herself. He can hear the kids as they come along. And each time he fades back behind the bandstand . . ."

"Tracks," Johnny said.

"Not this morning. There was no snow-cover this morning. Just frozen ground. So here's this crazy shitbag that ought to have his own testicles carved off and served to him for dinner, here he is, skulking behind the bandstand. At about 8:50 A.M., Peter Harrington and Melissa Loggins came along. School has been in session about twenty minutes at that time. When they're gone, he goes back to his bench. At 9:15 he fades back behind the bandstand again. This time it's two little girls, Susan Flarhaty and Katrina Bannerman.''

Johnny set his mug of tea down with a bang. Bannerman had taken off his spectacles and was polishing them savagely.

"Your *daughter* crossed this morning? Jesus!''

Bannerman put his glasses on again. His face was dark and dull with fury. And he's afraid, Johnny saw. Not afraid that the voters would turn him out, or that the *Union-Leader* would publish another editorial about nitwit cops in western Maine, but afraid because, if his daughter had happened to go to the library alone this morning—

"My daughter,'' Bannerman agreed softly. "I think she passed within forty feet of that . . . that animal. You know what that makes me feel like?''

"I can guess,'' Johnny said.

"No, I don't think you can. It makes me feel like I almost stepped into an empty elevator shaft. Like I passed up the mushrooms at dinner and someone else died of toadstool poisoning. And it makes me feel dirty. It makes me feel *filthy*. I guess maybe it also explains why I finally called you. I'd do anything right now to nail this guy. Anything at all.''

Outside, a giant orange plow loomed out of the snow like something from a horror movie. It parked and two men got out. They crossed the street to Jon's and sat at the counter. Johnny finished his tea. He no longer wanted the chili.

"This guy goes back to his bench,'' Bannerman resumed, "but not for long. Around 9:25 he hears the Harrington boy and the Loggins girl coming back from the library. So he goes back behind the bandstand again. It must have been around 9:25 because the librarian signed them out at 9:18. At 9:45 three boys from the fifth grade went past the bandstand on their way to the library. One of them thinks he might have seen 'some guy' standing on the other side of the bandstand. That's our whole description. 'Some guy.' We ought to put it out on the wire, what do you think? Be on the lookout for some guy.''

Bannerman uttered a short laugh like a bark.

"At 9:55 my daughter and her friend Susan go by on their

way back to school. Then, about 10:05, Mary Kate Hendrasen came along . . . by herself. Katrina and Sue met her going down the school steps as they were going up. They all said hi."

"Dear God," Johnny muttered. He ran his hands through his hair.

"Last of all, 10:30 A.M. The three fifth-grade boys are coming back. One of them sees something on the bandstand. It's Mary Kate, with her leotard and her underpants yanked down, blood all over her legs, her face . . . her face . . ."

"Take it easy," Johnny said, and put a hand on Bannerman's arm.

"No, I can't take it easy," Bannerman said. He spoke almost apologetically. "I've never seen anything like that, not in eighteen years of police work. He raped that little girl and that would have been enough . . . enough to, you know, kill her . . . the medical examiner said the way he did it . . . he ruptured something and it . . . yeah, it probably would have, well . . . killed her . . . but then he had to go on and choke her. Nine years old and choked and left . . . left on the bandstand with her underpants pulled down."

Suddenly Bannerman began to cry. The tears filled his eyes behind his glasses and then rolled down his face in two streams. At the counter, the two guys from the Bridgton road crew were talking about the Super Bowl. Bannerman took his glasses off again and mopped his face with his handkerchief. His shoulders shook and heaved. Johnny waited, stirring his chili aimlessly.

After a little while, Bannerman put his handkerchief away. His eyes were red, and Johnny thought how oddly naked his face looked without his glasses.

"I'm sorry, man," he said. "It's been a very long day."

"It's all right," Johnny said.

"I knew I was going to do that, but I thought I could hold on until I got home to my wife."

"Well, I guess that was just too long to wait."

"You're a sympathetic ear." Bannerman slipped his glasses back on. "No, you're more than that. You've got something. I'll be damned if I know just what it is, but it's something."

"What else have you got to go on?"

"Nothing. I'm taking most of the heat, but the state police haven't exactly distinguished themselves. Neither has the attorney general's special investigator, or our pet FBI man. The county M.E. has been able to type the sperm, but that's no good to us at this stage of the game. The thing that bothers me the most is the lack of hair or skin under the victims' fingernails. They all must have struggled, but we don't have as much as a centimeter of skin. The devil must be on this guy's side. He hasn't dropped a button or a shopping list or left a single damn track. We got a shrink from Augusta, also courtesy of the state A.G., and he tells us all these guys give themselves away sooner or later. Some comfort. What if it's later . . . say about twelve bodies from now?"

"The cigarette pack is in Castle Rock?"

"Yes."

Johnny stood up. "Well, let's take a ride."

"My car?"

Johnny smiled a little as the wind rose, shrieking, outside. "On a night like this, it pays to be with a policeman," he said.

◆ 7 ◆

The snowstorm was at its height and it took them an hour and a half to get over to Castle Rock in Bannerman's cruiser. It was twenty past ten when they came in through the foyer of the Town Office Building and stamped the snow off their boots.

There were half a dozen reporters in the lobby, most of them sitting on a bench under a gruesome oil portrait of some town founding father, telling each other about previous night watches. They were up and surrounding Bannerman and Johnny in no time.

"Sheriff Bannerman, is it true there has been a break in the case?"

"I have nothing for you at this time," Bannerman said stolidly.

"There's been a rumor that you've taken a man from Oxford into custody, Sheriff, is that true?"

"No. If you folks will pardon us . . ."

But their attention had turned to Johnny, and he felt a sinking sensation in his belly as he recognized at least two faces from the press conference at the hospital.

"Holy God!" one of them exclaimed. "You're John Smith, aren't you?"

Johnny felt a crazy urge to take the fifth like a gangster at a Senate committee hearing.

"Yes," he said. "That's me."

"The psychic guy?" another asked.

"Look, let us pass!" Bannerman said, raising his voice. "Haven't you guys got anything better to do than . . ."

"According to *Inside View,* you're a fake," a young man in a heavy topcoat said. "Is that true?"

"All I can say about that is *Inside View* prints what they want," Johnny said. "Look, really . . ."

"You're denying the *Inside View* story?"

"Look, I really can't say anything more."

As they went through the frosted glass door and into the sheriff's office, the reporters were racing toward the two pay phones on the wall by the dog warden's office.

"Now the shit has truly hit the fan," Bannerman said unhappily. "I swear before God I never thought they'd still be here on a night like this. I should have brought you in the back."

"Oh, didn't you know?" Johnny asked bitterly. "We love the publicity. All of us psychics are in it for the publicity."

"No, I don't believe that," Bannerman said. "At least not of you. Well, it's happened. Can't be helped now."

But in his mind, Johnny could visualize the headlines: a little extra seasoning in a pot of stew that was already bubbling briskly. CASTLE ROCK SHERIFF DEPUTIZES LOCAL PSYCHIC IN STRANGLER CASE. "NOVEMBER KILLER" TO BE INVESTIGATED BY SEER. HOAX ADMISSION STORY A FABRICATION, SMITH PROTESTS.

There were two deputies in the outer office, one of them snoozing, the other drinking coffee and looking glumly through a pile of reports.

"His wife kick him out or something?" Bannerman asked sourly, nodding toward the sleeper.

"He just got back from Augusta," the deputy said. He was little more than a kid himself, and there were dark circles of weariness under his eyes. He glanced over at Johnny curiously.

"Johnny Smith, Frank Dodd. Sleeping beauty over there is Roscoe Fisher."

Johnny nodded hello.

"Roscoe says the A.G. wants the whole case," Dodd told Bannerman. His look was angry and defiant and somehow pathetic. "Some Christmas present, huh?"

Bannerman put a hand on the back of Dodd's neck and shook him gently. "You worry too much, Frank. Also, you're spending too much time on the case."

"I just keep thinking there must be something in these reports . . ." He shrugged and then flicked them with one finger. "*Something.*"

"Go home and get some rest, Frank. And take sleeping beauty with you. All we need is for one of those photographers to get a picture of him. They'd run it in the papers with a caption like 'In Castle Rock the Intensive Investigation Goes On,' and we'd all be out sweeping streets."

Bannerman led Johnny into his private office. The desk was awash in paperwork. On the windowsill was a triptych showing Bannerman, his wife, and his daughter Katrina. His degree hung neatly framed on the wall, and beside it, in another frame, the front page of the Castle Rock *Call* which had announced his election.

"Coffee?" Bannerman asked him, unlocking a file cabinet.

"No thanks. I'll stick to tea."

"Mrs. Sugarman guards her tea jealously," Bannerman said. "Takes it home with her every day, sorry. I'd offer you a tonic, but we'd have to run the gauntlet out there again to get to the machine. Jesus Christ, I wish they'd go home."

"That's okay."

Bannerman came back with a small clasp envelope. "This is it," he said. He hesitated for a moment, then handed the envelope over.

Johnny held it but did not immediately open it. "As long as you understand that nothing comes guaranteed. I can't promise. Sometimes I can and sometimes I can't."

Bannerman shrugged tiredly and repeated: "No venture, no gain."

Johnny undid the clasp and shook an empty Marlboro cigarette box out into his hand. Red and white box. He held it in his left hand and looked at the far wall. Gray wall. Industrial gray wall. Red and white box. Industrial gray box. He put the cigarette package in his other hand, then cupped it in both. He waited for something, anything to come. Nothing did. He held it longer, hoping against hope, ignoring the knowledge that when things came, they came at once.

At last he handed the cigarette box back. "I'm sorry," he said.

"No soap, huh?"

"No."

There was a perfunctory tap at the door and Roscoe Fisher stuck his head in. He looked a bit shamefaced. "Frank and I are going home, George. I guess you caught me coopin."

"As long as I don't catch you doing it in your cruiser," Bannermann said. "Say hi to Deenie for me."

"You bet." Fisher glanced at Johnny for a moment and then closed the door.

"Well," Bannerman said. "It was worth the try, I guess. I'll run you back . . ."

"I want to go over to the common," Johnny said abruptly.

"No, that's no good. It's under a foot of snow."

"You can find the place, can't you?"

"Of course I can. But what'll it gain?"

"I don't know. But let's go across."

"Those reporters are going to follow us, Johnny. Just as sure as God made little fishes."

"You said something about a back door."

"Yeah, but it's a fire door. Getting in that way is okay, but if we use it to go out, the alarm goes off."

Johnny whistled through his teeth. "Let them follow along, then."

Bannermann looked at him thoughtfully for several moments and then nodded. "Okay."

◆ 8 ◆

When they came out of the office, the reporters were up and surrounding them immediately. Johnny was reminded of a rundown kennel over in Durham where a strange old woman kept collies. The dogs would all run out at you when you went past with your fishing pole, yapping and snarling and generally scaring the hell out of you. They would nip but not actually bite.

"Do you know who did it, Johnny?"

"Have any ideas at all?"

"Got any brainwaves, Mr. Smith?"

"Sheriff, was calling in a psychic your idea?"

"Do the state police and the A.G.'s office know about this development, Sheriff Bannerman?"

"Do you think you can break the case, Johnny?"

"Sheriff, have you deputized this guy?"

Bannerman pushed his way slowly and solidly through them, zipping his coat. "No comment, no comment." Johnny said nothing at all.

The reporters clustered in the foyer as Johnny and Bannerman went down and snowy steps. It wasn't until they bypassed the cruiser and began wading across the street that one of them realized they were going to the common. Several of them ran back for their topcoats. Those who had been dressed for outside when Bannerman and Johnny emerged from the office now floundered down the Town Office steps after them, calling like children.

◆ 9 ◆

Flashlights bobbing in the snowy dark. The wind howled, blowing snow past them this way and that in errant sheets.

"You're not gonna be able to see a damn thing," Bannerman said. "You w . . . *holy shit!*" He was almost knocked off his feet as a reporter in a bulky overcoat and a bizarre tam o'shanter sprawled into him.

"Sorry, Sheriff," he said sheepishly. "Slippery. Forgot my galoshes."

Up ahead a yellow length of nylon rope appeared out of the gloom. Attached to it was a wildly swinging sign reading POLICE INVESTIGATION.

"You forgot your brains, too," Bannerman said. "Now you keep back, all of you! Keep right back!"

"Town common's public property, Sheriff!" one of the reporters cried.

"That's right, and this is police business. You stay behind this rope here or you'll spend the night in my holding cell."

With the beam of his flashlight he traced the course of the rope for them and then held it up so Johnny could pass beneath. They walked down the slope toward the snowmounded shapes of the benches. Behind them the reporters gathered at the rope, pooling their few lights so that Johnny and George Bannerman walked in a dull sort of spotlight.

"Flying blind," Bannerman said.

"Well, there's nothing to see, anyway," Johnny said. "Is there?"

"No, not now. I told Frank he could take that rope down

anytime. Now I'm glad he didn't get around to it. You want to go over to the bandstand?"

"Not yet. Show me where the cigarette butts were."

They went on a little farther and then Bannerman stopped. "Here," he said, and shone his light on a bench that was little more than a vague hump poking out of a drift.

Johnny took off his gloves and put them in his coat pockets. Then he knelt and began to brush the snow away from the seat of the bench. Again Bannerman was struck by the haggard pallor of the man's face. On his knees before the bench he looked like a religious penitent, a man in desperate prayer.

Johnny's hands went cold, then mostly numb. Melted snow ran off his fingers. He got down to the splintered, weather-beaten surface of the bench. He seemed to see it very clearly, almost with magnifying power. It had once been green, but now much of the paint had flaked and eroded away. Two rusted steel bolts held the seat to the backrest.

He seized the bench in both hands, and sudden weirdness flooded him—he had felt nothing so intense before and would feel something so intense only once ever again. He stared down at the bench, frowning, gripping it tightly in his hands. It was . . .

(A summer bench)

How many hundreds of different people had sat here at one time or another, listening to "God Bless America," to "Stars and Stripes Forever" *("Be kind to your web-footed friends . . . for a duck may be somebody's mooooother . . ."),* to the Castle Rock Cougars' fight song? Green summer leaves, smoky haze of fall like a memory of cornhusks and men with rakes in mellow dusk. The thud of the big snare drum. Mellow gold trumpets and trombones. School band uniforms . . .

(for a duck . . . may be . . . somebody's mother . . .)

Good summer people sitting here, listening, applauding, holding programs that had been designed and printed in the Castle Rock High School graphic arts shop.

But this morning a killer had been sitting here. Johnny could *feel* him.

Dark tree branches etched against a gray snow-sky like runes. He (I) am sitting here, smoking, waiting, feeling good, feeling like he (I) could jump right over the roof of the world and land lightly on two feet. Humming a song. Something by the Rolling Stones. Can't get that, but very clearly everything is . . . is what?

All right. *Everything is all right, everything is gray and waiting for snow, and I'm . . .*

"Slick," Johnny muttered. "I'm slick, I'm so slick."

Bannerman leaned forward, unable to catch the words over the howling wind. "What?"

"Slick," Johnny repeated. He looked up at Bannerman and the Sheriff involuntarily took a step backward. Johnny's eyes were cool and somehow inhuman. His dark hair blew wildly around his white face, and overhead the winter wind screamed through the black sky. His hands seemed welded to the bench.

"*I'm so fucking slick,*" he said clearly. A triumphant smile had formed on his lips. His eyes stared through Bannerman. Bannerman believed. No one could be acting this, or putting it on. And the most terrible part of it was . . . he was *reminded* of someone. The smile . . . the tone of voice . . . Johnny Smith was gone; he seemed to have been replaced by a human blank. And lurking behind the planes of his ordinary features, almost near enough to touch, was another face. The face of the killer.

The face of someone he *knew.*

"Never catch me because I'm too slick for you." A little laugh escaped him, confident, lightly taunting. "I put it on every time, and if they scratch . . . or bite . . . they don't get a bit of me . . . because *I'm so SLICK!*" His voice rose to a triumphant, crazy shriek that competed with the wind, and Bannerman fell back another step, his flesh crawling helplessly, his balls tight and cringing against his guts.

Let it stop, he thought. *Let it stop now. Please.*

Johnny bent his head over the bench. Melting snow dripped between his bare fingers.

(Snow. Silent snow, secret snow—)

(She put a clothespin on it so I'd know how it felt. How it felt when you got a disease. A disease from one of those nasty-fuckers, they're all nasty-fuckers, and they have to be stopped, yes, stopped, stop them, stop, the stop, the STOP—OH MY GOD THE STOP SIGN—!)

He was little again. Going to school through the silent, secret snow. And there was a man looming out of the shifting whiteness, a terrible man, a terrible black grinning man with eyes as shiny as quarters, and there was a red STOP sign clutched in one gloved hand . . . him! . . . him! . . . *him!*

(OH MY GOD DON'T . . . DON'T LET HIM GET ME . . . MOMMA . . . DON'T LET HIM GET MEEEEE . . .)

Johnny screamed and fell away from the bench, his hands suddenly pressed to his cheeks. Bannerman crouched beside him, badly frightened. Behind the rope the reporters stirred and murmured.

"Johnny! Snap out of it! Listen, Johnny . . ."

"Slick," Johnny muttered. He looked up at Bannerman with hurt, frightened eyes. In his mind he still saw that black shape with the shiny-quarter eyes looming out of the snow. His crotch throbbed dully from the pain of the clothespin the killer's mother had made him wear. He hadn't been the killer then, oh no, not an animal, not a pusbag or a shitbag or whatever Bannerman had called him, he'd only been a scared little boy with a clothespin on his . . . his . . .

"Help me get up," he muttered.

Bannerman helped him to his feet.

"The bandstand now," Johnny said.

"No, I think we ought to go back, Johnny."

Johnny pushed past him blindly and began to flounder toward the bandstand, a big circular shadow up ahead. It bulked and loomed in the darkness, the death place. Bannerman ran and caught up to him.

"Johnny, who is it? Do you know who . . .?"

"You never found any scraps of tissue under their fingernails because he was wearing a raincoat," Johnny said. He panted the words out. "A raincoat with a hood. A slick vinyl raincoat. You go back over the reports. You go back over the reports and you'll see. It was raining or snowing every time. They clawed at him, all right. They fought him. Sure they did. But their fingers just slipped and slid over it."

"Who, Johnny? Who?"

"I don't know. But I'm going to find out."

He stumbled over the lowest of the six steps leading up to the bandstand, fumbled for his balance, and would have lost it if Bannerman had not gripped his arm. Then they were up on the stage. The snow was thin here, a bare dusting, kept off by the conical roof. Bannerman trained his flashlight beam on the floor and Johnny dropped to his hands and knees and began to crawl slowly across it. His hands were bright red. Bannerman thought that they must be like chunks of raw meat by now.

Johnny stopped suddenly and stiffened like a dog on point. "Here," he muttered. "He did it right here."

Images and textures and sensations flooded in. The copper taste of excitement, the possibility of being seen adding to it. The girl was squirming, trying to scream. He had covered her mouth with one gloved hand. Awful excitement. Never catch me, I'm the Invisible Man, is it dirty enough for you now, momma?

Johnny began to moan, shaking his head back and forth.

Sound of clothes ripping. Warmth. Something flowing. Blood? Semen? Urine?

He began to shudder all over. His hair hung in his face. His face. His smiling, open face caught inside the circular border of the raincoat's hood as his (my) hands close around the neck at the moment of orgasm and squeeze . . . and squeeze . . . and squeeze.

The strength left his arms as the images began to fade. He slipped forward, now lying on the stage full-length, sobbing. When Bannerman touched his shoulder he cried out and tried to scramble away, his face crazy with fear. Then, little by little, it loosened. He put his head back against the waist-high bandstand railing and closed his eyes. Shudders raced through his body like whippets. His pants and coat were sugared with snow.

"I know who it is," he said.

◆ 10 ◆

Fifteen minutes later Johnny sat in Bannerman's inner office again, stripped to his shorts and sitting as close as he could to a portable electric heater. He still looked cold and miserable, but he had stopped shaking.

"Sure you don't want some coffee?"

Johnny shook his head. "I can't abide the stuff."

"Johnny . . ." Bannerman sat down. "Do you really know something?"

"I know who killed them. You would have gotten him eventually. You were just too close to it. You've even seen him in his raincoat, that shiny all-over raincoat. Because he crosses the kids in the morning. He has a stop sign on a stick and he crosses the kids in the morning."

Bannerman looked at him, thunderstruck. "Are you talking about Frank? Frank *Dodd?* You're nuts!"

"Frank Dodd killed them," Johnny said. "Frank Dodd killed them all."

Bannerman looked as though he didn't know whether to laugh at Johnny or deal him a good swift kick. "That's the craziest goddam thing I've ever heard," he said finally. "Frank Dodd's a fine officer and a fine man. He's crossing over next November to run for municipal chief of police, and he'll do it with my blessing." Now his expression was one of amusement mixed with tired contempt. "Frank's twenty-five. That means he would have had to have started this crazy shit when he was just nineteen. He lives at home very quietly with his mother, who isn't very well—hypertension, thyroid, and a semidiabetic condition. Johnny, you put your foot in the bucket. Frank Dodd is no murderer. I'd stake my life on that."

"The murders stopped for two years," Johnny said. "Where was Frank Dodd then? Was he in town?"

Bannerman turned toward him, and now the tired amusement had left his face and he only looked hard. Hard and angry. "I don't want to hear any more about this. You were right the first time—you're nothing but a fake. Well, you got your press coverage, but that doesn't mean I have to listen to you malign a good officer, a man I . . ."

"A man you think of as your son," Johnny said quietly.

Bannerman's lips thinned, and a lot of the color that had risen in his cheeks during their time outside now faded out of his face. He looked like a man who has been punched low. Then it passed and his face was expressionless.

"Get out of here," he said. "Get one of your reporter friends to give you a ride home. You can hold a press conference on your way. But I swear to God, I swear to *holy God* that if you mention Frank Dodd's name, I'll come for you and I'll break your back. Understood?"

"Sure, my buddies from the press!" Johnny shouted at him suddenly. "That's right! Didn't you see me answering all their questions? Posing for their pictures and making sure they got my good side? Making sure they spelled my name right?"

Bannerman looked startled, then hard again. "Lower your voice."

"No, I'll be goddamned if I will!" Johnny said, and his voice rose even higher in pitch and volume. "I think you forgot who called who! I'll refresh your recollection for you. It was *you*, calling *me*. That's how eager I was to get over here!"

"That doesn't mean you're . . ."

Johnny walked over to Bannerman, pointing his index finger like a pistol. He was several inches shorter and probably eighty pounds lighter, but Bannerman backed up a step—as he had done on the common. Johnny's cheeks had flushed a dull red. His lips were drawn back slightly from his teeth.

"No, you're right, you calling me doesn't mean shit in à tin bucket," he said. "But you don't *want* it to be Dodd, do you? It can be somebody else, then we'll at least look into it, but it can't be good old Frank Dodd. Because Frank's upstanding, Frank takes care of his mother, Frank looks up to good old Sheriff George Bannerman, oh, Frank's bloody Christ down from the cross except when he's raping and strangling old ladies and little girls, and it could have been your *daughter,* Bannerman, don't you understand it could have been your *own dau* . . ."

Bannerman hit him. At the last moment he pulled the punch, but it was still hard enough to knock Johnny backward; he stumbled over the leg of a chair and then sprawled on the floor. Blood trickled from his cheek where Bannerman's Police Academy ring had grazed him.

"You had that coming," Bannerman said, but there was no real conviction in his voice. It occurred to him that for the first time in his life he had hit a cripple—or the next thing to a cripple.

Johnny's head felt light and full of bells. His voice seemed to belong to someone else, a radio announcer or a B-movie actor. "You ought to get down on your knees and thank God that he really didn't leave any clues, because you would have overlooked them, feeling like you do about Dodd. And then you could have held yourself responsible in Mary Kate Hendrasen's death, as an accessory."

"That is nothing but a damnable lie," Bannerman said slowly and clearly. "I'd arrest my own brother if he was the guy doing this. Get up off the floor. I'm sorry I hit you."

He helped Johnny to his feet and looked at the scrape on his cheek.

"I'll get the first-aid kit and put some iodine on that."

"Forget it," Johnny said. The anger had left his voice. "I guess I kind of sprang it on you, didn't I?"

"I'm telling you, it can't be Frank. You're not a publicity

hound, okay. I was wrong about that. Heat of the moment, okay? But your vibes or your astral plane or whatever it is sure gave you a bum steer this time."

"Then check," Johnny said. He caught Bannerman's eyes with his own and held them. "*Check it out*. Show me I got it wrong." He swallowed. "Check the times and dates against Frank's work schedule. Can you do that?"

Grudgingly, Bannerman said, "The time cards in the back closet there go back fourteen or fifteen years. I guess I could check it."

"Then do it."

"Mister . . ." He paused. "Johnny, if you *knew* Frank, you'd laugh at yourself. I mean it. It's not just me, you ask anybody . . ."

"If I'm wrong, I'll be glad to admit it."

"This is crazy," Bannerman muttered, but he went to the storage closet where the old time cards were kept and opened the door.

◆ 11 ◆

Two hours passed. It was now nearly one o'clock in the morning. Johnny had called his father and told him he would find a place to sleep in Castle Rock; the storm had leveled off at a single furious pitch, and driving back would be next to impossible.

"What's going on over there?" Herb asked. "Can you tell me?"

"I better not over the phone, Dad."

"All right, Johnny. Don't exhaust yourself."

"No."

But he *was* exhausted. He was more tired than he could remember being since those early days in physical therapy with Eileen Magown. A nice woman, he thought randomly. A nice *friendly* woman, at least until I told her that her house was burning down. After that she had become distant and awkward. She had thanked him, sure, but—had she ever touched him after that? Actually touched him? Johnny didn't think so. And it would be the same with Bannerman when this thing was over. Too bad. Like Eileen, he was a fine man. But people get very nervous around people who can just touch things and know all about them.

"It doesn't prove a thing," Bannerman was saying now. There was a sulky, little-boy rebelliousness in his voice that rattled. But he was too tired.

They were looking down at a rough chart Johnny had made on the back of a circular for used state police interceptors. Stacked untidily by Bannerman's desk were seven or eight cartons of old time cards, and sitting in the top half of Bannerman's in/out basket were Frank Dodd's cards, going back to 1971, when he had joined the sheriff's department. The chart looked like this:

THE MURDERS	FRANK DODD
Alma Frechette (waitress) 3:00 PM, 11/12/70	Then working at Main Street Gulf Station
Pauline Toothaker 10:00 AM, 11/17/71	Off-duty
Cheryl Moody (J.H.S. student) 2:00 PM, 12/16/71	Off-duty
Carol Dunbarger (H.S. student) 11/?/74	Two-week vacation period
Etta Ringgold (teacher) 10/29(?)/75	Regular duty tours
Mary Kate Hendrasen 10:10 AM, 12/17/75	Off-duty

All times are "estimated time of death" figures supplied by State Medical Examiner

"No, it doesn't prove anything," Johnny agreed, rubbing his temples. "But it doesn't exactly rule him out, either."

Bannerman tapped the chart. "When Miss Ringgold was killed, he was on duty."

"Yeah, if she really was killed on the twenty-ninth of October. But it might have been the twenty-eighth, or the twenty-seventh. And even if he was on duty, who suspects a cop?"

Bannerman was looking at the little chart very carefully.

"What about the gap?" Johnny said. "The two-year gap?"

Bannerman thumbed the time cards. "Frank was right here on duty all during 1973 and 1974. You saw that."

"So maybe the urge didn't come on him that year. At least, so far as we know."

"So far as we know, we don't know anything," Bannerman contradicted quickly.

"But what about 1972? Late 1972 and early 1973? There are no time cards for that period. Was he on vacation?"

"No," Bannerman said. "Frank and a guy named Tom Harrison took a semester course in Rural Law Enforcement at a branch of the University of Colorado in Pueblo. It's the only place in the country where they offer a deal like that. It's an eight-week course. Frank and Tom were out there from October 15 until just about Christmas. The state pays part, the county pays part, and the U.S. government pays part under the Law Enforcement Act of 1971. I picked Harrison—he's chief of police over in Gates Falls now—and Frank. Frank almost didn't go, because he was worried about his mother being alone. To tell you the truth, I think she tried to persuade him to stay home. I talked him into it. He wants to be a career officer, and something like the Rural Law Enforcement course looks damn good on your record. I remember that when he and Tom got back in December, Frank had a low-grade virus and he looked terrible. He'd lost twenty pounds. Claimed no one out there in cow country could cook like his mom."

Bannerman fell silent. Something in what he had just said seemed to disturb him.

"He took a week's sick leave around the holidays and then he was okay," Bannerman resumed, almost defensively. "He was back by the fifteenth of January at the latest. Check the time cards for yourself."

"I don't have to. Any more than I have to tell you what your next step is."

"No," Bannerman said. He looked at his hands. "I told you that you had a head for this stuff. Maybe I was righter than I knew. Or wanted to be."

He picked up the telephone and pulled out a thick directory with a plain blue cover from the bottom drawer of his desk. Paging through it without looking up, he told Johnny, "This is courtesy of that same Law Enforcement Act. Every sheriff's office in every county of the United States." He found the number he wanted and made his call.

Johnny shifted in his seat.

"Hello," Bannerman said. "Am I talking to the Pueblo sheriff's office? . . . All right. My name is George Bannerman, I'm the county sheriff of Castle County, in western Maine . . . yes, that's what I said. State of Maine. Who am I talking to, please? . . . All right, Officer Taylor, this is the situation. We've had a series of murders out here, rape-stranglings, six of them in the past five years. All of them have taken place in the late fall or early winter. We have a . . ." He looked up at Johnny for a moment, his eyes hurt and helpless. Then he looked down at the home phone again. "We have a suspect who was in Pueblo from October 15 of 1972 until . . . uh, December 17, I think. What I'd like to know is if you have an unsolved homicide on your books during that period, victim female, no particular age, raped, cause of death, strangulation. Further, I would like to know the perpetrator's sperm type if you have had such a crime and a sperm sample was obtained. What? . . . Yes, okay. Thanks . . . I'll be right here, waiting. Good-bye, Officer Taylor."

He hung up. "He's going to verify my bona fides, then check it through, then call me back. You want a cup of . . . no, you don't drink it, do you?"

"No," Johnny said. "I'll settle for a glass of water."

He went over to the big glass cooler and drew a paper cupful of water. Outside the storm howled and pounded.

Behind him, Bannerman said awkwardly: "Yeah, okay. You were right. He's the son I'd've liked to have had. My wife had Katrina by cesarian. She can never have another one, the doctor said it would kill her. She had the Band-Aid operation and I had a vasectomy. Just to be sure."

Johnny went to the window and looked out on darkness, his cup of water in his hand. There was nothing to see but snow, but if he turned around, Bannerman would break off— you didn't have to be psychic to know that.

"Frank's dad worked on the B&M line and died in an accident when Frank was five or so. He was drunk, tried to make a coupling in a state where he probably would have pissed down his own leg and never known it. He got crushed between two flatcars. Frank's had to be the man of the house ever since. Roscoe says he had a girl in high school, but Mrs. Dodd put paid to that in a hurry."

I bet she did, Johnny thought. *A woman who would do that thing . . . that clothespin thing . . . to her own son . . . that sort of woman would stop at nothing. She must be almost as crazy as he is.*

"He came to me when he was sixteen and asked if there was such a thing as a part-time policeman. Said it was the only thing he'd ever really wanted to do or be since he was a kid. I took a shine to him right off. Hired him to work around the place and paid him out of my own pocket. Paid him what I could, you know, he never complained about the wages. He was the sort of kid who would have worked for free. He put in an application for full-time work the month before he graduated from high school, but at that time we didn't have any vacancies. So he went to work at Donny Haggars' Gulf and took a night course in police work at the university down in Gorham. I guess Mrs. Dodd tried to put paid to that, too—felt she was alone too much of the time, or something—but that time Frank stood up to her . . . with my encouragement. We took him on in July of 1971 and he's been with the department ever since. Now you tell me this and I think of Katrina being out yesterday morning, walking right past whoever did it . . . and it's like some dirty kind of incest, almost. Frank's been at our house, he's eaten our food, babysat Katie once or twice . . . and you tell me . . ."

Johnny turned around. Bannerman had taken off his glasses and was wiping his eyes again.

"If you really can see such things, I pity you. You're a freak of God, no different from a two-headed cow I once saw in the carnival. I'm sorry. That's a shit thing to say, I know."

"The Bible says God loves all his creatures," Johnny said. His voice was a bit unsteady.

"Yeah?" Bannerman nodded and rubbed the red places on the sides of his nose where his glasses sat. "Got a funny way of showing it, doesn't he?"

◆ 12 ◆

About twenty minutes later the telephone rang and Bannerman answered it smartly. Talked briefly. Listened. Johnny watched his face get old. He hung up and looked at Johnny for a long time without speaking.

"November 12, 1972," he said. "A college girl. They found

her in a field out by the turnpike. Ann Simons, her name was. Raped and strangled. Twenty-three years old. No semen type obtained. It's still not proof, Johnny."

"I don't think, in your own mind, you need any more proof," Johnny said. "And if you confront him with what you have, I think he'll break down."

"And if he doesn't?"

Johnny remembered the vision of the bandstand. It whirled back at him like a crazy, lethal boomerang. The tearing sensation. The pain that was pleasant, the pain that recalled the pain of the clothespin, the pain that reconfirmed everything.

"Get him to drop his pants," Johnny said.

Bannerman looked at him.

◆ 13 ◆

The reporters were still out in the lobby. In truth, they probably wouldn't have moved even had they not suspected a break in the case—or at least a bizarre new development. The roads out of town were impassable.

Bannerman and Johnny went out the supply closet window.

"Are you sure this is the way to do it?" Johnny asked, and the storm tried to rip the words out of his mouth. His legs hurt.

"No," Bannerman said simply, "but I think you should be in on it. Maybe I think he should have the chance to look you in the face, Johnny. Come on. The Dodds are only two blocks from here."

They set off, hooded and booted, a pair of shadows in the driving snow. Beneath his coat Bannerman was wearing his service pistol. His handcuffs were clipped to his belt. Before they had gone a block through the deep snow Johnny was limping badly, but he kept his mouth grimly shut about it.

But Bannerman noticed. They stopped in the doorway of the Castle Rock Western Auto.

"Son, what's the matter with you?"

"Nothing," Johnny said. His head was starting to ache again, too.

"It sure is something. You act like you're walking on two broken legs."

"They had to operate on my legs after I came out of the coma. The muscles had atrophied. Started to melt is how Dr.

Brown put it. The joints were decayed. They fixed it up the
best they could with synthetics . . ."

"Like the Six Million Dollar Man, huh?"

Johnny thought of the neat piles of hospital bills back
home, sitting in the top drawer of the dining room hutch.

"Yes, something like that. When I'm on them too long,
they stiffen up. That's all."

"You want to go back?"

*You bet I do. Go back and not have to think about this
hellacious business anymore. Wish I'd never come. Not my
problem. This is the guy who compared me to a two-headed
cow.*

"No, I'm okay," he said.

They stepped out of the doorway and the wind grabbed
them and tried to bowl them along the empty street. They
struggled through the harsh, snow-choked flare of arc-sodium
streetlights, bent into the wind. They turned into a side street
and five houses down Bannerman stopped in front of a small
and neat New England saltbox. Like the other houses on the
street, it was dark and battened down.

"This is the house," Bannerman said, his voice oddly color-
less. They worked their way through the snowdrift that the
wind had thrown against the porch and mounted the steps.

◆ 14 ◆

Mrs. Henrietta Dodd was a big woman who was carrying a
dead weight of flesh on her frame. Johnny had never seen a
woman who looked any sicker. Her skin was a yellowish-gray.
Her hands were nearly reptilian with an eczemalike rash. And
there was something in her eyes, narrowed to glittering slits
in their puffy sockets, that reminded him unpleasantly of the
way his mother's eyes had sometimes looked when Vera
Smith was transported into one of her religious frenzies.

She had opened the door to them after Bannerman had
rapped steadily for nearly five minutes. Johnny stood beside
him on his aching legs, thinking that this night would never
end. It would just go on and on until the snow had piled up
enough to avalanche down and bury them all.

"What do you want in the middle of the night, George
Bannerman?" she asked suspiciously. Like many fat women,

her voice was a high, buzzy reed instrument—it sounded a bit like a fly or a bee caught in a bottle.

"Have to talk to Frank, Henrietta."

"Then talk to him in the morning," Henrietta Dodd said, and started to close the door in their faces.

Bannerman stopped the door's swing with a gloved hand. "I'm sorry, Henrietta. Has to be now."

"Well, I'm not going to wake him up!" she cried, not moving from the doorway. "He sleeps like the dead anyway! Some nights I ring my bell for him, the palpitations are terrible sometimes, and does he come? No, he sleeps right through it and he could wake up some morning to find me dead of a heart attack in my bed instead of getting him his goddam runny poached egg! Because you work him too hard!"

She grinned in a sour kind of triumph; the dirty secret exposed and hats over the windmill.

"All day, all night, swing shift, chasing after drunks in the middle of the night and any one of them could have a .32 gun under the seat, going out to the ginmills and honkytonks, oh, they're a rough trade out there but a lot you mind! I guess I know what goes on in those places, those cheap slutty women that'd be happy to give a nice boy like my Frank an incurable disease for the price of a quarter beer!"

Her voice, that reed instrument, swooped and buzzed. Johnny's head pumped and throbbed in counterpoint. He wished she would shut up. It was a hallucination, he knew, just the tiredness and stress of this awful night catching up, but it began to seem more and more to him that this was his mother standing here, that at any moment she would turn from Bannerman to him and begin to huckster him about the wonderful talent God had given him.

"Mrs. Dodd . . . Henrietta . . ." Bannerman began patiently.

Then she did turn to Johnny, and regarded him with her smart-stupid little pig's eyes.

"Who's this?"

"Special deputy," Bannerman said promptly. "Henrietta, I'll take the responsibility for waking Frank up."

"Oooh, the *responsibility!*" she cooed with monstrous, buzzing sarcasm, and Johnny finally realized she was afraid. The fear was coming off her in pulsing, noisome waves—that was what was making his headache worse. Couldn't Bannerman feel it? "The ree-spon-si-*bil*-i-tee! Isn't that *biiig* of you, my God yes! Well, I won't have my boy waked up in the middle of the night, George Bannerman, so you and your *special deputy* can just go peddle your goddam papers!"

She tried to shut the door again and this time Bannerman shoved it all the way open. His voice showed tight anger and beneath that terrible tension. "Open up, Henrietta, I mean it, now."

"You can't do this!" she cried. "This isn't no police state! I'll have your job! Let's see your warrant!"

"No, that's right, but I'm going to talk to Frank," Bannerman said, and pushed past her.

Johnny, barely aware of what he was doing, followed. Henrietta Dodd made a grab for him. Johnny caught her wrist— and a terrible pain flared in his head, dwarfing the sullen thud of the headache. *And the woman felt it, too.* The two of them stared at each other for a moment that seemed to last forever, an awful, perfect understanding. For that moment they seemed welded together. Then she fell back, clutching at her ogre's bosom.

"My heart . . . my heart . . ." She scrabbled at her robe pocket and pulled out a phial of pills. Her face had gone to the color of raw dough. She got the cap off the phial and spilled tiny pills all over the floor getting one into her palm. She slipped it under her tongue. Johnny stood staring at her in mute horror. His head felt like a swelling bladder full of hot blood.

"You *knew*?" he whispered.

Her fat, wrinkled mouth opened and closed, opened and closed. No sound came out. It was the mouth of a beached fish.

"All of this time *you knew*?"

"You're a devil!" she screamed at him. "You're a monster . . . devil . . . oh my heart . . . oh, I'm dying . . . think I'm dying . . . call the doctor . . . *George Bannerman don't you go up there and wake my baby!*"

Johnny let go of her, and unconsciously rubbing his hand back and forth on his coat as if to free it of a stain, he stumbled up the stairs after Bannerman. The wind outside sobbed around the eaves like a lost child. Halfway up he glanced back. Henrietta Dodd sat in a wicker chair, a sprawled mountain of meat, gasping and holding a huge breast in each hand. His head still felt as if it were swelling and he thought dreamily: *Pretty soon it'll just pop and that'll be the end. Thank God.*

An old and threadbare runner covered the narrow hall

floor. The wallpaper was watermarked. Bannerman was
pounding on a closed door. It was at least ten degrees colder
up here.

"Frank? Frank! It's George Bannerman! Wake up, Frank!"

There was no response. Bannerman turned the knob and
shoved the door open. His hand had fallen to the butt of his
gun, but he had not drawn it. It could have been a fatal mistake, but Frank Dodd's room was empty.

The two of them stood in the doorway for a moment, looking in. It was a child's room. The wallpaper—also watermarked—was covered with dancing clowns and rocking
horses. There was a child-sized chair with a Raggedy Andy
sitting in it, looking back at them with its shiny blank eyes.
In one corner was a toybox. In the other was a narrow maple
bed with the covers thrown back. Hooked over one of the
bedposts and looking out of place was Frank Dodd's hol-
stered gun.

"My God," Bannerman said softly. "What is this?"

"Help," Mrs. Dodd's voice floated up. "Help me . . ."

"She knew," Johnny said. "She knew from the beginning,
from the Frechette woman. He told her. And she covered up
for him."

Bannerman backed slowly out of the room and opened another door. His eyes were dazed and hurt. It was a guest
bedroom, unoccupied. He opened the closet, which was empty
except for a neat tray of D-Con rat-killer on the floor. Another door. This bedroom was unfinished and cold enough to
show Bannerman's breath. He looked around. There was another door, this one at the head of the stairs. He went to it,
and Johnny followed. This door was locked.

"Frank? Are you in there?" He rattled the knob. "Open
it, Frank!"

There was no answer. Bannerman raised his foot and
kicked out, connecting with the door just below the knob.
There was a flat cracking sound that seemed to echo in Johnny's head like a steel platter dropped on a tile floor.

"Oh God," Bannerman said in a flat, choked voice.
"Frank."

Johnny could see over his shoulder; could see too much.
Frank Dodd was propped on the lowered seat of the toilet.
He was naked except for the shiny black raincoat, which he
had looped over his shoulders; the raincoat's black hood (*exe-
cutioner's hood*, Johnny thought dimly) dangled down on the

top of the toilet tank like some grotesque, deflated black pod. He had somehow managed to cut his own throat—Johnny would not have thought that possible. There was a package of Wilkinson Sword Blades on the edge of the washbasin. A single blade lay on the floor, glittering wickedly. Drops of blood had beaded on its edge. The blood from his severed jugular vein and carotid artery had splashed everywhere. There were pools of it caught in the folds of the raincoat which dragged on the floor. It was on the shower curtain, which had a pattern of paddling ducks with umbrellas held over their heads. It was on the ceiling.

Around Frank Dodd's neck on a string was a sign crayoned in lipstick. It read: I CONFESS.

The pain in Johnny's head began to climb to a sizzling, insupportable peak. He groped out with a hand and found the doorjamb.

Knew, he thought incoherently. *Knew somehow when he saw me. Knew it was all over. Came home. Did this.*

Black rings overlaying his sight, spreading like evil ripples. *What a talent God has given you, Johnny.*

(I CONFESS)

"Johnny?"

From far away.

"Johnny, are you all . . ."

Fading. Everything fading away. That was good. Would have been better if he had never come out of the coma at all. Better for all concerned. Well, he had had his chance.

"—Johnny—"

Frank Dodd had come up here and somehow he had slit his throat from the ear to the proverbial ear while the storm howled outside like all the dark things of the earth let loose. Gone a gusher, as his father had said that winter twelve years or so ago, when the pipes in the basement had frozen and burst. Gone a gusher. Sure as hell had. All the way up to the ceiling.

He believed that he might have screamed then, but afterward was never sure. It might only have been in his own head that he screamed. But he had *wanted* to scream; to scream out all the horror and pity and agony in his heart.

Then he was falling forward into darkness, and grateful to go. Johnny blacked out.

◆ 15 ◆

From the *New York Times,* December 19, 1975:

MAINE PSYCHIC DIRECTS SHERIFF TO KILLER DEPUTY'S HOME AFTER VISITING SCENE OF THE CRIME

(Special to the times) John Smith of Pownal may not actually be psychic, but one would have difficulty persuading Sheriff George F. Bannerman of Castle County, Maine, to believe that. Desperate after a sixth assault-murder in the small western Maine town of Castle Rock, Sheriff Bannerman called Mr. Smith on the phone and asked him to come over to Castle Rock and lend a hand, if possible. Mr. Smith, who received national attention earlier this year when he recovered from a deep coma after fifty-five months of unconsciousness, had been condemned by the weekly tabloid *Inside View* as a hoaxer, but at a press conference yesterday Sheriff Bannerman would only say, "We don't put a whole lot of stock up here in Maine in what those New York reporters think."

According to Sheriff Bannerman, Mr. Smith crawled on his hands and knees around the scene of the sixth murder, which occurred on the Castle Rock town common. He came up with a mild case of frostbite and the murderer's name—Sheriff's Deputy Franklin Dodd, who had been on the Castle County Sheriff's payroll five years, as long as Bannerman himself.

Earlier this year Mr. Smith stirred controversy in his native state when he had a psychic flash that his physical therapist's house had caught fire. The flash turned out to be nothing but the truth. At a press conference following, a reporter challenged him to . . .

From *Newsweek,* page 41, week of December 24, 1975:

THE NEW HURKOS

It may be that the first genuine psychic since Peter Hurkos has been uncovered in this country—Hurkos was

the German-born seer who has been able to tell question-
ers all about their private lives by touching their hands,
silverware, or items from their handbags.

John Smith is a shy and unassuming young man from
the south-central Maine town of Pownal. Earlier this year
he returned to consciousness after a period of more than
four years in a deep coma following a car accident (see
photo). According to the consulting neurologist in the
case, Dr. Samuel Weizak, Smith made a "perfectly
astounding recovery." Today he is recovering from a mild
case of frostbite and a four-hour blackout following the
bizarre resolution of a long-unsolved multiple murder
case in the town of . . .

December 27, 1975

Dear Sarah,

*Dad and I both enjoyed your letter, which arrived just this
afternoon. I'm really fine, so you can stop worrying, okay?
But I thank you for your concern. The "frostbite" was greatly
exaggerated in the press. Just a couple of patches on the tips
of three fingers of my left hand. The blackout was really nothing much more than a fainting spell "brought on by emotional
overload," Weizak says. Yes, he came down himself and insisted on driving me to the hospital in Portland. Just watching
him in action is nearly worth the price of admission. He bullied
them into giving him a consultation room and an EEG machine and a technician to run it. He says he can find no new
brain damage or signs of progressive brain damage. He wants
to do a whole series of tests, some of them sound utterly inquis-
itorial—"Renounce, heretic, or we'll give you another pneumo-
brainscan!" (Ha-ha, and are you still sniffin' that wicked cocaine, darlin'?) Anyway, I turned down the kind offer to be
pumped and prodded some more. Dad is rawther pissed at me
about turning the tests down, keeps trying to draw a parallel
between my refusal to have them and my mother's refusal to
take her hypertension medicine. It's very hard to make him see
that, if Weizak did find something, the odds would be nine-to-
one against him being able to do anything about it.*

Yes, I saw the Newsweek *article. That picture of me is from
the press conference, only cropped. Don't look like anyone you'd
like to meet in a dark alley, do I? Ha-ha! Holy Gee (as your
buddy Anne Strafford is so fond of saying), but I wish they*

hadn't run that story. The packages, cards, and letters have started coming again. I don't open any of them anymore unless I recognize the return address, just mark them "Return to Sender." They are too pitiful, too full of hope and hate and belief and unbelief, and somehow they all remind me of the way my Mom was.

Well, I don't mean to sound so gloomy, it ain't all that bad. But I don't want to be a practicing psychic, I don't want to go on tour or appear on TV (some yahoo from NBC got our phone number, who knows how, and wanted to know if I'd consider "doing the Carson show." Great idea, huh? Don Rickles could insult some people, some starlet could show her jugs, and I could make a few predictions. All brought to you by General Foods.) I don't want to do any of that S*H*I*T. What I am really looking forward to is getting back to Cleaves Mills and sinking into the utter obscurity of the H.S. English teacher. And save the psychic flashes for football pep rallies.

Guess that's all for this time. Hope you and Walt and Denny had yourself a merry little Christmas and are looking forward eagerly (from what you said I'm sure Walt is, at the very least) to the Brave Bicentennial Election Year now stretching before us. Glad to hear your spouse has been picked to run for the state senate seat there, but cross your fingers, Sarey—'76 doesn't exactly look like a banner year for elephant-lovers. Send your thanks for that one across to San Clemente.

My dad sends best and wants me to tell you thanks for the picture of Denny, who really impressed him. I send my best, also. Thanks for writing, and for your misplaced concern (misplaced, but very welcome) I'm fine, and looking forward to getting back in harness.

Love and good wishes,
Johnny,

P.S. for the last time, kiddo, get off that cocaine.

J.

December 29, 1975

Dear Johnny,

I think this the hardest, bitterest letter I've had to write in my sixteen years of school administration—not only because you're a good friend but because you're a damned good teacher. There is no way to gild the lily on this, so guess I won't even try.

There was a special meeting of the school board last evening (at the behest of two members I won't name, but they were on

*the board when you were teaching here and I think you can
probably guess the names), and they voted 5–2 to ask that your
contract be withdrawn. The reason: you're too controversial to
be effective as a teacher. I came very close to tendering my
own resignation; I was that disgusted. If it wasn't for Maureen
and the kids, I think I would have. This abortion isn't even on
a par with tossing* Rabbit, Run *or* Catcher in the Rye *out of
the classroom. This is worse. It stinks.*

*I told them that, but I might as well have been talking in Espe-
ranto or igpay atinlay. All they can see is that your picture was
in* Newsweek *and the* New York Times *and that the Castle Rock
story was on the national network news broadcasts. Too controversial! Five old men in trusses, the kind of men who are more
interested in hair length than in textbooks, more involved in finding out who might smoke pot on the faculty than in finding out
how to get some twentieth-century equipment for the Sci Wing.*

*I have written a strong letter of protest to the board-at-large,
and with a little arm-twisting I believe I can get Irving Finegold
to cosign it with me. But I'd also be less than truthful if I told
you there was a hope in hell of getting those five old men to
change their minds.*

*My honest advice to you is to get yourself a lawyer, Johnny.
You signed that blueback in good faith, and I believe you can
squeeze them for every last cent of your salary, whether you
ever step into a Cleaves Mills classroom or not. And call me
when you feel like talking.*

With all my heart, I'm sorry.

*Your friend,
Dave Pelsen*

◆ 16 ◆

Johnny stood beside the mailbox with Dave's letter in his
hand, looking down at it unbelievingly. It was the last day of
1975, clear and bitingly cold. His breath came out of his nostrils in fine white jets of smoke.

"Shit," he whispered. "Oh man, oh shit."

Numbly, still not assimilating it totally, he leaned down to
see what else the mailman had brought him. As usual, the
box was crammed full. It had just been luck that Dave's letter
had been sticking out at the end.

There was a white, fluttering slip of paper telling him to

call at the post office for the packages, the inevitable packages. My husband deserted me in 1969, here is a pair of his socks, tell me where he is so I can get child-support out of the bastard. My baby choked to death last year, here is his rattle, please write and tell me if he is happy with the angels. I didn't have him baptized because his father did not approve and now my heart is breaking. The endless litany.

What a talent God has given you, Johnny.

The reason: You're too controversial to be effective as a teacher.

In a sudden vicious spasm he began to rake letters and manila envelopes out of the box, dropping some in the snow. The inevitable headache began to form around his temples like two dark clouds that would slowly draw together, enveloping him in pain. Sudden tears began to slip down his cheeks, and in the deep, still cold, they froze to glittering tracks almost immediately.

He bent and began to pick up the letters he had dropped; he saw one, doubled and trebled through the prisms of his tears, addressed in heavy dark pencil to JOHN SMITH SIKIK SEER.

Sikik seer, that's me. His hands began to tremble wildly and he dropped everything, including Dave's letter. It fluttered down like a leaf and landed print side up among the other letters, all the other letters. Through his helpless tears he could see the letterhead, and the motto below the torch: TO TEACH, TO LEARN, TO KNOW, TO SERVE.

"Serve my ass, you cheap bastards," Johnny said. He fell on his knees and began to gather up the letters, sweeping them together with his mittens. His fingers ached dully, a reminder of the frostbite, a reminder of Frank Dodd riding a dead toilet seat into eternity, blood in his all-American blond hair. I CONFESS.

He swept the letters up and heard himself muttering over and over, like a defective record: "Killing me, you people are killing me, let me alone, can't you see you're killing me?"

He made himself stop. This was no way to behave. Life would go on. One way or another, life would most certainly go on.

Johnny started back to the house, wondering what he could do now. Perhaps something would come along. At any rate, he had fulfilled his mother's prophecy. If God had had a mission for him, then he had done it. No matter now that it had been a kamikaze mission. He had done it.

He was quits.

· II ·

The Laughing Tiger

Chapter 17

The boy read slowly, following the words with his finger, his long brown football-player's legs stretched out on the chaise by the pool in the bright clear light of June.

" 'Of course young Danny Ju . . . Juniper . . . young Danny Juniper was dead and I suh . . . suppose that there were few in the world who would say he had not de . . . duh . . . dee . . .' Oh, shit, I don't know."

" 'Few in the world who would say he had not deserved his death,' " Johnny Smith said. "Only a slightly fancier way of saying that most would agree that Danny's death was a good thing."

Chuck was looking at him, and the familiar mix of emotions was crossing his usually pleasant face: amusement, resentment, embarrassment, and a trace of sullenness. Then he sighed and looked down at the Max Brand Western again.

" 'Deserved his death. But it was my great trah . . . truhjud . . .' "

"Tragedy," Johnny supplied.

" 'But it was my great *tragedy* that he had died just as he was about to redeem some of his e-e-evil work by one great service to the world.

" 'Of course that . . . suh . . . that sih . . . sih . . .' "

Chuck closed the book, looked up at Johnny, and smiled brilliantly.

"Let's quit for the day, Johnny, what do you say?" Chuck's smile was his most winning, the one that had probably tumbled cheerleaders into bed all over New Hampshire. "Doesn't that pool look good? You bet it does. The sweat is running right off your skinny, malnourished little bod."

Johnny had to admit—at least to himself—that the pool did look good. The first couple of weeks of the Bicentennial Summer of '76 had been uncommonly hot and sticky. From behind them, around on the other side of the big, gracious white house, came the soporific drone of the riding lawnmower as Ngo Phat, the Vietnamese groundsman, mowed what Chuck called the front forty. It was a sound that made you want to drink two glasses of cold lemonade and then nod off to sleep.

"No derogatory comments about my skinny bod," he said. "Besides, we just started the chapter."

"Sure, but we read two before it." Wheedling.

Johnny sighed. Usually he could keep Chuck at it, but not this afternoon. And today the kid had fought his way gamely through the way John Sherburne had set up his net of guards around the Amity jail and the way the evil Red Hawk had broken through and killed Danny Juniper.

"Yeah, well, just finish this page, then," he said. "That word you're stuck on's 'sickened.' No teeth in that one, Chuck."

"Good man!" The grin widened. "And no questions, right?"

"Well . . . maybe just a few."

Chuck scowled, but it was a put-on; he was getting off easy and knew it. He opened the paperback with the picture of the gunslinger shouldering his way through a set of saloon batwings again and began to read in his slow, halting voice . . . a voice so different from his normal speaking voice that it could have belonged to a different young man altogether.

" 'Of course that suh . . . sickened me at once. But it was . . . was nothing to what waited for me at the bedside of poor Tom Keyn . . . Kenyon.

" 'He had been shot through the body and he was fast dry-ing when I . . .' "

"Dying," Johnny said quietly. "Context, Chuck. Read for context."

"Fast drying," Chuck said, and giggled. Then he resumed: " ' . . . and he was fast *dying* when I ar-ar . . . when I arrived.' "

Johnny felt a sadness for Chuck steal over him as he watched the boy, hunched over the paperback copy of *Fire Brain,* a good oat opera that should have read like the wind—and instead, here was Chuck, following Max Brand's simple point-to-point prose with a laboriously moving finger. His father, Roger Chatsworth, owned Chatsworth Mills and Weaving, a very big deal indeed in southern New Hampshire. He owned this sixteen-room house in Durham, and there were five people on the staff, including Ngo Phat, who went down to Portsmouth once a week to take United States citizenship

classes. Chatsworth drove a restored 1957 Cadillac convert-
ible. His wife, a sweet, clear-eyed woman of forty-two, drove
a Mercedes. Chuck had a Corvette. The family fortune was
in the neighborhood of five million dollars.

And Chuck, at seventeen, was what God had really meant
when he breathed life into the clay, Johnny often thought. He
was a physically lovely human being. He stood six-two and
weighed a good muscular one hundred and ninety pounds.
His face was perhaps not quite interesting enough to be truly
handsome, but it was acne- and pimple-free and set off by a
pair of striking green eyes—which had caused Johnny to think
that the only other person he knew with really green eyes
was Sarah Hazlett. At his high school, Chuck was the apotheosis of the BMOC, almost ridiculously so. He was captain of
the baseball and football teams, president of the junior class
during the school year just ended, and president-elect of the
student council this coming fall. And most amazing of all,
none of it had gone to his head. In the words of Herb Smith,
who had been down once to check out Johnny's new digs,
Chuck was "a regular guy." Herb had no higher accolade in
his vocabulary. In addition, he was someday going to be an
exceedingly rich regular guy.

And here he sat, bent grimly over his book like a machine
gunner at a lonely outpost, shooting the words down one by
one as they came at him. He had taken Max Brand's exciting,
fast-moving story of drifting John "Fire Brain" Sherburne and
his confrontation with the outlaw Comanche Red Hawk and
had turned it into something that sounded every bit as exciting
as a trade advertisement for semiconductors or radio
components.

But Chuck wasn't stupid. His math grades were good, his
retentive memory was excellent, and he was manually adept.
His problem was that he had great difficulty storing printed
words. His oral vocabulary was fine, and he could grasp the
theory of phonics but apparently not its practice; and he
would sometimes reel a sentence off flawlessly and then come
up totally blank when you asked him to rephrase it. His father
had been afraid that Chuck was dyslexic, but Johnny didn't
think so—he had never met a dyslexic child that he was aware
of, although many parents seized on the word to explain or
excuse the reading problems of their children. Chuck's problem seemed more general—a loose, across-the-board reading
phobia.

It was a problem that had become more and more apparent over the last five years of Chuck's schooling, but his parents had only begun to take it seriously—as Chuck had—when his sports eligibility became endangered. And that was not the worst of it. This winter would be Chuck's last good chance to take the Scholastic Achievement Tests, if he expected to start college in the fall of 1977. The maths were not much of a problem, but the rest of the exam . . . well . . . if he could have the questions read aloud to him, he would do an average-to-good job. Five hundreds, no sweat. But they don't let you bring a reader with you when you take the SATs, not even if your dad is a biggie in the world of New Hampshire business.

" 'But I found him a ch . . . a changed man. He knew what lay before him and his courage was supp . . . supper . . . superb. He asked for nothing; he regretted nothing. All the terror and the nerv . . . nervousness which had puss . . . possett . . . *possessed* him so long as he was cuh . . . cuh . . . cuhfronted . . . *confronted* by an unknown fate . . .' "

Johnny had seen the ad for a tutor in the *Maine Times* and had applied without too much hope. He had moved down to Kittery in mid-February, needing more than anything else to get away from Pownal, from the boxful of mail each day, the reporters who had begun to find their way to the house in ever-increasing numbers, the nervous women with the wounded eyes who had just "dropped by" because "they just happened to be in the neighborhood" (one of those who had just dropped by because she just happened to be in the neighborhood had a Maryland license plate; another was driving a tired old Ford with Arizona tags). Their hands, stretching out to touch him . . .

In Kittery he had discovered for the first time that an anonymous name like John-no-middle-initial-Smith had its advantages. His third day in town he had applied for a job as a short-order cook, putting down his experience in the UMO commons and one summer cooking at a boys' camp in the Rangely Lakes as experience. The diner's owner, a tough-as-nails widow named Ruby Pelletier, had looked over his application and said, "You're a teensy bit overeducated for slinging hash. You know that, don't you, slugger?"

"That's right," Johnny said. "I went and educated myself right out of the job market."

Ruby Pelletier put her hands on her scrawny hips, threw her head back, and bellowed laughter. "You think you can

keep your shit together at two in the morning when twelve
CB cowboys pull in all at once and order scrambled eggs,
bacon, sausage, french toast, and flapjacks?"

"I guess maybe," Johnny said.

"I guess maybe you don't know what the eff I'm talking
about just yet," Ruby said, "but I'll give you a go, college
boy. Go get yourself a physical so we're square with the board
of health and bring me back a clean bill. I'll put you right on."

He had done that, and after a harum-scarum first two weeks
(which included a painful rash of blisters on his right hand
from dropping a french-fry basket into a well of boiling fat a
little too fast), he had been riding the job instead of the other
way around. When he saw Chatsworth's ad, he had sent his
resumé to the box number. In the course of the resumé he
had listed his special ed credentials, which included a one-
semester seminar in learning disabilities and reading
problems.

In late April, as he was finishing his second month at the
diner, he had gotten a letter from Roger Chatsworth, asking
him to appear for an interview on May 5. He made the necessary arrangements to take the day off, and at 2:10 on a lovely
midspring afternoon he had been sitting in Chatsworth's
study, a tall, ice-choked glass of Pepsi-Cola in one hand, listening to Stuart talk about his son's reading problems.

"That sound like dyslexia to you?" Stuart asked.

"No. It sounds like a general reading phobia."

Chatsworth had winced a little. "Jackson's Syndrome?"

Johnny had been impressed—as he was no doubt supposed
to be. Michael Carey Jackson was a reading-and-grammar spe-
cialist from the University of Southern California who had
caused something of a stir nine years ago with a book called
The Unlearning Reader. The book described a loose basket of
reading problems that had since become known as Jackson's
Syndrome. The book was a good one if you could get past
the dense academic jargon. The fact that Chatsworth apparently had done so told Johnny a good deal about the man's
commitment to solving his son's problem.

"Something like it," Johnny agreed. "But you understand
I haven't even met your son yet, or listened to him read."

"He's got course work to make up from last year. American
Writers, a nine-week history block, and *civics,* of all things.
He flunked his final exam there because he couldn't read the

beastly thing. Have you got a New Hampshire teacher's certificate?"

"No," Johnny said, "but getting one is no problem."

"And how would you handle the situation?"

Johnny outlined the way he would deal with it. A lot of oral reading on Chuck's part, leaning heavily on high-impact materials such as fantasy, science fiction, Westerns, and boy-meets-car juvenile novels. Constant questioning on what had just been read. And a relaxation technique described in Jackson's book. "High achievers often suffer the most," Johnny said. "They try too hard and reinforce the block. It's a kind of mental stutter that . . ."

"Jackson says that?" Chatsworth interposed sharply.

Johnny smiled. "No, I say that," he said.

"Okay. Go on."

"Sometimes, if the student can totally blank his mind right after reading and not feel the pressure to recite back right away, the circuits seem to clear themselves. When that begins to happen, the student begins to rethink his line of attack. It's a positive thinking kind of thing . . ."

Chatsworth's eyes had gleamed. Johnny had just touched on the linchpin of his own personal philosophy—probably the linchpin for the beliefs of most self-made men. "Nothing succeeds like success," he said.

"Well, yes. Something like that."

"How long would it take you to get a New Hampshire certificate?"

"No longer than it takes them to process my application. Two weeks, maybe."

"Then you could start on the twentieth?"

Johnny blinked. "You mean I'm hired?"

"If you want the job, you're hired. You can stay in the guest house, it'll keep the goddam relatives at bay this summer, not to mention Chuck's friends—and I want him to really buckle down. I'll pay you six hundred dollars a month, not a king's ransom, but if Chuck gets along, I'll pay you a substantial bonus. Substantial."

Chatsworth removed his glasses and rubbed a hand across his face. "I love my boy, Mr. Smith. I only want the best for him. Help us out a little if you can."

"I'll try."

Chatsworth put his glasses back on and picked up Johnny's

resumé again. "You haven't taught for a helluva long time. Didn't agree with you?"

Here it comes, Johnny thought.

"It agreed," he said, "but I was in an accident."

Chatsworth's eyes had gone to the scars on Johnny's neck where the atrophied tendons had been partially repaired. "Car crash?"

"Yes."

"Bad one?"

"Yes."

"You seem fine now," Chatsworth said. He picked up the resumé, slammed it into a drawer and, amazingly, that had been the end of the questions. So after five years Johnny was teaching again, although his student load was only one.

◆ 2 ◆

" 'As for me, who had i . . . indirectly br . . . brog . . . brought his death upon him, he took my hand with a weak grip and smiled his for . . . forgiveness up to me. It was a hard moment, and I went away feeling that I had done more harm in the world than I could ever ma . . . make up to it.' "

Chuck snapped the book closed. "There. Last one in the pool's a green banana."

"Hold it a minute, Chuck."

"Ahhhhhhh . . ." Chuck sat down again, heavily, his face composing itself into what Johnny already thought of as his *now the questions* expression. Long-suffering good humor predominated, but beneath it he could sometimes see another Chuck: sullen, worried, and scared. Plenty scared. Because it was a reader's world, the unlettered of America were dinosaurs lumbering down a blind alley, and Chuck was smart enough to know it. And he was plenty afraid of what might happen to him when he got back to school this fall.

"Just a couple of questions, Chuck."

"Why bother? You know I won't be able to answer them."

"Oh yes. This time you'll be able to answer them all."

"I can never understand what I read, you ought to know that by now." Chuck looked morose and unhappy. "I don't even know what you stick around for, unless it's the chow."

"You'll be able to answer these questions because they're not about the book."

Chuck glanced up. "Not about the book? Then why ask em? I thought . . ."

"Just humor me, okay?"

Johnny's heart was pounding hard, and he was not totally surprised to find that he was scared. He had been planning this for a long time, waiting for just the right confluence of circumstances. This was as close as he was ever going to get. Mrs. Chatsworth was not hovering around anxiously, making Chuck that much more nervous. None of his buddies were splashing around in the pool, making him feel self-conscious about reading aloud like a backward fourth grader. And most important, his father, the man Chuck wanted to please above all others in the world, was not here. He was in Boston at a New England Environmental Commission meeting on water pollution.

From Edward Stanney's *An Overview of Learning Disabilities:*

"The subject, Rupert J., was sitting in the third row of a movie theater. He was closest to the screen by more than six rows, and was the only one in a position to observe that a small fire had started in the accumulated litter on the floor. Rupert J. stood up and cried, 'F-F-F-F-F—' while the people behind him shouted for him to sit down and be quiet.

" 'How did that make you feel?' I asked Rupert J.

" 'I could never explain in a thousand years how it made me feel,' he answered. 'I was scared, but even more than being scared, I was frustrated. I felt inadequate, not fit to be a member of the human race. The stuttering always made me feel that way, but now I felt impotent, too.'

" 'Was there anything else?'

" 'Yes, I felt jealousy, because someone else would see the fire and—you know—'

" 'Get the glory of reporting it?'

" 'Yes, that's right. I saw the fire starting, I was the only one. And all I could say was F-F-F-F like a stupid broken record. Not fit to be a member of the human race describes it best.'

" 'And how did you break the block?'

" 'The day before had been my mother's birthday. I got her half a dozen roses at the florist's. And I stood there with all of them yelling at me and I thought: I am going to open my mouth and scream ROSES! just as loud as I can. I got that word all ready.'

" 'Then what did you do?'

" '*I opened my mouth and screamed FIRE! at the top of my lungs.*' "

It had been eight years since Johnny had read that case history in the introduction to Stanney's text, but he had never forgotten it. He had always thought that the key word in Rupert J.'s recollection of what had happened was *impotent*. If you feel that sexual intercourse is the most important thing on earth at this point in time, your risk of coming up with a limp penis increases ten or a hundredfold. And if you feel that reading is the most important thing on earth . . .

"What's your middle name, Chuck?" he asked casually.

"Murphy," Chuck said with a little grin. "How's that for bad? My mother's maiden name. You tell Jack or Al that, and I'll be forced to do gross damage to your skinny body."

"No fear," Johnny said. "When's your birthday?"

"September 8."

Johnny began to throw the questions faster, not giving Chuck a chance to think—but they weren't questions you had to think about.

"What's your girl's name?"

"Beth. You know Beth, Johnny . . ."

"What's her middle name?"

Chuck grinned. "Alma. Pretty horrible, right?"

"What's your paternal grandfather's name?"

"Richard."

"Who do you like in the American League East this year?"

"Yankees. In a walk."

"Who do you like for president?"

"I'd like to see Jerry Brown get it."

"You planning to trade that Vette?"

"Not this year. Maybe next."

"Your mom's idea?"

"You bet. She says it outraces her peace of mind."

"How did Red Hawk get past the guards and kill Danny Juniper?"

"Sherburne didn't pay enough attention to that trapdoor leading into the jail attic," Chuck said promptly, without thinking, and Johnny felt a sudden burst of triumph that hit him like a knock of straight bourbon. It had worked. He had gotten Chuck talking about roses, and he had responded with a good, healthy yell of *fire!*

Chuck was looking at him in almost total surprise.

"Red Hawk got into the attic through the skylight. Kicked

open the trapdoor. Shot Danny Juniper. Shot Tom Kenyon, too."

"That's right, Chuck."

"I remembered," he muttered, and then looked up at Johnny, eyes widening, a grin starting at the corners of his mouth. "You tricked me into remembering!"

"I just took you by the hand and led you around the side of whatever has been in your way all this time," Johnny said. "But whatever it is, it's still there, Chuck. Don't kid yourself. Who was the girl Sherburne fell for?"

"It was . . ." His eyes clouded a little, and he shook his head reluctantly. "I don't remember." He struck his thigh with sudden viciousness. I can't remember *anything!* I'm so fucking *stupid!*"

"Can you remember ever having been told how your dad and mom met?"

Chuck looked up at him and smiled a little. There was an angry red place on his thigh where he had struck himself. "Sure. She was working for Avis down in Charleston, South Carolina. She rented my dad a car with a flat tire." Chuck laughed. "She still claims she only married him because number two tries harder."

"And who was that girl Sherburne got interested in?"

"Jenny Langhorne. Big-time trouble for him. She's Gresham's girl. A redhead. Like Beth. She . . ." He broke off, staring at Johnny as if he had just produced a rabbit from the breast pocket of his shirt. "You did it again!"

"No. You did it. It's a simple trick of misdirection. Why do you say Jenny Langhorne is big-time trouble for John Sherburne?"

"Well, because Gresham's the big wheel there in that town . . ."

"What town?"

Chuck opened his mouth, but nothing came out. Suddenly he cut his eyes away from Johnny's face and looked at the pool. Then he smiled and looked back. "Amity. The same as in the flick *Jaws.*"

"Good! How did you come up with the name?"

Chuck grinned. "This makes no sense at all, but I started thinking about trying out for the swimming team, and there it was. What a trick. What a great trick."

"Okay. That's enough for today, I think." Johnny felt tired, sweaty, and very, very good. "You just made a breakthrough, in case you didn't notice. Let's swim. Last one in's a green banana."

"Johnny?"

"What?"

"Will that always work?"

"If you make a habit of it, it will," Johnny said. "And every time you go around that block instead of trying to bust through the middle of it, you're going to make it a little smaller. I think you'll begin to see an improvement in your word-to-word reading before long, also. I know a couple of other little tricks." He fell silent. What he had just given Chuck was less the truth than a kind of hypnotic suggestion.

"Thanks," Chuck said. The mask of long-suffering good humor was gone, replaced by naked gratitude. "If you get me over this, I'll . . . well, I guess I'd get down and kiss your feet if you wanted me to. Sometimes I get so scared, I feel like I'm letting my dad down . . ."

"Chuck, don't you know that's part of the problem?"

"It is?"

"Yeah. You're . . . you're overswinging. Overthrowing. Overeverything. And it may not be just a psychological block, you know. There are people who believe that some reading problems, Jackson's Syndrome, reading phobias, all of that, may be some kind of . . . mental birthmark. A fouled circuit, a faulty relay, a d . . ." He shut his mouth with a snap.

"A what?" Chuck asked.

"A dead zone," Johnny said slowly. "Whatever. Names don't matter. Results do. The misdirection trick really isn't a trick at all. It's educating a fallow part of your brain to do the work of that small faulty section. For you, that means getting into an oral-based train of thought every time you hit a snag. You're actually changing the location in your brain from which your thought is coming. It's learning to switch-hit."

"But can I do it? You think I can do it?"

"I know you can," Johnny said.

"All right. Then I will." Chuck dived low and flat into the pool and came up, shaking water out of his long hair in a fine spray of droplets. "Come on in! It's fine!"

"I will," Johnny said, but for the moment he was content just to stand on the pool's tile facing and watch Chuck swim powerfully toward the pool's deep end and to savor this success. There had been no good feeling like this when he had suddenly known Eileen Magown's kitchen curtains were taking fire, no good feeling like this when he had uncovered the name of Frank Dodd. If God had given him a talent, it was teaching, not knowing things he had no business knowing. This was the sort of thing he had been made for, and when he had been teaching at Cleaves Mills back in 1970, he had known it. More important, the kids had known it and responded to it, as Chuck had done just now.

"You gonna stand there like a dummy?" Chuck asked. Johnny dived into the pool.

Chapter 18

Warren Richardson came out of his small office building at quarter to five as he always did. He walked around to the parking lot and hoisted his two-hundred-pound bulk behind the wheel of his Chevy Caprice and started the engine. All according to routine. What was not according to routine was the face that appeared suddenly in the rear-view mirror—an olive-skinned, stubbled face framed by long hair and set off by eyes every bit as green as those of Sarah Hazlett or Chuck Chatsworth. Warren Richardson had not been so badly scared since he was a kid, and his heart took a great, unsteady leap in his chest.

"Howdy," said Sonny Elliman, leaning over the seat.

"Who . . ." was all Richardson managed, uttering the word in a terrified hiss of breath. His heart was pounding so hard that dark specks danced and pulsed before his eyes in rhythm with its beat. He was afraid he might have a heart attack.

"Easy," the man who had been hiding in his back seat said. "Go easy, man. Lighten up."

And Warren Richardson felt an absurd emotion. It was gratitude. The man who had scared him wasn't going to scare him anymore. He must be a nice man, he must be—

"Who are you?" he managed this time.

"A friend," Sonny said.

Richardson started to turn and fingers as hard as pincers bit into the sides of his flabby neck. The pain was excruciating. Richardson drew breath in a convulsive, heaving whine.

"You don't need to turn around, man. You can see me as well as you need to see me in your rear-view. Can you dig that?"

"Yes," Richardson gasped. "Yes yes yes just let go!"

The pincers began to ease up, and again he felt that irrational sense of gratitude. But he no longer doubted that the man in the back seat was dangerous, or that he was in this car on purpose although he couldn't think why anyone would—

And then he *could* think why someone would, at least why someone *might,* it wasn't the sort of thing you'd expect any ordinary candidate for office to do, but Greg Stillson wasn't ordinary, Greg Stillson was a crazy man, and—

Very softly, Warren Richardson began to blubber.

"Got to talk to you, man," Sonny said. His voice was kind and regretful, but in the rear-view mirror his eyes glittered green amusement. "Got to talk to you like a Dutch uncle."

"It's Stillson, isn't it? It's . . ."

The pincers were suddenly back, the man's fingers were buried in his neck, and Richardson uttered a high-pitched shriek.

"No names," the terrible man in the back seat told him in that same kind-yet-regretful voice. "You draw your own conclusions, Mr. Richardson, but keep the names to yourself. I've got one thumb just over your carotid artery and my fingers are over by your jugular, and I can turn you into a human turnip, if I want to."

"What do you want?" Richardson asked. He did not exactly moan, but it was a near thing; he had never felt more like moaning in his life. He could not believe that this was happening in the parking lot behind his real estate office in Capital City, New Hampshire, on a bright summer's day. He could see the clock set into the red brick of the town hall tower. It said ten minutes to five. At home, Norma would be putting the pork chops, nicely coated with Shake 'n Bake, into the oven to broil. Sean would be watching Sesame Street on TV. And there was a man behind him threatening to cut off the flow of blood to his brain and turn him into an idiot. No, it wasn't real; it was like a nightmare. The sort of nightmare that makes you moan in your sleep.

"I don't want anything." Sonny Elliman said. "It's all a matter of what you want."

"I don't understand what you're talking about." But he was terribly afraid that he did.

"That story in the New Hampshire *Journal* about funny real estate deals," Sonny said. "You surely did have a lot to say, Mr. Richardson, didn't you? Especially about . . . certain people."

"I . . ."

"That stuff about the Capital Mall, for instance. Hinting around about kickbacks and payoffs and one hand washing the other. All that *horseshit*." The fingers tightened on Richardson's neck again, and this time he did moan. But he hadn't been identified in the story, he had just been "an informed source." How had they known? How had *Greg Stillson* known?

The man behind him began to speak rapidly into Warren Richardson's ear now, his breath warm and ticklish.

"You could get certain people into trouble talking horseshit like that, Mr. Richardson, you know it? People running for public office, let's say. Running for office, it's like playing bridge, you dig it? You're vulnerable. People can sling mud and it sticks, especially these days. Now, there's no trouble yet. I'm happy to tell you that, because if there *was* trouble, you might be sitting here picking your teeth out of your nose instead of having a nice little talk with me."

In spite of his pounding heart, in spite of his fear, Richardson said: "This . . . this person . . . young man, you're crazy if you think you can protect him. He's played it as fast and loose as a snake-oil salesman in a southern town. Sooner or later . . ."

A thumb slammed into his ear, grinding. The pain was immense, unbelievable. Richardson's head slammed into his window and he cried out. Blindly, he groped for the horn ring.

"You blow that horn, I'll kill you," the voice whispered.

Richardson let his hands drop. The thumb eased up.

"You ought to use Q-tips in there, man," the voice said. "I got wax all over my thumb. Pretty gross."

Warren Richardson began to cry weakly. He was powerless to stop himself. Tears coursed down his fat cheeks. "Please don't hurt me anymore," he said. "Please don't. Please."

"It's like I said," Sonny told him. "It's all a matter of what you want. Your job isn't to worry what someone else might say about these . . . these certain people. Your job is to watch what comes out of your own mouth. Your job is to think before you talk the next time that guy from the *Journal* comes around. You might think about how easy it is to find out who 'an informed source' is. Or you might think about what a bummer it would be if your house burned down. Or you might think about how you'd pay for plastic surgery if someone threw some battery acid in your wife's face."

The man behind Richardson was panting now. He sounded like an animal in a jungle.

"Or you might think, you know, dig it, how easy it would be for someone to come along and pick up your son on his way home from kindergarten."

"Don't you say that!" Richardson cried hoarsely. "Don't you say that, you slimy bastard!"

"All I'm saying is that you want to think about what you want," Sonny said. "An election, it's an all-American thing, you know? Especially in a Bicentennial year. Everyone should have a good time. No one has a good time if dumb fucks like you start telling a lot of lies. Numb *jealous* fucks like you."

The hand went away altogether. The rear door opened. Oh thank God, thank God.

"You just want to think," Sonny Elliman repeated. "Now do we have an understanding?"

"Yes," Richardson whispered. "But if you think Gr . . . a certain person can be elected using these tactics, you're badly mistaken."

"No," Sonny said. "You're the one who's mistaken. Because everyone's having a good time. Make sure that you're not left out."

Richardson didn't answer. He sat rigid behind the steering wheel, his neck throbbing, staring at the clock on the Town Office Building as if it were the only sane thing left in his life. It was now almost five of five. The pork chops would be in by now.

The man in the back seat said one more thing and then he was gone, striding away rapidly, his long hair swinging against the collar of his shirt, not looking back. He went around the corner of the building and out of sight.

The last thing he had said to Warren Richardson was: "Q-Tips."

Richardson began to shake all over and it was a long time before he could drive. His first clear feeling was anger—terrible anger. The impulse that came with it was to drive directly to the Capital City police department (housed in the building below the clock) and report what had happened—the threats on his wife and son, the physical abuse—and on whose behalf it had been done.

You might think about how you'd pay for plastic surgery . . . or how easy it would be for someone to come along and pick up your son . . .

But why? Why take the chance? What he had said to that thug was just the plain, unvarnished truth. Everyone in southern New Hampshire real estate knew that Stillson had been running a shell game, reaping short-term profits that would land him in jail, not sooner or later, but sooner or even sooner. His campaign was an exercise in idiocy. And now strong-arm tactics! No one could get away with that for long in America—and especially not in New England.

But let someone else blow the whistle.

Someone with less to lose.

Warren Richardson started his car and went home to his pork chops and said nothing at all. Someone else would surely put a stop to it.

Chapter 19

◆ 1 ◆

On a day not long after Chuck's first breakthrough, Johnny Smith stood in the bathroom of the guest house, running his Norelco over his cheeks. Looking at himself closeup in a mirror always gave him a weird feeling these days, as if he were looking at an older brother instead of himself. Deep horizontal lines had grooved themselves across his forehead. Two more bracketed his mouth. Strangest of all, there was that streak of white, and the rest of his hair was beginning to go gray. It seemed to have started almost overnight.

He snapped off the razor and went out into the combination kitchen-living room. Lap of luxury, he thought, and smiled a little. Smiling was starting to feel natural again. He turned on the TV, got a Pepsi out of the fridge, and settled down to watch the news. Roger Chatsworth was due back later in the evening, and tomorrow Johnny would have the distinct pleasure of telling him that his son was beginning to make real progress.

Johnny had been up to see his own father every two weeks or so. He was pleased with Johnny's new job and listened with keen interest as Johnny told him about the Chatsworths, the house in the pleasant college town of Durham, and Chuck's problems. Johnny, in turn, listened as his father told him about the gratis work he was doing at Charlene MacKenzie's house in neighboring New Gloucester.

"Her husband was a helluva doctor but not much of a handyman," Herb said. Charlene and Vera had been friends before Vera's deepening involvement in the stranger offshoots of fundamentalism. That had separated them. Her husband, a GP, had died of a heart attack in 1973. "Place was practically falling down around that woman's ears," Herb said. "Least I could do. I go up on Saturdays and she gives me a dinner before I come back home. I have to tell the truth, Johnny, she cooks better than you do."

"Looks better, too," Johnny said blandly.

"Sure, she's a fine-looking woman, but it's nothing like *that*, Johnny. Your mother's not even in her grave a year . . ."

But Johnny suspected that maybe it *was* something like that, and secretly couldn't have been more pleased. He didn't fancy the idea of his father growing old alone.

On the television, Walter Cronkite was serving up the evening's political news. Now, with the primary season over and the conventions only weeks away, it appeared that Jimmy Carter had the Democratic nomination sewed up. It was Ford who was in a scrap for his political life with Ronald Reagan, the ex-governor of California and ex-host of "GE Theater." It was close enough to have the reporters counting individual delegates, and in one of her infrequent letters Sarah Hazlett had written: "Walt's got his fingers (and toes!) crossed that Ford gets it. As a candidate for state senate up here, he's already thinking about coattails. And he says that, in Maine at least, Reagan hasn't any."

While he was short-order cooking in Kittery, Johnny had gotten into the habit of going down to Dover or Portsmouth or any number of smaller surrounding towns in New Hampshire a couple of times a week. All of the candidates for president were in and out, and it was a unique opportunity to see those who were running closeup and without the nearly regal trappings of authority that might later surround any one of them. It became something of a hobby, although of necessity a short-lived one; when New Hampshire's first-in-the-nation primary was over, the candidates would move on to Florida without a glance back. And of course a few of their number would bury their political ambitions somewhere between Portsmouth and Keene. Never a political creature before—except during the Vietnam era—Johnny became an avid politician-watcher in the healing aftermath of the Castle Rock business—and his own particular talent, affliction, whatever it was, played a part in that, too.

He shook hands with Morris Udall and Henry Jackson. Fred Harris clapped him on the back. Ronald Reagan gave him a quick and practiced politico's double-pump and said, "Get out to the polls and help us if you can." Johnny had nodded agreeably enough, seeing no point in disabusing Mr. Reagan of his notion that he was a bona fide New Hampshire voter.

He had chatted with Sarge Shriver just inside the main entrance to the monstrous Newington Mall for nearly fifteen minutes. Shriver, his hair freshly cut and smelling of aftershave and perhaps desperation, was accompanied by a single aide with his pockets stuffed full of leaflets, and a Secret Service man who kept scratching furtively at his acne. Shriver had seemed inordinately pleased to be recognized. A minute or two before Johnny said good-bye, a candidate in search of some local office had approached Shriver and asked him to sign his nominating papers. Shriver had smiled gently.

Johnny had sensed things about all of them, but little of a specific nature. It was as if they had made the act of touching such a ritual thing that their true selves were buried beneath a layer of tough, clear lucite. Although he saw most of them—with the exception of President Ford—Johnny had felt only once that sudden, electrifying snap of knowledge that he associated with Eileen Magown—and, in an entirely different way, with Frank Dodd.

It was a quarter of seven in the morning. Johnny had driven down to Manchester in his old Plymouth. He had worked from ten the evening before until six this morning. He was tired, but the quiet winter dawn had been too good to sleep through. And he liked Manchester, Manchester with its narrow streets and timeworn brick buildings, the gothic textile mills strung along the river like mid-Victorian beads. He had not been consciously politician-hunting that morning; he thought he would cruise the streets for a while, until they began to get crowded, until the cold and silent spell of February was broken, then go back to Kittery and catch some sacktime.

He turned a corner and there had been three nondescript sedans pulled up in front of a shoe factory in a no-parking zone. Standing by the gate in the cyclone fencing was Jimmy Carter, shaking hands with the men and women going on shift. They were carrying lunch buckets or paper sacks, breathing out white clouds, bundled into heavy coats, their faces still asleep. Carter had a word for each of them. His grin, then not so publicized as it became later, was tireless and fresh. His nose was red with the cold.

Johnny parked half a block down and walked toward the factory gate, his shoes crunching and squeaking on the packed snow. The Secret Service agent with Carter sized him up quickly and then dismissed him—or seemed to.

"I'll vote for anyone who's interested in cutting taxes," a man in an old ski parka was saying. The parka had a constellation of what looked like battery-acid burns in one sleeve. "The goddam taxes are killing me, I kid you not."

"Well, we're gonna see about that," Carter said. "Lookin over the tax situation is gonna be one of our first priorities when I get into the White House." There was a serene self-confidence in his voice that struck Johnny and made him a little uneasy.

Carter's eyes, bright and almost amazingly blue, shifted to Johnny. "Hi there," he said.

"Hello, Mr. Carter," Johnny said. "I don't work here. I was driving by and saw you."

"Well I'm glad you stopped. I'm running for President."

"I know."

Carter put his hand out. Johnny shook it.

Carter began: "I hope you'll . . ." And broke off.

The flash came, a sudden, powerful zap that was like sticking his finger in an electric socket. Carter's eyes sharpened. He and Johnny looked at each other for what seemed a very long time.

The Secret Service guy didn't like it. He moved toward

Carter, and suddenly he was unbuttoning his coat. Somewhere behind them, a million miles behind them, the shoe factory's seven o'clock whistle blew its single long note into the crisp blue morning.

Johnny let go of Carter's hand, but still the two of them looked at each other.

"What the *hell* was that?" Carter asked, very softly.

"You've probably got someplace to go, don't you?" the Secret Service guy said suddenly. He put a hand on Johnny's shoulder. It was a very big hand. "Sure you do."

"It's all right," Carter said.

"You're going to be president," Johnny said.

The agent's hand was still on Johnny's shoulder, more lightly now but still there, and he was getting something from him, too. The Secret Service guy

(eyes)

didn't like his eyes. He thought they were

(assassin's eyes, psycho's eyes)

cold and strange, and if this guy put so much as one hand in his coat pocket, if he even looked as if he might be going in that direction, he was going to put him on the sidewalk. Behind the Secret Service guy's second-to-second evaluation of the situation there ran a simple, maddening litany of thought:

(laurel maryland laurel maryland laurel maryland laurel)

"Yes," Carter said.

"It's going to be closer than anyone thinks . . . closer than *you* think, but you'll win. He'll beat himself. Poland. Poland will beat him."

Carter only looked at him, half-smiling.

"You've got a daughter. She's going to go to a public school in Washington. She's going to go to . . ." But it was in the dead zone. "I think . . . it's a school named after a freed slave."

"Fellow, I want you to move on," the agent said.

Carter looked at him and the agent subsided.

"It's been a pleasure meeting you," Carter said. "A little disconcerting, but a pleasure."

Suddenly, Johnny was himself again. It had passed. He was aware that his ears were cold and that he had to go to the bathroom. "Have a good morning," he said lamely.

"Yes. You too, now."

He had gone back to his car, aware of the Secret Service guy's eyes still on him. He drove away, bemused. Shortly after, Carter had put away the competition in New Hampshire and went on to Florida.

◆ 2 ◆

Walter Cronkite finished with the politicians and went on to the civil war in Lebanon. Johnny got up and freshened his glass of Pepsi. He tipped the glass at the TV. *Your good health, Walt. To the three Ds—death, destruction, and destiny. Where would we be without them?*

There was a light tap at the door. "Come in," Johnny called, expecting Chuck, probably with an invitation to the drive-in over in Somersworth. But it wasn't Chuck. It was Chuck's father.

"Hi, Johnny," he said. He was wearing wash-faded jeans and an old cotton sports shirt, the tails out. "May I come in?"

"Sure. I thought you weren't due back until late."

"Well, Shelley gave me a call." Shelley was his wife. Roger came in and shut the door. "Chuck came to see her. Burst into tears, just like a little kid. He told her you were doing it, Johnny. He said he thought he was going to be all right."

Johnny put his glass down. "We've got a ways to go," he said.

"Chuck met me at the airport. I haven't seen him looking like he did since he was . . . what? Ten? Eleven? When I gave him the .22 he'd been waiting for for five years. He read me a story out of the newspaper. The improvement is . . . almost eerie. I came over to thank you."

"Thank Chuck," Johnny said. "He's an adaptable boy. A lot of what's happening to him is positive reinforcement. He's psyched himself into believing he can do it and now he's tripping on it. That's the best way I can put it."

Roger sat down. "He says you're teaching him to switch-hit."

Johnny smiled. "Yeah, I guess so."

"Is he going to be able to take the SATs?"

"I don't know. And I'd hate to see him gamble and lose. The SATs are a heavy pressure situation. If he gets in that lecture hall with an answer sheet in front of him and an IBM pencil in his hand and then freezes up, it's going to be a real setback for him. Have you thought about a good prep school for a year? A place like Pittsfield Academy?"

"We've kicked the idea around, but frankly I always thought of it as just postponing the inevitable."

"That's one of the things that's been giving Chuck trouble. This feeling that he's in a make-or-break situation."

"I've never pressured Chuck."

"Not on purpose, I know that. So does he. On the other hand, you're a rich, successful man who graduated from college *summa cum laude*. I think Chuck feels a little bit like he's batting after Hank Aaron."

"There's nothing I can do about that, Johnny."

"I think a year at a prep school, away from home, after his senior year might put things in perspective for him. And he wants to go to work in one of your mills next summer. If he were my kid and if they were my mills, I'd let him."

"Chuck wants to do that? How come he never told me?"

"Because he didn't want you to think he was ass-kissing," Johnny said.

"He told you that?"

"Yes. He wants to do it because he thinks the practical experience will be helpful to him later on. The kid wants to follow in your footsteps, Mr. Chatsworth. You've left some big ones behind you. That's what a lot of the reading block has been about. He's having buck fever."

In a sense, he had lied. Chuck had hinted around these things, had even mentioned some of them obliquely, but he had not been as frank as Johnny had led Roger Chatsworth to believe. Not verbally, at least. But Johnny had touched him from time to time, and he had gotten signals that way. He had looked through the pictures Chuck kept in his wallet and knew how Chuck felt about his dad. There were things he could never tell this pleasant but rather distant man sitting across from him. Chuck idolized the ground his father walked on. Beneath his easy-come easy-go exterior (an exterior that was very similar to Roger's), the boy was eaten up by the secret conviction that he could never measure up. His father had built a ten percent interest in a failing woolen mill into a New England textile empire. He believed that the issue of his father's love hung on his own ability to move similar mountains. To play sports. To get into a good college. To *read*.

"How sure are you about all of this?" Roger asked.

"I'm pretty sure. But I'd appreciate it if you never mentioned to Chuck that we talked this way. They're his secrets I'm telling." *And that's truer than you'll ever know.*

"All right. And Chuck and his mother and I will talk over the prep school idea. In the meantime, this is yours." He took a plain white business envelope from his back pocket and passed it to Johnny.

"What is it?"

"Open it and see."

Johnny opened it. Inside the envelope was a cashier's check for five hundred dollars.

"Oh, hey . . .! I can't take this."

"You can, and you will. I promised you a bonus if you could perform, and I keep my promises. There'll be another when you leave."

"Really, Mr. Chatsworth, I just . . ."

"Shh. I'll tell you something, Johnny." He leaned forward. He was smiling a peculiar little smile, and Johnny suddenly felt he could see beneath the pleasant exterior to the man who had made all of this happen—the house, the grounds, the pool, the mills. And, of course, his son's reading phobia, which could probably be classified a hysterical neurosis.

"It's been my experience that ninety-five percent of the people who walk the earth are simply inert, Johnny. One percent are saints, and one percent are assholes. The other three percent are the people who do what they say they can do. I'm in that three percent, and so are you. You earned that money. I've got people in the mills that take home eleven thousand dollars a year for doing little more than playing with their dicks. But I'm not bitching. I'm a man of the world, and all that means is I understand what powers the world. The fuel mix is one part high-octane to nine parts pure bullshit. You're no bullshitter. So you put that money in your wallet and next time try to value yourself a little higher."

"All right," Johnny said. "I can put it to good use, I won't lie to you about that."

"Doctor bills?"

Johnny looked up at Roger Chatsworth, his eyes narrowed.

"I know all about you," Roger said. "Did you think I wouldn't check back on the guy I hired to tutor my son?"

"You know about . . ."

"You're supposed to be a psychic of some kind. You helped to solve a murder case in Maine. At least, that's what the papers say. You had a teaching job lined up for last January, but they dropped you like a hot potato when your name got in the papers."

"You *knew?* For how long?"

"I knew before you moved in."

"And you still hired me?"

"I wanted a tutor, didn't I? You looked like you might be able to pull it off. I think I showed excellent judgment in engaging your services."

"Well, thanks," Johnny said. His voice was hoarse.

"I told you you didn't have to say that."

As they talked, Walter Cronkite had finished up with the real news of the day and had gone on to the man-bites-dog stories that sometimes turn up near the end of a newscast. He was saying, ". . . voters in western New Hampshire have an independent running in the third district this year . . ."

"Well, the cash will come in handy," Johnny said. "That's . . ."

"Shh. I want to hear this."

Chatsworth was leaning forward, hands dangling between his knees, a pleasant smile of expectation on his face. Johnny turned to look at the TV.

". . . Stillson," Cronkite said. "This forty-three-year-old insurance and real estate agent is surely running one of the most eccentric races of Campaign '76, but both the third-district Republican candidate, Harrison Fisher, and his Democratic opponent, David Bowes, are running scared, because the polls have Greg Stillson running comfortably ahead. George Herman has the story."

"Who's Stillson?" Johnny asked.

Chatsworth laughed. "Oh, you gotta see this guy, Johnny. He's as crazy as a rat in a drainpipe. But I do believe the sober-sided electorate of the third district is going to send him to Washington this November. Unless he actually falls down and starts frothing at the mouth. And I wouldn't completely rule that out."

Now the TV showed a picture of a handsome young man in a white open-throated shirt. He was speaking to a small crowd from a bunting-hung platform in a supermarket parking lot. The young man was exhorting the crowd. The crowd looked less than thrilled. George Herman voiced over: "This is David Bowes, the Democratic candidate—sacrificial offering, some would say—for the third-district seat in New Hamp-

shire. Bowes expected an uphill fight because New
Hampshire's third district has *never* gone Democratic, not
even in the great LBJ blitz of 1964. But he expected his competition to come from this man."

Now the TV showed a man of about sixty-five. He was
speaking to a plushy fund-raising dinner. The crowd had that
plump, righteous, and slightly constipated look that seems the
exclusive province of businessmen who belong to the GOP.
The speaker bore a remarkable resemblance to Edward Gurney of Florida, although he did not have Gurney's slim,
tough build.

"This is Harrison Fisher," Herman said. "The voters of the
third district have been sending him to Washington every two
years since 1960. He is a powerful figure in the House, sitting
on five committees and chairing the House Committee on
Parks and Waterways. It had been expected that he would
beat young David Bowes handily. But neither Fisher nor
Bowes counted on a wild card in the deck. This wild card."

The picture switched.

"Holy God!" Johnny said.

Beside him, Chatsworth roared laughter and slapped his
thighs. "Can you *believe* that guy?"

No lackadaisical supermarket parking-lot crowd here. No
comfy fund raiser in the Granite State Room of the Portsmouth Hilton, either. Greg Stillson was standing on a platform
outside in Ridgeway, his home town. Behind him there
loomed the statue of a Union soldier with his rifle in his hand
and his kepi tilted down over his eyes. The street was blocked
off and crowded with wildly cheering people, predominantly
young people. Stillson was wearing faded jeans and a two-
pocket Army fatigue shirt with the words GIVE PEACE A
CHANCE embroidered on one pocket and MOM'S APPLE
PIE on the other. There was a hi-impact construction worker's
helmet cocked at an arrogant, rakish angle on his head, and
plastered to the front of it was a green American flag ecology
sticker. Beside him was a stainless steel cart of some kind.
From the twin loudspeakers came the sound of John Denver
singing "Thank God I'm a Country Boy."

"What's that cart?" Johnny asked.

"You'll see," Roger said, still grinning hugely.

Herman said: "The wild card is Gregory Ammas Stillson,
forty-three, ex-salesman for the Truth Way Bible Company

of America, ex-housepainter, and, in Oklahoma, where he grew up, one-time rainmaker."

"Rainmaker," said Johnny, bemused.

"Oh, that's one of his planks," Roger said. "If he's elected, we'll have rain whenever we need it."

George Herman went on: "Stillson's platform is . . . well, refreshing."

John Denver finished singing with a yell that brought answering cheers from the crowd. Then Stillson started talking, his voice booming at peak amplification. His PA system at least was sophisticated; there was hardly any distortion. His voice made Johnny vaguely uneasy. The man had the high, hard, pumping delivery of a revival preacher. You could see a fine spray of spittle from his lips as he talked.

"What are we gonna do in Washington? Why do we want to go to Washington?" Stillson roared. "What's our platform? Our platform got five boards, my friends n neighbors, five old boards! And what are they? I'll tell you up front! First board: *THROW THE BUMS OUT!*"

A tremendous roar of approval ripped out of the crowd. Someone threw double handfuls of confetti into the air and someone else yelled, "*Yaaaah-HOO!*" Stillson leaned over his podium.

"You wanna know why I'm wearin this helmet, friends n neighbors? I'll tell you why. I'm wearin it because when you send me up to Washington, I'm gonna go through em like *you-know-what* through a canebrake! Gonna go through em *just like this!*"

And before Johnny's wondering eyes, Stillson put his head down and began to charge up and down the podium stage like a bull, uttering a high, yipping Rebel yell as he did so. Roger Chatsworth simply dissolved in his chair, laughing helplessly. The crowd went wild. Stillson charged back to the podium, took off his construction helmet, and spun it into the crowd. A minor riot over possession of it immediately ensued.

"Second board!" Stillson yelled into the mike. "We're gonna throw out anyone in the government, from the highest to the lowest, who is spending time in bed with some gal who ain't his wife! If they wanna sleep around, they ain't gonna do it on the public tit!"

"What did he say?" Johnny asked, blinking.

"Oh, he's just getting warmed up," Roger said. He wiped

his streaming eyes and went off into another gale of laughter. Johnny wished it seemed that funny to him.

"Third board!" Stillson roared. "We're gonna send all the pollution right into outer space! Gonna put it in Hefty bags! Gonna put it in Glad bags! Gonna send it to Mars, to Jupiter, and the rings of Saturn! We're gonna have clean air and we're gonna have clean water and we're gonna have it in *SIX MONTHS!*"

The crowd was in paroxysms of joy. Johnny saw many people in the crowd who were almost killing themselves laughing, as Roger Chatsworth was presently doing.

"Fourth board! We're gonna have all the gas and oil we need! We're gonna stop playing games with these Ayrabs and get down to brass tacks! Ain't gonna be no old people in New Hampshire turned into Popsicles this coming winter like there was last winter!"

This brought a solid roar of approval. The winter before an old woman in Portsmouth had been found frozen to death in her third-floor apartment, apparently following a turn-off by the gas company for nonpayment.

"We got the muscle, friends n neighbors, we can do it! Anybody out there think we can't do it?"

"*NO!*" The crowd bellowed back.

"Last board," Stillson said, and approached the metal cart. He threw back the hinged lid and a cloud of steam puffed out. "*HOT DOGS!!*"

He began to grab double handfuls of hot dogs from the cart, which Johnny now recognized as a portable steam table. He threw them into the crowd and went back for more. Hot dogs flew everywhere. "Hot dogs for every man, woman, and child in America! And when you put Greg Stillson in the House of Representatives, you gonna say *HOT DOG! SOMEONE GIVES A RIP AT LAST!*"

The picture changed. The podium was being dismantled by a crew of long-haired young men who looked like rock band roadies. Three more of them were cleaning up the litter the crowd had left behind. George Herman resumed: "Democratic candidate David Bowes calls Stillson a practical joker who is trying to throw a monkeywrench into the workings of the democratic process. Harrison Fisher is stronger in his criticism. He calls Stillson a cynical carnival pitchman who is playing the whole idea of the free election as a burlesquehouse joke. In speeches, he refers to independent candidate Stillson as the only member of the American Hot Dog party. But the fact is this: the latest CBS poll in New Hampshire's third district showed David Bowes with twenty percent of the vote, Harrison Fisher with twenty-six—and maverick Greg Stillson with a whopping forty-two percent. Of course election day is still quite a way down the road, and things may change. But for now, Greg Stillson has captured the hearts—if not the minds—of New Hampshire's third-district voters."

The TV showed a shot of Herman from the waist up. Both hands had been out of sight. Now he raised one of them, and in it was a hot dog. He took a big bite.

"This is George Herman, CBS News, in Ridgeway, New Hampshire."

Walter Cronkite came back on in the CBS newsroom, chuckling. "Hot dogs," he said, and chuckled again. "And that's the way it is . . ."

Johnny got up and snapped off the set. "I just can't believe that," he said. "That guy's really a candidate? It's not a joke?"

"Whether it's a joke or not is a matter of personal interpretation," Roger said, grinning, "but he really is running. I'm a Republican myself, born and bred, but I must admit I get a kick out of that guy Stillson. You know he hired half a dozen ex-motorcycle outlaws as bodyguards? Real iron horsemen. Not Hell's Angels or anything like that, but I guess they were pretty rough customers. He seems to have reformed them."

Motorcycle freaks as security. Johnny didn't like the sound of that very much. The motorcycle freaks had been in charge of security when the Rolling Stones gave their free concert at Altamont Speedway in California. It hadn't worked out so well.

"People put up with a . . . a motorcycle goon squad?"

"No, it really isn't like that. They're quite clean-cut. And Stillson has a helluva reputation around Ridgeway for reforming kids in trouble."

Johnny grunted doubtfully.

"You saw him," Roger said, gesturing at the TV set. "The man is a clown. He goes charging around the speaking platform like that at every rally. Throws his helmet into the crowd—I'd guess he's gone through a hundred of them by now—and gives out hot dogs. He's a clown, so what? Maybe people need a little comic relief from time to time. We're running out of oil, the inflation is slowly but surely getting out of control, the average guy's tax load has never been heavier, and we're apparently getting ready to elect a fuzzy-minded Georgia cracker president of the United States. So people want a giggle or two. Even more, they want to thumb their noses at a political establishment that doesn't seem able to solve anything. Stillson's harmless."

"He's in orbit," Johnny said, and they both laughed.

"We have plenty of crazy politicians around," Roger said. "In New Hampshire we've got Stillson, who wants to hot dog his way into the House of Representatives, so what? Out in California they've got Hayakawa. Or take our own governor, Meldrim Thomson. Last year he wanted to arm the New Hampshire National Guard with tactical nuclear weapons. I'd call that big-time crazy."

"Are you saying it's okay for those people in the third district to elect the village fool to represent them in Washington?"

"You don't get it," Chatsworth said patiently. "Take a voter's-eye-view, Johnny. Those third-district people are mostly all blue-collars and shopkeepers. The most rural parts of the district are just starting to develop some recreational potential. Those people look at David Bowes and they see a hungry young kid who's trying to get elected on the basis of some slick talk and a passing resemblance to Dustin Hoffman. They're supposed to think he's a man of the people because he wears blue jeans.

"Then take Fisher. My man, at least nominally. I've organized fund raisers for him and the other Republican candidates around this part of New Hampshire. He's been on the Hill so long he probably thinks the Capitol dome would split in two pieces if he wasn't around to give it moral support. He's never had an original thought in his life, he never went against the party line in his life. There's no stigma attached to his name because he's too stupid to be very crooked, although he'll probably wind up with some mud on him from this Koreagate thing. His speeches have all the excitement of the copy in the National Plumbers Wholesale Catalogue. People don't *know* all those things, but they can sense them sometimes. The idea that Harrison Fisher is doing anything for his constituency is just plain ridiculous."

"So the answer is to elect a loony?"

Chatsworth smiled indulgently. "Sometimes these loonies turn out doing a pretty good job. Look at Bella Abzug.

There's a damn fine set of brains under those crazy hats. But even if Stillson turns out to be as crazy in Washington as he is down in Ridgeway, he's only renting the seat for two years. They'll turn him out in '78 and put in someone who understands the lesson."

"The lesson?"

Roger stood up. "Don't fuck the people over for too long," he said. "That's the lesson. Adam Clayton Powell found out. Agnew and Nixon did, too. Just . . . don't fuck the people for too long." He glanced at his watch. "Come on over to the big house and have a drink, Johnny. Shelley and I are going out later on, but we've got time for a short one."

Johnny smiled and got up. "Okay," he said. "You twisted my arm."

Chapter 20

◆ 1 ◆

In mid-August, Johnny found himself alone at the Chatsworth estate except for Ngo Phat, who had his own quarters over the garage. The Chatsworth family had closed up the house and had gone to Montreal for three weeks of r & r before the new school year and the fall rush at the mills began.

Roger had left Johnny the keys to his wife's Mercedes and he motored up to his dad's house in Pownal, feeling like a potentate. His father's negotiations with Charlene MacKenzie had entered the critical stage, and Herb was no longer bothering to protest that his interest in her was only to make sure that the house didn't fall down on top of her. In fact, he was in full courting plumage and made Johnny a little nervous. After three days of it Johnny went back to the Chatsworth house, caught up on his reading and his correspondence, and soaked up the quiet.

He was sitting on a rubber chair-float in the middle of the pool, drinking a Seven-Up and reading the *New York Times Book Review,* when Ngo came over to the pool's apron, took off his zori, and dipped his feet into the water.

"Ahhhh," he said. "Much better." He smiled at Johnny. "Quiet, huh?"

"Very quiet," Johnny agreed. "How goes the citizenship class, Ngo?"

"Very nice going," Ngo said. "We are having a field trip on Saturday. First one. Very exciting. The whole class will be tripping."

"Going," Johnny said, smiling at an image of Ngo Phat's whole citizenship class freaking on LSD or psilocybin.

"Pardon?" He raised his eyebrows politely.

"Your whole class will be going."

"Yes, thanks. We are going to the political speech and rally in Trimbull. We are all thinking how lucky it is to be taking the citizenship class in an election year. It is most instructive."

"Yes, I'll bet it is. Who are you going to see?"

"Greg Stirrs . . ." He stopped and pronounced it again, very carefully. "Greg Stillson, who is running independently for a seat in the U.S. House of Representatives."

"I've heard of him," Johnny said. "Have you discussed him in class at all, Ngo?"

"Yes, we have had some conversation of this man. Born in 1933. A man of many jobs. He came to New Hampshire in 1964. Our instructor has told us that now he is here long enough so people do not see him as a carpetfogger."

"Bagger," Johnny said.

Ngo looked at him with blank politeness.

"The term is carpetbagger."

"Yes, thanks."

"Do you find Stillson a bit odd?"

"In America perhaps he is odd," Ngo said. "In Vietnam there were many like him. People who are . . ." He sat thinking, swishing his small and delicate feet in the blue-green water of the pool. Then he looked up at Johnny again.

"I do not have the English for what I wish to say. There is a game the people of my land play, it is called the Laughing Tiger. It is old and much loved, like your baseball. One child is dressing up as the tiger, you see. He puts on a skin. And the other children tries to catch him as he runs and dances. The child in the skin laughs, but he is also growling and biting, because that is the game. In my country, before the Communists, many of the village leaders played the Laughing Tiger. I think this Stillson knows that game, too."

Johnny looked over at Ngo, disturbed.

Ngo did not seem disturbed at all. He smiled. "So we will all go and see for ourselves. After, we are having the picnic foods. I myself am making two pies. I think it will be nice."

"It sounds great."

"It will be very great," Ngo said, getting up. "Afterward, in class, we will talk over all we saw in Trimbull. Maybe we will be writing the compositions. It is much easier to write the compositions, because one can look up the exact word. *Le mot juste.*"

"Yes, sometimes writing can be easier. But I never had a high school comp class that would believe it."

Ngo smiled. "How does it go with Chuck?"

"He's doing quite well."

"Yes, he is happy now. Not just pretending. He is a good boy." He stood up. "Take a rest, Johnny. I'm going to take a nap."

"All right."

He watched Ngo walk away, small, slim, and lithe in blue jeans and a faded chambray work shirt.

The child in the skin laughs, but he is also growling and biting, because that is the game . . . I think this Stillson knows that game, too.

That thread of disquiet again.

The pool chair bobbed gently up and down. The sun beat pleasantly on him. He opened his *Book Review* again, but the article he had been reading no longer engaged him. He put it down and paddled the little rubber float to the edge of the pool and got out. Trimbull was less than thirty miles away. Maybe he would just hop into Mrs. Chatsworth's Mercedes and drive down this Saturday. See Greg Stillson in person. Enjoy the show. Maybe . . . maybe shake his hand.

No. No!

But why not? After all, he had more or less made politicians his hobby this election year. What could possibly be so upsetting about going to see one more?

But he *was* upset, no question about that. His heart was knocking harder and more rapidly than it should have been, and he managed to drop his magazine into the pool. He fished it out with a curse before it was saturated.

Somehow, thinking about Greg Stillson made him think about Frank Dodd.

Utterly ridiculous. He couldn't have any feeling at all about

Stillson one way or the other from having just seen him on
TV.

Stay away.

Well, maybe he would and maybe he wouldn't. Maybe he
would go down to Boston this Saturday instead. See a film.

But a strange, heavy feeling of fright had settled on him by
the time he got back to the guest house and changed his
clothes. In a way the feeling was like an old friend—the sort
of old friend you secretly hate. Yes, he would go down to
Boston on Saturday. That would be better.

Although he relived that day over and over in the months
afterward, Johnny could never remember exactly how or why
it was that he ended up in Trimbull after all. He had set out
in another direction, planning to go down to Boston and take
in the Red Sox at Fenway Park, then maybe go over to Cam-
bridge and nose through the bookshops. If there was enough
cash left over (he had sent four hundred dollars of Chatsworth's bonus to his father, who in turn sent it on to Eastern
Maine Medical—a gesture tantamount to a spit in the ocean)
he planned to go to the Orson Welles Cinema and see that
reggae movie, *The Harder They Come.* A good day's program,
and a fine day to implement it; that August 19 had dawned
hot and clear and sweet, the distillation of the perfect New
England summer's day.

He had let himself into the kitchen of the big house and
made three hefty ham-and-cheese sandwiches for lunch, put
them in an old-fashioned wicker picnic basket he found in the
pantry, and after a little soul-searching, had topped off his
haul with a sixpack of Tuborg Beer. At that point he had
been feeling fine, absolutely first-rate. No thought of either
Greg Stillson or his homemade bodyguard corps of iron
horsemen had so much as crossed his mind.

He put the picnic basket on the floor of the Mercedes and
drove southeast toward I-95. All clear enough up to that
point. But then other things had begun to creep in. Thoughts
of his mother on her deathbed first. His mother's face, twisted
into a frozen snarl, the hand on the counterpane hooked into
a claw, her voice sounding as if it were coming through a big
mouthful of cotton wadding.

Didn't I tell you? Didn't I say it was so?

Johnny turned the radio up louder. Good rock 'n' roll
poured out of the Mercedes's stereo speakers. He had been

asleep for four-and-a-half years but rock 'n' roll had remained alive and well, thank you very much. Johnny sang along.

He has a job for you. Don't run from him, Johnny.

The radio couldn't drown out his dead mother's voice. His dead mother was going to have her say. Even from beyond the grave she was going to have her say.

Don't hide away in a cave or make him have to send a big fish to swallow you.

But he had been swallowed by a big fish. Its name was not leviathan but coma. He had spent four-and-a-half years in that particular fish's black belly, and that was enough.

The entrance ramp to the turnpike came up—and then slipped behind him. He had been so lost in his thoughts that he had missed his turn. The old ghosts just wouldn't give up and let him alone. Well, he would turn around and go back as soon as he found a good place.

Not the potter but the potter's clay, Johnny.

"Oh, come on," he muttered. He had to get this crap off his mind, that was all. His mother had been a religious crazy, not a very kind way of putting it, but true all the same. Heaven out in the constellation Orion, angels driving flying saucers, kingdoms under the earth. In her way she had been at least as crazy as Greg Stillson was in his.

Oh for Christ's sake, don't get off on that guy.

"*And when you send Greg Stillson to the House of Representatives, you gonna say HOT DOG! SOMEONE GIVES A RIP AT LAST!*"

He came to New Hampshire Route 63. A left turn would take him to Concord, Berlin, Ridder's Mill, Trimbull. Johnny made the turn without even thinking about it. His thoughts were elsewhere.

Roger Chatsworth, no babe in the woods, had laughed over Greg Stillson as if he were this year's answer to George Carlin and Chevy Chase all rolled up into one. *He's a clown, Johnny.*

And if that was all Stillson was, then there was no problem, was there? A charming eccentric, a piece of blank paper on which the electorate could write its message: *You other guys are so wasted that we decided to elect this fool for two years instead.* That was probably all Stillson was, after all. Just a harmless crazy, there was no need at all to associate him with the patterned, destructive madness of Frank Dodd. And yet . . . somehow . . . he did.

The road branched ahead. Left branch to Berlin and Ridder's Mill, right branch to Trimbull and Concord. Johnny turned right.

But it wouldn't hurt to just shake his hand, would it?

Maybe not. One more politician for his collection. Some people collected stamps, some coins, but Johnny Smith collects handshakes and—

—and admit it. You've been looking for a wild card in the deck all along.

The thought shook him so badly that he almost pulled over to the side of the road. He caught a glimpse of himself in the rear-view mirror and it wasn't the contented, everything-is-resting-easy face he had gotten up with that morning. Now it was the press conference face, and the face of the man who had crawled through the snow of the Castle Rock town common on his hands and knees. The skin was too white, the eyes circled with bruised-looking brown rings, the lines etched too deep.

No. It isn't true.

But it was. Now that was out, it couldn't be denied. In the first twenty-three years of his life he had shaken hands with exactly one politician; that was when Ed Muskie had come to talk to his high school government class in 1966. In the last seven months he had shaken hands with over a dozen big names. And hadn't the thought flashed across the back of his mind as each one struck out his hand—*What's this guy all about? What's he going to tell me?*

Hadn't he been looking, all along, for the political equivalent of Frank Dodd?

Yes. It was true.

But the fact was, none of them except Carter had told him much of anything, and the feelings that he had gotten from Carter were not particularly alarming. Shaking hands with Carter had not given him that sinking feeling he had gotten just from watching Greg Stillson on TV. He felt as if Stillson might have taken the game of the Laughing Tiger a step further inside the beast-skin, a man, yes.

But inside the man-skin, a beast.

◆ **2** ◆

Whatever the progression had been, Johnny found himself eating his picnic lunch in the Trimbull town park instead of the Fenway bleachers. He had arrived shortly after noon and had seen a sign on the community notice board announcing the rally at three P.M.

He drifted over to the park, expecting to have the place pretty much to himself so long before the rally was scheduled to begin, but others were already spreading blankets, unlimbering Frisbees, or settling down to their own lunches.

Up front, a number of men were at work on the bandstand. Two of them were decorating the waist-high railings with bunting. Another was on a ladder, hanging colorful crepe streamers from the bandstand's circular eave. Others were setting up the sound system, and as Johnny had guessed when he watched the CBS newsclip, it was no four-hundred-dollar podium PA set. The speakers were Altec-Lansings, and they were being carefully placed to give surround-sound.

The advance men (but the image that persisted was that of roadies setting up for an Eagles or Geils band concert) went about their work with businesslike precision. The whole thing had a practiced, professional quality to it that jarred with Stillson's image of the amiable Wild Man of Borneo.

The crowd mostly spanned about twenty years, from midteens to midthirties. They were having a good time. Babies toddled around clutching melting Dairy Queens and Slush Puppies. Women chatted together and laughed. Men drank beer from styrofoam cups. A few dogs bounced around, grabbing what there was to be grabbed, and the sun shone benignly down on everyone.

"Test," one of the men on the bandstand said laconically into the two mikes. "Test-one, test-two . . ." One of the speakers in the park uttered a loud feedback whine, and the guy on the podium motioned that he wanted it moved backward.

This isn't the way you set up for a political speech and rally, Johnny thought. *They're setting up for a love-feast . . . or a group grope.*

"Test-one, test-two . . . test, test, test."

They were *strapping* the big speakers to the trees, Johnny saw. Not *nailing* them but *strapping* them. Stillson was an ecology booster, and someone had told his advance men not to hurt so much as one tree in one town park. The operation gave him the feeling of having been honed down to the smallest detail. This was no grab-it-and-run-with-it deal.

Two yellow school buses pulled into the turnaround left of the small (and already full) parking lot. The doors folded open and men and women got out, talking animatedly to one another. They were in sharp contrast to those already in the park because they were dressed in their best—men in suits or sports coats, ladies in crisp skirt-and-blouse combinations or smart dresses. They were gazing around with expressions of nearly childlike wonder and anticipation, and Johnny grinned. Ngo's citizenship class had arrived.

He walked over to them. Ngo was standing with a tall man in a corduroy suit and two women, both Chinese.

"Hi, Ngo," Johnny said.

Ngo grinned broadly. "Johnny!" he said. "Good to see you, man! It is being a great day for the state of New Hampshire, right?"

"I guess so," Johnny said.

Ngo introduced his companions. The man in the corduroy suit was Polish. The two women severe sisters from Taiwan. One of the women told Johnny that she was much hoping for shaking hands with the candidate after the program and then, shyly, she showed Johnny the autograph book in her handbag.

"I am so glad to be here in America," she said. "But it is strange, is it not, Mr. Smith?"

Johnny, who thought the whole thing was strange, agreed.

The citizenship class's two instructors were calling the group together. "I'll see you later, Johnny," Ngo said. "I've got to be tripping."

"Going," Johnny said.

"Yes, thanks."

"Have a fine time, Ngo."

"Oh, yes, I am sure I will." And Ngo's eyes seemed to glint with a secret amusement. "I am sure it will be most entertaining, Johnny."

The group, about forty in all, went over to the south side of the park to have their picnic lunch. Johnny went back to his own place and made himself eat one of his sandwiches. It tasted like a combination of paper and library paste.

A thick feeling of tension had begun to creep into his body.

◆ **3** ◆

By two-thirty the park was completely full; people were jammed together nearly shoulder to shoulder. The town police, augmented by a small contingent of State Police, had closed off the streets leading to the Trimbull town park. The resemblance to a rock concert was stronger than ever. Bluegrass music poured from the speakers, cheery and fast. Fat white clouds drifted across the innocent blue sky.

Suddenly, people started getting to their feet and craning their necks. It was a ripple effect passing through the crowd. Johnny got up too, wondering if Stillson was going to be early. Now he could hear the steady roar of motorcycle engines, the beat swelling to fill the summer afternoon as they grew closer. Johnny got an eyeful of sun-arrows reflecting off chrome, and a few moments later about ten cycles swung into the turn-around where the citizenship buses were parked. There was no car with them. Johnny guessed they were an advance guard.

His feeling of disquiet deepened. The riders were neat enough, dressed for the most part in clean, faded jeans and white shirts, but the bikes themselves, mostly Harleys and BSAs, had been customized almost beyond recognition: ape-hanger handlebars, raked chromium manifolds, and strange fairings abounded.

Their owners killed the engines, swung off, and moved away toward the bandstand in single file. Only one of them looked back. His eyes moved without haste over the big crowd; even from some distance away Johnny could see that the man's irises were a brilliant bottle green. He seemed to be counting the house. He glanced left, at four or five town cops leaning against the chain-link backstop of the Little League ballfield. He waved. One of the cops leaned over and spit. The act had a feeling of ceremony to it, and Johnny's disquiet deepened further. The man with the green eyes sauntered to the bandstand.

Above the disquiet, which now lay like an emotional floor to his other feelings, Johnny felt predominantly a wild mix of horror and hilarity. He had a dreamlike sense of having some-how entered one of those paintings where steam engines are coming out of brick fireplaces or clockfaces are lying limply over tree limbs. The cyclists looked like extras in an American-International bikie movie who had all decided to Get Clean For Gene. Their fresh, faded jeans were snugged down over square-toed engineer boots, and on more than one pair Johnny could see chromed chains strapped down over the insteps. The chrome twinkled savagely in the sun. Their ex-pressions were nearly all the same: a sort of vacuous good humor that seemed directed at the crowd. But beneath it there might have been simple contempt for the young mill workers, the summer students who had come over from UNH in Durham, and the factory workers who were standing to give them a round of applause. Each of them wore a pair of political buttons. One of them showed a construction worker's yellow hard hat with a green ecology sticker on the front. The other bore the motto STILLSON'S GOT 'EM IN A FULL-NELSON.

And sticking out of every right hip pocket was a sawed-off pool cue.

Johnny turned to the man next to him, who was with his wife and small child. "Are those things legal?" he asked.

"Who the hell cares," the young guy responded, laughing. "They're just for show, anyway." He was still applauding. "*Go-get-em-Greg!*" he yelled.

The motorcycle honor guard deployed themselves around the bandstand in a circle and stood at parade rest.

The applause tapered off, but conversation went on at a louder level. The crowd's mass mouth had received the meal's appetizer and had found it good.

Brownshirts, Johnny thought, sitting down. *Brownshirts is all they are.*

Well, so what? Maybe that was even good. Americans had a rather low tolerance for the fascist approach—even rock-ribbed righties like Reagan didn't go for that stuff; nothing but a pure fact no matter how many tantrums the New Left might want to throw or how many songs Joan Baez wrote. Eight years before, the fascist tactics of the Chicago police had helped lose the election for Hubert Humphrey. Johnny didn't care how clean-cut these fellows were; if they were in the employ of a man running for the House of Representatives, then Stillson couldn't be more than a few paces from overstepping himself. *If it wasn't quite so weird, it really would be funny.*

All the same, he wished he hadn't come.

◆ **4** ◆

Just before three o'clock, the thud of a big brass drum impressed itself on the air, felt through the feet before actually heard by the ears. Other instruments gradually began to surround it, and all of them resolved into a marching band playing a Sousa tune. Small-town election hoopla, all of a summer's day.

The crowd came to its feet again and craned in the direction of the music. Soon the band came in sight—first a baton-twirler in a short skirt, high-stepping in white kidskin boots with pompons on them, then two majorettes, then two pimply boys with grimly set faces carrying a banner that proclaimed this was THE TRIMBULL HIGH SCHOOL MARCHING BAND and you had by-God better not forget it. Then the band itself, resplendent and sweaty in blinding white uniforms and brass buttons.

The crowd cleared a path for them, and then broke into a wave of applause as they began to march in place. Behind them was a white Ford van, and standing spread-legged on the roof, face sunburned and split into a mammoth grin under his cocked-back construction hat, was the candidate himself. He raised a battery-powered bullhorn and shouted into it with leather-lunged enthusiasm: "*HI, Y'ALL!*"

"*Hi, Greg!*" The crowd gave it right back.

Greg, Johnny thought a little hysterically. *We're on first-name terms with the guy.*

Stillson leaped down from the roof of the van, managing to make it look easy. He was dressed as Johnny had seen him on the news, jeans and a khaki shirt. He began to work the crowd on his way to the bandstand, shaking hands, touching other hands outstretched over the heads of those in the first ranks. The crowd lurched and swayed deliriously toward him, and Johnny felt an answering lurch in his own guts.

I'm not going to touch him. No way.

But in front of him the crowd suddenly parted a little and he stepped into the gap and suddenly found himself in the front row. He was close enough to the tuba player in the Trimbull High School Marching Band to have reached out and rapped his knuckles on the bell of his horn, had he wanted to.

Stillson moved quickly through the ranks of the band to shake hands on the other side, and Johnny lost complete sight of him except for the bobbing yellow helmet. He felt relief. That was all right, then. No harm, no foul. Like the pharisee in that famous story, he was going to pass by on the other side. Good. Wonderful. And when he made the podium, Johnny was going to gather up his stuff and steal away into the afternoon. Enough was enough.

The bikies had moved up on both sides of the path through the crowd to keep it from collapsing in on the candidate and drowning him in people. All the chunks of pool cue were still in the back pockets, but their owners looked tense and alert for trouble. Johnny didn't know exactly what sort of trouble they expected—a Brownie Delight thrown in the candidate's face, maybe—but for the first time the bikies looked really interested.

Then something did happen, but Johnny was unable to tell exactly what it had been. A female hand reached for the bobbing yellow hard hat, maybe just to touch it for good luck, and one of Stillson's fellows moved in quickly. There was a yell of dismay and the woman's hand disappeared quickly. But it was all on the other side of the marching band.

The din from the crowd was enormous, and he thought again of the rock concerts he had been to. This was what it would be like if Paul McCartney or Elvis Presley decided to shake hands with the crowd.

They were screaming his name, chanting it: "*GREG . . . GREG . . . GREG . . .*"

The young guy who had billeted his family next to Johnny was holding his son up over his head so the kid could see. A young man with a large, puckered burn scar on one side of his face was waving a sign that read: LIVE FREE OR DIE, HERE'S GREG IN YER EYE! An achingly beautiful girl of maybe eighteen was waving a chunk of watermelon, and pink juice was running down her tanned arm. It was all mass confusion. Excitement was humming through the crowd like a series of high-voltage electrical cables.

And suddenly there was Greg Stillson, darting back through the band, back to Johnny's side of the crowd. He didn't pause, but still found time to give the tuba player a hearty clap on the back.

Later, Johnny mulled it over and tried to tell himself that there really hadn't been any chance or time to melt back into the crowd; he tried to tell himself that the crowd had practically *heaved* him into Stillson's arms. He tried to tell himself that Stillson had done everything but abduct his hand. None of it was true. There was time, because a fat woman in absurd, yellow clamdiggers threw her arms around Stillson's neck and gave him a hearty kiss, which Stillson returned with a laugh and a "You bet I'll remember *you,* hon." The fat woman screamed laughter.

Johnny felt the familiar compact coldness come over him, the trance feeling. The sensation that nothing mattered except to *know*. He even smiled a little, but it wasn't his smile. He put his hand out, and Stillson seized it in both of his and began to pump it up and down.

"Hey, man, hope you're gonna support us in . . ."

Then Stillson broke off. The way Eileen Magown had. The way Dr. James (just like the soul singer) Brown had. The way Roger Dussault had. His eyes went wide, and then they filled with—fright? No. It was *terror* in Stillson's eyes.

The moment was endless. Objective time was replaced by something else, a perfect cameo of time as they stared into each other's eyes. For Johnny it was like being in that dull chrome corridor again, only this time Stillson was with him and they were sharing . . . sharing

(everything)

For Johnny it had never been this strong, never. Everything came at him at once, crammed together and screaming like some terrible black freight train highballing through a narrow tunnel, a speeding engine with a single glaring headlamp mounted up front, and the headlamp was *knowing everything*, and its light impaled Johnny Smith like a bug on a pin. There was nowhere to run and perfect knowledge ran him down, plastered him as flat as a sheet of paper while that night-running train raced over him.

He felt like screaming, but had no taste for it, no voice for it.

The one image he never escaped

(as the blue filter began to creep in)

was Greg Stillson taking the oath of office. It was being administered by an old man with the humble, frightened eyes of a fieldmouse trapped by a terribly proficient, battlescarred

(tiger)

barnyard tomcat. One of Stillson's hands clapped over a Bible, one upraised. It was years in the future because Stillson had lost most of his hair. The old man was speaking, Stillson was following. Stillson was saying

(the blue filter is deepening, covering things, blotting them out bit by bit, merciful blue filter, Stillson's face is behind the blue . . . and the yellow . . . the yellow like tiger-stripes)

he would do it "So help him God." His face was solemn, grim, even, but a great hot joy clapped in his chest and roared in his brain. Because the man with the scared fieldmouse eyes was the Chief Justice of the United States Supreme Court and

(O dear God the filter the filter the blue filter the yellow stripes)

now all of it began to disappear slowly behind that blue filter—except it wasn't a filter; it was something real. It was

(in the future in the dead zone)

something in the future. His? Stillson's? Johnny didn't know.

There was the sense of flying—flying through the blue—above scenes of utter desolation that could not quite be seen. And cutting through this came the disembodied voice of Greg Stillson, the voice of a cut-rate God or a comic-opera engine of the dead: *"I'M GONNA GO THROUGH THEM LIKE BUCKWHEAT THROUGH A GOOSE! GONNA GO THROUGH THEM LIKE SHIT THROUGH A CANEBRAKE!"*

"The tiger," Johnny muttered thickly. "The tiger's behind the blue. Behind the yellow."

Then all of it, pictures, images, and words, broke up in the swelling, soft roar of oblivion. He seemed to smell some sweet, coppery scent, like burning high-tension wires. For a moment that inner eye seemed to open even wider, searching; the blue and yellow that had obscured everything seemed about to solidify into . . . into something, and from somewhere inside, distant and full of terror, he heard a woman shriek: *"Give him to me, you bastard!"*

Then it was gone.

How long did we stand together like that? he would ask himself later. His guess was maybe five seconds. Then Stillson was pulling his hand away, *ripping* it away, staring at Johnny with his mouth open, the color draining away from beneath the deep tan of the summertime campaigner. Johnny could see the fillings in the man's back teeth.

His expression was one of revolted horror.

Good! Johnny wanted to scream. *Good! Shake yourself to pieces! Total yourself! Destruct! Implode! Disintegrate! Do the world a favor!*

Two of the motorcycle guys were rushing forward and now the sawed-off pool cues *were* out and Johnny felt a stupid kind of terror because they were going to hit him, hit him over the head with their cues, they were going to make believe Johnny Smith's head was the eight ball and they were going to blast it right into the side pocket, right back into the blackness of coma and he would never come out of it this time, he would never be able to tell anyone what he had seen or change anything.

That sense of destruction—God! It had been *everything*!

He tried to backpedal. People scattered, pressed back, yelled with fear (or perhaps with excitement). Stillson was turning toward his bodyguards, already regaining his composure, shaking his head, restraining them.

Johnny never saw what happened next. He swayed on his feet, head lowered, blinking slowly like a drunk at the bitter end of a week-long binge. Then the soft, swelling roar of oblivion overwhelmed him and Johnny let it; he gladly let it. He blacked out.

Chapter 21

◆ 1 ◆

"No," the Trimbull chief of police said in answer to Johnny's question, "you're not charged with anything. You're not under detention. And you don't have to answer any questions. We'd just be very grateful if you would."

"*Very* grateful," the man in the conservative business suit echoed. His name was Edgar Lancte. He was with the Boston office of the Federal Bureau of Investigation. He thought that Johnny Smith looked like a very sick man. There was a puffed bruise above his left eyebrow that was rapidly turning purple. When he blacked out, Johnny had come down very hard— either on the shoe of a marching-bandsman or on the squared-off toe of a motorcycle boot. Lancte mentally favored the latter possibility. And possibly the motorcycle boot had been in motion at the instant of contact.

Smith was too pale, and his hands trembled badly as he drank the paper cup of water that Chief Bass had given him. One eyelid was ticking nervously. He looked like the classic would-be assassin, although the most deadly thing in his personal effects had been a nailclipper. Still, Lancte would keep that impression in mind, because he was what he was.

"What can I tell you?" Johnny asked. He had awakened

on a cot in an unlocked cell. He'd had a blinding headache. It was draining away now, leaving him feeling strangely hollow inside. He felt a little as if his legitimate innards had been scooped out and replaced with Reddi Wip. There was a high, constant sound in his ears—not precisely a ringing; more like a high, steady hum. It was nine P.M. The Stillson entourage had long since swept out of town. All the hot dogs had been eaten.

"You can tell us exactly what happened back there," Bass said.

"It was hot. I guess I got overexcited and fainted."

"You an invalid or something?" Lancte asked casually.

Johnny looked at him steadily. "Don't play games with me, Mr. Lancte. If you know who I am, then say so."

"I know," Lancte said. "Maybe you *are* psychic."

"Nothing psychic about guessing an FBI agent might be up to a few games," Johnny said.

"You're a Maine boy, Johnny. Born and bred. What's a Maine boy doing down in New Hampshre?"

"Tutoring."

"The Chatsworth boy?"

"For the second time: if you know, why ask? Unless you suspect me of something."

Lancte lit a Vantage Green. "Rich family."

"Yes. They are."

"You a Stillson fan, are you, Johnny?" Bass asked. Johnny didn't like fellows who used his first name on first acquaintance, and both of these fellows were doing it. It made him nervous.

"Are you?" he asked.

Bass made an obscene blowing sound. "About five years ago we had a day-long folk-rock concert in Trimbull. Out on Hake Jamieson's land. Town council had their doubts, but they went ahead because the kids have got to have something. We thought we were going to have maybe two hundred local kids in Hake's east pasture listening to music. Instead we got sixteen hundred, all of em smoking pot and drinking hard stuff straight out from the neck of the bottle. They made a hell of a mess and the council got mad and said there'd never be another one and they turned around all hurt and wet-eyed and said, 'Whassa matter? No one got hurt, did they?' It was supposed to be okay to make a helluva mess because no one got hurt. I feel the same way about this guy Stillson. I remember once . . ."

"You don't have any sort of grudge against Stillson, do you, Johnny?" Lancte asked. "Nothing personal between you and him?" He smiled a fatherly, you-can-get-it-off-your-chest-if-you-want-to smile.

"I didn't even know who he was until six weeks ago."

"Yes, well, but that really doesn't answer my question, does it?"

Johnny sat silent for a little while. "He disturbs me," he said finally.

"That doesn't really answer my question, either."

"Yes, I think it does."

"You're not being as helpful as we'd like," Lancte said regretfully.

Johnny glanced over at Bass. "Does anybody who faints in your town at a public gathering get the FBI treatment, Chief Bass?"

Bass looked uncomfortable. "Well . . . no. Course not."

"You were shaking hands with Stillson when you keeled over," Lancte said. "You looked sick. Stillson himself looked scared green. You're a very lucky young man, Johnny. Lucky his goodbuddies there didn't turn your head into a votive urn. They thought you'd pulled a piece on him."

Johnny was looking at Lancte with dawning surprise. He looked at Bass, then back to the FBI man. "You were *there*," he said. "Bass didn't call you up on the phone. You were *there*. At the rally."

Lancte crushed out his cigarette. "Yes. I was."

"Why is the FBI interested in Stillson?" Johnny nearly barked the question.

"Let's talk about you, Johnny. What's your . . ."

"No, let's talk about Stillson. Let's talk about his goodbuddies, as you call them. Is it legal for them to carry around sawed-off pool cues?"

"It is," Bass said. Lancte threw him a warning look, but Bass either didn't see it or ignored it. "Cues, baseball bats, golf clubs. No law against any of them."

"I heard someone say those guys used to be iron riders. Bike gang members."

"Some of them used to be with a New Jersey club, some used to be with a New York club, that's . . ."

"Chief Bass," Lancte interrupted, "I hardly think this is the time . . ."

"I can't see the harm of telling him," Bass said. "They're bums, rotten apples, hairbags. Some of them ganged together in the Hamptons back four or five years ago, when they had the bad riots. A few of them were affiliated with a bike club called the Devil's Dozen that disbanded in 1972. Stillson's ramrod is a guy named Sonny Elliman. He used to be the president of the Devil's Dozen. He's been busted half a dozen times but never convicted of anything."

"You're wrong about that, Chief," Lancte said, lighting a fresh cigarette. "He was cited in Washington State in 1973 for making an illegal left turn against traffic. He signed the waiver and paid a twenty-five-dollar fine."

Johnny got up and went slowly across the room to the water cooler, where he drew himself a fresh cup of water. Lancte watched him go with interest.

"So you just fainted, right?" Lancte said.

"No," Johnny said, not turning around. "I was going to shoot him with a bazooka. Then, at the critical moment, all my bionic circuits blew."

Lancte sighed.

Bass said, "You're free to go any time."

"Thank you."

"But I'll tell you just the same way Mr. Lancte here would tell you. In the future, I'd stay away from Stillson rallies, if I were you. If you want to keep a whole skin, that is. Things have a way of happening to people Greg Stillson doesn't like . . ."

"Is that so?" Johnny asked. He drank his water.

"Those are matters outside your bailiwick, Chief Bass," Lancte said. His eyes were like hazy steel and he was looking at Bass very hard.

"All right," Bass said mildly.

"I don't see any harm in telling you that there have been other rally incidents," Lancte said. "In Ridgeway a young pregnant woman was beaten so badly she miscarried. This was just after the Stillson rally there that CBS filmed. She said she couldn't ID her assailant, but we feel it may have been one of Stillson's bikies. A month ago a kid, he was fourteen, got himself a fractured skull. He had a little plastic squirtgun. He couldn't ID his assailant, either. But the squirtgun makes us believe it may have been a security overreaction."

How nicely put, Johnny thought.

"You couldn't find anyone who saw it happen?"

"Nobody who would talk." Lancte smiled humorlessly and tapped the ash off his cigarette. "He's the people's choice."

Johnny thought of the young guy holding his son up so that the boy could see Greg Stillson *Who the hell cares? They're just for show, anyway.*

"So he's got his own pet FBI agent."

Lancte shrugged and smiled disarmingly. "Well, what can I say? Except, FYI, it's no tit assignment, Johnny. Sometimes I get scared. The guy generates one hell of a lot of magnetism. If he pointed me out from the podium and told the crowd at one of those rallies who I was, I think they'd run me up the nearest lamppost."

Johnny thought of the crowd that afternoon, and of the pretty girl hysterically waving her chunk of watermelon. "I think you might be right," he said.

"So if there's something you know that might help me . . ." Lancte leaned forward. The disarming smile had become slightly predatory. "Maybe you even had a psychic flash about him. Maybe that's what messed you up."

"Maybe I did," Johnny said, unsmiling.

"Well?"

For one wild moment Johnny considered telling them everything. Then he rejected it. "I saw him on TV. I had nothing in particular to do today, so I thought I'd come over here and check him out in person. I bet I wasn't the only out-of-towner who did that."

"You sure *wasn't,*" Bass said vehemently.

"And that's all?" Lancte asked.

"That's all," Johnny said, and then hesitated. "Except . . . I think he's going to win his election."

"We're sure he is," Lancte said. "Unless we can get something on him. In the meantime, I'm in complete agreement with Chief Bass. Stay away from Stillson rallies."

"Don't worry." Johnny crumpled up his paper cup and threw it away. "It's been nice talking to you two gentlemen, but I've got a long drive back to Durham."

"Going back to Maine soon, Johnny?" Lancte asked casually.

"Don't know." He looked from Lancte, slim and impeccable, tapping out a fresh cigarette on the blank face of his digital watch, to Bass, a big, tired man with a basset hound's face. "Do either of you think he'll run for a higher office? If he gets this seat in the House of Representatives?"

"Jesus wept," Bass uttered, and rolled his eyes.

"These guys come and go," Lancte said. His eyes, so brown they were nearly black, had never stopped studying Johnny. "They're like one of those rare radioactive elements that are so unstable that they don't last long. Guys like Stillson have no permanent political base, just a temporary coalition that holds together for a little while and then falls apart. Did you see that crowd today? College kids and mill hands yelling for the same guy? That's not politics, that's something on the order of hula hoops or coonskin caps or Beatle wigs. He'll get his term in the House and he'll free-lunch until 1978 and that'll be it. Count on it."

But Johnny wondered.

♦ 2 ♦

The next day, the left side of Johnny's forehead had become very colorful. Dark purple—almost black—above the eyebrow shaded to red and then to a morbidly gay yellow at the temple and hairline. His eyelid had puffed slightly, giving him a leering sort of expression, like the second banana in a burlesque revue.

He did twenty laps in the pool and then sprawled in one of the deck chairs, panting. He felt terrible. He had gotten less than four hours' sleep the night before, and all of what he had gotten had been dream-haunted.

"Hi, Johnny . . . how you doing, man?"

He turned around. It was Ngo, smiling gently. He was dressed in his work clothes and wearing gardening gloves. Behind him was a child's red wagon filled with small pine trees, their roots wrapped in burlap. Recalling what Ngo called the pines, he said: "I see you're planting more weeds."

Ngo wrinkled his nose. "Sorry, yes. Mr. Chatsworth is loving them. I tell him, but they are junk trees. Everywhere there are these trees in New England. His face goes like this . . ." Now Ngo's whole face wrinkled and he looked like a caricature of some late show monster. ". . . and he says to me, 'Just plant them.' "

Johnny laughed. That was Roger Chatsworth, all right. He liked things done his way. "How did you enjoy the rally?"

Ngo smiled gently. "Very instructive," he said. There was no way to read his eyes. He might not have noticed the sunrise on the side of Johnny's face. "Yes, very instructive, we are all enjoying ourselves."

"Good."

"And you?"

"Not so much," Johnny said, and touched the bruise lightly with his fingertips. It was very tender.

"Yes, too bad, you should put a beefsteak on it," Ngo said, still smiling gently.

"What did you think about him, Ngo? What did your class think? Your Polish friend? Or Ruth Chen and her sister?"

"Going back we did not talk about it, at our instructors' request. Think about what you have seen, they say. Next Tuesday we will write in class, I think. Yes, I am thinking very much that we will. A class composition."

"What will you say in your composition?"

Ngo looked at the blue summer sky. He and the sky smiled at each other. He was a small man with the first threads of gray in his hair. Johnny knew almost nothing about him; didn't know if he had been married, had fathered children, if he had fled before the Vietcong, if he had been from Saigon or from one of the rural provinces. He had no idea what Ngo's political leanings were.

"We talked of the game of the Laughing Tiger," Ngo said. "Do you remember?"

"Yes," Johnny said.

"I will tell you of a real tiger. When I was a boy there was a tiger who went bad near my village. He was being *le manger d'homme,* eater of men, you understand, except he was not that, he was an eater of boys and girls and old women because this was during the war and there were no men to eat. Not the war you know of, but the Second World War. He had gotten the taste for human meat, this tiger. Who was there to kill such an awful creature in a humble village where the youngest man is being sixty and with only one arm, and the oldest boy is myself, only seven years of age? And one day this tiger was found in a pit that had been baited with the body of a dead woman. It is a terrible thing to bait a trap with a human being made in the image of God, I will say in my composition, but it is more terrible to do nothing while a bad tiger carries away small children. And I will say in my composition that this bad tiger was still alive when we found it. It was having a stake pushed through its body but it was still alive. We beat it to death with hoes and sticks. Old men and women and children, some children so excited and frightened they are wetting themselves in their pants. The tiger fell in the pit and we beat it to death with our hoes because the men of the village had gone to fight the Japanese. I am thinking that this Stillson is like that bad tiger with its taste for human meat. I think a trap should be made for him, and I think he should be falling into it. And if he still lives, I think he should be beaten to death."

He smiled gently at Johnny in the clear summer sunshine.

"Do you really believe that?" Johnny asked.

"Oh, yes," Ngo said. He spoke lightly, as if it were a matter of no consequence. "What my teacher will say when I am handing in such a composition, I don't know." He shrugged his shoulders. "Probably he will say, 'Ngo, you are not ready for the American Way.' But I will say the truth of what I feel. What did *you* think, Johnny?" His eyes moved to the bruise, then moved away.

"I think he's dangerous," Johnny said. "I . . . I know he's dangerous."

"Do you?" Ngo remarked. "Yes, I believe you do know it. Your fellow New Hampshires, they see him as an engaging clown. They see him the way many of this world are seeing this black man, Idi Amin Dada. But you do not."

"No," Johnny said. "But to suggest he should be killed . . ."

"*Politically* killed," Ngo said, smiling. "I am only suggesting he should be politically killed."

"And if he can't be politically killed?"

Ngo smiled at Johnny. He unfolded his index finger, cocked his thumb, and then snapped it down. "Bam," he said softly. "Bam, bam, bam."

"No," Johnny said, surprised at the hoarseness in his own voice "That's never an answer. *Never.*"

"No? I thought it was an answer you Americans used quite often." Ngo picked up the handle of the red wagon. "I must be planting these weeds, Johnny. So long, man."

Johnny watched him go, a small man in suntans and moccasins, pulling a wagonload of baby pines. He disappeared around the corner of the house.

No. Killing only sows more dragon's teeth. I believe that. I believe it with all my heart.

◆ 3 ◆

On the first Tuesday in November, which happened to be the
second day in the month, Johnny Smith sat slumped in the
easy chair of his combined kitchen-living room and watched
the election returns. Chancellor and Brinkley were featuring
a large electronic map that showed the results of the presidential race in a color-code as each state came in. Now, at nearly
midnight, the race between Ford and Carter looked very
close. But Carter would win; Johnny had no doubt of it.

Greg Stillson had also won.

His victory had been extensively covered on the local news-
breaks, but the national reporters had also taken some note
of it, comparing his victory to that of James Longley, Maine's
independent governor, two years before.

Chancellor said, "Late polls showing that the Republican
candidate and incumbent Harrison Fisher was closing the gap
were apparently in error; NBC predicts that Stillson, who
campaigned in a construction worker's hard hat and on a platform that included the proposal that all pollution be sent into
outer space, ended up with forty-six percent of the vote, to
Fisher's thirty-one percent. In a district where the Democrats
have always been poor relations, David Bowes could only poll
twenty-three percent of the vote."

"And so," Brinkley said, "it's hot dog time down in New
Hampshire . . . for the next two years, at least." He and
Chancellor grinned. A commercial came on. Johnny didn't
grin. He was thinking of tigers.

The time between the Trimbull rally and election night had
been busy for Johnny. His work with Chuck had continued,
and Chuck continued to improve at a slow but steady pace.
He had taken two summer courses, passed them both, and
retained his sports eligibility. Now, with the football season
just ending, it looked very much as if he would be named to
the Gannett newspaper chain's All New England team. The
careful, almost ritualistic visits from the college scouts had
already begun, but they would have to wait another year; the
decision had already been made between Chuck and his father
that he would spend a year at Stovington Prep, a good private
school in Vermont. Johnny thought Stovington would probably be delirious at the news. The Vermont school regularly

fielded great soccer teams and dismal football teams. They would probably give him a full scholarship and a gold key to the girl's dorm in the bargain. Johnny felt that it had been the right decision. After it had been reached and the pressure on Chuck to take the SATs right away had eased off, his progress had taken another big jump.

In late September, Johnny had gone up to Pownal for the weekend and after an entire Friday night of watching his father fidget and laugh uproariously at jokes on TV that weren't particularly funny, he had asked Herb what the trouble was.

"No trouble," Herb said, smiling nervously and rubbing his hands together like an accountant who has discovered that the company he just invested his life savings with is bankrupt. "No trouble at all, what makes you think that, son?"

"Well, what's on your mind, then?"

Herb stopped smiling, but he kept rubbing his hands together. "I don't really know how to tell you, Johnny. I mean . . ."

"Is it Charlene?"

"Well, yes. It is."

"You popped the question."

Herb looked at Johnny humbly. "How do you feel about coming into a stepmother at the age of twenty-nine, John?"

Johnny grinned. "I feel fine about it. Congratulations, Dad."

Herb smiled, relieved. "Well, thanks. I was a little scared to tell you, I don't mind admitting it. I know what you said when we talked about it before, but people sometimes feel one way when something's maybe and another way when it's gonna be. I loved your mom, Johnny. And I guess I always will."

"I know that, dad."

"But I'm alone and Charlene's alone and . . . well, I guess we can put each other to good use."

Johnny went over to his father and kissed him. "All the best. I know you'll have it."

"You're a good son, Johnny." Herb took his handkerchief out of his back pocket and swiped at his eyes with it. "We thought we'd lost you. I did, anyway. Vera never lost hope. She always believed. Johnny, I . . ."

"Don't, Daddy. It's over."

"I have to," he said. "It's been in my gut like a stone for a year and a half now. I prayed for you to die, Johnny. My

own son, and I prayed for God to take you." He wiped his
eyes again and put his handkerchief away. "Turned out God
knew a smidge more than I did. Johnny . . . would you stand
up with me? At my wedding?"

Johnny felt something inside that was almost but not quite
like sorrow. "That would be my pleasure," he said.

"Thanks. I'm glad I've . . . that I've said everything that's
on my mind. I feel better than I have in a long, long time."

"Have you set a date?"

"As a matter of fact, we have. How does January 2 sound
to you?"

"Sounds good," Johnny said. "You can count on me."

"We're going to put both places on the market, I guess,"
Herb said. "We've got our eye on a farm in Biddeford. Nice
place. Twenty acres. Half of it woodlot. A new start."

"Yes. A new start, that's good."

"You wouldn't have any objections to us selling the home
place?" Herb asked anxiously.

"A little tug," Johnny said. "That's all."

"Yeah, that's what I feel. A little tug." He smiled. "Somewhere around the heart, that's where mine is. What about
you?"

"About the same," Johnny said.

"How's it going down there for you?"

"Good."

"Your boy's getting along?"

"Amazin well," Johnny said, using one of his father's pet
expressions and grinning.

"How long do you think you'll be there?"

"Working with Chuck? I guess I'll stick with it through the
school year, if they want me. Working one-on-one has been
a new kind of experience. I like it. And this has been a really
good job. Atypically good, I'd say."

"What are you going to do after?"

Johnny shook his head. "I don't know yet. But I know
one thing."

"What's that?"

"I'm going out for a bottle of champagne. We're going to
get bombed."

His father had stood up on that September evening and
clapped him on the back. "Make it two," he said.

He still got the occasional letter from Sarah Hazlett. She
and Walt were expecting their second child in April. Johnny

wrote back his congratulations and his good wishes for Walt's canvass. And he thought sometimes about his afternoon with Sarah, the long, slow afternoon. It wasn't a memory he allowed himself to take out too often; he was afraid that constant exposure to the sunlight of recollection might cause it to wash out and fade, like the reddish-tinted proofs they used to give you of your graduation portraits.

He had gone out a few times this fall, once with the older and newly divorced sister of the girl Chuck was seeing, but nothing had developed from any of those dates.

Most of his spare time that fall he had spent in the company of Gregory Ammas Stillson.

He had become a Stillsonphile. He kept three loose-leaf notebooks in his bureau under his socks and underwear and T-shirts. They were filled with notes, speculations, and Xerox copies of news items.

Doing this had made him uneasy. At night, as he wrote around the pasted-up clippings with a fine-line Pilot pen, he sometimes felt like Arthur Bremmer or the Moore woman who had tried to shoot Jerry Ford. He knew that if Edgar Lancte, Fearless Minion of the Effa Bee Eye, could see him doing this, his phone, living room, and bathroom would be tapped in a jiffy. There would be an Acme Furniture van parked across the street, only instead of being full of furniture it would be loaded with cameras and mikes and God knew what else.

He kept telling himself that he wasn't Bremmer, that Stillson wasn't an obsession, but that got harder to believe after the long afternoons at the UNH library, searching through old newspapers and magazines and feeding dimes into the photocopier. It got harder to believe on the nights he burned the midnight oil, writing out his thoughts and trying to make valid connections. It grew well-nigh impossible to believe on those graveyard-ditch three A.M.s when he woke up sweating from the recurring nightmare.

The nightmare was nearly always the same, a naked replay of his handshake with Stillson at the Trimbull rally. The sudden blackness. The feeling of being in a tunnel filled with the glare of the onrushing headlight, a headlight bolted to some black engine of doom. The old man with the humble, frightened eyes administering an unthinkable oath of office. The nuances of feeling, coming and going like tight puffs of smoke. And a series of brief images, strung together in a flapping row like the plastic pennants over a used-car dealer's lot. His mind whispered to him that these images were all related, that they told a picture-story of a titanic approaching doom, perhaps even the Armageddon of which Vera Smith had been so endlessly confident.

But what were the images? What were they exactly? They were hazy, impossible to see except in vague outline, because there was always that puzzling blue filter between, the blue filter that was sometimes cut by those yellow markings like tiger stripes.

The only clear image in these dream-replays came near the end: the screams of the dying, the smell of the dead. And a single tiger padding through miles of twisted metal, fused glass, and scorched earth. This tiger was always laughing, and it seemed to be carrying something in its mouth—something blue and yellow and dripping blood.

There had been times in the fall when he thought that dream would send him mad. Ridiculous dream; the possibility it seemed to point to was impossible, after all. Best to drive it totally out of his mind.

But because he couldn't, he researched Gregory Stillson and tried to tell himself it was only a harmless hobby and not a dangerous obsession.

Stillson had been born in Tulsa. His father had been an oil-field roughneck who drifted from job to job, working more often than some of his colleagues because of his tremendous size. His mother might once have been pretty, although there was only a hint of that in the two pictures that Johnny had been able to unearth. If she had been, the times and the man she had been married to had dimmed her prettiness quickly. The pictures showed little more than another dust-bowl face, a southeast United States depression woman who was wearing a faded print dress and holding a baby—Greg—in her scrawny arms, and squinting into the sun.

His father had been a domineering man who didn't think much of his son. As a child, Greg had been pallid and sickly. There was no evidence that his father had abused the boy either mentally or physically, but there was the suggestion that at the very least, Greg Stillson had lived in a disapproving shadow for the first nine years of his life. The one picture Johnny had of the father and son together was a happy one, however; it showed them together in the oil fields, the father's arm slung around the son's neck in a careless gesture of comradeship. But it gave Johnny a little chill all the same. Harry Stillson was dressed in working clothes, twill pants and a double-breasted khaki shirt, and his hard hat was cocked jauntily back on his head.

Greg had begun school in Tulsa, then had been switched to Oklahoma City when he was ten. The previous summer his father had been killed in an oil-derrick flameout. Mary Lou Stillson had gone to Okie City with her boy because it was where her mother lived, and where the war work was. It was 1942, and good times had come around again.

Greg's grades had been good until high school, and then he began to get into a series of scraps. Truancy, fighting, hustling snooker downtown, maybe hustling stolen goods uptown, although that had never been proved. In 1949, when he had been a high-school junior, he had pulled a two-day suspension for putting a cherry-bomb firecracker in a locker-room toilet.

In all of these confrontations with authority, Mary Lou Stillson took her son's part. The good times—at least for the likes of the Stillsons—had ended with the war work in 1945, and Mrs. Stillson seemed to think of it as a case of her and her boy against the rest of the world. Her mother had died, leaving her the small frame house and nothing else. She hustled drinks in a roughneck bar for a while, then waited table in an all-night beanery. And when her boy got in trouble, she went to bat for him, never checking (apparently) to see if his hands were dirty or clean.

The pale sickly boy that his father had nicknamed Runt was gone by 1949. As Greg Stillson's adolescence progressed, his father's physical legacy came out. The boy shot up six inches and put on seventy pounds between thirteen and seventeen. He did not play organized school sports but somehow managed to acquire a Charles Atlas body-building gym and then a set of weights. The Runt became a bad guy to mess with.

Johnny guessed he must have come close to dropping out of school on dozens of occasions. He had probably avoided a bust out of sheer dumb luck. If only he *had* taken at least one serious bust, Johnny thought often. It would have ended all these stupid worries, because a convicted felon can't aspire to high public office.

Stillson had graduated—near the bottom of his class, it was true—in June, 1951. Grades notwithstanding, there was nothing wrong with his brains. His eye was on the main chance.

He had a glib tongue and a winning manner. He worked briefly that summer as a gas jockey. Then, in August of that year, Greg Stillson had gotten Jesus at a tent-revival in Wildwood Green. He quit his job at the 76 station and went into business as a rainmaker "through the power of Jesus Christ our Lord."

Coincidentally or otherwise, that had been one of the driest summers in Oklahoma since the days of the dust bowl. The crops were already a dead loss, and the livestock would soon follow if the shallowing wells went dry. Greg had been invited to a meeting of the local ranchers' association. Johnny had found a great many stories about what had followed; it was one of the high points of Stillson's career. None of the stories completely jibed, and Johnny could understand why. It had all the attributes of an American myth, not much different from some of the stories about Davy Crockett, Pecos Bill, Paul Bunyan. That *something* had happened was undeniable. But the strict truth of it was already beyond reach.

One thing seemed sure. That meeting of the ranchers' association must have been one of the strangest ever held. The ranchers had invited over two dozen rainmakers from various parts of the southeast and southwest. About half of them were Negroes. Two were Indians—a half-breed Pawnee and a full-blooded Apache. There was a peyote-chewing Mexican. Greg was one of about nine white fellows, and the only home-town boy.

The ranchers heard the proposals of the rainmakers and dowsers one by one. They gradually and naturally divided themselves into two groups: those who would take half of their fee up front (nonrefundable) and those who wanted their entire fee up front (nonrefundable).

When Greg Stillson's turn came, he stood up, hooked his thumbs into the belt loops of his jeans, and was supposed to have said: "I guess you fellows know I got in the way of being able to make it rain after I gave my heart to Jesus. Before that I was deep in sin and the ways of sin. Now one of the main ways of sin is the way we've seen tonight, and you spell that kind of sinning mostly with dollar signs."

The ranchers were interested. Even at nineteen Stillson had been something of a comic spellbinder. And he had made them an offer they couldn't refuse. Because he was a born-again Christian and because he knew that the love of money was the root of all evil, he would make it rain and afterward they could pay him whatever they thought the job had been worth.

He was hired by acclamation, and two days later he was down on his knees in the back of a flatbed farm truck, cruising slowly along the highways and byways of central Oklahoma, dressed in a black coat and a preacher's low-crowned hat, praying for rain through a pair of loudspeakers hooked up to a Delco tractor battery. People turned out by the thousands to get a look at him.

The end of the story was predictable but satisfying. The skies grew cloudy during the afternoon of Greg's second day on the job, and the next morning the rains came. The rains came for three days and two nights, flash floods killed four people, whole houses with chickens perched on the roof peaks were washed down the Greenwood River, the wells were filled, the livestock was saved, and The Oklahoma Ranchers' and Cattlemen's Association decided it probably would have happened anyway. They passed the hat for Greg at their next meeting and the young rainmaker was given the princely sum of seventeen dollars.

Greg was not put out of countenance. He used the seventeen dollars to place an ad in the Oklahoma City *Herald*. The ad pointed out that about the same sort of thing had happened a certain rat-catcher in the town of Hamlin. Being a Christian, the ad went on, Greg Stillson was not in the way of taking children, and he surely knew he had no legal recourse against a group as large and powerful as the Oklahoma Ranchers' and Cattlemen's Association. But fair was fair, wasn't it? He had his elderly mother to support, and she was in failing health. The ad suggested that he had prayed his ass off for a bunch of rich, ungrateful snobs, the same sort of men that had tractored poor folks like the Joads off their land in the thirties. The ad suggested that he had saved tens of thousands of dollars' worth of livestock and had got seventeen dollars in return. Because he was a good Christian, this sort of ingratitude didn't bother him, but maybe it ought to give the good citizens of the county some pause. Right-thinking people could send contributions to Box 471, care of the *Herald*.

Johnny wondered how much Greg Stillson had actually received as a result of that ad. Reports varied. But that fall, Greg had been tooling around town in a brand-new Mercury. Three years' worth of back taxes were paid on the small house left to them by Mary Lou's mother. Mary Lou herself (who was not particularly sickly and no older than forty-five), blossomed out in a new raccoon coat. Stillson had apparently discovered one of the great hidden muscles of principle which move the earth: if those who receive will not pay, those who have not often will, for no good reason at all. It may be the same principle that assures the politicians there will always be enough young men to feed the war machine.

The ranchers discovered they had stuck their collective hand into a hornets' nest. When members came into town, crowds often gathered and jeered at them. They were denounced from pulpits all across the county. They found it suddenly difficult to sell the beef the rain had saved without shipping it a considerable distance.

In November of that memorable year, two young men with brass knucks on their hands and nickel-plated .32s in their pockets had turned up on Greg Stillson's doorstep, apparently hired by the Ranchers' and Cattlemen's Association to suggest—as strenuously as necessary—that Greg would find the climate more congenial elsewhere. Both of them ended up in the hospital. One of them had a concussion. The other had lost four of his teeth and was suffering a rupture. Both had been found on the corner of Greg Stillson's block, *sans* pants. Their brass knucks had been inserted in an anatomical location most commonly associated with sitting down, and in the case of one of these two young men, minor surgery was necessary to remove the foreign objects.

The Association cried off. At a meeting in early December, an appropriation of $700 was made from its general fund, and a check in that amount was forwarded to Greg Stillson.

He got what he wanted.

In 1953 he and his mother moved to Nebraska. The rainmaking business had gone bad, and there were some who said the pool-hall hustling had also gone bad. Whatever the reason for moving, they turned up in Omaha where Greg opened a house-painting business that went bust two years later. He did better as a salesman for the Truth Way Bible Company of America. He crisscrossed the cornbelt, taking dinner with hundreds of hard-working, God-fearing farm families, telling the story of his conversion and selling Bibles, plaques, luminous plastic Jesuses, hymn books, records, tracts, and a rabidly right-wing paperback called *America the TruthWay: The Communist-Jewish Conspiracy Against Our United States*. In

1957 the aging Mercury was replaced with a brand new Ford ranch wagon.

In 1958 Mary Lou Stillson died of cancer, and late that year Greg Stillson got out of the born-again Bible business and drifted east. He spent a year in New York City before moving upstate to Albany. His year in New York had been devoted to an effort at cracking the acting business. It was one of the few jobs (along with house painting) that he hadn't been able to turn a buck at. But probably not from lack of talent, Johnny thought cynically.

In Albany he had gone to work for Prudential, and he had stayed in the capital city until 1965. As an insurance salesman he was an aimless sort of success. There was no offer to join the company at the executive level, no outbursts of Christian fervor. During that five-year period, the brash and brassy Greg Stillson of yore seemed to have gone into hibernation. In all of his checkered career, the only woman in his life had been his mother. He had never married, had not even dated regularly as far as Johnny had been able to find out.

In 1965, Prudential had offered him a position in Ridgeway, New Hampshire, and Greg had taken it. At about the same time, his period of hibernation seemed to end. The gogo Sixties were gathering steam. It was the era of the short skirt and do your own thing. Greg became active in Ridgeway community affairs. He joined the Chamber of Commerce and the Rotary Club. He got state-wide coverage in 1967, during a controversy over the parking meters downtown. For six years, various factions had been wrangling over them. Greg suggested that all the meters be taken out and that collection boxes be put up in their stead. Let people pay what they want. Some people had said that was the craziest idea they had ever heard. Well, Greg responded, you might just be surprised. Yes sir. He was persuasive. The town finally adopted the proposal on a provisional basis, and the ensuing flood of nickels and dimes had surprised everyone but Greg. He had discovered the principle years ago.

In 1969 he made New Hampshire news again when he suggested, in a long and carefully worked-out letter to the Ridgeway newspaper, that drug offenders be put to work on town public works projects such as parks and bike paths, even weeding the grass on the traffic islands. That's the craziest idea I ever heard, many said. Well, Greg responded, try her out and if she don't work, chuck her. The town tried it out.

One pothead reorganized the entire town library from the outmoded Dewey decimal system to the more modern Library of Congress cataloguing system, at no charge to the town. A number of hippies busted at an hallucinogenic house party relandscaped the town park into an area showplace, complete with duckpond and a playground scientifically designed to maximize effective playtime and minimize danger. As Greg pointed out, most of these drug-users got interested in all those chemicals in college, but that was no reason why they shouldn't utilize all the other things they had learned in college.

At the same time Greg was revolutionizing his adopted home town's parking regulations and its handling of drug offenders, he was writing letters to the Manchester *Union-Leader,* the Boston *Globe,* and the *New York Times,* espousing hawkish positions on the war in Vietnam, mandatory felony sentences for heroin addicts, and a return to the death penalty, especially for heroin pushers. In his campaign for the House of Representatives, he had claimed on several occasions to have been against the war from 1970 on, but the man's own published statements made that a flat lie.

In 1970, Greg Stillson had opened his own insurance and realty company. He was a great success. In 1973 he and three other businessmen had financed and built a shopping mall on the outskirts of Capital City, the county seat of the district he now represented. That was the year of the Arabian oil boycott, also the year Greg started driving a Lincoln Continental. It was also the year he ran for mayor of Ridgeway.

The mayor enjoyed a two-year term, and two years before, in 1971, he had been asked by both the Republicans and Democrats of the largish (population 8,500) New England town to run. He had declined both of them with smiling thanks. In '73 he ran as an independent, taking on a fairly popular Republican who was vulnerable because of his fervent support of President Nixon, and a Democratic figure-head. He donned his construction helmet for the first time. His campaign slogan was *Let's Build A Better Ridgeway!* He won in a landslide. A year later, in New Hampshire's sister state of Maine, the voters turned away from both the Democrat, George Mitchell, and the Republican, James Erwin, and elected an insurance man from Lewiston named James Longley their governor.

The lesson had not been lost on Gregory Ammas Stillson.

♦ 4 ♦

Around the Xerox clippings were Johnny's notes and the questions he regularly asked himself. He had been over his chain of reasoning so often that now, as Chancellor and Brinkley continued to chronicle the election results, he could have spouted the whole thing word for word.

First, Greg Stillson shouldn't have been able to get elected. His campaign promises were, by and large, jokes. His background was all wrong. His education was all wrong. It stopped at the twelfth-grade level, and, until 1965, he had been little more than a drifter. In a country where the voters have decided that the lawyers should make the laws, Stillson's only brushes with that force had been from the wrong side. He wasn't married. And his personal history was decidedly freaky.

Second, the press had left him almost completely—and very puzzlingly—alone. In an election year when Wilbur Mills had admitted to a mistress, when Wayne Hays had been dislodged from his barnacle-encrusted House seat because of his, when even those in the houses of the mighty had not been immune from the rough-and-ready frisking of the press, the reporters should have had a field day with Stillson. His colorful, controversial personality seemed to stir only amused admiration from the national press, and he seemed to make no one— except maybe Johnny Smith—nervous. His bodyguards had been Harley-Davidson beach-boppers only a few years ago, and people had a way of getting hurt at Stillson rallies, but no investigative reporter had done an in-depth study of that. At a campaign rally in Capital City—at that same mall Stillson had had a hand in developing—an eight-year-old girl had suffered a broken arm and a dislocated neck; her mother swore hysterically that one of those "motorcycle maniacs" had pushed her from the stage when the girl tried to climb up on the podium and get the Great Man's signature for her autograph book. Yet there had only been a squib in the paper— *Girl Hurt at Stillson Rally*—quickly forgotten.

Stillson had made a financial disclosure that Johnny thought too good to be true. In 1975 Stillson had paid $11,000 in Federal taxes on an income of $36,000—no state income tax at all, of course; New Hampshire didn't have one. He claimed all of his income came from his insurance and real estate agency, plus a small pittance that was his salary as mayor. There was no mention of the lucrative Capital City mall. No explanation of the fact that Stillson lived in a house with an assessed value of $86,000, a house he owned free and clear. In a season when the president of the United States was being dunned over what amounted to greens fees, Stillson's weird financial disclosure statement raised zero eyebrows.

Then there was his record as mayor. His performance on the job was a lot better than his campaign performances would have led anyone to expect. He was a shrewd and canny man with a rough but accurate grasp of human, corporate, and political psychology. He had wound up his term in 1975 with a fiscal surplus for the first time in ten years, much to the delight of the taxpayers. He pointed with justifiable pride to his parking program and what he called his Hippie Work-Study Program. Ridgeway had also been one of the first towns in the whole country to organize a Bicentennial Committee. A company that made filing cabinets had located in Ridgeway, and in recessionary times, the unemployment rate locally was an enviable 3.2 percent. All very admirable.

It was some of the other things that had happened while Stillson was mayor that made Johnny feel scared.

Funds for the town library had been cut from $11,500 to $8,000, and then, in the last year of Stillson's term, to $6,500. At the same time, the municipal police appropriation had risen by forty percent. Three new police cruisers had been added to the town motor pool, and a collection of riot equipment. Two new officers had also been added, and the town council had agreed, at Stillson's urging, to institute a 50 50 policy on purchasing officers' personal sidearms. As a result, several of the cops in this sleepy New England town had gone out and bought .357 Magnums, the gun immortalized by Dirty Harry Callahan. Also during Stillson's term as mayor, the teen rec center had been closed, a supposedly voluntary but police-enforced ten o'clock curfew for people under sixteen had been instituted, and welfare had been cut by thirty-five percent.

Yes, there were lots of things about Greg Stillson that scared Johnny.

The domineering father and laxly approving mother. The political rallies that felt more like rock concerts. The man's way with a crowd, his bodyguards—

Ever since Sinclair Lewis people had been crying woe and

doom and beware of the fascist state in America, and it just didn't happen. Well, there had been Huey Long down there in Louisiana, but Huey Long had—

Had been assassinated.

Johnny closed his eyes and saw Ngo cocking his finger. Bam, Bam, bam. Tiger, tiger, burning bright in the forests of the night. What fearful hand or eye—

But you don't sow dragon's teeth. Not unless you want to get right down there with Frank Dodd in his hooded vinyl raincoat. With the Oswalds and the Sirhans and the Bremmers. Crazies of the world, unite. Keep your paranoid notebooks up-to-date and thumb them over at midnight and when things start to reach a head inside you, send away the coupon for the mail-order gun. Johnny Smith, meet Squeaky Fromme. Nice to meet you, Johnny, everything you've got in that notebook makes perfect sense to me. Want you to meet my spiritual master. Johnny, meet Charlie. Charlie, this is Johnny. When you finish with Stillson, we're going to get together and off the rest of the pigs so we can save the redwoods.

His head was swirling. The inevitable headache was coming on. It always led to this. Greg Stillson always led him to this. It was time to go to sleep and please God, no dreams.

Still: The Question.

He had written it in one of the notebooks and kept coming back to it. He had written it in neat letters and then had drawn a triple circle around it, as if to keep it in. The Question was this: *If you could jump into a time machine and go back to 1932, would you kill Hitler?*

Johnny looked at his watch. Quarter of one. It was November 3 now, and the Bicentennial election was a part of history. Ohio was still undecided, but Carter was leading. No contest, baby. The hurly burly's done, the election's lost and won. Jerry Ford could hang up his jock, at least until 1980.

Johnny went to the window and looked out. The big house was dark, but there was a light burning in Ngo's apartment over the garage. Ngo, who would shortly be an American citizen, was still watching the great American quadrennial ritual: Old Bums Exit There, New Bums Enter Here. Maybe Gordon Strachan hadn't given the Watergate Committee such a bad answer at that.

Johnny went to bed. After a long time he slept.

And dreamed of the laughing tiger.

Chapter 22

◆ 1 ◆

Herb Smith took Charlene MacKenzie as his second wife on the afternoon of January 2, 1977, just as planned. The ceremony took place in the Congregational Church at Southwest Bend. The bride's father, an eighty-year-old gentleman who was almost blind, gave her away. Johnny stood up with his dad and produced the ring flawlessly at the proper moment. It was a lovely occasion.

Sarah Hazlett attended with her husband and their son, who was leaving his babyhood behind now. Sarah was pregnant and radiant, a picture of happiness and fulfillment. Looking at her, Johnny was surprised by a stab of bitter jealousy like an unexpected attack of gas. After a few moments it went away, and Johnny went over and spoke to them at the reception following the wedding.

It was the first time he had met Sarah's husband. He was a tall, good-looking man with a pencil-line moustache and prematurely graying hair. His canvass for the Maine state senate had been successful, and he held forth on what the national elections had really meant, and the difficulties of working with an independent governor, while Denny pulled at the leg of his trousers and demanded more-drink, Daddy, more-drink, more-*drink!*

Sarah said little, but Johnny felt her brilliant eyes on him— an uncomfortable sensation, but somehow not unpleasant. A little sad, maybe.

The liquor at the reception flowed freely, and Johnny went two drinks beyond his usual two-drink stopping point—the shock of seeing Sarah again, maybe, this time with her family, or maybe only the realization, written on Charlene's radiant face, that Vera Smith really was gone, and for all time. So when he approached Hector Markstone, father of the bride, some fifteen minutes after the Hazletts had left, he had a pleasant buzz on.

The old man was sitting in the corner by the demolished remains of the wedding cake, his arthritis-gnarled hands folded over his cane. He was wearing dark glasses. One bow had been mended with black electricians' tape. Beside him there stood two empty bottles of beer and another that was half-full. He peered closely at Johnny.

"Herb's boy, ain't you?"

"Yes, sir."

A longer scrutiny. Then Hector Markstone said, "Boy, you don't look well."

"Too many late nights, I guess."

"Look like you need a tonic. Something to build you up."

"You were in World War I, weren't you?" Johnny asked. A number of medals, including a Croix de Guerre, were pinned to the old man's blue serge suit coat.

"Indeed I was," Markstone said, brightening. "Served under Black Jack Pershing. AEF, 1917 and 18. We went through the mud and the crud. The wind blew and the shit flew. Belleau Wood, my boy. Belleau Wood. It's just a name in the history books now. But I was there. I saw men die there. The wind blew and the shit flew and up from the trenches came the whole damn crew."

"And Charlene said that your boy . . . her brother . . ."

"Buddy. Yep. Would have been your stepuncle, boy. Did we love that boy? I guess we did. His name was Joe, but everyone called him Buddy almost from the day he was born. Charlie's mother started to die the day the telegram came."

"Killed in the war, wasn't he?"

"Yes, he was," the old man said slowly. "St. Lô, 1944. Not that far from Belleau Wood, not the way we measure things over here, anyway. They ended Buddy's life with a bullet. The Nazis."

"I'm working on an essay," Johnny said, feeling a certain drunken cunning at having brought the conversation around to his real object at last. "I'm hoping to sell it to the *Atlantic* or maybe *Harper's* . . ."

"Writer, are you?" The dark glasses glinted up at Johnny with renewed interest.

"Well, I'm trying," Johnny said. Already he was beginning to regret his glibness. *Yes, I'm a writer. I write in my notebooks, after the dark of night his fallen.* "Anyway, the essay's going to be about Hitler."

"Hitler? What about Hitler?"

"Well . . . suppose . . . just suppose you could hop into a time machine and go back to the year 1932. In Germany. And suppose you came across Hitler. Would you kill him or let him live?"

The old man's blank black glasses tilted slowly up to Johnny's face. And now Johnny didn't feel drunk or glib or clever at all. Everything seemed to depend on what this old man had to say.

"Is it a joke, boy?"

"No. No joke."

One of Hector Markstone's hands left the head of his cane. It went to the pocket of his suit pants and fumbled there for what seemed an eternity. At last it came out again. It was holding a bone-handled pocket knife that had been rubbed as smooth and mellow as old ivory over the course of years. The other hand came into play, folding the knife's one blade out with all the incredible delicacy of arthritis. It glimmered with bland wickedness under the light of the Congregational parish hall: a knife that had traveled to France in 1917 with a boy, a boy who had been part of a boy-army ready and willing to stop the dirty hun from bayoneting babies and raping nuns, ready to show the Frenchies a thing or two in the bargain, and the boys had been machine-gunned, the boys had gotten dysentery and the killer flu, the boys had inhaled mustard gas and phosgene gas, the boys had come out of Belleau Wood looking like haunted scarecrows who had seen the face of Lord Satan himself. And it had all turned out to be for nothing; it turned out that it all had to be done over again.

Somewhere music was playing. People were laughing. People were dancing. A flashbar popped warm light. Somewhere far away. Johnny stared at the naked blade, transfixed, hypnotized by the play of the light over its honed edge.

"See this?" Markstone asked softly.

"Yes," Johnny breathed.

"I'd seat this in his black, lying, murderer's heart," Markstone said. "I'd put her in as far as she'd go . . . and then I'd twist her." He twisted the knife slowly in his hand, first clock, then counterclock. He smiled, showing baby-smooth gums and one leaning yellow tooth.

"But first," he said, "I'd coat the blade with rat poison."

◆ 2 ◆

"Kill Hitler?" Roger Chatsworth said, his breath coming out in little puffs. The two of them were snowshoeing in the woods behind the Durham house. The woods were very silent. It was early March, but this day was as smoothly and coldly silent as deep January.

"Yes, that's right."

"Interesting question," Roger said. "Pointless, but interesting. No. I wouldn't. I think I'd join the party instead. Try to change things from within. It might have been possible to purge him or frame him, always granting the foreknowledge of what was going to happen."

Johnny thought of the sawed-off pool cues. He thought of the brilliant green eyes of Sonny Elliman.

"It might also be possible to get yourself killed," he said. "Those guys were doing more than singing beer-hall songs back in 1933."

"Yes, that's true enough." He cocked an eyebrow at Johnny. "What would you do?"

"I really don't know," Johnny said.

Roger dismissed the subject. "How did your dad and his wife enjoy their honeymoon?"

Johnny grinned. They had gone to Miami Beach, hotel-workers' strike and all. "Charlene said she felt right at home, making her own bed. My dad says he feels like a freak, sporting a sunburn in March. But I think they both enjoyed it."

"And they've sold the houses?"

"Yes, both on the same day. Got almost what they wanted, too. Now if it wasn't for the goddam medical bills still hanging over my head, it'd be plain sailing."

"Johnny . . ."

"Hmmm?"

"Nothing. Let's go back. I've got some Chivas Regal, if you've got a taste."

"I believe I do," Johnny said.

◆ 3 ◆

They were reading *Jude the Obscure* now, and Johnny had been surprised at how quickly and naturally Chuck had taken to it (after some moaning and groaning over the first forty pages or so). He confessed he had been reading ahead at night on his own, and he intended to try something else by Hardy when he finished. For the first time in his life he was reading for pleasure. And like a boy who has just been initiated into the pleasures of sex by an older woman, he was wallowing in it.

Now the book lay open but facedown in his lap. They were by the pool again, but it was still drained and both he and Johnny were wearing light jackets. Overhead, mild white clouds scudded across the sky, trying desultorily to coalesce enough to make it rain. The feel of the air was mysterious and sweet; spring was somewhere near. It was April 16.

"Is this one of those trick questions?" Chuck asked.

"Nope."

"Well, would they catch me?"

"Pardon?" That was a question none of the others had asked.

"If I killed him. Would they catch me? Hang me from a lamppost? Make me do the funky chicken six inches off the ground?"

"Well, I don't know," Johnny said slowly. "Yes, I suppose they would catch you."

"I don't get to escape in my time machine to a gloriously changed world, huh? Back to good old 1977?"

"No, I don't think so."

"Well, it wouldn't matter. I'd kill him anyway."

"Just like that?"

"Sure." Chuck smiled a little. "I'd rig myself up with one of those hollow teeth filled with quick-acting poison or a razor blade in my shirt collar or something like that. So if I did get caught they couldn't do anything too gross to me. But I'd do it. If I didn't, I'd be afraid all those millions of people he ended up killing would haunt me to my grave."

"To your grave," Johnny said a little sickly.

"Are you okay, Johnny?"

Johnny made himself return Chuck's smile. "Fine. I guess my heart just missed a beat or something."

Chuck went on with *Jude* under the mildly cloudy sky.

◆ **4** ◆

May.

The smell of cut grass was back for yet another return engagement—also those long-running favorites, honeysuckle, dust, and roses. In New England spring really only comes for one priceless week and then the deejays drag out the Beach Boys golden oldies, the buzz of the cruising Honda is heard throughout the land, and summer comes down with a hot thud.

On one of the last evenings of that priceless spring week, Johnny sat in the guest house, looking out into the night. The spring dark was soft and deep. Chuck was off at the senior prom with his current girl friend, a more intellectual type than the last half-dozen. She *reads,* Chuck had confided to Johnny, one man of the world to another.

Ngo was gone. He had gotten his citizenship papers in late March, had applied for a job as head groundskeeper at a North Carolina resort hotel in April, had gone down for an interview three weeks ago, and had been hired on the spot. Before he left, he had come to see Johnny.

"You worry too much about tigers that are not there, I think," he said. "The tiger has stripes that will fade into the background so he will not be seen. This makes the worried man see tigers everywhere."

"There's a tiger," Johnny had answered.

"Yes," Ngo agreed. "Somewhere. In the meantime, you grow thin."

Johnny got up, went to the fridge, and poured himself a Pepsi. He went outside with it to the little deck. He sat down and sipped his drink and thought how lucky everyone was that time travel was a complete impossibility. The moon came up, an orange eye above the pines, and beat a bloody path across the swimming pool. The first frogs croaked and thumped. After a little while Johnny went inside and poured a hefty dollop of Ron Rico into his Pepsi. He went back outside and sat down again, drinking and watching as the moon rose higher in the sky, changing slowly from orange to mystic, silent silver.

Chapter 23

On June the 23rd, 1977, Chuck graduated from high school. Johnny, dressed in his best suit, sat in the hot auditorium with Roger and Shelley Chatsworth and watched as he graduated forty-third in his class. Shelley cried.

Afterward, there was a lawn party at the Chatsworth home. The day was hot and humid. Thunderheads with purple bellies had formed in the west; they dragged slowly back and forth across the horizon, but seemed to come no closer. Chuck, flushed with three screwdrivers, came over with his girl friend, Patty Strachan, to show Johnny his graduation present from his parents—a new Pulsar watch.

"I told them I wanted that R2D2 robot, but this was the best they could do," Chuck said, and Johnny laughed. They talked a while longer and then Chuck said with almost rough abruptness: "I want to thank you, Johnny. If it hadn't been for you, I wouldn't be graduating today at all."

"No, that isn't true," Johnny said. He was a little alarmed to see that Chuck was on the verge of tears. "Class always tells, man."

"That's what I keep telling him," Chuck's girl said. Behind her glasses, a cool and elegant beauty was waiting to come out.

"Maybe," Chuck said. "Maybe it does. But I think I know which side my diploma is buttered on. Thanks a hell of a lot." He put his arms around Johnny and gave him a hug.

It came suddenly—a hard, bright bolt of image that made Johnny straighten up and clap his hand against the side of his head as if Chuck had struck him instead of hugging him. The image sank into his mind like a picture done by electroplate.

"No," he said. "No *way*. You two stay right away from there."

Chuck drew back uneasily. He had felt *something*. Something cold and dark and incomprehensible. Suddenly he didn't want to touch Johnny; at that moment he never wanted to touch Johnny again. It was as if he had found out what it would be like to lie in his own coffin and watch the lid nailed down.

"Johnny," he said, and then faltered. "What . . . what's . . ."

Roger had been on his way over with drinks, and now he paused, puzzled. Johnny was looking over Chuck's shoulder, at the distant thunderheads. His eyes were vague and hazy.

He said: "You want to stay away from that place. There are no lightning rods."

"*Johnny* . . ." Chuck looked at his father, frightened. "It's like he's having some kind of . . . *fit,* or something."

"Lightning," Johnny proclaimed in a carrying voice. People turned their heads to look at him. He spread his hands. "Flash fire. The insulation in the walls. The doors . . . jammed. Burning people smell like hot pork."

"*What's he talking about?*" Chuck's girl cried, and conversation trickled to a halt. Now everyone was looking at Johnny, as they balanced plates of food and glasses.

Roger stepped over. "John! Johnny! What's wrong? Wake up" He snapped his fingers in front of Johnny's vague eyes. Thunder muttered in the west, the voice of giants over gin rummy, perhaps. "What's wrong?"

Johnny's voice was clear and moderately loud, carrying to each of the fifty-some people who were there—businessmen and their wives, professors and their wives, Durham's upper middle class. "Keep your son home tonight or he's going to burn to death with the rest of them. There is going to be a fire, a terrible fire. Keep him away from Cathy's. It's going to be struck by lightning and it will burn flat before the first fire engine can arrive. The insulation will burn. They will find charred bodies six and seven deep in the exits and there will be no way to identify them except by their dental work. It . . . it . . ."

Patty Strachan screamed then, her hand going to her mouth, her plastic glass tumbling to the lawn, the ice cubes spilling out onto the grass and gleaming there like diamonds of improbable size. She stood swaying for a moment and then she fainted, going down in a pastel billow of party dress, and her mother ran forward, crying at Johnny as she passed: "What's *wrong* with you? What in God's name is *wrong* with you?"

Chuck stared at Johnny. His face was paper-white.

Johnny's eyes began to clear. He looked around at the staring knots of people. "I'm sorry," he muttered.

Patty's mother was on her knees, holding her daughter's head in her arms and patting her cheeks lightly. The girl began to stir and moan.

"Johnny?" Chuck whispered, and then, without waiting for an answer, went to his girl.

It was very still on the Chatsworth back lawn. Everyone was looking at him. They were looking at him because it had happened again. They were looking at him the way the nurses had. And the reporters. They were crows strung out on a telephone line. They were holding their drinks and their plates of potato salad and looking at him as if he were a bug, a freak. They were looking at him as if he had suddenly opened his pants and exposed himself to them.

He wanted to run, he wanted to hide. He wanted to puke.

"Johnny," Roger said, putting an arm around him. "Come on in the house. You need to get off your feet for . . ."

Thunder rumbled, far off.

"What's Cathy's?" Johnny said harshly, resisting the pressure of Roger's arm over his shoulders. "It isn't someone's house, because there were exit signs. What is it? Where is it?"

"Can't you get him out of here?" Patty's mother nearly screamed. "He's upsetting her all over again!"

"Come on, Johnny."

"But . . ."

"*Come on.*"

He allowed himself to be led away toward the guest house. The sound of their shoes on the gravel drive was very loud. There seemed to be no other sound. They got as far as the pool, and then the whispering began behind them.

"Where's Cathy's?" Johnny asked again.

"How come you don't know?" Roger asked. "You seemed to know everything else. You scared poor Patty Strachan into a faint."

"I can't see it. It's in the dead zone. What is it?"

"Let's get you upstairs first."

"I'm not sick!"

"Under strain, then," Roger said. He spoke softly and soothingly, the way people speak to the hopelessly mad. The sound of his voice made Johnny afraid. And the headache started to come. He willed it back savagely. They went up the stairs to the guest house.

◆ 2 ◆

"Feel any better?" Roger asked.

"What's Cathy's?"

"It's a very fancy steakhouse and lounge in Somersworth. Graduation parties at Cathy's are something of a tradition, God knows why. Sure you don't want these aspirin?"

"No. Don't let him go, Roger. It's going to be hit by lightning. It's going to burn flat."

"Johnny," Roger Chatsworth said, slowly and very kindly, "you can't know a thing like that."

Johnny drank ice water a small sip at a time and set the glass back down with a hand that shook slightly. "You said you checked into my background I thought . . ."

"Yes, I did. But you're drawing a mistaken conclusion. I knew you were supposed to be a psychic or something, but I didn't want a psychic. I wanted a tutor. You've done a fine job as a tutor. My personal belief is that there isn't any difference between good psychics and bad ones, because I don't believe in any of that business. It's as simple as that. I don't believe it."

"That makes me a liar, then."

"Not at all," Roger said in that same kind, low voice. "I have a foreman at the mill in Sussex who won't light three on a match, but that doesn't make him a bad foreman. I have friends who are devoutly religious, and although I don't go to church myself, they're still my friends. Your belief that you can see into the future or sight things at a distance never entered into my judgment of whether or not to hire you. No . . . that isn't quite true. It never entered into it once I'd decided that it wouldn't interfere with your ability to do a good job with Chuck. It hasn't. But I no more believe that Cathy's is going to burn down tonight than I believe the moon is green cheese."

"I'm not a liar, just crazy," Johnny said. In a dull sort of way it was interesting. Roger Dussault and many of the people who wrote Johnny letters had accused him of trickery, but Chatsworth was the first to accuse him of having a Jeanne d'Arc complex.

"Not that, either," Roger said. "You're a young man who was involved in a terrible accident and who has fought his way back against terrible odds at what has probably been a terrible price. That isn't a thing I'd ever flap my jaw about freely, Johnny, but if any of those people out there on the lawn—including Patty's mother—want to jump to a lot of stupid conclusions, they'll be invited to shut their mouths about things they don't understand."

"Cathy's," Johnny said suddenly. "How did I know the name, then? And how did I know it wasn't someone's house?"

"From Chuck. He's talked about the party a lot this week."

"Not to me."

Roger shrugged. "Maybe he said something to Shelley or me while you were in earshot. Your subconscious happened to pick it up and file it away . . ."

"That's right," Johnny said bitterly. "Anything we don't understand, anything that doesn't fit into our scheme of the way things are, we'll just file it under *S* for subconscious, right? The twentieth-century god. How many times have you done that when something ran counter to your pragmatic view of the world, Roger?"

Roger's eyes might have flickered a little—or it might have been imagination.

"You associated lightning with the thunderstorm that's coming," he said. "Don't you see that? It's perfectly sim . . ."

"Listen," Johnny said. "I'm telling you this as simply as I can. That place is going to be struck by lightning. It's going to burn down. *Keep Chuck home.*"

Ah, God, the headache was coming for him. Coming like a tiger. He put his hand to his forehead and rubbed it unsteadily.

"Johnny, you've been pushing much too hard."

"Keep him home," Johnny repeated.

"It's his decision, and I wouldn't presume to make it for him. He's free, white, and eighteen."

There was a tap at the door. "Johnny?"

"Come in," Johnny said, and Chuck himself came in. He looked worried.

"How are you?" Chuck asked.

"I'm all right," Johnny said. "I've got a headache, that's all. Chuck . . . please stay away from that place tonight. I'm asking you as a friend. Whether you think like your dad or not. *Please.*"

"No problem, man," Chuck said cheerfully, and whumped

down on the sofa. He hooked a hassock over with one foot. "Couldn't drag Patty within a mile of that place with a twenty-foot towin chain. You put a scare into her."

"I'm sorry," Johnny said. He felt sick and chilly with relief. "I'm sorry but I'm glad."

"You had some kind of a flash, didn't you?" Chuck looked at Johnny, then at his father, and then slowly back to Johnny. "I felt it. It was bad."

"Sometimes people do. I understand it's sort of nasty."

"Well, I wouldn't want it to happen again," Chuck said. "But hey . . . that place isn't really going to burn down, is it?"

"Yes," Johnny said. "You want to just keep away."

"But . . ." He looked at his father, troubled. "The senior class reserved the whole damn place. The school encourages that, you know. It's safer than twenty or thirty different parties and a lot of people drinking on the back roads. There's apt to be . . ." Chuck fell silent for a moment and then began to look frightened. "There's apt to be two hundred couples there," he said. "Dad . . ."

"I don't think he believes any of this," Johnny said.

Roger stood up and smiled. "Well, let's take a ride over to Somersworth and talk to the manager of the place," he said. "It was a dull lawn party, anyway. And if you two still feel the same coming back, we can have everyone over here tonight."

He glanced at Johnny.

"Only condition being that you have to stay sober and help chaperon, fellow."

"I'll be glad to," Johnny said. "But why, if you don't believe it?"

"For your peace of mind," Roger said, "and for Chuck's. And so that, when nothing happens tonight, I can say I told you so and then just *laaaugh* my ass off."

"Well, whatever, thanks." He was trembling worse than ever now that the relief had come, but his headache had retreated to a dull throb.

"One thing up front, though," Roger said. "I don't think we stand a snowball's chance in hell of getting the owner to cancel on your unsubstantiated word, Johnny. This is probably one of his big business nights each year."

Chuck said, "Well, we could work something out . . ."

"Like what!"

"Well, we could tell him a story . . . spin some kind of yarn . . ."

"Lie, you mean? No, I won't do that. Don't ask me, Chuck."

Chuck nodded. "All right."

"We better get going," Roger said briskly. "It's quarter of five. We'll take the Mercedes over to Somersworth."

◆ 3 ◆

Bruce Carrick, the owner-manager, was tending bar when the three of them came in at five-forty. Johnny's heart sank a little when he read the sign posted outside the lounge doors: PRIVATE PARTY THIS EVENING ONLY 7 PM TO CLOSING SEE YOU TOMORROW.

Carrick was not exactly being run into the ground. He was serving a few workmen who were drinking beer and watching the early news, and three couples who were having cocktails. He listened to Johnny's story with a face that grew ever more incredulous. When he had finished, Carrick said: "You say Smith's your name?"

"Yes, that's right."

"Mr. Smith, come on over to this window with me."

He led Johnny to the lobby window, by the cloakroom door.

"Look out there Mr. Smith and tell me what you see."

Johnny looked out, knowing what he would see. Route 9 ran west, now drying from a light afternoon sprinkle. Above, the sky was perfectly clear. The thunderheads had passed.

"Not much. At least, not now. But . . ."

"But nothing," Bruce Carrick said. "You know what I think? You want to know frankly? I think you're a nut. Why you picked me for this royal screwing I don't know or care. But if you got a second, sonny, I'll tell you the facts of life. The senior class has paid me six hundred and fifty bucks for this bash. They've hired a pretty good rock 'n' roll band, Oak, from up in Maine. The food's out there in the freezer, all ready to go into the microwave. The salads are on ice. Drinks are extra, and most of these kids are over eighteen and can drink all they want . . . and tonight they will, who can blame them, you only graduate from high school once. I'll take in two thousand dollars in the lounge tonight, no sweat. I got two extra barmen coming in. I got six waitresses and a hostess. If I should cancel this thing now, I lose the whole night, plus

I got to pay back the six-fifty I already took for the meal. I don't even get my regular dinner crowd because that sign's been there all week. Do you get the picture?"

"Are there lightning rods on this place?" Johnny asked.

Carrick threw his hands up. "I tell this guy the facts of life and he wants to discuss lightning rods! Yeah, I got lightning rods! A guy came in here, before I added one, must be five years ago now. He gave me a song-and-dance about improving my insurance rates. So I bought the goddam lightning rods! Are you happy? Jesus *Christ*!" He looked at Roger and Chuck. "What are you two guys doing? Why are you letting this asshole run around loose? Get out, why don't you? I got a business to run."

"Johnny . . ." Chuck began.

"Never mind," Roger said. "Let's go. Thank you for your time, Mr. Carrick, and for your polite and sympathetic attention."

"Thanks for nothing," Carrick said. "Bunch of nuts!" He strode back toward the lounge.

The three of them went out. Chuck looked doubtfully at the flawless sky. Johnny started toward the car, looking only at his feet, feeling stupid and defeated. His headache thudded sickly against his temples. Roger was standing with his hands in his back pockets, looking up at the long, low roof of the building.

"What are you looking at, Dad?" Chuck asked.

"There are no lightning rods up there," Roger Chatsworth said thoughtfully. "No lightning rods at all."

◆ 4 ◆

The three of them sat in the living room of the big house, Chuck by the telephone. He looked doubtfully at his father. "Most of them won't want to change their plans this late," he said.

"They've got plans to go out, that's all," Roger said. "They can just as easily come here."

Chuck shrugged and began dialing.

They ended up with about half the couples who had been planning to go to Cathy's that graduation evening, and Johnny was never really sure why they came. Some probably came simply because it sounded like a more interesting party and because the drinks were on the house. But word traveled fast, and the parents of a good many of the kids here had been at the lawn party that afternoon—as a result, Johnny spent much of the evening feeling like an exhibit in a glass case. Roger sat in the corner on a stool, drinking a vodka martini. His face was a studied mask.

Around quarter of eight he walked across the big bar play-room combination that took up three-quarters of the base-ment level, bent close to Johnny and bellowed over the roar of Elton John, "You want to go upstairs and play some cribbage?"

Johnny nodded gratefully.

Shelley was in the kitchen, writing letters. She looked up when they came in, and smiled. "I thought you two masochists were going to stay down there all night. It's not really neces-sary, you know."

"I'm sorry about all of this," Johnny said. "I know how crazy it must seem."

"It does seem crazy," Shelley said. "No reason not to be candid about that. But having them here is really rather nice. I don't mind."

Thunder rumbled outside. Johnny looked around. Shelley saw it and smiled a little. Roger had left to hunt for the cribbage board in the dining room welsh dresser.

"It's just passing over, you know," she said. "A little thun-der and a sprinkle of rain."

"Yes," Johnny said.

She sighed her letter in a comfortable scrawl, folded it, sealed it, addressed it, stamped it. "You really experienced something, didn't you, Johnny?"

"Yes."

"A momentary faintness," she said. "Possibly caused by a dietary deficiency. You're much too thin, Johnny. It might have been a hallucination, mightn't it?"

"No, I don't think so."

Outside, thunder growled again, but distantly.

"I'm just as glad to have him home. I don't believe in as-trology and palmistry and clairvoyance and all of that, but . . . I'm just as glad to have him home. He's our only chick . . . a pretty damned big chick now, I suspect you're thinking, but it's easy to remember him riding the little kids' merry-go-round in the town park in his short pants. Too easy, perhaps.

And it's nice to be able to share the . . . the last rite of his boyhood with him."

"It's nice that you feel that way," Johnny said. Suddenly he was frightened to find himself close to tears. In the last six or eight months it seemed to him that his emotional control had slipped several notches.

"You've been good for Chuck. I don't mean just teaching him to read. In a lot of ways."

"I like Chuck."

"Yes," she said quietly. "I know you do."

Roger came back with the cribbage board and a transistor radio tuned to WMTQ, a classical station that broadcast from the top of Mount Washington.

"A little antidote for Elton John, Aerosmith, Foghat, et al," he said. "How does a dollar a game sound, Johnny?"

"It sounds fine."

Roger sat down, rubbing his hands. "Oh you're goin home poor," he said.

◆ 5 ◆

They played cribbage and the evening passed. Between each game one of them would go downstairs and make sure no one had decided to dance on the pool table or go out back for a little party of their own. "No one is going to impregnate anyone else at this party if I can help it," Roger said.

Shelley had gone into the living room to read. Once an hour the music on the radio would stop and the news would come on and Johnny's attention would falter a little. But there was nothing about Cathy's in Somersworth—not at eight, nine, or ten.

After the ten o'clock news, Roger said: "Getting ready to hedge your prediction a little, Johnny?"

"No."

The weather forecast was for scattered thundershowers, clearing after midnight.

The steady bass signature of K.C. and the Sunshine Band came up through the floor.

"Party's getting loud," Johnny remarked.

"The hell with that," Roger said, grinning. "The party's getting drunk. Spider Parmeleau is passed out in the corner and somebody's using him for a beer coaster. Oh, they'll have big heads in the morning, you want to believe it. I remember at my own graduation party . . ."

"Here is a bulletin from the WMTQ newsroom," the radio said.

Johnny, who had been shuffling, sprayed cards all over the floor.

"Relax, it's probably just something about that kidnapping down in Florida."

"I don't think so," Johnny said.

The broadcaster said: "It appears at this moment that the worst fire in New Hampshire history has claimed more than seventy-five young lives in the border town of Somersworth, New Hampshire. The fire occurred at a restaurant-lounge called Cathy's. A graduation party was in progress when the fire broke out. Somersworth fire chief Milton Hovey told reporters they have no suspicions of arson; they believe that the fire was almost certainly caused by a bolt of lightning."

Roger Chatsworth's face was draining of all color. He sat bolt upright in his kitchen chair, his eyes fixed on a point somewhere above Johnny's head. His hands lay loosely on the table. From below them came the babble of conversation and laughter, intermingled now with the sound of Bruce Springsteen.

Shelley came into the room. She looked from her husband to Johnny and then back again. "What is it? What's wrong?"

"Shut up," Roger said.

". . . is still blazing, and Hovey said that a final tally of the dead will probably not be known until early morning. It is known that over thirty people, mostly members of the Durham High School senior class, have been taken to hospitals in surrounding areas to be treated for burns. Forty people, also mostly graduating students, escaped from small bathroom windows at the rear of the lounge, but others were apparently trapped in fatal pile-ups at the . . ."

"*Was it Cathy's?*" Shelley Chatsworth screamed. "*Was it that place?*"

"Yes," Roger said. He seemed eerily calm. "Yes, it was."

Downstairs there had been a momentary silence. It was followed by a running thud of footsteps coming up the stairs. The kitchen door burst open and Chuck came in, looking for his mother.

"Mom? What is it? What's wrong?"

"It appears that we may owe you for our son's life," Roger

said in that same eerily calm voice. Johnny had never seen a face that white. Roger looked like a ghastly living waxwork.

"It *burned*?" Chuck's voice was incredulous. Behind him, others were crowding up the stairs now, whispering in low, affrighted voices. "Are you saying it burned *down*?"

No one answered. And then, suddenly, from somewhere behind him Patty Strachan began to talk in a high hysterical voice. "It's his fault, that guy there! He made it happen! He set it on fire by his mind, just like in that book *Carrie*. You murderer! Killer! You . . ."

Roger turned toward her. *"SHUT UP!"* he roared.

Patty collapsed into wild sobs.

"Burned?" Chuck repeated. He seemed to be asking himself now, inquiring if that could possibly be the right word.

"Roger?" Shelley whispered. "Rog? Honey?"

There was a growing mutter on the stairs, and in the playroom below, like a stir of leaves. The stereo clicked off. The voices murmured.

Was Mike there? Shannon went, didn't she? Are you sure? Yes, I was all ready to leave when Chuck called me. My mother was there when that guy freaked out and she said she felt like a goose was walking on her grave, she asked me to come here instead. Was Casey there? Was Ray there? Was Maureen Ontello there? Oh my God, was she? Was . . .

Roger stood up slowly and turned around. "I suggest," he said, "that we find the soberest people here to drive and that we all go down to the hospital. They'll need blood donors."

Johnny sat like a stone. He found himself wondering if he would ever move again. Outside, thunder rumbled. And followed on its heels like an inner clap, he heard his dying mother's voice:

Do your duty, John.

Chapter 24

August 12, 1977

Dear Johnny,

Finding you wasn't much of a trick—I sometimes think if you have enough free cash, you can find anyone in this country, and the cash I got. Maybe I'm risking your resentment stating it as badly as that, but Chuck and Shelley and I owe you too much to tell you less than the truth. Money buys a lot, but it can't buy off the lightning. They found twelve boys still in the men's room opening off the restaurant, the one where the window had been nailed shut. The fire didn't reach there but the smoke did, and all twelve of them were suffocated. I haven't been able to get that out of my mind, because Chuck could have been one of those boys. So I had you "tracked down," as you put it in your letter. And for the same reason, I can't leave you alone as you requested. At least not until the enclosed check comes back canceled with your endorsement on the back.

You'll notice that it's a considerably smaller check than the one you received about a month ago. I got in touch with the EMMC Accounts Department and paid your outstanding hospital bills with the balance of it. You're free and clear that way, Johnny. That I could do, and I did it—with great pleasure, I might add.

You protest you can't take the money. I say you can and you will. You will, Johnny. I traced you to Ft. Lauderdale, and if you leave there I will trace you to the next place you go, even if you decide on Nepal. Call me a louse who won't let go if you want to; I see myself more as "the Hound of Heaven." I don't want to hound you, Johnny. I remember you telling me that day not to sacrifice my son. I almost did. And what about the others? Eighty-one dead, thirty more terribly maimed and burned. I think of Chuck saying maybe we could work out some kind of a story, spin a yarn or something, and me saying with all the righteousness of the totally stupid, "I won't do that, Chuck. Don't ask me." Well I could have done something. That's what haunts me. I could have given that butcher Carrick $3,000 to pay off his help and shut down for the night. It would have come to about $37 a life. So believe me when I say I don't want to hound you; I'm really too busy hounding myself to want to spare the time. I think I'll be doing it for quite a few years to come. I'm paying up for refusing to believe anything I couldn't touch with one of my five senses. And please don't believe that paying the bills and tendering this check is just a sop to my conscience. Money can't buy off the lightning, and it can't buy an end to bad dreams, either. The money is for Chuck, although he knows nothing about it.

Take the check and I'll leave you in peace. That's the deal. Send it on to UNICEF, if you want, or give it to a home for orphan bloodhounds, or blow it all on the ponies. I don't care. Just take it.

I'm sorry you felt you had to leave in such a hurry, but I believe I understand. We all hope to see you soon. Chuck leaves for Stovington Prep on September 4.

Johnny, take the check. Please.

All regards,
Roger Chatsworth

September 1, 1977

Dear Johnny,

Will you believe that I'm not going to let this go? Please. Take the check.

Regards,
Roger

September 10, 1977

Dear Johnny,

Charlie and I were both so glad to know where you are, and it was a relief to get a letter from you that sounded so natural and like yourself. But there was one thing that bothered me very much, son. I called up Sam Weizak and read him that part of your letter about the increasing frequency of your headaches. He advises you to see a doctor, Johnny, without delay. He is afraid that a clot may have formed around the old scar tissue. So that worries me, and it worries Sam, too. You've never looked really *healthy since you came out of the coma, Johnny, and when I last saw you in early June, I thought you looked very tired. Sam didn't say, but I know what he'd really like you to do is to catch a plane out of Phoenix and come on home and let him be the one to look at you. You certainly can't plead poverty now!*

Roger Chatsworth has called here twice, and I tell him what I can. I think he's telling the truth when he says it isn't conscience-money or a reward for saving his son's life. I believe your mother would have said that the man is doing penance the only way he knows how. Anyway, you've taken it, and I hope you don't mean it when you say you only did it to "get him off your back." I believe you have too much grit in you to do anything for a reason like that.

Now this is very hard for me to say, but I will do the best I can. Please come home, Johnny. The publicity has died down again—I can hear you saying, "Oh bullshit, it will never die down again, not after this" and I suppose you are right in a way, but you are also wrong. Over the phone Mr. Chatsworth said, "If you talk to him, try to make him understand that no psychic except Nostradamus has ever been much more than a nine-days' wonder." I worry about you a lot, son. I worry about you blaming yourself for the dead instead of blessing yourself for the living, the ones you saved, the ones that were at the Chatsworths' house that night. I worry and I miss you, too. "I miss you like the dickens," as your grandmother used to say. So please come home as soon as you can.

Dad

P.S. I'm sending the clippings about the fire and about your part in it. Charlie collected them up. As you will see, you were correct in guessing that "everyone who was at that lawn party will spill their guts to the papers." I suppose these clippings may just upset you more, and if they do, just toss them away. But Charlie's idea was that you may look at them and say, "That wasn't as bad as I thought, I can face that." I hope it turns out that way.

Dad

September 29, 1977

Dear Johnny,

I got your address from my dad. How is the great American desert. Seen any redskins (ha-ha)? Well here I am at Stovington

*Prep. This place isn't so tough. I am taking sixteen hours of
credit. Advanced chemistry is my favorite although it's really
something of a tit after the course at DHS. I always had the
feeling that our teacher there, old Fearless Farnham, would really
have been more happy making doomsday weapons and blowing
up the world. In English we are reading three things by J. D.
Salinger this first four weeks,* Catcher in the Rye, Franny and
Zooey, *and* Raise High the Roof Beams, Carpenters. *I like him
a lot. Our teacher told us he still lives over in N.H. but has given
up writing. That blows my mind. Why would someone just give
up when they are going great guns? Oh well. The football team
here really sucks but I'm learning to like soccer. The coach says
soccer is football for smart people and football is football for
assholes. I can't figure out yet if he's right or just jealous.*

*I'm wondering if it would be ok to give out your address to
some people who were at our party graduation night. They
want to write and say thanks. One of them is Patty Strachan's
mother, you will remember her, the one that made such a piss-
head of herself when her "precious daughter" fainted at the
lawn party that afternoon. She now figures that you're an ok
person. I'm not going with Patty anymore, by the way. I'm not
much on long-distance courtships at my "tender age" (ha-ha),
and Patty is going to Vassar, as you might have expected. I've
met a foxy little chick right here.*

*Well, write when you can, my man. My dad made it sound
like you were really "bummed out" for what reason I do not
know since it seems to me that you did everything you could
to make things turn out right. He's wrong, isn't he, Johnny?
You're really not bummed out, are you? Please write and tell
me you are ok, I worry about you. That's a laugh, isn't it, the
original Alfred E. Neuman worried about you, but I am.*

*When you write, tell me why Holden Caulfield always has
to have the blues so much when he isn't even black.*

Chuck

*P.S. The foxy chick's name is Stephanie Wyman, and I have
already turned her on to* Something Wicked This Way Comes.
*She also likes a punk-rock group called The Ramones, you
should hear them, they are hilarious.*

C

October 17, 1977

Dear Johnny,

Okay that's better, you sound ok. Laughed my ass off about your job with the Phoenix Public Works Dept. I have no sympathy at all for your sunburn after four outings as a Stovington Tiger. Coach is right, I guess, football is football for assholes, at least at this place. Our record is 1–3 and in the game we won I scored three touchdowns, hyperventilated my stupid self and blacked out. Scared Steff into a tizzy (ha-ha).

I waited to write so I could answer your question about how the Home Folks feel about Greg Stillson now that he is "on the job." I was home this last weekend, and I'll tell you all I can. Asked my dad first and he said, "Is Johnny still interested in that guy?" I said, "He's showing his fundamental bad taste by wanting your opinion." Then he goes to my mother, "See, prep school is turning him into a smartass. I thought it would."

Well, to make a long story short, most people are pretty surprised by how well Stillson's doing. My dad said this: "If people of a congressman's home district had to give a report card on how well the guy was doing after 10 months, Stillson would get mostly Bs, plus an A for his work on Carter's energy bill and his own home heating-oil ceiling bill. Also an A for effort." Dad told me to tell you that maybe he was wrong about Stillson being the village fool.

Other comments from people I talked to when I was home: they like it around here that he doesn't dress up in a business suit. Mrs. Jarvis who runs the Quik-Pik (sorry about the spelling, man, but that's what they call it) says she thinks Stillson is not afraid of "the big interests." Henry Burke, who runs The Bucket—that el scuzzo tavern downtown—says he thinks Stillson has done "a double-damn good job." Most other comments are similar. They contrast what Stillson has done with what Carter hasn't done, most of them are really disappointed in him and are kicking themselves for having voted for him. I asked some of them if they weren't worried that those iron horsemen were still hanging around and that fellow Sonny Elliman was serving as one of Stillson's aides. None of them seemed too upset. The guy who runs the Record Rock put it to me this way: "If Tom Hayden can go straight and Eldridge Cleaver can get Jesus, why can't some bikies join the establishment? Forgive and forget."

So there you are. I would write more, but football practice

*is coming up. This weekend we are scheduled to be trounced
by the Barre Wildcats. I just hope I survive the season. Keep
well, my man.*

Chuck

From the *New York Times,* March 4, 1978:

FBI AGENT MURDERED IN OKLAHOMA

Special to the Times—Edgar Lancte, 37, a ten-year veteran of the FBI, was apparently murdered last night in
an Oklahoma City parking garage. Police say that a dyna-
mite bomb wired to the ignition of his car exploded when
Mr. Lancte turned the key. The gangland-style execution
was similar in style to the murder of Arizona investigative
reporter Don Bolles two years ago, but FBI chief William
Webster would not speculate on any possible connection.
Mr. Webster would also neither confirm nor deny that
Mr. Lancte had been investigating shady land deals and
possible links to local politicians.

There appears to be some mystery surrounding exactly
what Mr. Lancte's current assignment was, and one
source in the Justice Department claims that Mr. Lancte
was not investigating possible land fraud at all but a national security matter.

Mr. Lancte joined the Federal Bureau of Investigation
in 1968 and . . .

Chapter 25

◆ 1 ◆

The notebooks in Johnny's bureau drawer grew from four to
five, and by the fall of 1978 to seven. In the fall of 1978,
between the deaths of two Popes in rapid succession, Greg
Stillson had become national news.

He was reelected to the House of Representatives in a landslide, and with the country tending toward Proposition 13 conservatism, he had formed the America Now party. Most startling, several members of the House had reneged on their original party standing and had "jined up," as Greg liked to put it. Most of them held very similar beliefs, which Johnny had defined as superficially liberal on domestic issues and moderate to very conservative on issues of foreign policy. There was not a one of them who had voted on the Carter side of the Panama Canal treaties. And when you peeled back the liberal veneer on domestic positions, they turned out to be pretty conservative, too. The America Now party wanted bad trouble for big-time dopers, they wanted the cities to have to sink or swim on their own ("There is no need for a struggling dairy farmer to have to subsidize New York City's methadone programs with his taxes," Greg proclaimed), they wanted a crackdown on welfare benefits to whores, pimps, bums, and people with a felony bust on their records, they wanted sweeping tax reforms to be paid for by sweeping social services cutbacks. All of it was an old song, but Greg's America Now party had set it to a pleasing new tune.

Seven congressmen swung over before the off-year elections, and two senators. Six of the congressmen were reelected, and both of the senators. Of the nine, eight had been Republicans whose base had been whittled away to a pinhead. Their switch of party and subsequent reelections, one wag had quipped, was a better trick than the one that had followed "Lazarus, come forth!"

Some were already saying that Greg Stillson might be a power to be reckoned with, and not that many years down the road, either. He had not been able to send all the world's pollution out to Jupiter and the rings of Saturn, but he had succeeded in running at least two of the rascals out—one of them a congressman who had been feathering his nest as the silent partner in a parking-lot kickback scheme, and one of them a presidential aide with a penchant for gay bars. His oil-ceiling bill had shown vision and boldness, and his careful guidance of its passage from committee to final vote had shown a down-home country-boy shrewdness. Nineteen-hundred eighty would be too early for Greg, and 1984 might be too tempting to resist, but if he managed to stay cool until 1988, if he continued to build his base and the winds of change did not shift radically enough to blow his fledgling party away, why, anything might happen. The Republicans had fallen to squabbling splinters, and assuming that Mondale or Jerry Brown or even Howard Baker might follow Carter as president, who was to follow then? Even 1992 might not be too late for him. He was a relatively young man. Yes, 1992 sounded about right . . .

There were several political cartoons in Johnny's notebooks. All of them showed Stillson's infectious slantwise grin, and in all of them he was wearing his construction helmet. One by Oliphant showed Greg rolling a barrel of oil marked PRICE CEILINGS straight down the middle aisle of the House, the helmet cocked back on his head. Up front was Jimmy Carter, scratching his head and looking puzzled; he was not looking Greg's way at all and the implication seemed to be that he was going to get run down. The caption read: OUTTA MY WAY, JIMMY!

The helmet. The helmet somehow bothered Johnny more than anything else. The Republicans had their elephant, the Democrats their donkey, and Greg Stillson had his construction helmet. In Johnny's dreams it sometimes seemed that Stillson was wearing a motorcycle helmet. And sometimes it was a coal-scuttle helmet.

◆ 2 ◆

In a separate notebook he kept the clippings his father had sent him concerning the fire at Cathy's. He had gone over them again and again, although for reasons that Sam, Roger, or even his father could not have suspected. PSYCHIC PREDICTS FIRE. "MY DAUGHTER WOULD HAVE DIED TOO," TEARFUL, THANKFUL MOM PROCLAIMS (the tearful, thankful mom in question had been Patty Strachan's). *Psychic Who Cracked Castle Rock Murders Predicts Flash Fire.* ROADHOUSE DEATH-TOLL REACHES 90. FATHER SAYS JOHN SMITH HAS LEFT NEW ENGLAND, REFUSES TO SAY WHY. Pictures of him. Pictures of his father. Pictures of that long-ago wreck on Route 6 in Cleaves Mills, back in the days when Sarah Bracknell had been his girl. Now Sarah was a woman, the mother of two, and in his last letter Herb had said Sarah was showing a few gray hairs. It seemed impossible to believe that he himself was thirty-one. Impossible, but true.

Around all these clippings were his own jottings, his painful efforts to get it straight in his mind once and for all. None of them understood the true importance of the fire, its implication on the much larger matter of what to do about Greg Stillson.

He had written: "I have to do something about Stillson. I *have* to. I was right about Cathy's, and I'm going to be right about this. There is absolutely no question in my mind. He is going to become president and he is going to start a war—or cause one through simple mismanagement of the office, which amounts to the same thing.

"The question is: *How drastic are the measures that need to be taken?*

"Take Cathy's as a test-tube case. It almost could have been sent to me as a sign, God I'm starting to sound like my mother, but there it is. Okay, I *knew* there was going to be a fire and that people were going to die. Was that sufficient to save them? Answer: it was not sufficient to save *all* of them, because *people only truly believe after the fact.* The ones who came to the Chatsworth house instead of going to Cathy's were saved, but it's important to remember that R.C. didn't have the party because he believed my prediction. He was very upfront about that. He had the party because he thought it would help me have peace of mind. He was . . . humoring me. He believed *after.* Patty Strachan's mother believed *after.* After-after-after. By then it was too late for the dead and the burned.

"So, Question 2: Could I have changed the outcome?

"Yes. I could have driven a car right through the front of the place. Or, I could have burned it down myself that afternoon.

"Question 3: What would the results of either action have been to me?

"Imprisonment, probably. If I took the car option and then lightning struck it later that night, I suppose I could have argued . . . no, it doesn't wash. Common experience may recognize some sort of psychic ability in the human mind, but the law sure as hell doesn't. I think now, if I had it to do over again, I would do one of those things and never mind the consequences to me. Is it possible that I didn't completely believe my own prediction?

"The matter of Stillson is horribly similar in all respects, except, thank God, that I have a lot more lead time.

"So, back to square one. I don't want Greg Stillson to become President. How can I change that outcome?

"1. Go back to New Hampshire and 'jine up,' as he puts it. Try to throw a few monkey wrenches into the America Now party. Try to sabotage *him*. There's dirt enough under the rug. Maybe I could sweep some of it out.

"2. Hire someone else to get the dirt on him. There's enough of Roger's money left over to hire someone good. On the other hand, I got the feeling that Lancte was pretty good. And Lancte's dead.

"3. Wound or cripple him. The way Arthur Bremmer crippled Wallace, the way whoever-it-was crippled Larry Flynt.

"4. Kill him. Assassinate him.

"Now, some of the drawbacks. The first option isn't sure enough. I could end up doing nothing more constructive than getting myself trounced, the way Hunter Thompson did when he was researching his first book, that one on the Hell's Angels. Even worse, this fellow Elliman may be familiar with what I look like, as a result of what happened at the Trimbull rally. Isn't it more or less S.O.P. to keep a file on people who may be dangerous to your guys? I wouldn't be surprised to find out that Stillson had one guy on his payroll whose only job was to keep updated files on weird people and kooks. Which definitely includes me.

"Then there's the second option. Suppose all the dirt has already come out? If Stillson has already formed his higher political aspirations—and all his actions seem to point that way—he may already have cleaned up his act. And another thing: dirt under the rug is only as dirty as the press wants to make it, and the press likes Stillson. He cultivates them. In a novel I suppose I would turn private detective myself and 'get the goods on him,' but the sad fact is that I wouldn't know where to begin. You could argue that my ability to 'read' people, to find things that have been lost (to quote Sam) would give me a boost. If I could find out something about Lancte, that would turn the trick. But isn't it likely that Stillson delegates all that to Sonny Elliman? And I cannot even be sure, despite my suspicions, that Edgar Lancte was still on Stillson's trail when he was murdered. It is possible that I might hang Sonny Elliman and still not finish Stillson.

"Overall, the second alternative *is just not sure enough*. The stakes are *enormous*, so much so that I don't even dare let myself think about 'the big picture' very often. It brings on a very bitch-kitty of a headache every time.

"I have even considered, in my wilder moments, trying to hook him on drugs the way the character Gene Hackman played in *The French Connection II* was, or driving him batty with LSD slipped into his Dr Pepper or whatever it is he drinks. But all of that is cop-show make-believe. Gordon Liddy shit. The problems are so great that this 'option' doesn't even bear much talking about. Maybe I could kidnap him. After all, the guy is only a U.S. representative. I wouldn't know where to get heroin or morphine, but I could get plenty of LSD from Larry McNaughton right here in the good old Phoenix Public Works Department. He has pills for every purpose. But suppose (if we're willing to suppose the foregoing) that he just enjoyed his trip(s)?

"Shooting and crippling him? Maybe I could and maybe I couldn't. I guess under the right circumstances, I could—like the rally in Trimbull. Suppose I did. After what happened in Laurel, George Wallace was never really a potent political force again. On the other hand, FDR campaigned from his wheelchair and even turned it into an asset.

"That leaves assassination, the Big Casino. This is the one unarguable alternative. You can't run for president if you're a corpse.

"If I could pull the trigger.

"And if I could, what would the results be to me?

"As Bob Dylan says 'Honey do you have to ask me that?' "

There were a great many other notes and jottings, but the only other really important one was written out and neatly boxed: "Suppose outright murder does turn out to be the only alternative? And suppose it turned out that I could pull the trigger? Murder is still wrong. Murder is wrong. Murder is wrong. There may yet be an answer. Thank God there's years of time."

◆ **3** ◆

But for Johnny, there wasn't.

In early December of 1978, shortly after another congressman, Leo Ryan of California, had been shot to death on a jungle airstrip in the South American country of Guayana, Johnny Smith discovered he had almost run out of time.

Chapter 26

◆ 1 ◆

At 2:30 P.M. on December 26, 1978, Bud Prescott waited on a tall and rather haggard-looking young man with graying hair and badly bloodshot eyes. Bud was one of three clerks working in the 4th Street Phoenix Sporting Goods Store on the day after Christmas, and most of the business was exchanges—but this fellow was a paying customer.

He said he wanted to buy a good rifle, light-weight, bolt-action. Bud showed him several. The day after Christmas was a slow one on the gun-counter; when men got guns for Christmas, very few of them wanted to exchange them for something else.

This fellow looked them all over carefully and finally settled on a Remington 700, .243 caliber, a very nice gun with a light kick and a flat trajectory. He signed the gunbook John Smith and Bud thought, *If I never saw me an alias before in my life, there's one there.* "John Smith" paid cash—took the twenties right out of a wallet that was bulging with them. Took the riffle right over the counter. Bud, thinking to poke him a little, told him he could have his initials burned into the stock, no extra charge. "John Smith" merely shook his head.

When "Smith" left the store, Bud noticed that he was limping noticeably. Would never be any problem identifying that guy again, he thought, not with that limp and those scars running up and down his neck.

◆ 2 ◆

At 10:30 A.M. on December 27, a thin man who walked with a limp came into Phoenix Office Supply, Inc., and approached Dean Clay, a salesman there. Clay said later that he noticed what his mother had always called a "fire-spot" in one of the man's eyes. The customer said he wanted to buy a large attaché case, and eventually picked out a handsome cowhide item, top of the line, priced at $149.95. And the man with the limp qualified for the cash discount by paying with new twenties. The whole transaction, from looking to paying, took no more than ten minutes. The fellow walked out of the store, and turned right toward the downtown area, and Dean Clay never saw him again until he saw his picture in the Phoenix *Sun*.

◆ 3 ◆

Late that same afternoon a tall man with graying hair approached Bonita Alvarez's window in the Phoenix Amtrak terminal and inquired about traveling from Phoenix to New York by train. Bonita showed him the connections. He followed them with his finger and then carefully jotted them all down. He asked Bonnie Alvarez if she could ticket him to depart on January 3. Bonnie danced her fingers over her computer console and said that she could.

"Then why don't you . . ." the tall man began, and then faltered. He put one hand up to his head.

"Are you all right, sir?"

"Fireworks," the tall man said. She told the police later on that she was quite sure that was what he said. *Fireworks*.

"Sir? Are you all right?"

"Headache," he said. "Excuse me." He tried to smile, but the effort did not improve his drawn, young-old face much.

"Would you like some aspirin? I have some."

"No, thanks. It'll pass."

She wrote the tickets and told him he would arrive at New York's Grand Central Station on January 6, at midafternoon.

"How much is that?"

She told him and added: "Will that be cash or charge, Mr. Smith?"

"Cash," he said, and pulled it right out of his wallet—a whole handful of twenties and tens.

She counted it, gave him his change, his receipt, his tickets. "Your train leaves at 10:30 A.M., Mr. Smith," she said. "Please be here and ready to entrain at 10:10."

"All right," he said. "Thank you."

Bonnie gave him the big professional smile, but Mr. Smith was already turning away. His face was very pale, and to Bonnie he looked like a man who was in a great deal of pain.

She was very sure that he had said *fireworks*.

◆ 4 ◆

Elton Curry was a conductor on Amtrak's Phoenix-Salt Lake
run. The tall man appeared promptly at 10:00 A.M. on January
3, and Elton helped him up the steps and into the car because
he was limping quite badly. He was carrying a rather old
tartan traveling bag with scuffmarks and fraying edges in one
hand. In the other hand he carried a brand-new cowhide attaché case. He carried the attaché case as if it were quite heavy.

"Can I help you with that, sir?" Elton asked, meaning the
attaché case but it was the traveling bag that the passenger
handed him, along with his ticket.

"No, I'll take that when we're underway, sir."

"All right. Thank you."

A very polite sort of fellow, Elton Curry told the FBI
agents who questioned him later. And he tipped well.

◆ 5 ◆

January 6, 1979, was a gray, overcast day in New York—snow
threatened but did not fall. George Clements' taxi was parked
in front of the Biltmore Hotel, across from Grand Central.

The door opened and a fellow with graying hair got in,
moving carefully and a little painfully. He placed a traveling
bag and an attaché case beside him on the seat, closed the
door, then put his head back against the seat and closed his
eyes for a moment, as if he was very, very tired.

"Where we goin, my friend?" George asked.

His fare looked at a slip of paper. "Port Authority Terminal," he said.

George got going. "You look a little white around the gills,
my friend. My brother-in-law looked like that when he was
havin his gallstone attacks. You got stones?"

"No."

"My brother-in-law, he says gallstones hurt worse than anything. Except maybe kidney stones. You know what I told
him? I told him he was full of shit. Andy, I says, you're a
great guy, I love ya, but you're full of shit. You ever had
cancer, Andy? I says. I asks him that, you know, did he ever
have cancer. I mean, everybody knows cancer's the worst."

George took a long look in his rear-view mirror. "I'm asking you sincerely, my friend . . . are you okay? Because, I'm telling you the truth, you look like death warmed over."

The passenger answered, "I'm fine. I was . . . thinking of another taxi ride. Several years ago."

"Oh, right," George said sagely, exactly as if he knew what the man was talking about. Well, New York was full of kooks, there was no denying that. And after this brief pause for reflection, he went on talking about his brother-in-law.

◆ 6 ◆

"Mommy, is that man sick?"

"Shhh."

"Yeah, but is he?"

"Danny, be quiet."

She smiled at the man on the other side of the Greyhound's aisle, an apologetic, kids-will-say-anything-won't-they smile, but the man appeared not to have heard. The poor guy did look sick. Danny was only four, but he was right about that. The man was looking listlessly out at the snow that had begun to fall shortly after they crossed the Connecticut state line. He was much too pale, much too thin, and there was a hideous Frankenstein scar running up out of his coat collar to just under his jaw. It was as if someone had tried taking his head clean off at sometime in the not-too-distant past—tried and almost succeeded.

The Greyhound was on its way to Portsmouth, New Hampshire, and they would arrive at 9:30 tonight if the snow didn't slow things down too much. Julie Brown and her son were going to see Julie's mother-in-law, and as usual the old bitch would spoil Danny rotten—and Danny didn't have far to go.

"I wanna go see him."

"No, Danny."

"I wanna see if he's sick."

"No!"

"Yeah, but what if he's *dine,* ma?" Danny's eyes positively glowed at this entrancing possibility. "He might be dine right now!"

"Danny, shut up."

"Hey, mister!" Danny cried. "You dine, or anything?"

"Danny, you *shut your mouth!*" Julie hissed, her cheeks burning with embarrassment.

Danny began to cry then, not real crying but that snotty, I-can't-get-my-own-way whining that always made her want to grab him and pinch his arms until he *really* had something to cry about. At times like this, riding the bus into evening through another cruddy snowstorm with her son whining beside her, she wished her own mother had sterilized her several years before she had reached the age of consent.

That was when the man across the aisle turned his head and smiled at her—a tired, painful smile, but rather sweet for all that. She saw that his eyes were terribly bloodshot, as if he had been crying. She tried to smile back, but it felt false and uneasy on her lips. That red left eye—and the scar running up his neck—made that half of his face look sinister and unpleasant.

She hoped that the man across the aisle wasn't going all the way to Portsmouth, but as it turned out, he was. She caught sight of him in the terminal as Danny's gram swept the boy, giggling happily, into her arms. She saw him limping toward the terminal doors, a scuffed traveling bag in one hand, a new attaché case in the other. And for just a moment, she felt a terrible chill cross her back. It was really worse than a limp—it was very nearly a headlong lurch. But there was something implacable about it, she told the New Hampshire state police later. It was as if he knew exactly where he was going and nothing was going to stop him from getting there.

Then he passed out into the darkness and she lost sight of him.

◆ 7 ◆

Timmesdale, New Hampshire, is a small town west of Durham, just inside the third congressional district. It is kept alive by the smallest of the Chatsworth Mills, which hulks like a soot-stained brick ogre on the edge of Timmesdale Stream. Its one modest claim to fame (according to the local Chamber of Commerce) is that it was the first town in New Hampshire to have electric streetlights.

One evening in early January, a young man with prematurely graying hair and a limp walked into the Timmesdale Pub, the town's only beer joint. Dick O'Donnell, the owner, was tending the bar. The place was almost empty because it was the middle of the week and another norther was brewing. Two or three inches had piled up out there already, and more was on the way.

The man with the limp stamped off his shoes, came to the bar, and ordered a Pabst. O'Donnell served him. The fellow had two more, making them last, watching the TV over the bar. The color was going bad, had been for a couple of months now, and The Fonz looked like an aging Rumanian ghoul. O'Donnell couldn't remember having seen this guy around.

"Like another?" O'Donnell asked, coming back to the bar after serving the two old bags in the corner.

"One more won't hurt," the fellow said. He pointed to a spot above the TV. "You met him, I guess."

It was a framed blowup of a political cartoon. It showed Greg Stillson, his construction helmet cocked back on his head throwing a fellow in a business suit down the Capitol steps. The fellow in the business suit was Louis Quinn, the congressman who had been caught taking kickbacks in the parking-lot scam some fourteen months ago. The cartoon was titled GIVING EM THE BUM'S RUSH, and across the corner it had been signed in a scrawling hand: *For Dick O'Donnell, who keeps the best damn saloon in the third district! Keep drawing them, Dick—Greg Stillson.*

"Betcha butt I did," O'Donnell said. "He gave a speech in here the last time he canvassed for the House. Had signs out all over town, come on into the Pub at two o'clock Saturday afternoon and have one on Greg. That was the best damn day's business I've ever done. People was only supposed to have one on him, but he ended up grabbing the whole tab. Can't do much better than that, can you?"

"Sounds like you think he's one hell of a guy."

"Yeah, I do," O'Donnell said. "I'd be tempted to put my bare knuckles on anyone who said the other way."

"Well, I won't try you." The fellow put down three quarters. "Have one on me."

"Well, okay. Don't mind if I do. Thanks, mister . . . ?"

"Johnny Smith is my name."

"Why, pleased to meet you, Johnny. Dicky O'Donnell, that's me." He drew himself a beer from the tap. "Yeah, Greg's done this part of New Hampshire a lotta good. And there's a lotta people afraid to come right out and say it, but

I'm not. I'll say it right out loud. Some day Greg Stillson's apt to be president."

"You think so?"

"I do," O'Donnell said, coming back to the bar. "New Hampshire's not big enough to hold Greg. He's one hell of a politician, and coming from me, that's something. I thought the whole crew was nothin but a bunch of crooks and lolly-gags. I still do, but Greg's an exception to the rule. He's a square shooter. If you told me five years ago I'd be sayin somethin like that, I woulda laughed in your face. You'd be more likely to find me readin poitry than seein any good in a politician, I woulda said. But, goddammit, he's a man."

Johnny said, "Most of these guys want to be your buddy while they're running for office, but when they get in it's fuck you, Jack, I got mine until the next election. I come from Maine myself, and the one time I wrote Ed Muskie, you know what I got? A form letter!"

"Ah, that's a Polack for you," O'Donnell said. "What do you expect from a Polack? Listen, Greg comes back to the district every damn weekend! Now does that sound like fuck you, Jack, I got mine, to you?"

"Every weekend huh?" Johnny sipped his beer. "Where? Trimbull? Ridgeway? The big towns?"

"He's got a system," O'Donnell said in the reverent tones of a man who has never quite been able to work one out for himself. "Fifteen towns, from the big places like Capital City right down to the little burgs like Timmesdale and Coorter's Notch. He hits one a week until he's gone through the whole list and then he starts at the top again. You know how big Coorter's Notch is? They got eight hundred souls up there. So what do you think about a guy who takes a weekend off from Washington and comes down to Coorter's Notch to freeze his balls off in a cold meetin hall? Does that sound like fuck you, Jack, I got mine, to you?"

"No, it doesn't," Johnny said truthfully. "What does he do? Just shake hands?"

"No, he's got a hall in every town. Reserves it for all day Saturday. He gets in there about ten in the morning, and people can come by and talk to him. Tell him their idears, you know. If they got questions, he answers them. If he can't answer them, he goes back to Washington and *finds* the answer!" He looked at Johnny triumphantly.

"When was he here in Timmesdale last?"

"Couple of months ago," O'Donnell said. He went to the cash register and rummaged through a pile of papers beside it. He came up with a dog-eared clipping and laid it on the bar beside Johnny.

"Here's the list. You just take a look at that and see what you think."

The clipping was from the Ridgeway paper. It was fairly old now. The story was headlined STILLSON ANNOUNCES "FEEDBACK CENTERS." The first paragraph looked as though it might have been lifted straight from the Stillson press kit. Below it was the list of towns where Greg would be spending his weekends, and the proposed dates. He was not due in Timmesdale again until mid-March.

"I think it looks pretty good," Johnny said.

"Yeah, I think so. Lotta people think so."

"By this clipping, he must have been in Coorter's Notch just last weekend."

"That's right," O'Donnell said and laughed. "Good old Coorter's Notch. Want another beer, Johnny?"

"Only if you'll join me," Johnny said, and laid a couple of bucks on the bar.

"Well, I don't care if I do."

One of the two bar-bags had put some money in the juke and Tammy Wynette, sounding old and tired and not happy to be here, began singing, "Stand By Your Man."

"Hey Dick!" the other cawed. "You ever hear of service in this place?"

"Shut your head!" he hollered back.

"Fuck——YOU," she called, and cackled.

"Goddammit, Clarice, I told you about saying the effword in my bar! I told you . . ."

"Oh get off it and let's have some beer."

"I hate those two old cunts," O'Donnell muttered to Johnny. "Couple of old alky diesel-dykes, that's what they are. They been here a million years, and I wouldn't be surprised if they both lived to spit on my grave. It's a hell of a world sometimes."

"Yes, it is."

"Pardon me, I'll be right back. I got a girl, but she only comes in Fridays and Saturdays in the winter."

O'Donnell drew two schooners of beer and brought them over to the table. He said something to them and Clarice replied "Fuck——YOU!" and cackled again. The beerjoint was filled with the ghosts of dead hamburgers. Tammy Wynette sang through the popcorn-crackle of an old record. The radiators thudded dull heat into the room and outside snow spatted dryly against the glass. Johnny rubbed his temples. He had been in this bar before, in a hundred other small towns. His head ached. When he had shaken O'Donnell's hand he knew that the barkeep had a big old mongrel dog that he had trained to sic on command. His one great dream was that some night a burglar would break into his house and he would legally be able to sic that big old dog onto him and there would be one less goddam hippie pervo junkie in the world.

Oh, his head ached.

O'Donnell came back, wiping his hands on his apron. Tammy Wynette finished up and was replaced with Red Sovine, who had a CB call for the Teddy Bear.

"Thanks again for the suds," O'Donnell said, drawing two.

"My pleasure," Johnny said, still studying the clipping. "Coorter's Notch last week, Jackson this coming weekend. I never heard of that one. Must be a pretty small town, huh?"

"Just a burg," O'Donnell agreed. "They used to have a ski resort, but it went broke. Lotta unemployment up that way. They do some wood-pulping and a little shirttail farming. But he goes up there, by the Jesus. Talks to em. Listens to their bitches. Where you from up in Maine, Johnny?"

"Lewiston," Johnny lied. The clipping said that Greg Stillson would meet with interested persons at the town hall.

"Guess you came down from the skiing, huh?"

"No, I hurt my leg a while back. I don't ski anymore. Just passing through. Thanks for letting me look at this." Johnny handed the clipping back. "It's quite interesting."

O'Donnell put it carefully back with his other papers. He had an empty bar, a dog back home that would sic on command, and Greg Stillson. Greg had been in his bar.

Johnny found himself abruptly wishing himself dead. If this talent was a gift from God, then God was a dangerous lunatic who ought to be stopped. If God wanted Greg Stillson dead, why hadn't he sent him down the birth canal with the umbilical cord wrapped around his throat? Or strangled him on a piece of meat? Or electrocuted him while he was changing the radio station? Drowned him in the ole swimming hole? Why did God have to have Johnny Smith to do his dirty work? It wasn't his responsibility to save the world, that was for the psychos and only psychos would presume to try it. He suddenly decided he would let Greg Stillson live and spit in God's eye.

"You okay, Johnny?" O'Donnell asked.

"Huh? Yeah, sure."

"You looked sorta funny for just a second there."

Chuck Chatsworth saying: *If I didn't, I'd be afraid all those people he killed would haunt me to my grave.*

"Out woolgathering, I guess," Johnny said. "I want you to know it's been a pleasure drinking with you."

"Well, the same goes back to you," O'Donnell said, looking pleased. "I wish more people passing through felt that way. They go through here headed for the ski resorts, you know. The big places. That's where they take their money. If I thought they'd stop in, I'd fix this place up like they'd like. Posters, you know, of Switzerland and Colorado. A fireplace. Load the juke up with rock 'n' roll records instead of that shitkicking music. I'd . . . you know, I'd like that." He shrugged. "I'm not a bad guy, hell."

"Of course not," Johnny said, getting off the stool and thinking about the dog trained to sic, and the hoped-for hippie junkie burglar.

"Well, tell your friends I'm here," O'Donnell said.

"For sure," Johnny said.

"Hey Dick!" one of the bar-bags hollered. "Ever hear of service-with-a-smile in this place?"

"Why don't you get stuffed?" O'Donnell yelled at her, flushing.

"Fuck——*YOU!*" Clarice called back, and cackled.

Johnny slipped quietly out into the gathering storm.

◆ 8 ◆

He was staying at the Holiday Inn in Portsmouth. When he got back that evening, he told the desk clerk to have his bill ready for checkout in the morning.

In his room, he sat down at the impersonal Holiday Inn writing desk, took out all the stationery, and grasped the Holiday Inn pen. His head was throbbing, but there were letters to be written. His momentary rebellion—if that was what it had been—had passed. His unfinished business with Greg Stillson remained.

I've gone crazy, he thought. *That's really it. I've gone entirely off my chump.* He could see the headlines now. PSYCHO SHOOTS N.H. REP. MADMAN ASSASSINATES STILLSON. HAIL OF BULLETS CUTS DOWN U.S. REPPRESENTATIVE IN NEW HAMPSHIRE. And *Inside View,* of course, would have a field day. SELF-PROCLAIMED "SEER" KILLS STILLSON, 12 NOTED PSYCHIATRISTS TELL WHY SMITH DID IT. With a sidebar by that fellow Dees, maybe, telling how Johnny had threatened to get his shotgun and "shoot me a trespasser."

Crazy.

The hospital debt was paid, but this would leave a new bill of particulars behind, and his father would have to pay for it. He and his new wife would spend a lot of days in the limelight of his reflected notoriety. They would get the hate mail. Everyone he had known would be interviewed—the Chatsworths, Sam, Sheriff George Bannerman. Sarah? Well, maybe they wouldn't get as far as Sarah. After all, it wasn't as though he were planning to shoot the president. At least, not yet. *There's a lotta people afraid to come right out and say it, but I'm not. I'll say it right out loud. Some day Greg Stillson's apt to be president.*

Johnny rubbed his temples. The headache came in low, slow waves, and none of this was getting his letters written. He drew the first sheet of stationery toward him, picked up the pen, and wrote *Dear Dad.* Outside, snow struck the window with that dry, sandy sound that means serious business. Finally the pen began to move across the paper, slowly at first, then gaining speed.

Chapter 27

◆ 1 ◆

Johnny came up wooden steps that had been shoveled clear of snow and salted down. He went through a set of double doors and into a foyer plastered with specimen ballots and notices of a special town meeting to be held here in Jackson on the third of February. There was also a notice of Greg Stillson's impending visit and a picture of The Man Who himself, hard hat cocked back on his head grinning that hard slantwise "We're wise to em ain't we pard?" grin. Set a little to the right of the green door leading into the meeting hall itself was a sign that Johnny hadn't expected, and he pondered it in silence for several seconds, his breath pluming white from his lips. DRIVER EXAMINATIONS TODAY, this sign read. It was set on a wooden easel. HAVE PAPERS READY.

He opened the door, went into the stuporous glow of heat thrown by a big woodstove, and there sat a cop at a desk. The cop was wearing a ski parka, unzipped. There were papers scattered across his desk, and there was also a gadget for examining visual acuity.

The cop looked up at Johnny, and he felt a sinking sensation in his gut.

"Can I help you, sir?"

Johnny fingered the camera slung around his neck. "Well, I wondered if it would be all right to look around a little bit," he said. "I'm on assignment from *Yankee* magazine. We're doing a spread on town hall architecture in Maine, New Hampshire, and Vermont. Taking a lot of pictures, you know."

"Go right to it," the cop said. "My wife reads *Yankee* all the time. Puts me to sleep."

Johnny smiled. "New England architecture has a tendency toward . . . well, starkness."

"Starkness," the cop repeated doubtfully, and then let it go. "Next please."

A young man approached the desk the cop was sitting behind. He handed an examination sheet to the cop, who took it and said, "Look into the viewer, please, and identify the traffic signs and signals which I will show you."

A young man peered into the viewing machine. The cop put an answer-key over the young man's exam sheet. Johnny moved down the center aisle of the Jackson town hall and clicked a picture of the rostrum at the front.

"Stop sign," the young man said from behind him. "The next one's a yield sign . . . and the next one is a traffic information sign . . . no right turn, no left turn, like that . . ."

He hadn't expected a cop in the town hall; he hadn't even bothered to buy film for the camera he was using as a prop. But now it was too late to back out anyway. This was Friday, and Stillson would be here tomorrow if things went the way they were supposed to go. He would be answering questions and listening to suggestions from the good people of Jackson. There would be a fair-sized entourage with him. A couple of aides, a couple of advisors—and several others, young men in sober suits and sports jackets who had been wearing jeans and riding motorcycles not so long ago. Greg Stillson was still a firm believer in guards for the body. At the Trimbull rally they had been carrying sawed-off pool cues. Did they carry guns now? Would it be so difficult for a U.S. representative to get a permit to carry a concealed weapon? Johnny didn't think so. He could count on one good chance only; he would have to make the most of it. So it was important to look the place over, to try and decide if he could take Stillson in here or if it would be better to wait in the parking lot with the window rolled down and the rifle on his lap.

So he had come and here he was, casing the joint while a state cop gave driver-permit exams not thirty feet away.

There was a bulletin board on his left, and Johnny snapped his unloaded camera at it—why in God's name hadn't he taken another two minutes and bought himself a roll of film? The board was covered with chatty small-town intelligence concerning baked-bean suppers, an upcoming high school play, dog-licensing information, and, of course, more on Greg. A file card said that Jackson's first selectman was looking for someone who could take shorthand, and Johnny studied this as though it were of great interest to him while his mind moved into high gear.

Of course if Jackson looked impossible—or even chancy—he could wait until next week, where Stillson would be doing the whole thing all over again in the town of Upson. Or the week after, in Trimbull. Or the week after that. Or never.

It should be this week. It ought to be tomorrow.

He snapped the big woodstove in the corner, and then glanced upward. There was a balcony up there. No—not precisely a balcony, more like a gallery with a waist-high railing and wide, white-painted slats with small, decorative diamonds and curlicues cut into the wood. It would be very possible for a man to crouch behind that railing and look through one of those doodads. At the right moment, he could just stand up and—

"What kind of camera is that?"

Johnny looked around, sure it was the cop. The cop would ask to see his filmless camera—and then he would want to see some ID—and then it would be all over.

But it wasn't the cop. It was the young man who had been taking his driver's permit test. He was about twenty-two, with long hair and pleasant, frank eyes. He was wearing a suede coat and faded jeans.

"A Nikon," Johnny said.

"Good camera, man. I'm a real camera nut. How long have you been working for *Yankee*?"

"Well, I'm a free lance," Johnny said. "I do stuff for them, sometimes for *Country Journal*, sometimes for *Downeast*, you know."

"Nothing national, like *People* or *Life*?"

"No. At least, not yet."

"What f-stop do you use in here?"

What in hell is an f-stop?

Johnny shrugged. "I play it mostly by ear."

"By eye, you mean," the young man said, smiling.

"That's right, by eye." *Get lost, kid, please get lost.*

"I'm interested in free-lancing myself," the young man said, and grinned. "My big dream is to take a picture some day like the flag-raising at Iwo Jima."

"I heard that was staged," Johnny said.

"Well, maybe. Maybe. But it's a classic. Or how about the first picture of a UFO coming in for a landing? I'd sure like that. Anyway, I've got a portfolio of stuff I've taken around here. Who's your contact at *Yankee*?"

Johnny was sweating now. "Actually, they contacted me on this one," he said. "It was a . . ."

"Mr. Clawson, you can come over now," the cop said, sounding impatient. "I'd like to go over these answers with you."

"Whoops, his master's voice," Clawson said. "See you later, man." He hurried off and Johnny let out his breath in a silent, whispering sigh. It was time to get out, and quickly.

He snapped another two or three "pictures" just so it wouldn't look like a complete rout, but he was barely aware of what he was looking at through the viewfinder. Then he left.

The young man in the suede jacket—Clawson—had forgotten all about him. He had apparently flunked the written part of his exam. He was arguing strenuously with the cop, who was only shaking his head.

Johnny paused for a moment in the town hall's entryway. To his left was a cloakroom. To his right was a closed door. He tried it and found it unlocked. A narrow flight of stairs led upward into dimness. The actual offices would be up there, of course. And the gallery.

◆ 2 ◆

He was staying at the Jackson House, a pleasant little hotel on the main drag. It had been carefully renovated and the renovations had probably cost a lot of money, but the place would pay for itself, the owners must have reckoned, because of the new Jackson Mountain ski resort. Only the resort had gone bust and now the pleasant little hotel was barely hanging on. The night clerk was dozing over a cup of coffee when Johnny went out at four o'clock on Saturday morning, the attaché case in his left hand.

He had slept little last night, slipping into a short, light doze after midnight. He had dreamed. It was 1970 again. It was carnival time. He and Sarah stood in front of the Wheel of Fortune and again he had that feeling of crazy, enormous power. In his nostrils he could smell burning rubber.

"Come on," a voice said softly behind him, "I love to watch this guy take a beatin." He turned and it was Frank Dodd, dressed in his black vinyl raincoat, his throat slit from ear to ear in a wide red grin, his eyes sparkling with dead vivaciousness. He turned back to the booth, scared—but now the pitchman was Greg Stillson, grinning knowingly at him, his yellow hard hat tipped cockily back on his skull. "Hey-hey-hey," Stillson chanted, his voice deep and resonant and ominous. "Lay em down where you want em down fella. What do you say! Want to shoot the moon?"

Yes, he wanted to shoot the moon. But as Stillson set the Wheel in motion he saw that the entire outer circle had turned green. Every number was double-zero. Every number was a house number.

He had jerked awake and spent the rest of the night looking out the frost-rimmed window into darkness. The headache he'd had ever since arriving in Jackson the day before was gone, leaving him feeling weak but composed. He sat with his hands in his lap. He didn't think about Greg Stillson; he thought about the past. He thought about his mother putting a Band-Aid on a scraped knee; he thought about the time the dog had torn off the back of Grandma Nellie's absurd sundress and how he had laughed and how Vera had swatted him one and cut his forehead with the stone in her engagement ring; he thought about his father showing him how to bait a fishing hook and saying. *It doesn't hurt the worms, Johnny . . . at least, I don't think it does.* He thought about his father giving him a pocketknife for Christmas when he was seven and saying very seriously, *I'm trusting you, Johnny.* All those memories had come back in a flood.

Now he stepped off into the deep cold of the morning, his shoes squeaking on the path shoveled through the snow. His breath plumed out in front of him The moon was down but the stars were sprawled across the black sky in idiot's profusion. God's jewel box, Vera always called it. You're looking into God's jewel box, Johnny.

He walked down Main Street, and he stopped in front of the tiny Jackson post office and fumbled the letters out of his coat pocket. Letters to his father, to Sarah, to Sam Weizak, to Bannerman. He set the attaché case down between his feet, opened the mailbox that stood in front of the neat little brick building, and after one brief moment of hesitation, dropped them in. He could hear them drop down inside, surely the first letters mailed in Jackson this new day, and the sound gave him a queer sense of finality. The letters were mailed, there was no stopping now.

He picked up the case again and walked on. The only sound was the squeak of his shoes on the snow. The big thermometer over the door of the Granite State Savings Bank stood at 3 degrees, and the air had that feeling of total silent inertia that belongs exclusively to cold New Hampshire mornings. Noting moved. The roadway was empty. The windshields of the parked cars were blinded with cataracts of frost. Dark windows, drawn shades. To Johnny it all seemed somehow dreadful and at the same time holy. He fought the feeling, This was no holy business he was on.

He crossed Jasper Street and there was the town hall, standing white and austerely elegant behind its plowed banks of twinkling snow.

What you going to do if the front door's locked, smart guy?

Well, he would find a way to cross that bridge if he had to. Johnny looked around, but there was no one to see him. If this had been the president coming for one of his famous town meetings, everything would have been different, of course. The place would have been blocked off since the night before, and men would have been stationed inside already. But this was only a U.S. representative, one of over four hundred, no big deal. No big deal yet.

Johnny went up the steps and tried the door. The knob turned easily and he stepped into the cold entryway and pulled the door shut behind him. Now the headache was coming back, pulsing along with the steady thick beat of his heart. He set his case down and massaged his temples with his gloved fingers.

There was a sudden low scream. The coat-closet door was opening, very slowly, and then something white was falling out of the shadows toward him.

Johnny barely held back a cry. For one moment he thought it was a body, falling out of the closet like something from a spook movie. But it was only a heavy cardboard sign that read PLEASE HAVE PAPERS IN ORDER BEFORE APPEARING FOR EXAMINATION.

He set it back in place and then turned to the doorway giving upon the stairs.

This door was now locked.

He leaned down to get a better look at it in the dim white glow of the streetlight that filtered in the one window. It was a spring lock, and he thought he might be able to open it with a coat hanger. He found one in the coat closet and hooked the neck of it into the crack between the door and the jamb. He worked it down to the lock and began to fumble around. His head was thudding fiercely now. At last he heard the bolt snap back as the wire caught it. He pulled the door open. He picked up his attaché case and went through, still holding the coat hanger. He pulled the door closed behind him and heard it lock again. He went up the narrow stairs, which creaked and groaned under his weight.

At the top of the stairs there was a short hallway with several doors on either side. He walked down the hall, past TOWN MANAGER and TOWN SELECTMEN, past TAX ASSESSOR and MEN'S and O'SEER OF THE POOR and LADIES'.

There was an unmarked door at the end. It was unlocked and he came out onto the gallery above the rear of the meeting hall, which was spread out below him in a crazy quilt of shadows. He closed the door behind him and shivered a little at the soft stir of echoes in the empty hall. His footfalls also echoed back as he walked to the right along the rear gallery, then turned left. Now he was walking along the right-hand side of the hall, about twenty-five feet above the floor. He stopped at a point above the woodstove and directly across from the podium where Stillson would be standing in about five-and-a-half hours.

He sat down cross-legged and rested for a while. Tried to get in control of the headache with some deep breathing. The woodstove wasn't operating and he felt the cold settling steadily against him—and then into him. Previews of the winding shroud.

When he had begun to feel a little better, he thumbed the catches on the attaché case. The double click echoed back as his footfalls had done, and this time it was the sound of cocking pistols.

Western justice, he thought, for no reason at all. That was what the prosecutor had said when the jury found Claudine Longet guilty of shooting her lover. *She's found out what western justice means.*

Johnny looked down into the case and rubbed his eyes. His vision doubled briefly and then things came together again. He was getting an impression from the very wood he was sitting on. A very old impression; if it had been a photograph, it would have been sepia-toned. Men standing here and smoking cigars, talking and laughing and waiting for town meeting to begin. Had it been 1920? 1902? There was something ghostly about it that made him feel uneasy. One of them had been talking about the price of whiskey and cleaning his nose with a silver toothpick and

(*and two years before he had poisoned his wife*)

Johnny shivered. Whatever the impression was, it didn't matter. It was an impression of a man who was long dead now.

The rifle gleamed up at him.

When men do it in wartime, they give them medals, he thought.

He began to assemble the rifle. Each *click!* echoed back, just once, solemnly, the sound of a cocking pistol.

He loaded the Remington with five bullets.

He placed it across his knees.

And waited.

◆ 3 ◆

Dawn came slowly. Johnny dozed a little, but he was too cold now to do more than doze. Thin, sketchy dreams haunted what sleep he did get.

He came fully awake at a little past seven. The door below was thrown open with a crash, and he had to bite his tongue to keep from crying out, *Who's there?*

It was the custodian. Johnny put his eye to one of the diamond shapes cut into the balustrade and saw a burly man who was bundled up in a thick Navy pea coat. He was coming up the center aisle with an armload of firewood. He was humming "Red River Valley." He dropped the armload of wood into the woodbox with a crash and then disappeared below Johnny. A second later he heard the thin screeing noise of the stove's firebox door being swung open.

Johnny suddenly thought of the plume of vapor he was producing every time he exhaled. Suppose the custodian looked up? Would he be able to see that?

He tried to slow the rate of his breathing, but that made his head ache worse and his vision doubled alarmingly.

Now there was the crackle of paper being crumpled, then the scratch of a match. A faint whiff of sulphur in the cold air. The custodian went on humming "Red River Valley," and then broke into loud and tuneless song: "From this valley they say you are going . . . we will miss your bright eyes and sweet smiiiiile . . ."

Now a different crackling sound. Fire.

"That's got it, you sucker," the custodian said from directly below Johnny, and then there was the sound of the firebox door being slammed shut again. Johnny pressed both hands over his mouth like a bandage, suddenly afflicted with suicidal amusement. He saw himself rising up from the floor of the gallery, as thin and white as any self-respecting ghost. He saw himself spreading his arms like wings and his fingers like talons and calling down in hollow tones: "That's got *you*, you sucker."

He held the laughter behind his hands. His head throbbed like a tomato full of hot, expanding blood. His vision jittered and blurred crazily. Suddenly he wanted very badly to move away from the impression of the man who had been cleaning his nose with the silver toothpick, but he didn't dare make a sound. Dear Jesus, what if he had to sneeze?

Suddenly, with no warning a terrible wavering shriek filled the hall, drilling into Johnny's ears like thin silver nails, climbing, making his head vibrate. He opened his mouth to scream—

It cut off.

"Oh, you whore," the custodian said conversationally.

Johnny looked through the diamond and saw the custodian standing behind the podium and fiddling with a microphone. The mike cord snaked down to a small portable amp. The custodian went down the few steps from the podium to the floor and pulled the amplifier farther from the mike, then fooled with the dials on top of it. He went back to the mike and turned it on again. There was another feedback whine, this one lower and then tapering away entirely. Johnny pressed his hands tight against his forehead and rubbed them back and forth.

The custodian tapped on the mike with his thumb, and the sound filled the big empty room. It sounded like a fist knocking on a coffin lid. Then his voice, still tuneless, but now amplified to the point of monstrosity, a giant's voice bludgeoning into Johnny's head: "*FROM THIS VAL-LEEE THEY SAY YOU ARE GOING . . .*"

Stop it, Johnny wanted to scream. *Oh, please stop it, I'm going crazy, can't you stop it?*

The singing ended with a loud, amplified *snap!* and the custodian said in his own voice, "That's got you, whore."

He walked out of Johnny's line of sight again. There was a sound of tearing paper and the low popping sounds of twine being snapped. Then the custodian reappeared, whistling and holding a large stack of booklets. He began to place them at close intervals along the benches.

When he had finished that chore, the custodian buttoned his coat and left the hall. The door slammed hollowly shut behind him. Johnny looked at his watch. It was 7:45. The town hall was warming up a little. He sat and waited. The headache was still very bad, but oddly enough, it was easier to bear than it had ever been before. All he had to do was tell himself that he wouldn't have to bear it for long.

◆ 4 ◆

The doors slammed open again promptly at nine o'clock, startling him out of a catnap. His hands clamped tightly over the rifle and then relaxed. He put his eye to the diamond-shaped peephole. Four men this time. One of them was the custodian, the collar of his pea coat turned up against his neck. The other three were wearing topcoats with suits underneath. Johnny felt his heartbeat quicken. One of them was Sonny Elliman. His hair was cut short now and handsomely styled, but the brilliant green eyes had not changed.

"Everything set?" he asked

"Check for yourself," the custodian said.

"Don't be offended, Dad," one of the others replied. They were moving to the front of the hall. One of them clicked the amplifier on and then clicked it off again, satisfied.

"People round these parts act like he was the bloody emperor," the custodian grumbled.

"He is, he is," the third man said—Johnny thought he also recognized this fellow from the Trimbull rally. "Haven't you got wise to that yet, Pop?"

"Have you been upstairs?" Elliman asked the custodian, and Johnny went cold.

"Stairway door's locked," the custodian answered. "Same as always. I gave her a shake."

Johnny silently gave thanks for the spring lock on the door.

"Ought to check it out," Elliman said.

The custodian uttered an exasperated laugh. "I don't know about you guys," he said. "Who are you expecting? The Phantom of the Opera?"

"Come on Sonny," the fellow Johnny thought he recognized said. "There's nobody up there. We just got time for a coffee if we shag ass down to that resrunt on the corner."

"That's not coffee," Sonny said. "Fucking mud is all that is. Just run upstairs first and make sure no one's there, Moochie. We go by the book."

Johnny licked his lips and clutched the gun. He looked up and down the narrow gallery. To his right it ended in a blank wall. To his left it went back to the suite of offices, and either way it made no difference. If he moved, they would hear him. This empty, the town hall served as a natural amplifier. He was stuck.

There were footfalls down below. Then the sound of the door between the hall and the entryway being opened and closed. Johnny waited, frozen and helpless. Just below him the custodian and the other two were talking, but he heard nothing they said. His head had turned on his neck like some slow engine and he stared down the length of the gallery, waiting for the fellow Sonny Elliman had called Moochie to appear at the end of it. His bored expression would suddenly turn to shock and incredulity, his mouth would open: *Hey Sonny, there's a guy up here!*

Now he could hear the muffled sound of Moochie climbing the stairs. He tried to think of something, anything. Nothing came. They were going to discover him, it was less than a minute away now, and he didn't have any idea of how to stop it from happening. No matter what he did, his one chance was on the verge of being blown.

Doors began to open and close, the sound of each drawing closer and less muffled. A drop of sweat spilled from Johnny's forehead and darkened the leg of his jeans. He could remember each door he had come past on his way here. Moochie had checked TOWN MANAGER and TOWN SELECTMEN and TAX ASSESSOR. Now he was opening the door of MEN'S, now he was glancing through the office that belonged to the O'SEER OF THE POOR, now the LADIES' room. The next door would be the one leading to the galleries.

It opened.

There was the sound of two footfalls as Moochie approached the railing of the short gallery that ran along the back of the hall. "Okay, Sonny? You satisfied?"

"Everything look good?"

"Looks like a fucking dump," Moochie responded, and there was a burst of laughter from below.

"Well, come on down and let's go for coffee," the third man said. And incredibly, that was it. The door slammed to. The footsteps retreated back down the hall, and then down the steps to the first floor.

Johnny went limp and for a moment everything swam away from him into shades of gray. The slam of the entryway door as they went out for their coffee brought him partially out of it.

Below, the custodian presented his judgment: "Bunch of whores." Then he left, too, and for the next twenty minutes or so, there was only Johnny.

♦ 5 ♦

Around 9:30 A.M., the people of Jackson began to file into their town hall. The first to appear was a trio of old ladies dressed in formal black, chattering together like magpies. Johnny watched them pick seats close to the stove—almost entirely out of the field of his vision—and pick up the booklets that had been left on the seats. The booklets appeared to be filled with glossy pictures of Greg Stillson.

"I just love that man," one of the three said. "I've gotten his autograph three times and I'll get it again today, I'll be bound."

That was all the talk there was about Greg Stillson. The ladies went on to discuss the impending Old Home Sunday at the Methodist Church.

Johnny, almost directly over the stove, went from very cold to very hot. He had taken advantage of the slack tide between the departure of Stillson's security people and the arrival of the first townsfolk, using it to shed both his jacket and his outer shirt. He kept wiping sweat from his face with a handkerchief, and the linen was streaked with blood as well as sweat. His bad eye was kicking up again, and his vision was constantly blurred and reddish.

The door below opened, there was the hearty tromp-tromp-

tromp of men stamping snow from their pacs, and then four men in checked woolen jackets came down the aisle and sat in the front row. One of them launched immediately into a Frenchman joke.

A young woman of about twenty-three arrived with her son, who looked about four. The boy was wearing a blue snowmobile suit with bright yellow markings, and he wanted to know if he could talk into the microphone.

"No, dear," the woman said, and they went down behind the men. The boy immediately began to kick his feet against the bench in front of him, and one of the men glanced back over his shoulder.

"Matt, stop that," she said.

Quarter of ten now. The door was opening and closing with a steady regularity. Men and women of all types and occupations and ages were filling up the hall. There was a drifting hum of conversation, and it was edged with an indefinable sense of anticipation. They weren't here to quiz their duly-elected representative; they were waiting for a bona-fide star turn in their small community. Johnny knew that most "meet-your-candidate" and "meet-your-representative" sessions were attended by a handful of die-hards in the nearly empty meeting halls. During the election of 1976 a debate between Maine's Bill Cohen and his challenger, Leighton Cooney, had attracted all of twenty-six people, press aside. The skull-sessions were so much window-dressing, a self-testimonial to wave when election time came around again. Most could have been held in a middling-sized closet. But by 10 A.M., every seat in the town hall was taken, and there were twenty or thirty standees at the back. Every time the door opened, Johnny's hands tensed down on the rifle. And he was still not positive he could do it, no matter what the stakes.

Five past, ten past. Johnny began to think Stillson had been held up, or was perhaps not coming at all. And the feeling which moved stealthily through him was one of relief.

Then the door opened again and a hearty voice called: "Hey! How ya doin, Jackson, N.H.?"

A startled, pleased murmur. Someone called ecstatically, "Greg! How are you?"

"Well, I'm feeling perky," Stillson came right back. "How the heck are you?"

A spatter of applause quickly swelled to a roar of approval.

"Hey, all right!" Greg shouted over it. He moved quickly down the aisle, shaking hands, toward the podium.

Johnny watched him through his loophole. Stillson was wearing a heavy rawhide coat with a sheepskin collar, and today the hard hat had been replaced with a woolen ski cap with a bright red tassel. He paused at the head of the aisle and waved at the three or four press in attendance. Flashpaks popped and the applause got its second wind, shaking the rafters.

And Johnny Smith suddenly knew it was now or never.

The feelings he had had about Greg Stillson at the Trimbull rally suddenly swept over him again with a certain and terrible clarity. Inside his aching, tortured head he seemed to hear a dull wooden sound, two things coming together with terrible force at one single moment. It was, perhaps, the sound of destiny. It would be too easy to delay, to let Stillson talk and talk. Too easy to let him get away, to sit up here with his head in his hands, waiting as the crowd thinned out, waiting as the custodian returned to dismantle the sound system and sweep up the litter, all the time kidding himself that there would be next week in another town.

The time was now, indisputably now, and every human being on earth suddenly had a stake in what happened in this backwater meetinghouse.

That thudding sound in his head, like poles of destiny coming together.

Stillson was mounting the steps to the podium. The area behind him was clear. The three men in their open topcoats were lounging against the far wall.

Johnny stood up.

◆ **6** ◆

Everything seemed to happen in slow motion.

There were cramps in his legs from sitting so long. His knees popped like dud firecrackers. Time seemed frozen, the applause went on and on even though heads were turning, necks were craning; someone screamed through the applause and still it went on; someone had screamed because there was a man in the gallery and the man was holding a rifle and this was something they had all seen on TV, it was a situation with classic elements that they all recognized. In its own way, it was as American as *The Wonderful World of Disney*. The politician and the man in a high place with the gun.

Greg Stillson turned toward him, his thick neck craning, wrinkling into creases. The red puff on the top of his ski cap bobbed.

Johnny put the rifle to his shoulder. It seemed to float up there and he felt the thud as it socketed home next to the joint there. He thought of shooting partridge with his dad as a boy. They had gone deer-hunting but the only time Johnny had ever seen one he had not been able to pull the trigger; the buck fever had gotten him. It was a secret, as shameful as masturbation, and he had never told anyone.

There was another scream. One of the old ladies was clutching her mouth and Johnny saw there was artificial fruit scattered along the wide brim of her black hat. Faces turned up to him, big white zeros. Open mouths, small black zeros. The little boy in the snowmobile suit was pointing. His mother was trying to shield him. Stillson was in the gunsight suddenly and Johnny remembered to flick off the rifle's safety. Across the way the men in the topcoats were reaching inside their jackets and Sonny Elliman, his green eyes blazing, was hollering: *Down! Greg, get DOWN!*"

But Stillson stared up into the gallery and for the second time their eyes locked together in a perfect sort of understanding, and Stillson only ducked at the same instant Johnny fired. The rifle's roar was loud, filling the place, and the slug took away nearly one whole corner of the podium, peeling it back to the bare, bright wood. Splinters flew. One of them struck the microphone, and there was another monstrous whine of feedback that suddenly ended in a guttural, low-key buzzing.

Johnny pumped another cartridge into the chamber and fired again. This time the slug punched a hole through the dusty carpeting of the dais.

The crowd had started to move, panicky as cattle. They all drove into the center aisle. The people who had been standing at the rear escaped easily, but then a bottleneck of cursing, screaming men and women formed in the double doorway.

There were popping noises from the other side of the hall, and suddenly part of the gallery railing splintered up in front of Johnny's eyes. Something screamed past his ear a second later. Then an invisible finger gave the collar of his shirt a flick. All three of them across the way were holding handguns, and because Johnny was up in the gallery, their field of fire was crystal clear—but Johnny doubted if they would have bothered overmuch about innocent bystanders anyway.

One of the trio of old women grabbed Moochie's arm. She was sobbing, trying to ask something. He flung her away and steadied his gun in both hands. There was a stink of gunpowder in the hall now. It had been about twenty seconds since Johnny had stood up.

"Down! Down, Greg!"

Stillson was still standing at the edge of the dais, crouching slightly, looking up. Johnny brought the rifle down, and for an instant Stillson was dead-bang in front sight. Then a pistol-slug grooved his neck, knocking him backward, and his own shot went wild into the air. The window across the way dissolved in a tinkling rain of glass. Thin screams drifted up from below. Blood poured down and across his shoulder and chest.

Oh, you're doing a great job of killing him, he thought hysterically, and pushed back to the railing again. He levered another cartridge into the breech and threw it to his shoulder again. Now Stillson was on the move. He darted down the steps to floor-level and then glanced up at Johnny again.

Another bullet whizzed by his temple. *I'm bleeding like a stuck pig,* he thought. *Come on. Come on and get this over.*

The bottleneck at the entryway broke, and now people began to pour out. A puff of smoke rose from the barrel of one of the pistols across the way, there was a bang, and the invisible finger that had flicked his collar a few seconds ago now drew a line of fire across the side of Johnny's head. It didn't matter. Nothing mattered except taking Stillson. He brought the rifle down again.

Make this one count—

Stillson moved with good speed for such a big man. The dark-haired young woman Johnny had noticed earlier was about halfway up the center aisle, holding her crying son in her arms, still trying to shield him with her body. And what Stillson did then so dumbfounded Johnny that he almost dropped the rifle altogether. He snatched the boy from his mother's arms, whirled toward the gallery, holding the boy's body in front of him. It was no longer Greg Stillson in the front sight but a small squirming figure in

(*the filter blue filter yellow stripes tiger stripes*)

a dark blue snowmobile suit with bright yellow piping.

Johnny's mouth dropped open. It was Stillson, all right. The tiger. *But he was behind the filter now.*

What does it mean? Johnny screamed, but no sound passed his lips.

The mother screamed shrilly then; but Johnny had heard it all somewhere before. "*Matt! Give him to me! MATT! GIVE HIM TO ME, YOU BASTARD!*"

Johnny's head was swelling blackly, expanding like a bladder. Everything was starting to fade. The only brightness left was centered around the notched gunsight, the gunsight now laid directly over the chest of that blue snowmobile suit.

Do it, oh for Christ's sake you have to do it he'll get away—

And now—perhaps it was only his blurring eyesight that made it seem so—the blue snowmobile suit began to spread, its color washing out to the light robin's-egg color of the vision, the dark yellow stretching, striping, until everything began to be lost in it.

(*behind the filter, yes, he's behind the filter, but what does it mean? does it mean it's safe or just that he's beyond my reach? what does it*)

Warm fire flashed somewhere below and was gone. Some dim part of Johnny's mind registered it as a flash-pak.

Stillson shoved the woman away and backed toward the door, eyes squeezed into calculating pirate's slits. He held the squirming boy firmly by the neck and the crotch.

Can't. Oh dear God forgive me, I can't.

Two more bullets struck him then, one high in the chest, driving him back against the wall and bouncing him off it, the second into the left side of his midsection, spinning him around into the gallery railing. He was dimly aware that he had lost the rifle. It struck the gallery floor and discharged point-blank into the wall. Then his upper thighs crashed into the balustrade and he was falling. The town hall turned over twice before his eyes and then there was a splintering crash as he struck two of the benches, breaking his back and both legs.

He opened his mouth to scream, but what came out was a great gush of blood. He lay in the splintered remains of the benches he had struck and thought: *It's over. I punked out. Blew it.*

Hands were on him, not gentle. They were turning him over. Elliman, Moochie, and the other guy were there. Elliman was the one who had turned him over.

Stillson came, shoving Moochie aside.

"Never mind this guy," he said harshly. "Find the son of a bitch that took that picture. Smash his camera."

Moochie and the other guy left. Somewhere close by the woman with the dark hair was crying out: ". . . *behind a kid, hiding behind a kid and I'll tell everybody . . .*"

"Shut her up, Sonny," Stillson said.

"Sure," Sonny said, and left Stillson's side.

Stillson got down on his knees above Johnny. "Do we know each other, Fella? No sense lying. You've had the course."

Johnny whispered, "We knew each other."

"It was that Trimbull rally, wasn't it?"

Johnny nodded.

Stillson got up abruptly, and with the last bit of his strength Johnny reached out and grasped his ankle. It was only for a second; Stillson pulled free easily. But it was long enough.

Everything had changed.

People were drawing near him now, but he saw only feet and legs no faces. It didn't matter. *Everything had changed.*

He began to cry a little. Touching Stillson this time had been like touching a blank. Dead battery. Fallen tree. Empty house. Bare bookshelves. Wine bottles ready for candles.

Fading. Going away. The feet and legs around him were becoming misty and indistinct. He heard their voices, the excited gabble of speculation, but not the words. Only the sound of the words, and even that was fading, blurring into a high, sweet humming sound.

He looked over his shoulder and there was the corridor he had emerged from so long ago. He had come out of that corridor and into this bright placental place. Only then his mother had been alive and his father had been there, calling him by name, until he broke through to them. Now it was only time to go back. Now it was right to go back.

I did it. Somehow I did it. I don't understand how, but I have.

He let himself drift toward that corridor with the dark chrome walls, not knowing if there might be something at the far end of it or not, content to let time show him that. The sweet hum of the voices faded. The misty brightness faded. But he was still *he*—Johnny Smith—intact.

Get into the corridor, he thought. *All right.*

He thought that if he could get into that corridor, he would be able to walk.

· III ·

Notes from the Dead Zone

◆ 1 ◆

Portsmouth, N.H.
January 23, 1979

Dear Dad,

This is a terrible letter to have to write, and I will try to keep it short. When you get it, I guess I will probably be dead. An awful thing has happened to me, and I think now that it may have started a long time before the car accident and the coma. You know about the psychic business, of course, and you may remember Mom swearing on her deathbed that God had meant for it to be this way, that God had something for me to do. She asked me not to run from it, and I promised her that I wouldn't—not meaning it seriously, but wanting her mind to be easy. Now it looks as if she was right, in a funny sort of way. I still don't really believe in God, not in a real Being who plans for us and gives us all little jobs to do, like Boy Scouts winning merit badges on The Great Hike of Life. But neither do I believe that all the things that have happened to me are blind chance.

In the summer of 1976, Dad, I went to a Greg Stillson rally in Trimbull, which is in New Hampshire's third district. He was running for the first time then, you may recall. When he was on his way to the speaker's rostrum he shook a lot of hands, and one of them was mine. This is the part you may find hard to believe even though you have seen the ability in action. I had one of my "flashes," only this one was no flash, Dad. It was a vision, either in the biblical sense or in something very near it. Oddly enough, it wasn't as clear as some of my other "insights" have been—there was a puzzling blue glow over everything that has never been there before—but it was incredibly powerful. I saw Greg Stillson as president of the United States. How far in the future I can't say, except that he had lost most of his hair. I would say fourteen years, or perhaps eighteen at the most. Now, my ability is to see and not to interpret, and in this case my ability to see was impeded by that funny blue filter, but I saw enough. If Stillson becomes president, he's going to worsen an international situation that is going to be pretty awful to begin with. If Stillson becomes president, he is going to end up precipitating a full-scale nuclear war. I believe that the initial flashpoint for this war is going to be in South Africa. And I also believe that in the short, bloody course of this war, it's not going to be just two or three nations throwing warheads, but maybe as many as twenty—plus terrorist groups.

Daddy, I know how crazy this must look. It looks crazy to me. But I have no doubts, no urge to look back over my shoulder and try to second-guess this thing into something less real and urgent than it is. You never knew—no one did—but I didn't run away from the Chatsworths because of that restaurant fire. I guess I was running away from Greg Stillson and the thing I am supposed to do. Like Elijah hiding in his cave or Jonah, who ended up in the fish's belly. I thought I would just wait and see, you know. Wait and see if the preconditions for such a horrible future began to come into place. I would probably be waiting still, but in the fall of last year the headaches began to get worse, and there was an incident on the road-crew I was working with. I guess Keith Strang, the foreman, would remember that . . .

◆ **2** ◆

Excerpt from testimony given before the so-called "Stillson Committee," chaired by Senator William Cohen of Maine. The questioner is Mr. Norman D. Verizer, the Committee's Chief Counsel. The witness is Mr. Keith Strang, of 1421 Desert Boulevard, Phoenix, Arizona.

Date of testimony: August 17, 1979.

Verizer: And at this time, John Smith was in the employ of the Phoenix Public Works Department, was he not?

Strang: Yes, Sir, he was.

V.: This was early December of 1978.

S.: Yes, Sir.

V.: And did something happen on December 7 that you particularly remember? Something concerning John Smith?

S.: Yes, Sir. It sure did.

V.: Tell the Committee about that, if you would.

S.: Well, I had to go back to the central motor pool to get

two forty-gallon drums of orange paint. We were lining roads, you understand. Johnny—that's Johnny Smith—was out on Rosemont Avenue on the day you're talking about, putting down new lane markings. Well, I got back out there at approximately four-fifteen—about forty-five minutes before knocking-off time—and this fellow Herman Joellyn that you've already talked to, he comes up to me and says, "You better check on Johnny, Keith. Something's wrong with Johnny. I tried to talk to him and he acted like he didn't hear. He almost run me down. You better get him straight." That's what he said. So I said, "What's wrong with him, Hermie?" And Hermie says, "Check it out for yourself, there's something offwhack with that dude." So I drove on up the road, and at first everything was all right, and then—wow!

V.: What did you see?

S.: Before I saw Johnny, you mean.

V.: Yes, that's right.

S.: The line he was putting down started to go haywire. Just a little bit at first—a jig here and there, a little bubble—it wasn't perfectly straight, you know. And Johnny had always been the best liner on the whole crew. Then it started to get really bad. It started to go all over the road in these big loops and swirls. Some places it was like he'd gone right around in circles a few times. For about a hundred yards he'd put the stripe right along the dirt shoulder.

V.: What did you do?

S.: I stopped him. That is, eventually I stopped him. I pulled up right beside the lining machine and started yelling at him. Must have yelled half a dozen times. It was like he didn't hear. Then he swooped that thing toward me and put a helluva ding in the side of the car I was driving. Highway Department property, too. So I laid on the horn and yelled at him again, and that seemed to get through to him. He threw it in neutral and looked over at me. I asked him what in the name of God he thought he was doing.

V.: And what was his response?

S.: He said hi. That was all. "Hi, Keith." Like everything was hunky-dory.

V.: And your response was . . . ?

S.: My response was pretty blue. I was mad. And Johnny is just standing there, looking all around and holding onto the side of the liner like he would fall down if he let go. That was when I realized how sick he looked. He was always thin, you know, but now he looked as white as paper, and the side of his mouth was kind of . . . you know . . . drawn down. At first he didn't even seem to get what I was saying. Then he looked around and saw the way that line was—all over the road.

V.: And he said . . . ?

S.: Said he was sorry. Then he kind of—I don't know—staggered, and put one hand up to his face. So I asked him what was wrong with him and he said . . . oh, a lot of confused stuff. It didn't mean anything.

Cohen: Mr. Strang, the Committee is particularly interested in *anything* Mr. Smith said that might cast a light on this matter. Can you remember what he said?

S.: Well, at first he said there was nothing wrong except that it smelled like rubber tires. Tires on fire. Then he said, "That battery will explode if you try to jump it." And something like, "I got potatoes in the chest and both radios are in the sun. So it's all out for the trees." That's the best I can remember. Like I say, it was all confused and crazy.

V.: What happened then?

S.: He started to fall down. So I grabbed him by the shoulder and his hand—he had been holding it against the side of his face—it came away. And I saw his right eye was full of blood. Then he passed out.

V.: But he said one more thing before he passed out, did he not?

S.: Yes, Sir, he did.

V.: And what was that?

S.: He said, "We'll worry about Stillson later, Daddy, he's in the dead zone now."

V.: Are you sure that's what he said?

S.: Yes, Sir, I am. I'll never forget it.

◆ 3 ◆

. . . and when I woke up I was in the small equipment shed at the base of Rosemont Drive. Keith said I'd better get to see a doctor right away, and I wasn't to come back to work until I did. I was scared, Dad, but not for the reasons Keith thought, I guess. Anyway, I made an appointment to see a neurologist that Sam Weizak had mentioned to me in a letter he wrote in

*early November. You see, I had written to Sam telling him that
I was afraid to drive a car because I was having some incidents
of double vision. Sam wrote back right away and told me to
go see this Dr. Vann—said he considered the symptoms very
alarming, but wouldn't presume to diagnose long-distance.*

*I didn't go right away. I guess your mind can screw you
over pretty well, and I kept thinking—right up to the incident
with the road-lining machine—that it was just a phase I was
going through and that it would get better. I guess I just didn't
want to think about the alternative. But the road-lining incident
was too much, I went, because I was getting scared—not just
for myself, because of what I knew.*

*So I went to see this Dr. Vann, and he gave me the tests,
and then he laid it out for me. It turned out I didn't have as
much time as I thought, because . . .*

◆ **4** ◆

Excerpt from testimony given before the so-called "Stillson
Committee," chaired by Senator William Cohen of Maine.
The questioner is Mr. Norman D. Verizer, the Committee's
Chief Counsel. The witness is Dr. Quentin M. Vann, of 17
Parkland Drive, Phoenix, Arizona.

   Date of testimony: August 22, 1979.

Verizer: After your tests were complete and your diagnosis
   was complete, you saw John Smith in your office, didn't
   you?

Vann: Yes. It was a difficult meeting. Such meetings are always difficult.

Ve: Can you give us the substance of what passed between
   you?

Va: Yes. Under these unusual circumstances, I believe that
   the doctor-patient relationship may be waived. I began by
   pointing out to Smith that he had had a terribly frightening
   experience. He agreed. His right eye was still extremely
   bloodshot, but it was better. He had ruptured a small capil-
   lary. If I may refer to the chart . . .

   (Material deleted and condensed at this point)

Ve: And after making this explanation to Smith?
Va: He asked me for the bottom line. That was his phrase;

"the bottom line." In a quiet way he impressed me with his calmness and his courage.

Ve: And the bottom line was what, Dr. Vann?

Va: Ah? I thought that would be clear by now. John Smith had an extremely well-developed brain tumor in the parietal lobe.

(Disorder among spectators; short recess)

Ve: Doctor, I'm sorry about this interruption. I'd like to remind the spectators that this Committee is in session, and that it is an investigatory body, not a freak-show. I'll have order or I'll have the Sergeant-at-Arms clear the room.

Va: That is quite all right, Mr. Verizer.

Ve: Thank you, Doctor. Can you tell the Committee how Smith took the news?

Va: He was calm. Extraordinarily calm. I believe that in his heart he had formed his own diagnosis, and that his and mine happened to coincide. He said that he was badly scared, however. And he asked me how long he had to live.

Ve: What did you tell him?

Va: I said that at that point such a question was meaningless, because our options were all still open. I told him he would need an operation. I should point out that at this time I had no knowledge of his coma and his extraordinary—almost miraculous—recovery.

Ve: And what was his response?

Va: He said there would be no operation. He was quiet but very, very firm. No operation. I said that I hoped he would reconsider, because to turn such an operation down would be to sign his own death-warrant.

Ve: Did Smith make any response to this?

Va: He asked me to give him my best opinion on how long he could live without such an operation.

Ve: Did you give him your opinion?

Va: I gave him a ballpark estimate, yes. I told him that tumors have extremely erratic growth patterns, and that I had known patients whose tumors had fallen dormant for as long as two years, but that such a dormancy was quite rare. I told him that without an operation he might reasonably expect to live from eight to twenty months.

Ve: But he still declined the operation, is that right?

Va: Yes, that is so.

Ve: Did something unusual happen as Smith was leaving?

Va: I would say it was extremely unusual.

Ve: Tell the Committee about that, if you would.

Va: I touched his shoulder, meaning to restrain him, I suppose. I was unwilling to see the man leave under those circumstances, you understand. And I felt something coming from him when I did . . . it was a sensation like an electric shock, but it was also an oddly draining, debilitating sensation. As if he were *drawing* something from me. I will grant you that this is an extremely subjective description, but it comes from a man trained in the art and craft of professional observation. It was not pleasant, I assure you. I . . . drew away from him . . . and he suggested I call my wife because Strawberry had hurt himself seriously.

Ve: Strawberry?

Va: Yes, that's what he said. My wife's brother . . . his name is Stanbury Richards. My youngest son always called him Uncle Strawberry when he was very small. That association didn't occur until later, by the way. That evening I suggested to my wife that she call her brother, who lives in the town of Coose Lake, New York.

Ve: Did she call him?

Va: Yes, she did. They had a very nice chat.

Ve: And was Mr. Richards—your brother-in-law—was he all right?

Va: Yes, he was fine. But the following week he fell from a ladder while painting his house and broke his back.

Ve: Dr. Vann, do you believe John Smith saw that happen? Do you believe that he had a precognitive vision concerning your wife's brother?

Va: I don't know. But I believe . . . that it may have been so.

Ve: Thank you, Dr.

Va: May I say one more thing?

Ve: Of course.

Va: If he did have such a curse—yes, I would call it a curse— I hope God will show pity to that man's tortured soul.

◆ **5** ◆

. . . *and I know, Dad, that people are going to say that I did what I am planning to do because of the tumor, but Daddy, don't believe them. It isn't true. The tumor is only the accident finally catching up with me, the accident which I now believe never stopped happening. The tumor lies in the same area that was injured in the crash, the same area that I now believe was probably bruised when I was a child and took a fall one day while skating on Runaround Pond. That was when I had the first of my "flashes," although even now I cannot remember exactly what it was. And I had another just before the accident, at the Esty Fair. Ask Sarah about that one; I'm sure she remembers. The tumor lies in that area which I always called "the dead zone." And that turned out to be right, didn't it? All too bitterly right. God . . . destiny . . . providence . . . fate . . . whatever you want to call it, seems to be reaching out with its steady and unarguable hand to put the scales back in balance again. Perhaps I was meant to die in that car-crash, or even earlier, that day on the Runaround. And I believe that when I've finished what I have to finish, the scales will come completely back into balance again.*

Daddy, I love you. The worst thing, next to the belief that the gun is the only way out of this terrible deadlock I find myself in, is knowing that I'll be leaving you behind to bear the grief and hate of those who have no reason to believe Stillson is anything but a good and just man . . .

◆ 6 ◆

Excerpt from testimony given before the so-called "Stillson Committee," chaired by Senator William Cohen of Maine. The questioner is Mr. Albert Renfrew, the Committee's Deputy Counsel. The witness is Dr. Samuel Weizak, of 26 Harlow Court, Bangor, Maine.

Date of testimony: August 23, 1979.

Renfrew: We are now approaching the hour of adjournment, Dr. Weizak, and on behalf of the Committee, I would like to thank you for the last four long hours of testimony. You have offered a great deal of light on the situation.

Weizak: That is quite all right.

R: I have one final question for you, Dr. Weizak, one which seems to me to be of nearly ultimate importance; it speaks to an issue which John Smith himself raised in the letter to his father which has been entered into evidence. That question is . . .

W: No.

R: I beg your pardon?

W: You are preparing to ask me if Johnny's tumor pulled the trigger that day in New Hampshire, are you not?

R: In a manner of speaking, I suppose . . .

W: The answer is no. Johnny Smith was a thinking, reasoning human being until the end of his life. The letter to his father shows this; his letter to Sarah Hazlett also shows this. He was a man with a terrible, Godlike power—perhaps a curse, as my colleague Dr. Vann has called it—but he was neither unhinged nor acting upon fantasies caused by cranial pressure—if such a thing is even possible.

R: But isn't it true that Charles Witman, the so-called "Texas Tower Sniper," had . . .

W: Yes, yes, he had a tumor. So did the pilot of the Eastern Airlines airplane that crashed in Florida some years ago. And it has never been suggested that the tumor was a precipitating cause in either case. I would point out to you that other infamous creatures—Richard Speck; the so-called "Son of Sam," and Adolf Hitler—needed no brain tumors to cause them to act in a homicidal manner. Or Frank Dodd, the murderer Johnny himself uncovered in the town of Castle Rock. However misguided this Committee may find Johnny's act to have been, it was the act of a man who was sane. In great mental agony, perhaps . . . but sane.

◆ 7 ◆

. . . and most of all, don't believe that I did this without the longest and most agonizing reflection. If by killing him I could be sure that the human race was gaining another four years, another two, even another eight months in which to think it over, it would be worth it. It's wrong, but it may turn out right. I don't know. But I won't play Hamlet any longer. I know *how dangerous Stillson is.*

Daddy, I love you very much. Believe it.

*Your son,
Johnny*

◆ 8 ◆

Excerpt from testimony given before the so-called "Stillson Committee," chaired by Senator William Cohen of Maine. The questioner is Mr. Albert Renfrew, the Committee's Deputy Counsel. The witness is Mr. Stuart Clawson, of the Blackstrap Road in Jackson, New Hampshire.

Renfrew: And you say you just happened to grab your camera, Mr. Clawson?

Clawson: Yeah! Just as I went out the door. I almost didn't even go that day, even though I like Greg Stillson—well, I did like him before all of this, anyway. The town hall just seemed like a bummer to me, you know?

R: Because of your driver's exam.

C: You got it. Flunking that permit test was one colossal bummer. But at the end, I said what the hell. And I got the picture. Wow! I got it. That picture's going to make me rich, I guess. Just like the flag-raising on Iwo Jima.

R: I hope you don't get the idea that the entire thing was staged for your benefit, young man.

C: Oh, no! Not at all! I only meant . . . well . . . I don't know what I meant. But it happened right in front of me, and . . . I don't know. Jeez, I was just glad I had my Nikon, that's all.

R: You just snapped the photo when Stillson picked up the child?

C: Matt Robeson, yessir.

R: And this is a blowup of that photo?

C: That's my picture, yes.

R: And after you took it, what happened?

C: Two of those goons ran after me. They were yelling "Give us the camera, kid! Drop it." Shi—uh, stuff like that.

R: And you ran.

C: Did I run? Holy God, I guess I ran. They chased me almost all the way to the town garage. One of them almost had me, but he slipped on the ice and fell down.

Cohen: Young man, I'd like to suggest that you won the most important footrace of your life when you outran those two thugs.

C: Thank you, Sir. What Stillson did that day . . . maybe you had to be there, but . . . holding a little kid in front of you, that's pretty low. I bet the people in New Hampshire wouldn't vote for that guy for dog-catcher. Not for . . .

R: Thank you, Mr. Clawson. The witness is excused.

◆ 9 ◆

October again.

Sarah had avoided this trip for a very long time, but now the time had come and it could be put off no longer. She felt that. She had left both children with Mrs. Ablanap—they had house-help now, and two cars instead of the little red Pinto; Walt's income was scraping near thirty thousand dollars a year—and had come by herself to Pownal through the burning blaze of late autumn.

Now she pulled over on the shoulder of a pretty little country road, got out, and crossed to the small cemetery on the other side. A small, tarnished plaque on one of the stone posts announced that this was THE BIRCHES. It was enclosed by a rambling rock wall, and the grounds were neatly kept. A few faded flags remained from Memorial Day five months ago. Soon they would be buried under snow.

She walked slowly, not hurrying, the breeze catching the hem of her dark green skirt and fluttering it. Here were generations of BOWDENS; here was a whole family of MARSTENS; here, grouped around a large marble memorial were PILLSBURYS going back to 1750.

And near the rear wall, she found a relatively new stone, which read simply JOHN SMITH. Sarah knelt beside it, hesitated, touched it. She let her fingertips skate thoughtfully over its polished surface.

◆ **10** ◆

January 23, 1979

Dear Sarah,

I've just written my father a very important letter, and it took me nearly an hour and a half to work my way through it. I just don't have the energy to repeat the effort, so I am going to suggest that you call him as soon as you receive this. Go do it now, Sarah, before you read the rest of this. . . .

So now, in all probability, you know. I just wanted to tell you that I've been thinking a lot about our date at the Esty Fair just recently. If I had to guess the two things that you remember most about it, I'd guess the run of luck I had on the Wheel of Fortune (remember the kid who kept saying "I love to see this guy take a beatin"?), and the mask I wore to fool you. That was supposed to be a big joke, but you got mad and our date damn near went right down the drain. Maybe if it had, I wouldn't be here now and that taxi driver would still be alive. On the other hand, maybe nothing at all of importance

*changes in the future, and I would have been handed the same
bullet to eat a week or a month or a year later.*

*Well, we had our chance and it came up on one of the house
numbers—double zero, I guess. But I wanted you to know that
I think of you, Sarah. For me there really hasn't been anyone
else, and that night was the best night for us . . .*

◆ 11 ◆

"Hello, Johnny," she murmured and the wind walked softly
through the trees that burned and blazed; a red leaf flipped
its way across the bright blue sky and landed, unnoticed in
her hair. "I'm here. I finally came."

Speaking out loud should have also seemed wrong; speaking to the dead in a graveyard was the act of a crazy person,
she would have said once. But now emotion surprised her,
emotion of such force and intensity that it caused her throat
to ache and her hands to suddenly clap shut. It was all right
to speak to him, maybe; after all, it had been nine years, and
this was the end of it. After this there would be Walt and the
children and lots of smiles from one of the chairs behind her
husband's speaking podium; the endless smiles from the background and an occasional feature article in the Sunday supple-
ments, if Walt's political career skyrocketed as he so calmly
expected it to do. The future was a little more gray in her
hair each year, never going braless because of the sag, becoming more careful about makeup; the future was exercise
classes at the YWCA in Bangor and shopping and taking
Denny to the first grade and Janis to nursery school; the future was New Year's Eve parties and funny hats as her life
rolled into the science-fictiony decade of the 1980s and also
into a queer and almost unsuspected state—middle age.

She saw no county fairs in her future.

The first slow, scalding tears began to come. "Oh, Johnny,"
she said. "Everything was supposed to be different, wasn't it?
It wasn't supposed to end like this."

She lowered her head, her throat working painfully—and
to no effect. The sobs came anyway, and the bright sunlight
broke into prisms of light. The wind, which had seemed so
warm and Indian summery, now seemed as chill as February
on her wet cheeks.

"Not *fair!*" she cried into the silence of BOWDENS and

MARSTENS and PILLSBURYS, that dead congregation of listeners who testified to nothing more or less than life is quick and dead is dead. "Oh God, not *fair!*"

And that was when the hand touched her neck.

♦ 12 ♦

. . . and that night was the best night for us, although there are still times when it's hard for me to believe there ever was such a year as 1970 and upheaval on the campuses and Nixon was president, no pocket calculators, no home video tape recorders, no Bruce Springsteen or punk-rock bands either. And at other times it seems like that time is only a handsbreadth away, that I can almost touch it, that if I could put my arms around you or touch your cheek or the back of your neck, I could carry you away with me into a different future with no pain or darkness or bitter choices.

Well, we all do what we can, and it has to be good enough . . . and if it isn't good enough, it has to do. I only hope that you will think of me as well as you can, dear Sarah. All my best,

and all my love,
Johnny

♦ 13 ♦

She drew her breath in raggedly, her back straightening, her eyes going wide and round. "Johnny . . . ?"

It was gone.

Whatever it had been, it was gone. She stood and turned around and of course there was nothing there. But she could see him standing there, his hands jammed deep into his pockets, that easy, crooked grin on his pleasant-rather-than-handsome face, leaning lanky and at ease against a monument or one of the stone gateposts or maybe just a tree gone red with fall's dying fire. No big deal, Sarah—you still sniffin that wicked cocaine?

Nothing there but Johnny; somewhere near, maybe everywhere.

We all do what we can, and it has to be good enough . . .

and if it isn't good enough, it has to do. Nothing is ever lost, Sarah. Nothing that can't be found.

"Same old Johnny," she whispered, and walked out of the cemetery and crossed the road. She paused for a moment, looking back. The warm October wind gusted strongly and great shades of light and shadow seemed to pass across the world. The trees rustled secretly.

Sarah got in her car and drove away.